Dear Reader,

Another Quinn trilogy is coming to a close and this one has been a lot of fun to write, especially since it took me back to one of my favorite places, Ireland.

Though I've only been to Ireland once, I've spent the last year thinking about all the wonderful and picturesque towns I visited. Someday, I hope to return for another visit, maybe even during the holidays. I could even search out my one lonely Irish ancestor. I'd drive past the spot on the coast where Ballykirk should be and wander down the country road where Winterhill might have stood. And if I'm lucky, I might even meet a man who looks a little bit like Kellan Quinn. You couldn't ask for a better Christmas present than that.

If you've never had a chance to visit the Emerald Isle, I hope this Quinn trilogy has given you a little taste of one of my favorite places.

Happy holidays,

Kate Hoffmann

THE MIGHTY QUINNS: KELLAN

BY
KATE HOFFMANN

First published in Great Britain 2012
by Mills & Boon, an imprint of Harlequin (UK) Limited,
Eton House, 18-24 Paradise Road, Richmond, Surrey TW9 1SR

© Peggy A. Hoffmann 2011

ISBN: 978 0 263 89395 3
ebook ISBN: 978 1 408 96950 2

14-1212

Harlequin (UK) policy is to use papers that are natural, renewable and recyclable products and made from wood grown in sustainable forests. The logging and manufacturing processes conform to the legal environmental regulations of the country of origin.

Printed and bound in Spain
by Blackprint CPI, Barcelona

Kate Hoffmann began writing for Mills & Boon in 1993. Since then she's published sixty-five books. When she isn't writing, she enjoys music, theater and musical theater. She is active working with high school students in the performing arts. She lives in southeastern Wisconsin with her cat, Chloe.

Prologue

Prologue

KELLAN STARED out at the water from the narrow beach, the morning sun gleamed off the glassy surface of the Atlantic. He drew a deep breath and smiled. It was the perfect summer day. Warm without a hint of the damp wind that usually roared along the coast.

"We should sleep here tonight," he said to his brothers. "Up on the cliff. Da would let us take the tent." Glancing over his shoulder, he found Riley and Danny squatting down and digging in the sand.

Smuggler's Cove had become their secret getaway. Just five or six kilometers from their cottage outside Ballykirk, the hidden cove could only be reached from the water. But Danny, Kellan's youngest brother, had discovered a path down through the rocks, making the spot accessible.

"I'm not spendin' the night," Riley said. "There's ghosts in that old house up there." He was talking about the abandoned castle and manor house that overlooked the cliff. None of them had ever been brave enough to venture inside, although Kellan had heard the older kids used the place for parties all the time.

"Me, neither," Danny said.

"What the feck are you two about?" Kellan asked, watching as they scraped sand aside with their fingers.

"There's something buried in the sand," Danny said, burrowing after it like a terrier after a bone. "Come here and help, ya lazy git."

"No way. You've been digging in that sand for two years now and you haven't found a thing. Considering the smugglers are long gone, it's probably just an old piece of wood. You and your fantasies. They're a waste of time."

Riley stopped for a moment. "If Kell doesn't dig and it is treasure, then he doesn't get a share."

"Agreed," Danny said.

"Yeah," Kellan said. "Agreed." But to Kellan's surprise, Danny and Riley pulled a small tin box out of the sand. "What the feck," he muttered, striding over to them.

"See," Danny said smugly. "Told you. Now you don't get a share." He brushed the sand off the top of the old biscuit tin.

"Open it," Riley urged.

Danny reached for the top, then hesitated. "I don't know. What if it's cursed? It could be like…like…"

"Pandora's box," Kellan told him. "Jaysus, you two are always letting your imagination run away with you. It's a feckin' biscuit tin."

"Should we open it?" Danny asked, looking to

Kellan for an answer. They always looked to him for answers. That's what it was to be the oldest boy in the Quinn family.

Kellan shrugged. "You found it. You open it." He turned away, determined not to show his interest. But as he did, he caught sight of a movement among the rocks on the cliffside. He stared at the spot for a long moment, then shook his head. But there it was again. A flutter of pale green fabric in the breeze and a slender form scrambling behind another rock.

"There's someone up there," he muttered. "Watching us."

The boys looked up from their examination of the box, following Kellan's nod. "Right up there."

"Maybe it's a fairy," Riley said. "And maybe this is her box of magic. Let's go see if we can catch her." Riley shoved the box at Danny and leaped to his feet, then took off for the path at the bottom of the rocks.

"Wait," Danny called. "What if it's a ghost from the house?"

Kellan heard a tiny cry from above him and he watched the girl scamper along the path, climbing up and over the rocks. She looked like a fairy, her long, golden hair draped over her back and crowned by a wreath of wildflowers. But she didn't have wings, at least none that he could see. She was dressed in an old gown made of a sheer fabric so light it floated around her.

Cursing to himself, Kellan followed his brothers. What was he thinking? He knew fairies weren't real.

Maybe his little brothers believed, but Kellan was far too pragmatic to put any faith in Irish myths and legends. "Leave me to it," he said, hurrying past Riley. "I can climb faster than you."

Kellan scrambled up the path, but each time he looked for her, she was putting more distance between them. If she really were a fairy, she'd just fly away. No, this was a girl, a girl he'd never seen before. Kellan knew all the girls living around Ballykirk and not one of them was half as beautiful as this one.

Breathless, he reached the top of the cliff only to find her halfway across the meadow. She turned once and laughed, then took her crown of wildflowers and threw it into the air.

"Wait!" Kellan called. "Don't go. I want to talk to you."

She spun around and stood, staring at him, waiting as he ran toward her. When he reached her, Kellan stopped, his heart pounding, gasping for breath. She *was* the most beautiful thing he'd ever seen, features so perfect that they couldn't belong to anything human.

"Open the box," she said, the musical tone of her voice ringing in the still summer air. "I put it there for you."

Kellan heard his brothers behind him, calling his name. "Who are you?"

With a laugh, she came closer and dropped a kiss on his lips. "I'm a dream," she said. "Close your eyes and I'll disappear."

Kellan glanced back to see his brothers quickly approaching, but when he turned to the girl again, she had already run from him. This time, Kellan decided not to follow.

"You're letting her get away," Danny called. "Go after her, Kellan."

"She's not a fairy," Kellan said when Danny and Riley reached him. He touched his lips, still warm from her kiss. "She's just a girl. A silly old girl."

They watched her retreat together, then Kellan grabbed the tin from beneath Riley's arm. "Let's see what's inside."

"I thought Danny said it might be cursed."

"Do you believe everything he says?" Kellan asked. "Riley, sometimes you're as thick as a post."

He tugged off the top and peered inside. The tin was filled with a variety of items—a seashell, a few pretty stones, a necklace made of flowers, braided string.

"Aw, it's nothing but junk," Riley said.

Danny swore. "I was hoping it might at least be worth a few quid."

"I think we should bury it again," Kellan said. If they did, she might come back for it. He could hide in the rocks and watch for her. Catching a fairy was powerful luck, wasn't it?

"I'm not climbing back down." Danny started off toward home. "I'm hungry. And Ma will have lunch for us soon."

Riley followed him, a dejected look on his face. "I thought it would be treasure. I thought we'd be rich."

Kellan sighed softly, then plopped down onto the

grass. Crossing his legs in front of him, he reopened the tin and carefully picked through the contents. There were jeweled buttons and a penny whistle, a scrap of lace and three pieces of butterscotch candy. Why the girl had decided to bury it in the sand, he didn't know. But he couldn't help but be intrigued.

Who was she? Would she return to the cove or was she really a visitor from another world? For the first time in his life, Kellan felt an odd attraction, a strange fascination with a girl.

Would he ever understand the opposite sex? The girls in school were annoying. Though they were constantly following him about, whispering and giggling, they were all uninteresting to his eyes. And his two older sisters, Shanna and Claire, were a complete mystery and a royal pain in his arse. But this...this lovely creature was magical. He closed his eyes and lay in the grass, letting his imagination wander, back to the kiss she'd given him.

He'd never kissed a girl. He was nearly fifteen years old and though most of his friends had enjoyed the experience at least once or twice, Kellan had never taken advantage of his opportunities, until now.

He grinned. If he ever saw the fairy girl again, he'd do it even better. He'd grab her and kiss her, right on the lips, and see what she had to say about that. Now that he knew exactly what he wanted in a girl, what he'd been looking for, everything made sense.

She had to be...extraordinary. He'd settle for nothing less. Someday soon, maybe she'd come back to the cove, looking for her tin of treasures. He'd find a proper place to hide it until then.

1

THE WEATHER WAS unusually warm for late November. Kellan Quinn stared out at the sea from his spot above Smuggler's Cove. He walked over to the rocky edge of the cliff to look down at the narrow strip of beach where he and his brothers used to play. He hadn't been down the path in years, not since before he left for university.

But the little beach, sheltered from the wind, would be a perfect place to think, to find some solitude and clear his head. Life in Ballykirk had turned into a whirl of activity since his younger brothers had both found mates, and though he was happy for them, lately he'd felt like the odd man out.

Riley would be getting married in just over a month and though he and Nan had planned a simple New Year's Eve ceremony at the village church and a reception at the pub, it promised to be the biggest social event Ballykirk had seen in quite some time. Both Danny and Kellan would be standing up with Riley, which didn't sound like much. However, Kellan had learned that serving as a groomsman meant that you were at the beck and call of the groom until he left for his honeymoon.

Kellan still couldn't get over how quickly things had changed for the Quinn brothers. Riley and Danny had both fallen for American girls in the space of a few months. Of course, everyone assumed Kellan would be next and to that end, they'd started to put interested single girls in his path. But he knew better.

When it came to romance, Kellan Quinn was a realist. The chances of finding lasting love were slim at best. Though he'd turned thirty last year, he really hadn't ever come close to marriage, or enjoyed a longterm relationship. Perhaps it was because he'd never found a woman who could hold his attention. A woman who was more interesting than his career.

His reputation as an architect was growing with every project he completed and he was usually at the top of the list for any major historical renovation in Ireland. Though it wasn't really cutting-edge architecture, Kellan enjoyed doing his part to preserve pieces of Ireland's past.

Sixteen-hour days didn't leave much time for a social life, but he did manage to date occasionally when he stayed at his flat in Dublin. There were women who were happy to have him warm their bed, no strings, no expectations. But the relationships lacked an emotional component, existing purely for physical release.

Kellan drew a deep breath of the damp air. Riley

and Danny had found their perfect matches. It was as if both women had just dropped out of the sky and into their beds. Had they been searching, waiting, wondering?

The wind buffeted his body and Kellan pulled his canvas jacket closed. In the past few days, a strange restlessness had come over him. Something was about to change. He could feel it inside, like the sky darkening before a storm.

He'd had an offer to do a project in France and he'd been considering the opportunity. It would mean moving to Brittany for a year to supervise the renovation of an old armory into a World War II museum. Maybe it was time for a change. Maybe he needed something new in his life...just like his brothers.

Raking his hands through his windblown hair, Kellan walked to the rocks and searched for the way down. The descent was easy once he found the right path. As he clambered over the jagged traverse, he noticed something odd lying on the beach.

At first, it looked like a pile of debris and seaweed. But as he got closer, his heart started to pound. It was a body! He made out a long, slender arm and the unmistakable curve of a woman's hip. Kellan jumped down the last five feet and ran over to her, almost dreading what he was about to discover.

But the moment he touched her, she jerked, then sat up, brushing the damp strands of hair from her eyes. She looked at him through eyes so pale they were almost colorless.

"Are you all right?"

A tiny frown worried her brow, but she made no attempt to speak.

"What are you doing down here? How did you get here? Were you in the water?"

She reached out and smoothed her sand-covered palm over his cheek, her gaze studying the details of his face. And then, without warning, she leaned forward and touched her lips to his. She tasted of salt water and smelled of the ocean breeze.

The kiss was so surprising, he jerked back. But she was determined and slipped her hand around his nape, pulling him closer, drawing him down into the sand with her. Kellan normally exercised a great deal of self-restraint around women. But the moment her lips touched his, his control dissolved into an overwhelming need.

Her lips parted on a sigh and he took the chance to taste, his tongue delving into the sweet warmth of her mouth. She responded immediately, writhing beneath him as if trying to get closer. Her body trembled and when he finally drew back he realized it wasn't from the impact of their kiss but from the cold.

"Are you all right?" he asked again. "What's your name?"

Her eyes fluttered and then closed as she went limp in his arms. Kellan grabbed her chin and turned her head. She was still breathing, but just barely. Cursing, he scrambled to his feet and picked her up, hoping that she'd regain consciousness. She was dead weight in his arms, like a rag doll.

Kellan looked up to the top of the cliff. The only way to get her up was tossed over his shoulder. It wouldn't be comfortable, but there was no other option.

The dress she wore was barely enough to keep her warm in midsummer much less late autumn. Just a thin layer of green silk. He shrugged out of his canvas jacket and struggled to get her into it, buttoning it up once he had. "I don't know who the hell you are, but you should count yourself bloody lucky I came along."

He bent down and grabbed her thighs, her body folding over his shoulder. The path was narrow but navigable, even with a passenger. He had to be cautious of her head, careful not to bump her against the rocks. When he finally reached the top, Kellan set her down in the grass and took a deep breath.

Her eyes fluttered again and for a moment she opened them. "Can you stand up?" he asked.

Her lips curled into a sleepy smile and she shook her head and closed her eyes again.

"What the hell am I supposed to do with you?" he muttered. "If the hike home doesn't kill you, it will probably kill me."

He couldn't leave her here alone. But he could probably run home and fetch his car in less time than it would take to carry her. The hike to the road was only about half a kilometer. Home was nearly five.

He had his mobile. He'd ring the pub and see if one of his brothers could drive out. Meanwhile, he'd try to get her warm and awake. He flipped open his phone and to his relief, Danny answered almost immediately.

"I need your help," Kellan said. "I need you to drive up the coast road and park your car just around the bend by the dry stone fence, before you get to Castle Cnoc. Right where we used to leave our bikes when we'd come down to the cove."

"Why?" Danny asked.

"Just do it. I'll explain when you get here."

"Riley and Nan have me stuffing invitations for their engagement party. This is important stuff I'm workin' on, Kell. I can't just be hopping off for no good reason."

"It's an emergency. Maybe even life or death. Leave now. I'll meet you there in a few minutes."

"I'm on my way."

This time, when Kellan hefted her over his shoulder, she groaned and fought against him. "That's right," he said. "It's not so comfortable, is it? Maybe if you could summon the energy to walk, we might both be spared the trouble of me lugging you through this meadow like a lumpy sack of potatoes."

"Ow," she said.

"What were you doing on that beach, anyway? If I hadn't come along, you'd be on your way to dead right now. Dead and washed away by the tide. That's no way to leave this world. What about your family? They might never have known what happened to you."

"I— Oh, sick," she muttered. A few seconds later, she retched and he felt the back of his leg go damp. After that, she seemed to settle down.

"Lovely. Brilliant." Kellan tried to calm his own stomach. If there was one thing he couldn't handle it was— He felt a wave of nausea overtake him and he stopped and drew a deep breath through his mouth. "I don't know if you're drunk or just crazy, but you'll be thanking me for this later."

By the time he reached the road, Danny was waiting in his battered old Land Rover. His brother jumped out of the driver's side and ran up to him. "What the devil! Where did you find her?"

"On the beach at the cove. She's cold and I think she might be drunk. Or sick. I don't know."

"What are you going to do with her?"

"Take her back to the cottage. I'll get her warm and call Doc Finnerty."

"Maybe we should drive her directly to the hospital?"

"All the way to Cork? Let's get her out of these wet clothes first and warm her up. If she doesn't come round, I'll take her."

When they got her settled in the backseat, Kellan slid in beside her, resting her head on his lap. Danny turned the car around and raced back toward town. At the fork in the road, he turned up toward the cottage.

Kellan had been living in Ballykirk for the past couple weeks, taking a break from life in Dublin while his family planned for the upcoming wedding. The small, whitewashed cottage had been his childhood home, set on a high rise above the seaside village. On occasion, it was let out to tourists, but when it wasn't, Kellan often stayed there.

When Danny pulled the car to a stop, Kellan got out and carefully scooped the woman up into his arms. "Do me a favor. Give Doc Finnerty a call and if he doesn't answer, see if you can find him."

"I know where he is," Danny said. "He's having a pint at the pub. He was there when I left." He ran up the garden path and opened the door for Kellan. "I'll go get him, then."

Kellan turned toward the bedroom, then realized that the sofa was a better choice. He could light a fire and it would provide the warmth she needed. He set her down, then hurriedly laid peat and kindling in the hearth. A few minutes later, a flicker of flame licked at the sod, smoke curling up into the chimney.

"There," he said. He leaned back on his heels, then realized the fire would do only half the job. He had to get her out of her wet clothes and into something warm. Though he didn't relish undressing a woman without her permission, Kellan figured if he didn't look at her in a sexual way, it would remain a purely practical matter.

He strode into the bedroom and grabbed the quilt and a wool blanket off the bed, then returned to the sofa. She was so still, curled up in front of him. Kellan gently sat her up, then slipped his jacket off her shoulders.

If she were conscious, he could put her in a warm shower. But there was no way she could stand unless he joined her.

Her hair was tangled with sand and bits of debris from the beach. He managed to skim her damp dress up along her legs, but was forced to pull her to her feet to get it over her head. To his relief, she seemed able to stand on her own for a few seconds.

He tossed the dress aside, then grabbed the quilt, wrapping her up in it and trying not to dwell on the fact that she wasn't wearing any underwear. "Why should that surprise me?" he murmured.

She had a beautiful body, slender and long-limbed. Her skin was pale and soft as silk, but so cold to his touch. His gaze slipped lower, to her lovely breasts, the curve of her hips and the junction of her legs.

He drew a ragged breath and pulled her against him, rubbing her back with his palms until the friction created warmth. What she really needed was a long, hot bath. But the cottage had only a shower. A bath would require hauling in the old tub that they'd used as kids.

A sharp knock sounded on the door and a few seconds later, Danny stepped inside followed by Jimmy Finnerty. Dr. Finnerty was the closest thing the town had to a local doctor. He had retired from his practice in Cork three years ago and now lived a quiet life with his wife in his vacation home on the bay, spending his days fishing and only coming out of retirement for the occasional emergency.

"What have we here?" he asked, setting his bag on the end of the sofa.

"I found her on the beach," Kellan said.

"The beach? What beach?"

"A little spot I know just up the coast. She was lying in the sand."

"Naked?"

"No, she was dressed. I took her dress off to try to get her warm. I think she's a bit better. I had her standing. But she hasn't really opened her eyes."

The doctor reached into his bag and pulled out a small vial, then cracked it and held the smelling salts under her nose. She jerked back, then waved her hand in front of her face, moaning softly. "Well, she's not unconscious. She seems to be under the influence."

"Of what?" Danny asked.

"Pills. Liquor. Can't say for certain. Why don't we start with some nice hot coffee and see if that helps." He glanced over at Kellan. "You say you found her on the beach?"

Kellan nodded. "She threw up while I was carrying her out to the road."

"That's a positive sign."

"Not for me," he muttered.

"You don't suppose she's a—"

"A drunk?"

"No, a mermaid," Finnerty said with a chuckle. "She could be a mermaid washed up onshore."

"Look at her," Danny said. "She has that look about her."

Kellan stared at the woman, frowning. "She looks... I don't know. Pretty. But she has feet. Don't mermaids have...fins?"

"Naw. Not after they come ashore," Finnerty said

as he slipped on a blood pressure cuff. "The skin is so pale and the hair like spun silk. I've seen pictures. This is what they look like. Otherworldly. Was she combing her hair when you first saw her?" He looked up. "That's how they cast their spells, you know."

"I don't believe in mermaids," Kellan said. "And neither do you two. She was unconscious when I found her."

Finnerty listened to her pulse, then removed the cuff. "Well, she's here. And her vital signs are strong. What are you going to do with her?"

"I thought you could take her. To hospital, if need be."

"She appears to be slightly hypothermic and possibly hungover. Now that she's getting warm, she'll probably wake up and be just fine. I expect the best place for her is right here—at least until she's feeling better. Then you can take her back where you found her."

"What? I can't put her back on that beach."

"Well, I'm sure you'll sort it all out," Finnerty said as he rose from the sofa. "You're a smart lad, Kellan. Now, my wife has dinner waiting and I'm late. If you need me, give me a ring and I'll come back. Danny, let's be off and leave your brother to nurse this pretty merrow back to health."

Danny gave Kellan a shrug and followed the doctor out the door. "Bring me up some soup from the pub," Kellan called. "And a bottle of whiskey."

"No problem," Danny said. "And I'll fetch a bushel

of kelp and some herring, too." He was still chuckling as the door slammed behind him.

Kellan stared down at the woman lying on the sofa. He reached down and brushed the flaxen hair from her eyes, taking in the perfect features of her face. Finnerty was right. She had a look about her, something...extraordinary. "Otherworldly," he murmured.

And familiar. Kellan couldn't shake the feeling that he'd seen her somewhere before. And yet, he certainly would have remembered meeting her. A woman this beautiful would have stuck in his mind.

"If you are a mermaid," he murmured, smoothing his hand over her temple, "then we're going to have a very interesting conversation when you wake up."

GELSEY WOODSON SNUGGLED into the warm recesses of the blanket wrapped around her naked body. Her head ached from the bottle of champagne she'd drunk the night before and her skin itched from salt water and sand, but she couldn't bring herself to open her eyes.

She listened distractedly to the male voices, realizing they were talking about her. The one man was obviously a doctor and she stifled a moan as he took her blood pressure. There was another voice, her rescuer. The man who'd carried her up from the beach. She liked his voice. It was like liquid chocolate, smooth and dark and just a bit sweet.

Their conversation turned to mermaids and for a moment she was confused, until she realized that they thought she was a mermaid. That nearly made her laugh out loud. She'd always been one to indulge in fantasies. From the time she was a child, she'd woven a rich imaginary life for herself where she was a princess one day and a fairy queen the next, or a sorceress or an elf or a pixie with powers that could change her world in the blink of an eye.

And now she was a mermaid. Maybe that was for the best, she mused. For she certainly didn't want to be Gelsey Woodson anymore.

Her stomach growled and she winced, remembering the humiliation of vomiting over the man's shoulder. Though she was used to overindulging, bouncing around as he carried her had been a recipe for disaster.

She pulled the blanket up more tightly around her nose. Just a few more hours of rest would be enough. Then she could face the world again. But even though she wanted to sleep, she couldn't help but be curious about the man who'd plucked her off the beach.

When the house went quiet, she slowly opened her eyes and looked around. A fire flickered on the hearth and the acrid smell of peat teased at her nose. She glanced under the quilt. Though she was certain she hadn't undressed herself, she couldn't remember who had.

Her mind wandered back to the previous night. Though she'd done her share of stupid things, especially when it came to her relationships with men, this might just top the list. A late-night phone call, an argument with her ex-fiancé and too much to drink had ended with her tossing a nine carat diamond ring into the sea before passing out on the beach. It seemed as if all her problems had become too heavy to bear. Not just the breakup, but the everything that had come before it—the fights, the paparazzi, the Italian police and the "incident."

That's what she'd taken to calling it. That's what her Italian attorney called it. And that made it sound so benign. But punching a photographer was a serious offense, even if she'd done it while under the influence of another very expensive bottle of champagne and the misunderstanding that the photographer was trying to grope her.

And so she'd run away to Winterhill, to lick her wounds and await her hearing scheduled for late January. Her grandmother's country house in Ireland was a place she'd remembered so fondly from her childhood. The windswept cliffs and brilliant green meadows had been her playground every summer, creating fantasies for a girl used to a solitary existence. She'd come back to find the center in her life again, to hide from everything that confused and frightened her. Though she'd lived all over the world, Ireland had always felt the most like home.

She drew a deep breath and winced, her head throbbing and her mouth dry as dust. Was this what all her therapists had talked about? Everyone had been predicting it. Had Gigi Woodson, tabloid princess and celebrity heiress, finally hit rock bottom?

Her father, Ellery Woodson, was a diplomat for the British government, and her mother, an American socialite. She was their only child and after the first eight years of her life, a pawn in their very nasty divorce. Bad behavior had come easily. It had been the only way to get her parents' attention.

At age twelve, she'd been kicked out of her first boarding school. By seventeen, she'd been kicked out of more schools than she could remember. She had a brief spell of normalcy during her university years in Paris, when she worked on an art history degree and lived with a handsome French banker. But then her grandmother died, leaving her Winterhill and a large trust fund. At age twenty-one, the naughty Gelsey returned with a vengeance—and with a seemingly bottomless bank account.

She'd transformed herself from Gelsey Evangeline Woodson, well-educated daughter of a diplomat, to Gigi Woodson, party girl without a care in the world. For the first five years, it had been fun, like playing make-believe only with posh parties and exciting new friends. Even her mother had approved.

But in the past few years, her life had started to spiral out of control and she began to suspect that she really *did* care. That all the pretending didn't make the loneliness and the insecurities go away. Maybe she hadn't had the best family life and maybe her parents hadn't really wanted her around. But she'd come to realize that the life she was living would never make her happy and the friends she had weren't true friends at all.

Gelsey drew a ragged breath. So, perhaps this could

be a fresh start. Today, this morning. Or afternoon. When she opened her eyes again, she could forget the past and start all over again. She could use what was left of her trust fund and build a simple life for herself, away from the glare of the spotlight and the flash of the paparazzi's cameras.

Her thoughts dissolved and she fell back into a shallow sleep, content for the first time in a long time. Everything would be all right. She'd be safe here, in this tiny cottage. No one knew her in Ireland beyond the housekeeper at Winterhill. No one would care if she stayed away for a day or even a week.

She wasn't sure how long she slept, but the touch of a hand on her face brought her back from a dreamless state of exhaustion. She opened her eyes and found him sitting on the floor near the end of the sofa and staring at her intently.

"You're awake," he murmured.

"Yes," she said, her voice croaking. Gelsey cleared her throat.

"Would you like something warm to drink?" he asked. "I have coffee or tea. Or soup. Or maybe a bit of whiskey?"

Her stomach growled at the mention of food. "Yes, soup would be nice." As for the whiskey, she'd decided to take a new direction in her life. It was time to stop drinking…at least to excess.

"Soup," she said.

"I'll be right back," he murmured.

Gelsey clasped the quilt to her chest as she pulled

herself up to a sitting position. To her surprise, she didn't feel nearly as bad as she'd expected. Just a little bit weak and a tiny bit embarrassed. But she was here, being waited on by a devastatingly handsome man who was making her soup. The first day of her new life was beginning quite well.

As promised, he returned in a few moments with a huge mug and spoon. He sat down beside her and handed her the soup. "It's beef and barley," he said. "It's from the pub down in the village. My ma makes it."

Gelsey took a spoonful. The hearty warmth made her smile. "It's delicious."

"How are you feeling?"

"Fine."

"How is it you came to be on the beach?"

Gelsey opened her mouth to reply, then snapped it shut. She didn't want to explain it all, especially to this man. She didn't want him to think badly of her, to make assumptions and to write her off as some stupid girl without any limits.

"I—I don't know," she said.

"What does that mean?"

Gelsey shrugged. "I don't remember." She took another spoonful of the soup, waiting for him to question her. But he just continued to watch her suspiciously. "I'm not sure."

"Are you saying you have amnesia?"

Gelsey frowned. It sounded like a reasonable diagnosis and it happened all the time in the movies. If she didn't know who she was, then she wouldn't know where she came from. And she could stay here with this man. "I don't know. I just don't remember." She took another spoonful of soup and handed it to him. "I've had enough, thank you."

"You've barely eaten at all," he said.

"What is your name?" she asked.

"Kellan. Kellan Quinn."

A memory flashed in her mind, so clear it might have happened just yesterday. The boy that had chased her from the beach so many years before. His name had been Kellan. She'd heard his brothers yell it across the meadow and she'd committed it to memory. This was the same boy, all grown up.

She smiled to herself. How many times had she woven long and complicated fantasies around that boy? For at least a month after, she'd thought about returning to the beach to find him. But the summer had ended and she'd been sent back to school, leaving thoughts of him far behind.

"Kellan," she repeated. "I like that."

"And what's your name?"

"Gelsey," she replied.

He said it back to her. Softly. The sound of it on his lips caused a shiver to skitter through her body.

"Do you have a last name?" he asked.

"I'm not sure I do," Gelsey said.

A grin teased at the corners of his mouth. "Does that mean you don't remember it or you don't want to tell me what it is?"

"A little of both," she said. She drew in a sharp

breath as her gaze fell to his lips. Lord, he was handsome. She had dated an endless string of gorgeous men, but not one of them had captured her fancy like this man. He was just a regular guy, yet there was something so intriguing about him. "You kissed me," she murmured.

"No," Kellan said.

"You did. I remember. On the beach."

"You kissed me," he said.

"Yes." Gelsey reached out and touched his face, then leaned closer, curious to see if the kiss she remembered was really so good. Her lips found his. He didn't seem surprised or reluctant. Instead, he gently cupped her face in his hands and returned the kiss in full measure, his tongue tangling with hers.

Desire raced through her body, warming her blood and making her mind spin. Gelsey felt giddy, like that breathless young girl on the cliffs. He'd been such a handsome boy, but now he was a man, full grown and capable of making her weak with need.

"Does that help?" he asked.

"Help?"

"Your memory," Kellan said.

"Yes," she said. "I remember liking that very much." She peeked under the blanket. "I have no clothes. Did you undress me?"

Kellan nodded. "You were cold. I had to get you warm."

"I don't remember that." She reached out and took

his hand and placed it on her bare shoulder. "Maybe you should show me how that happened."

Kellan stared at the spot where he touched her, then slowly drew his hand away. "You—you should rest," he murmured. "You've had a long day."

"What time is it?"

"Nearly five," he replied. "Do you have a place to go? Someone who might be waiting for you?"

Gelsey shook her head. "No," she said. "No one is waiting for me." In truth, the only person who'd wonder where she was might be Caroline, the housekeeper at Winterhill. She'd call the first chance she got, but Caroline knew not to worry. Gelsey often disappeared for days at a time.

As for her parents, they'd given up worrying a long time ago. No. No one really cared at all. The only one who'd ever truly cared had been her grandmother and she'd been gone for years now.

"You can stay here until you're feeling better," he said.

"I wouldn't want to put you out," she said.

"You wouldn't be."

"You know what I'd really like? A hot bath. I've got sand in places I didn't even know I had. It feels like I slept in it."

"You did," Kellan said. "I found you on the beach." He stood. "We have a shower. The bathroom is just through the kitchen. Or we have an old tub that I can bring in and fill if you're set on a bath."

"I think a shower would do nicely," Gelsey said. "And I could use some clothes. Do you have my dress?"

"I'll find you something better to wear."

She slowly stood, wrapping the quilt more tightly around her naked body. "Thank you," she said. "For saving me." She paused. "You're a nice man, Kellan. I haven't known too many nice men in my life."

"I'm not all that nice," he replied.

"You can't fool me," she said, pushing up on her toes and placing a kiss on his cheek. Then Gelsey slowly walked toward the bathroom.

As she closed the bathroom door behind her, Gelsey leaned back against it and drew a deep breath. Had he been any other man in her life, she would have seduced him on the spot. She'd never been one to play coy when it came to satisfying her desires. And she'd never met a man who'd refused her.

But that was precisely how she'd gotten into trouble in the past. She'd led with her heart, not her head. Her argument with Antonio last night had been a prime example. She should have been nicer, considering his word would go a long way toward making the assault case disappear. Instead, all the anger and resentment over their breakup had come bubbling to the surface, and after a long predawn phone argument, she'd grabbed a bottle of champagne as the sun came up and wandered along the cliffs to the cove.

Her heart had told her to kiss Kellan that day in the meadow. And her heart had told her to do the same thing when he found her on the beach. And both times, it had felt so right and so real, not wicked or manipulative. Just…perfect.

She didn't have to live her life in brilliant swaths of color and chaos. She could be just like everyone else if she wanted to be—normal. From now on, she'd try to become the kind of woman who didn't indulge her every whim, a woman who controlled her desires and considered her actions.

"Except for kissing," she murmured. After all, what harm could it do to enjoy the lips of a man as handsome and sexy as Kellan Quinn? It was only a matter of time before he found out about her past, about the life she wanted to leave behind. And men like Kellan were not the type to put up with the kind of baggage she carried with her.

Gelsey turned on the shower, then let the quilt drop to the floor. She was warm now, and happy. It was time to take a breath and see life the way everyone else in the world did—without the endless drama and roller-coaster emotions.

2

KELLAN SET THE PILE of clothes down next to the bathroom. Though he was trying to keep his mind on other things, it wasn't difficult to imagine what was going on beyond the door. She was naked, obviously. And he'd seen her body when he'd undressed her, so there was no use trying to forget the sweet curves and soft flesh that had been hidden by the quilt.

She'd kissed him not once, but twice. She'd made it quite apparent that she'd welcome more. But Kellan wasn't one to play games when it came to sex and he knew damn well she was hiding something.

She'd refused to provide her last name, which made him suspect she might be running from something or someone—the authorities…or a jealous husband or boyfriend. That was more likely. She didn't seem like the criminal sort. And chances were that a woman as beautiful as Gelsey would have a man in her life. She possessed the kind of beauty that could make any male mad with jealousy.

Kellan cleared his throat, then rapped on the door. "I'm going to run down to the pub and get some supper for us," he called. "I'll be back in about twenty minutes."

"I'm really not very hungry," she replied.

"I am," Kellan said. "Don't make your shower too long. You'll run out of hot water. There are clothes on the floor outside the door."

The bathroom door opened and she poked her head out and smiled. Water droplets clung to her lashes and ran down her cheeks. "Thanks," she said. She bent down and grabbed the clothes and he caught sight of her naked body.

A current of desire raced through him as his gaze settled on a sleek leg, setting his nerves on edge. Kellan couldn't help but look. "Are these yours?" she asked, nodding at the clothes.

"Yes. They won't fit, but they'll keep you warm. For now. I'll see if Nan or Jordan might have something you can borrow."

"Who are Nan and Jordan?"

"Nan is my brother Riley's fiancée and Jordan is my brother Danny's girlfriend."

"I don't mind wearing your clothes," she said.

"But I do." With that, Kellan turned and strode to the door. If she wasn't going to walk around the cottage naked, then at least he'd make sure she had clothes that enhanced her beautiful body.

When he got outside, Kellan took a long deep breath of the cold evening air. The day had begun like any ordinary day, but suddenly, he'd found himself in possession of a beautiful woman, one who planned to spend the night.

A brisk walk into the village should clear his mind of any thoughts of seduction. But he couldn't seem to put Gelsey out of his head. There was something about her, something he found incredibly intriguing.

Kellan made a mental list of all her qualities—the long blond hair, perfectly balanced features, a body that was made to be touched and skin so flawless it made her seem unattainable. But it wasn't just the physical that he found attractive. It was what he didn't know about her that was even more tantalizing.

There was a certain appeal to the idea of a mystery woman, a complete stranger with a secret past. Though he was usually quite rational and fantasies weren't a regular indulgence, Gelsey seemed to bring out the devil in him. What would it be like to have her in his bed, to lose himself inside such a lovely creature?

The pub was busy when he walked in the front door. But the conversation softened to a low murmur the instant everyone saw him enter. He glanced around, then found Danny smiling at him from behind the bar. "There he is!" Danny shouted. "The hero of the day. So what did you do with your mermaid, Kell? Did ya toss her back? Or have you decided to keep her?"

Kellan cursed beneath his breath. No doubt everyone in town was aware of the situation unfolding at the cottage. Maybe that was for the best. Someone in town must know who she was or where she came from.

"She's not a mermaid," he shouted, crossing the room to the bar.

"Doc Finnerty says she is."

"Doc Finnerty should limit himself to one pint of the dark stuff." Kellan turned to Riley and Nan sitting at the end of the bar. Jordan was with them, the remains of their dinner littering the surface in front of them. "She is not a mermaid. She's just some girl who got drunk and ended up on the beach."

"Doc Finnerty says she doesn't look like a normal girl," Riley said.

"She was half frozen to death. Almost blue from the cold," Kellan explained. "Now I need some dinner." He glanced over at Danny. "Pack up some stew and some shepherd's pie. And soup. Lots of soup."

"You sure she wouldn't want a bucket of herring?" Danny teased.

"Just get my dinner," Kellan said.

Though he usually enjoyed his brothers' good-natured ribbing, he didn't want to turn this whole episode into something more than it was. He'd done a good deed and rescued a damsel in distress. And tomorrow, she'd find her way home and his life would get back to normal.

Danny poured him a Guinness before he went back into the kitchen to place Kellan's dinner order. A few moments later, Jordan and Nan sidled up to him, sitting down on stools on either side of him.

"Don't even ask," he growled.

"You told me you'd do the programs for our wedding ceremony," Nan said.

"Get Danny to do it," Kellan said. "He's a far better artist than I am."

"He hates using a computer. And he and Jordan are helping with the decorations." She reached over the bar to retrieve a box. "Please?"

Kellan smiled. "Of course I'll do them."

Nan clapped, her expression brightening. "There's plenty of paper. You'll have to print it all on one page and then fold the page in half and then punch it at the top and string the ribbon through. And then glue a tiny little red jewel on the end of each ribbon. But be careful not to get a lot of glue on it. And let it dry before you fold it again." She paused, forcing a smile. "It's easy. Really."

"Where's she from?" Jordan asked, unable to contain her curiosity.

Kellan shrugged. "No clue."

"She must be from close by," Jordan commented. "She knew how to get down to the cove. Danny says you three are the only ones who know where the path is."

Kellan took a sip of his beer, then slowly set it down in front of him. He did know of one other person who'd discovered the path. It had been so long ago, fifteen years, more or less. The girl he'd chased across the meadow. His first kiss. He'd seen her that day and then never again. And though his memory was a bit muddled, there was something about Gelsey that was oddly familiar.

"She could use some clothes," Kellan said. "I was hoping one of you might have something to lend her."

"Is she naked up there?" Jordan asked, her eyes wide.

"No, I gave her some of my clothes. But they'll be far too large for her."

"I can run home right now," Nan offered.

"I'm sure I can find something for her," Jordan said.

"Tomorrow morning will be fine," Kellan said. "I don't think she's going anywhere tonight."

Nan leaned closer, lowering her voice. "Was she wearing a red cap? Or a cloak? You can tell us. We won't say anything."

"I wouldn't have expected you to fall for all that mermaid rubbish," Kellan said. "She was wearing a green silk dress with nothing underneath."

"Hmm," Nan said, her brow furrowed. "The Irish legends about merrows say that they wear a red cap or a cloak and if the human steals either one, the merrow will forget her life in the sea and live on land with the human."

"If you want to keep her, maybe you should start looking for that cloak or hat," Jordan teased. "I'd definitely hide the green silk dress for safe measure."

"Yeah, I'll get right on that," Kellan said with a chuckle. "Because the best way to form a perfect relationship is to trap someone into staying with me. Especially some magical sea creature that isn't human in the first place."

Nan and Jordan giggled. "So she's probably not a real merrow," Nan said. "But if she's pretty and you like her, maybe you should ask her to stay a little longer. You need a date to our engagement party, don't you?"

He smiled. "I really don't think she'll hang around that long."

By the time he finished his beer, Danny had packed up his supper order in a paper sack and encouraged him to bring the "merrow" down to the pub for lunch the following day. Kellan put up with the last bit of teasing before making his escape.

As he walked back to the cottage, the wind nipped at his face. The thought that Gelsey might have died on the beach sent a shiver running through him. How long had she been there? Was there no one who'd missed her? Wouldn't her absence cause at least one person to wonder where she was sleeping for the night?

The cottage was dark and quiet when he stepped inside. The peat fire on the hearth had cooled and Kellan set the bag of food and box of paper on the table and slipped out of his jacket. When he saw Gelsey on the sofa, sound asleep, he kicked off his shoes and crossed to the hearth.

He silently tossed another brick of peat on the fire, then turned and looked at her. The light from the flame played across her beautiful face and he studied her for a long moment. Was she the girl he remembered from so long ago? If it was her, where had she been all this time? Why hadn't he seen her in the last fifteen years?

A sudden thought occurred to him and he walked into the bedroom and bent down at a spot beneath the window. The floorboard was still loose. He took his keys out of his pocket and pried the end up, peering into the dark space between the joists.

There it was. Where he'd hidden it all those years ago. Kellan reached down and pulled out the old biscuit tin, wiping the dust away with his palm. Did it belong to her? Is that why she'd come back to him? Or was he just fooling himself that there was something special about her?

Kellan sat down on the bed and pried off the lid, silently inventorying the contents and looking for a clue about the previous owner. When he found nothing, he tucked the tin into the bottom drawer of the bedside table, then walked to the kitchen and grabbed a cold beer.

Stretching out in the overstuffed chair across from the sofa, he watched her, thinking about what it would be like to have her in his bed. The heat from the hearth relaxed him and he sensed that whatever happened between them would be incredibly pleasurable.

This wasn't a woman who hid her passions. Whatever had sent her to that beach last night, dressed in almost nothing, and vulnerable to the wind and cold, had overwhelmed all common sense. Who or what had driven her to nearly kill herself?

He silently catalogued what he knew about her. She

was familiar enough with the area to know how to get down to the cove. He'd already ruled out the possibility that she'd washed ashore from the water. She wasn't wearing any underwear with her dress, so she probably hadn't been out in public before visiting the beach. She wasn't a local. Her accent was an odd mix of British and American and something else. Something more exotic.

She seemed well educated, maybe even coming from a posh background, though he wasn't sure what brought him to that conclusion. Maybe it was in the way she moved, with such self-assured grace and perfect posture. And in the way she ate, quietly sipping her soup from the spoon as if dining in some fancy restaurant.

Kellan sat in front of the fire for a long time, thinking about the women who'd populated his past. He'd always carefully chosen those he invited into his bed. Vulnerability wasn't a quality he sought. But looking at Gelsey, he felt a strange urge to protect her, to keep her from harm.

When he finished his beer, he got up and took the empty to the kitchen, then wandered back to the bedroom. He thought about waking her, but she seemed quite comfortable on the sofa.

He stripped off his clothes in the dark, then flopped down on the bed, dressed only in his boxers. He closed his eyes, but images of Gelsey plagued his thoughts. His fingers twitched as he remembered the feel of her naked body beneath his palms, recalled the soft swell of her breasts, the sweet curve of her backside. Just the thought of touching her brought an unwelcome reaction and Kellan groaned and rolled over on his stomach.

Unless he wanted to put up with this kind of torment for the rest of his stay in Ballykirk, he'd have to return Gelsey to where she belonged. He pulled the pillow over his head and quietly sang a familiar pub song that went on and on.

Like counting sheep, the song gradually relaxed him and he found himself drifting closer and closer to sleep. The image in his head slowly morphed into a dream as sleep overcame him.

THE WIND RATTLED the windows and Gelsey sat up and ran her hands through her tangled hair. Where was she? She squinted to see in the low light from the hearth. This wasn't her room at Winterhill. Or her room at her mother's apartment on Park Avenue. She didn't recognize anything.

She swung her feet off the sofa and stood, fighting a wave of dizziness. Running her hands over her clothes, she remembered that she was in Kellan Quinn's house. What time was it? How long had she slept? And where was Kellan?

The room was chilly and she rubbed her arms, then grabbed up the quilt and wrapped it around her body. She was normally a restless sleeper, preferring to nap during the day and stay awake during the darkest hours. Rain hissed at the windows and she crossed the room to the fireplace.

There was no more peat to feed the fire and the room

would only get colder. She raked her hands through her hair again, then wandered over to the bedroom, her bare feet silent on the rough wooden floor.

She found Kellan asleep in the bed, his form faintly visible in the dark. His long legs were twisted around the bedclothes and his arm was thrown over his head, his naked chest bare to the chilly room. Gelsey stood over him, deciding whether she ought to wake him, or just crawl into bed beside him.

She tossed the quilt over the bed, then stretched out along the length of his body. As she slipped under the covers, he jerked, then pushed up on his elbow, squinting into the dark.

"The fire went out," she whispered. "It's cold out there."

He cleared his throat. "I—I can fetch more peat," he said. "And there's a portable heater in the kitchen."

"This is all right," she said. "You're warm." She snuggled into that warmth. He had a beautiful body, slender but muscular, perfectly masculine in every way.

He grabbed her hand, pressing it to his heart and Gelsey felt his pulse beneath her palm, quick and sure. She held her breath, wondering what was going through his mind. "Maybe I should go find that heater," she murmured.

"No." Kellan held tight to her hand. "It's all right. You can stay."

She relaxed again and stretched out beside him. "I love nights like this," Gelsey whispered, "listening to the rain and the wind outside. It makes me feel safe, all warm and cozy and out of the weather."

"You weren't out of the weather last night," he said.

"I wasn't out there all night," Gelsey explained. "I walked out there after the sun came up."

"You were drunk at seven in the morning?"

"Not so much drunk as just…drained. Emotionally exhausted."

"Would you like to tell me why?"

Gelsey shook her head. That was the last thing she wanted to talk about. There was nothing about her past that she wanted to remember. "It's not important." She pushed up on an elbow and tried to make out his features in the dark. "Thank you for coming to my rescue. I don't know if I said that before, but I do appreciate what you did."

"Not a problem," Kellan said.

She leaned closer to kiss him on the cheek, but at the last moment, he turned and her lips came down on the corner of his mouth. Gelsey froze. She'd promised herself that she wasn't going to rush headlong into a sexual relationship again. She was going to think before she acted.

But Kellan made the next move and she was powerless to stop. He slipped his palms around her waist and pulled her beneath him. A sigh escaped from her throat as his mouth covered hers in a long and mind-numbing kiss.

Gelsey moaned softly as he stretched her arms out above her head. He was nearly naked and she was bun-dled up in a fleece sweatshirt and a pair of his cotton boxers. But she was glad for the barrier between them, at least for the moment. It was just a kiss and nothing more. Just a kiss, she reminded herself.

"Are you sure about this?" he whispered.

Then again, maybe it was something more. She arched against him, her movement instinctive. "I don't know," she said, the answer coming with a gasp.

Her hands skimmed over his back, her fingers exploring the rippled muscle that shifted with every movement of his body. Though she was ready to tear her clothes off, Kellan seemed more intent on seducing her slowly.

"Tell me to stop," he murmured.

But as his hands slipped beneath her clothes, Gelsey knew the battle was already lost. Desperate to feel that connection with another human being, she couldn't bring herself to say it. It was always this way with her, craving that intimacy she only found in bed with men. It wasn't always the right thing to do, but it was the only time she felt wanted and needed—and completely in control.

"Don't stop," she said, reaching for the hem of her sweatshirt.

"Relax." He took her hand and wove his fingers through hers, drawing it up to his lips. "We have time. Unless you're going to wander out into this storm all by yourself again."

Gelsey wriggled out from beneath him, then got up on her knees. "Maybe I should take my clothes off?"

"No," he said, shaking his head.

"I could take your clothes off," she suggested.

"No." He pulled her back down on top of him. "I get the feeling you usually take charge in the bedroom."

"No," Gelsey said. She paused. "Yes." He was right. She usually did do the seducing. The men she chose to seduce were always happy to be along for the ride. "But I've been told I'm really good."

"I've been told the same thing," Kellan said. He slipped his hand beneath her sweatshirt, running his palm along her belly until he cupped her breast. Gelsey's breath caught in her throat as his thumb grazed her nipple. "I do know what I'm doing. If you just trust me, I'm sure we'll make it through just fine."

She closed her eyes and tipped her head back as delicious sensation pulsed through her body. "Yes, I suppose we will."

He moved to the other breast. "And hasn't anyone ever told you that anticipation can sometimes be as much fun as the act itself?"

"No," she said. "In fact, you do more talking than anyone I've ever been with."

This brought a chuckle. He slipped his hands around her and pulled her back down on top of him. "Everyone in town thinks you're a mermaid."

Gelsey laughed softly. "Do you think I am?"

He slipped his hand around her nape and pulled her close. "Sweetheart, right now, I'll believe anything you tell me."

Kellan grabbed the hem of her sweatshirt and in one

smooth motion pulled it over her head and tossed it aside. He drew her closer, his lips teasing at her nipple. Gelsey sighed, furrowing her hands through his thick hair and arching against him. Inhaling deeply, she closed her eyes and relaxed, focusing on his touch.

As promised, Kellan took his time, slowly seducing her, learning what she liked, what made her shudder and what made her moan. No man had ever taken so much care to make her feel wanted. Sex had always been a race to the end. But this was a long, lazy stroll.

By the time they were both naked, Gelsey wasn't even in charge of her own reactions. As he kissed his way from her lips to her belly, she trembled, knowing exactly what was coming.

But he teased her a little longer, moving lower to gently kiss the inside of her thighs. When he finally found the spot between her legs, Gelsey was so close to the edge she knew she would lose control at the first caress. But, as if he read her distress, Kellan began slowly and deliberately.

Again and again, he brought her close, then slowly pulled back. He knew the signs of her impending release and never allowed her to tumble over the edge. A delicious tension grew inside her and with each flick of his tongue, she began to feel herself losing touch with reality.

Her fingers and toes tingled and her arms and legs felt boneless. She begged him to stop teasing and to give her what she needed, but Kellan seemed determined to prove his point. Her body belonged to him, at least for this one night and he was going to bend it to his will.

Gelsey finally ceded all control—she realized that fighting him was no use. All he wanted was to give her pleasure—deep, shattering, soul-stirring pleasure. And for the first time in her life, she trusted a man enough to allow it.

Though she didn't really know him, she sensed that he had no ulterior motive. He had no idea who she was or where she came from. He didn't know about her family or her money. And all the emotional baggage that she carried around was invisible to him, at least for now.

With this man, this stranger, she felt liberated. There were no fears hiding just beneath the surface, no doubts or insecurities. And when her release came, it was a perfect expression of what she felt—complete freedom.

Her body tensed and then dissolved into powerful spasms. He'd been right all along. It was worth the wait. Wave after wave of pleasure washed over her until she couldn't respond anymore. But though the orgasm re-laxed her, it also invigorated her. And when the last shudder was long gone, Gelsey was far from finished.

Kellan pulled her into the curve of his naked body, resting his chin on her shoulder, his breath warm against her ear. Gelsey wriggled her backside, testing the limits of his control. He was hard. She could feel it. But Kellan had other ideas.

"Go to sleep," he murmured.

"I've been sleeping all day," Gelsey replied.

"I haven't. And we have a busy day ahead of us tomorrow."

"What are we doing?"

"I have no idea. But I'm sure we'll have fun. I suspect it will require a lot of energy, though."

Gelsey smiled to herself and snuggled a little closer. She didn't need to hear anything else. She had another day and maybe another night to spend in this world, with this man. And that was all she really wanted.

"You can't resist me forever," she said.

"I can't?"

"No," she whispered. There'd come a moment when he'd ache for the touch of her hand or the feel of her mouth on his body. And then, she'd give him what he'd given her…sweet, shattering release. And after that—they'd see what happened. Right now, the possibilities seemed endless.

KELLAN ROLLED OVER in bed, stretching his arms over his head. His legs were tangled in the bed linens and he kicked them aside, then reached out to Gelsey. But the opposite side of the bed was cold and empty. He sat up and drew a deep breath. The soft sound of her voice drifted in through the open door. It sounded as if she was talking on the phone.

Kellan glanced over at the clock on the bedside table. It was just past 5:00 a.m. and dawn was still hours away. Swinging his legs over the edge of the bed, Kellan stood and tiptoed to the door. A floorboard creaked beneath his feet and he paused, waiting to see if she'd noticed.

"Really," Gelsey whispered. "I'm fine. I'm safe. I'm with friends. I just didn't want you to worry."

After a long silence, she spoke again. "Yes, I have everything I need for now."

Who was she speaking to? It sounded like a parent. But maybe it was a boyfriend. Or a husband.

"I—I lost my mobile," Gelsey said. "If Antonio calls again, tell him…tell him that…" She cursed softly. "Just put him off. Don't tell him anything." She paused again. "All right. I know you do. Take care."

He heard her set the phone back into the cradle. By the time she returned to the bed, his eyes were closed and the sheets pulled up around his waist. She sank down beside him and a moment later, he felt the warmth from her naked body against his. Kellan wrapped his arms around her and nuzzled his face into the curve of her neck.

"Are you awake?" she whispered.

"I wasn't…until now. Where were you?"

"Bathroom," she lied. Gelsey shuddered and wriggled back against him, her backside nestled into his lap. "I'm so cold. I just can't seem to stay warm."

It was a blatant invitation to touch her, to run his hands over her bare skin. Kellan considered his options. Why even bother to resist, he mused. She was offering herself to him without any conditions. Why not enjoy her company while she was here? He reached out and smoothed his hand over her shoulder, pushing her hair aside until he could kiss the curve of her neck.

The warmth of his lips on her skin was enough to get him aroused again, enough to make him forget all his doubts about who she was and where she came from. In truth, the mystery about this woman made it even more exciting, more dangerous.

She turned to face him and almost immediately, her mouth found his. She kissed him without any hesitation, her tongue tangling with his as he pulled her beneath his naked body. Everything about her was perfect, her long, slender limbs, her pale silken skin, the addictive taste of her lips….

Kellan groaned as she slid her leg up along his hip, his growing erection cradled at the juncture of her thighs. It would be so simple to just slip inside her and he ached to join in this way, to share such an intimate connection.

He hadn't planned on unplanned sex. Part of the reason he'd focused on her earlier was that he wasn't really sure he had any condoms with him. He usually kept a box in the side pocket of his duffel, but he'd put his emptied bag in the boot of his car to get it out of the way.

Gelsey pressed her palm to his chest. Kellan was sure she could feel his heart slamming against it. He'd always had such control around women, trying to figure out what they wanted, and what he was willing to surrender to get what he wanted. It was like a chess game, only with naked bodies and unsatisfied desires.

But he didn't want to think now. He just wanted to feel. And when Gelsey ran her palm between them, then wrapped her fingers around his shaft, Kellan closed his eyes and groaned. He didn't know anything about her, except her name. And one other thing. She could make his body ache like no other women ever had.

"I need to go get a condom," he murmured.

"You don't keep them in the bedroom?"

"They're in my duffel. I think."

"Where is your duffel?"

"In my car." Cursing softly, Kellan crawled out of bed. This would no doubt prove to her that he wasn't the smoothest guy on the planet.

"Aren't you going to put some clothes on?" she asked.

He shook his head. "No. That will take too long. I'm just going to make a run for it." Kellan hurried to the front door, grabbing his keys from the table as he passed. With a squeal of excitement, Gelsey followed him, tugging the quilt off the bed and wrapping it around them both.

"You don't have to come with me," he said. "It's freezing out there."

He wrapped his arm around her waist and pulled her body against his, kissing her deeply as his hand skimmed over her bare torso. When they finally pulled the front door open, a cold, wet wind hit them both in the face. Gelsey covered him with the blanket and stood in the doorway, naked and shivering. "Run," she cried. "Hurry."

Drawing a deep breath, Kellan started down the garden path. The bricks were freezing and slick under his feet and by the time he reached his car, he was already soaked. Fumbling with the keys, he tried to keep the quilt wrapped around himself, but a gust caught it and exposed his nude body to the full brunt of the storm.

When he reached the front door, duffel in his hand, Gelsey was waiting with a towel. She rubbed the rain from his face and hair, then slammed the door shut and gently pulled him along to the fireplace.

"It's bloody cold out there."

"You're stark naked," she said with a giggle. "What did you expect?"

He glanced down. "I think I've done irreparable damage to my manhood."

Gelsey looked up at him, sending him a coy smile. "I can take care of that."

As she continued to dry him off, he reached out and cupped her cheek in his palm. "Who are you? What are you doing here with me?"

"I'm not sure," she said. "But I do know that I don't want to leave yet."

He brought her lips to his and kissed her, a rush of warmth snaking through his body. It wasn't enough to possess only her mouth. Kellan pulled her against him, stumbling back against the door and dropping the leather duffel.

Grabbing her hips, he spun them around and pressed her against the door. Gelsey slipped her hand between them and slowly began to stroke. She'd been right all along. She had a very simple antidote for the cold. In little more than a minute, he was hard and ready and aching to bury himself in her warmth.

Outside, the weather raged, the wind roaring up from the sea and the rain pelting at the windowpanes. But inside the cottage, they found the storm between them just as powerful and overwhelming.

Kellan's mouth savaged Gelsey's and he felt himself losing all sense of control. The last time had been gentle and slow, but this time he didn't want to wait. For Kellan, there was no longer any point in pretending. Since he'd held her body against his on the beach, he'd known this moment would come. It felt as if he'd been waiting for this his entire adult life—waiting for a woman who could make him feel real raw passion.

"Condom," he murmured.

She reached down and picked up his duffel and he rummaged through it until he found the box. Saying a silent prayer that it wasn't empty, Kellan opened it. A single foil packet fell into his palm. "Stroke of luck there," he murmured.

Gelsey grabbed the packet and tore it open, then quickly sheathed him. She drew him along to the sofa, then pushed him down, straddling his hips with her knees. Gently, she guided him inside her. He wanted to slow down, to just take a moment and enjoy the anticipation. But the instant he felt her warmth close around him, Kellan was lost. He held his breath, marshaling his control, trying to fix his mind on something other than the woman above him.

Programs, he thought to himself. He had to do those damn wedding programs. Ribbon and little red jewels, Nan had said. He didn't know what the hell she'd been talking about, but as long as he focused on his brother's wedding plans, he'd be all right.

"Do you want me to move?" she whispered, her words soft against his ear.

"No," he said.

"It works better if I move."

He leaned back and found her smiling down at him. "I know. I have done this before."

"Really? It's hard to tell."

Chuckling softly, he clasped her hips and moved. "Better?"

"Do it again," she said with a laugh.

He did as she asked and she groaned softly. "See how good that feels?"

She leaned over him and touched her lips to his. "You were right," she whispered.

"About what?"

"You *are* very good at this."

3

GELSEY SNUGGLED into the soft covers of the bed. It was still warm with the heat from Kellan's body, even though he'd gotten up an hour before. She was beginning to feel almost normal and attributed part of that to the passionate interlude she'd shared with her rescuer.

Sex had always been an important part of Gelsey's life, but never for the right reasons. According to a long string of therapists, she used sex to create a false sense of security, the security she'd never enjoyed as a child.

Her early childhood had been spent with her nanny, Marie, a wonderful Frenchwoman who had been more of a mother than Dorothy Trent Woodson had ever been. And Gelsey had been happy with that life, even if she rarely spent time with her parents.

But after the divorce, Marie had been sent away, there one day and gone the next. And Gelsey had been packed and shipped off to a Swiss boarding school, a place where she was to be well educated and carefully prepared to take her place in society as some billion-aire's charming wife.

At first, she'd accepted her fate and done her best at school. But then, she'd discovered boys. And along with boys came a sense of exhilarating freedom. There was nothing to stop her from living her life exactly how she chose. That first spontaneous kiss with Kellan had been just the start of her pursuit of pleasure.

Thinking back on it, it had been a terribly bold move on her part. But her grandmother had always told her that if she wanted to be happy, she had to grab happi-ness wherever she could find it. At that moment in time, Kellan had represented everything that was wonderful about life.

She'd watched him and his brothers from afar, hidden behind the rocks on the cliff. He'd been the one she'd fashioned her silly schoolgirl dreams around, the dark, brooding, handsome boy with the pale blue eyes and the confident air about him.

He'd been her first, but he hadn't been her last. Schoolgirl fantasies gave way to teenage realities. Once back in Switzerland, she'd begun to sneak out after curfew. A few years later, there were ski weekends with college boys, older brothers of her schoolmates. She quickly learned to use her sex appeal to get whatever she wanted from handsome men.

After being kicked out of one boarding school, her parents sent to another and another. It was then she discovered that bad behavior was all it took to get at-tention from her parents.

Prep school was followed by university. She headed for Paris and studied art history at the Sorbonne, cooking at Le Cordon Bleu and apprenticed as a designer at Studio Berçot. Then she gained access to her trust fund and her life as a celebutante began.

Gelsey sighed and pulled the covers over her head. She was so tired of that life, completely exhausted playing the role she'd created for herself. The men, the money, the parties. It had all become a giant, crashing bore. And now she'd found an escape, a place to breathe, to take stock of the future and put her past behind her.

To the rest of the world, she was Gigi Woodson. She dated famous athletes and gorgeous male models and sexy actors. She moved from one man to another whenever she grew bored or restless. And every now and then, she got so drunk that she did something that landed her in the tabloids. But here, on the western coast of Ireland, she was a stranger without a past.

Very few people knew her well. Her parents had never bothered to try. But her grandmother had always been able to see inside her heart and say the words that made her feel loved and cherished. It had been the only truly good thing she'd remembered from her childhood. Gelsey felt emotion tighten her throat and she fought back the tears. If only her grandmother were here now, to help her through, to reassure her.

A knock sounded at the front door and Gelsey pushed up, bracing her hand beneath her. She raked her tousled hair out of her eyes and searched around for something to wear. The sweatshirt that Kellan had given her the night before was draped over the bedpost. She grabbed it and pulled it over her head, then tugged on his boxer shorts.

The house was warmer, a fresh peat fire burning in the hearth and the little space heater humming away in the corner. She pulled the door open expecting to see Kellan, his arms overloaded with breakfast. But two women were standing outside, friendly smiles pasted on their faces.

"Hello," Gelsey said, rubbing the sleep from her eyes. "I'm afraid Kellan isn't here."

"Better that," the brunette said cheerfully. "We've come to see you." She held a canvas bag in front of her. "We've brought you something to wear. I'm Jordan and this is Nan."

The raven-haired woman held out another bag. "And you must be Gelsey."

Gelsey stepped away from the door and the two strolled inside as if they were quite at home. Nan wrinkled her nose, then motioned toward the fire. "We really should talk to the boys about putting in central heat. Those peat fires make my eyes water."

"And they should put in a decent bathroom. That shower isn't any bigger than a broom closet."

"Could I offer either of you a cup of tea?" Gelsey asked. Although she'd been well schooled in etiquette, she wasn't quite sure what to do with strangers bearing gifts of secondhand clothing.

Nan stared at her for a long moment. "Have we met?"

"I'm sure we haven't," Gelsey said.

"You look so familiar." Nan plopped down on the end of the sofa. "Now, I'm not sure you'll like anything I brought. But Kellan said you didn't have any decent clothes to wear. I brought a pair of jeans and a couple sweaters—or jumpers, as he calls them. It's so damp in the winter."

"And I brought a jacket," Jordan said. "It's not very fashionable, but it will be warm. And underwear. It's new, still in the package."

Nan rummaged through her bag. "And I have gloves and a hat. And boots. Did you bring the boots, Jo?"

They were both talking so fast that Gelsey could do nothing more than nod and smile. When they finally finished, she drew a ragged breath. "And you're from… the church?"

"Oh, Kellan didn't tell you we'd be stopping by? He saw us both last night at the pub and explained your situation. I'm engaged to Kellan's brother Riley."

"They're getting married New Year's Eve. And I'm with Danny, the other brother."

"Right," Gelsey said. "I remember now." She frowned. "You're not Irish."

"American," Nan said. "And you're not Irish, either."

"No," Gelsey said. She thought it best to leave it at that, unwilling to go into a long explanation of her life. "Let me just put the water on for tea."

"Oh, we can't stay," Nan said. "We're on our way to Cork. I'm shopping for a wedding dress."

"Shopping," Gelsey murmured. She'd been an expert at that in her former life.

"You wouldn't want to come with, would you?" Nan asked.

Jordan clapped her hands. "You should come! We'll make a girls' day of it. And it will get you out of this cottage." She paused and the color rose on her cheeks. "That is, if you want to leave. But I can completely understand why you wouldn't. I'm sure Kell is keeping you—"

"Busy," Nan finished.

"I can't. I'm a bit broke right now."

The two women stared at her with uneasy smiles. "Perfectly understandable," Nan said. "Why would you have any use for— I mean, you've spent your life…"

"Living in the ocean," Jordan said.

"What— Oh!" Gelsey laughed. "Right. Kellan told me that everyone thinks I'm a mermaid."

Jordan nodded. "Of course, we don't really believe that. But when in Ireland…"

"I love that about Ireland," Gelsey said. "People still believe in magic here."

"And you do look the part, with all that long, wavy hair," Nan said. "Danny was right. You are beautiful."

"Danny?"

"He was there when Kellan rescued you," Jordan explained.

A slow smile curled the corners of Gelsey's mouth

and she shrugged. "I don't really remember meeting him."

"What size are your feet?" Jordan asked.

"Eight?" Gelsey said.

"Perfect! The boots are eight and a half. Just wear extra socks. Are you sure you won't come with us? We'll have lunch. Our treat."

"Maybe another time," Gelsey said. "Really. I'd love to go another time."

They both stood. "Good," Nan said. "I'm sure we'll see you around the pub. Tell Kellan to bring you down for dinner tonight."

Gelsey took the offered bags and walked them to the door. This was all very strange. Gelsey couldn't remember the last time she'd been able to be completely anonymous. No matter where she went, someone always recognized her.

But then, she was usually dressed quite differently and hiding behind an image that was regularly splashed across the pages of the tabloids. For the first time in a very long time, she had a chance to live life like an ordinary woman.

She had a fresh start, a chance to make real friends who didn't care about her notoriety or her money or her family connections. And Nan and Jordan seemed exactly like the kind of women she'd want for friends.

After she said goodbye, Gelsey quickly found an outfit to wear, then pulled on socks and the soft fleece-lined boots. Though she was a bit taller than Nan and Jordan, with longer arms, she couldn't complain. It was good enough to go out in public in and she needed some fresh air and exercise.

She'd walk down to the village and get her bearings. If she was going to stay for a while, she needed a source of income. She could just go get her bank cards at Winterhill, but if she was going to start over, then she needed to find a way to make a living. She needed a job.

But could she survive on her own? It was a challenge she'd never have thought of taking on in the past, but now it made sense. Gigi Woodson, celebrity heiress, was gone and Gelsey Woodson, ordinary working girl, had been born. For once, she didn't want to mess it all up.

Gelsey grabbed the jacket from the sofa and slipped into it. When she opened the door, the chilly air rushed in and she drew a deep breath and smiled. It was a beautiful day. She had no idea what was going to happen, but it was exciting to be completely unsure of her future.

She followed the road down to the village at a brisk walk, smiling to herself as she took in the beauty of the countryside. Everything looked so picturesque— the vivid green hills and the whitewashed village set against the slate-blue sea. Boats bobbed in the harbor and she watched one as it slowly moved out into the bay.

Gelsey had lived in many exotic places, but she'd never felt at home. Maybe this was where she'd belonged all along. She was destined to find Kellan all these years later and to begin where they'd left off as teenagers.

KELLAN SQUINTED against the late-morning sun as he drove out of Ballykirk toward the cottage. He'd left Gelsey naked and sound asleep in his bed. After last night, he'd figured she'd need her sleep. But it was nearly noon and he'd fetched lunch from the pub, hoping that they could spend the rest of the day in bed after a hearty meal.

It was the perfect day to spend curled up beneath the sheets, he mused. A winter chill had set in and the damp wind blowing off the sea made it feel colder than it was. Christmas was three weeks away and after that, the new year. He'd made a resolution last year on New Year's Eve to expand his professional horizons, to take jobs outside of Ireland and see a bit more of the world. And here he was, just a month away from his deadline and he still hadn't made a decision about the project in France.

As he rounded a bend in the road, Kellan caught sight of a figure striding toward him. As he drove closer, he recognized Gelsey, her pale hair blowing in the wind. She smiled and waved. He pulled the car to a stop and rolled down the window.

"What are you doing out here?"

"A couple of your friends brought me some clothes." She pointed to her feet. "And boots. I was coming to find you."

"Hop in," he said, leaning across the seat to open the passenger-side door.

She joined him inside the car, her color high, her eyes bright. Kellan knew she was a beautiful woman, but the sight of her in broad daylight was enough to take his breath away. An unbidden surge of hunger raced through him and he fought his instinct to drag her into his arms and kiss her. "So, I guess you slept well last night. You're clearly feeling better."

"I feel wonderful," Gelsey said. "Good sex always does that for me."

Kellan couldn't help but smile. "And what would you like to do today? I have lunch." He pointed to the paper sack in the backseat.

"Well, we could eat." She paused as she considered her options. "And then, I'd like…"

"What?"

"I'd like you to teach me how to drive this car."

"You don't know how to drive?"

"I never had a reason to."

Kellan groaned. "Don't start with that mermaid bollocks again. I know you're not a mermaid."

"I was going to say that I never had a reason to learn," she said. A tiny smile quirked at the corners of her mouth. "We don't have cars at the bottom of the ocean. And it's really difficult to work the pedals with flippers."

Kellan laughed. "I'll teach you how to drive if you tell me the truth about where you come from."

"Why? There's nothing wrong with exercising your imagination every now and then. Is it so hard to believe I came from the sea?"

"Why can't you tell me the truth? Is that so hard to do?"

She stared out the windscreen, her gaze fixed on the landscape passing by. "Have you ever wanted to change your life? Just start all over again?"

"I wish I could go back and change a few things," Kellan said.

She looked at him, curiosity filling her eyes. "Like what?"

"I had a chance to go into business with a developer a few years ago, to buy properties and fix them up and then sell them. I thought it was too risky, but now I'm thinking that risk might not be such a bad thing."

"Why don't you do it now?" she asked.

"I get paid a boatload to do exactly what I do best," he said, shaking his head. "And the economy hasn't been too good. In the end, I was right to trust my instincts."

"I always liked to take risks," she said. "It makes life more exciting."

"Or more chaotic," Kellan countered.

"A little chaos might be good for you," she said.

"You don't know me very well."

Gelsey smiled. "I'm a really good judge of people. It's one of my most amazing qualities."

"But you can't drive," he said.

"I'm not perfect," she teased.

"Close," Kellan replied. "All right, switch spots with me and we'll give this a go. You have to promise to listen to everything I say."

She crawled over him, stopping at the point where

she straddled his legs. "This is nice," she murmured, her breasts in his face.

"It's impossible to drive this way," he murmured, staring up at her, his gaze fixed on her lips. With a groan, Kellan shoved his fingers through the hair at her nape and dragged her into a long, deep kiss. This hunger for the taste of her was so difficult to deny, especially when she was so available and so willing.

When she finally drew back, a satisfied smile curled her lips. "Is that a gearshift in your pocket or are you just happy to see me?" she teased. Gelsey giggled as she moved over him, taunting him with the friction of her body against his. "I see I've got your engine running, don't I?"

Kellan held up his hands, chuckling softly. "Stop. The metaphors are torture enough. Do you want to learn to drive?"

"Yes," she said. "As long as we can get back to this lesson later."

"And what lesson is that?"

"The lesson that teaches you that you can't possibly resist me."

Kellan groaned. "I believe I learned that lesson the first day we met."

"And it's my duty to keep reminding you," she said.

There was no need to do that, Kellan mused. It was painfully evident the effect she had on his body. A single kiss was enough to set him off. But his reaction hadn't been just physical. He was developing a real affection for Gelsey.

She was smart and witty and managed to drag him out of his serious nature with just a smile. When he was with her, he didn't dwell on his professional worries. Hell, he'd barely thought about work at all. He liked the fact that he actually had a personal life now, a reason to relax and take time off.

But how long could that possibly last? Kellan wondered. Would there come a point where they grew bored with each other, where being together seemed more like a chore than a treat?

"Switch!" Gelsey said. When she'd finally settled herself behind the wheel, she glanced over at him. "Where are we going to go?"

"Back to the cottage."

Gelsey shook her head. "No, I want to go into town."

"But I have lunch right here. It's going to get cold."

"I'm not hungry. I need to look for a job."

Kellan frowned, taken aback by her request. "A job? What exactly is a mermaid qualified to do?"

"I don't know. I'm very good with people, I'm clever and I'm a fast learner. I expect I could do any number of jobs. Do you need a waitress at the pub? I could do that. And I can also cook. I'm a very good cook."

"You cook?"

She stared out the windscreen and nodded, her attention now absorbed with learning to drive. "I am very good with fish. It's my specialty." She looked at him and grinned. "Really. I'll cook you dinner sometime." Gelsey grabbed the gearshift and put it into Drive. "Ready?"

"Buckle your safety belt," he warned.

She did as she was told, then clutching the wheel, she slowly pressed on the accelerator. To Kellan's surprise, the car glided smoothly forward. After only a few minutes, he had reason to suspect that she'd driven before. Though she appeared a bit tense, she knew exactly what she was doing.

They came to a crossroad north of Ballykirk and she stopped and looked at him. "Which way?"

"You're in charge," he said. "You choose. Who taught you how to drive? Because I don't believe you've never driven before."

"A very nice octopus taught me when I was just a tadpole." She turned left, heading along the coast and for a moment, she drove on the wrong side of the road. But then, before he could speak, she corrected herself. "Sorry," she murmured. "We usually drive on the other side in...the ocean."

"You're doing well," he said.

"I'm going to need a car," she said. "How much does a car cost? I've never bought one."

"Varies," he said. "But before you get a car, you need a license. You'll have to take a test. In truth, you should have a permit now. The garda probably could stop you and—"

She slammed on the brakes and the car skidded to a stop. "That's enough for now," she said, putting the gearshift back into Park. Gelsey shoved the door open and hopped out. Kellan got out and they exchanged places.

"I didn't mean you had to stop," he said. "The garda usually doesn't patrol these roads during the day."

"I don't want to cause any trouble," she said. "I'm already in…" She paused, then pointed out the window. "Drive on."

They continued their drive along the coast and when they passed by Castle Cnoc, Kellan slowed the car and stopped at the gate. He pointed up the driveway. "That's one of my projects," he said. "Just finished last month. Jordan was the project manager."

"It's lovely," she said. "Do you like your job, then?"

"Sure. I've always loved historical properties. It's like mixing history with architecture. New buildings just don't have the same appeal to me."

"I wish I knew what I was meant to do," she murmured. "I've never had to choose a path for my life. It was chosen for me. How do you pick?"

"I didn't," he said. "It just always seemed like the right thing. You'll figure it out."

"I'm twenty-seven years old," she said.

"Is that in fish years or human years?" he teased.

"Human," she said. "Sometimes, I feel like I'm just starting my life. Like a baby taking her first steps."

An odd expression crossed her face and Kellan could only read it as regret. He knew nothing of her past or what she was running away from. But he knew that he cared enough to give her a safe place to stay for a while. "You won't need to buy a car," he said. "My family has a little Fiat that we lend out to tourists who rent the cot-

tage. It's parked behind Danny's smithy. You can use it
for as long as you like."

She glanced over at him, her expression shifting suddenly. "Thank you," she said. "That's very nice of you.
But I still think I should get a car of my own."

The smile she sent him was like a ray of sunshine,
warm and bright and full of everything that he needed
to survive. But Kellan got the uneasy feeling that his
affection for Gelsey would come at a price. The more
he got to know her, the more he needed her. So what
would happen when she decided to leave?

It wasn't a question that he'd thought about in any
great depth, but now, the idea of losing her outweighed
any fears he had of getting too close. "I suppose we
could drive into town and see if anyone is looking for
help."

"You really think someone would hire me?"

As Kellan turned the car around and headed back to
Ballykirk, he realized that Gelsey's job hunt might provide a bit more insight into who she really was. She'd
have to give a last name and if she wasn't an Irish citi-
zen, she'd have to give a whole lot more than that.

GELSEY HAD BEEN CURIOUS about the inhabitants of Kellan's hometown, but she'd never expected them to be
so curious about her. "Why is everyone staring at me?"
she murmured as she and Kellan strolled down the main
street of Ballykirk.

"Are they?" he asked.

"Yes! Haven't you noticed? They don't really think I'm a—"

"No," Kellan said. "I suspect they're just curious about what's going on between us. Everyone in this village is in everyone else's business. You can't sneeze in this town without a half-dozen people offering medical advice. It's kind of the same with romance."

She opened her mouth, then snapped it shut. Of course. She and Kellan been shacked up together for two days now, eating take-out food from the pub and no doubt creating all sorts of speculation. Now that they'd emerged from their den of passion, people were bound to be curious.

"I suppose I'll have to get used to that kind of thing," she murmured.

"They're just excited to have something new to gossip about. They'll move along to a new subject soon enough."

Gelsey forced a smile. Or maybe not. How long would it be before someone recognized her? Without the makeup and the skimpy dresses, she barely looked like the girl in the tabloids. But was Ballykirk really that isolated from the rest of the world? "I love this village," she said. "It's so…picturesque."

"Ballykirk? When I was a lad I couldn't wait to leave."

"You did leave," she said.

Kellan nodded. "For university. In Dublin and then a year in London."

"Why did you come back?" Gelsey asked.

"I'm not technically back. I just finished the job at Castle Cnoc and I don't have anything else lined up until after the new year. I usually live in Dublin."

"I ought to have finished university," Gelsey said. In truth, she hadn't given it much chance. She'd been too restless to sit in a class all day, so she'd decided to go to cooking school. When she'd grown bored with that, she'd tried fashion school. Paired with her lack of real work experience, she'd been left with a rather unconventional résumé.

"They have universities where you come from?" he asked. "Oh, wait. I don't know where you come from, do I?"

She slipped her arm through his and gave him a playful slap. "How do you think I learned to speak French?" she asked.

"You speak French?"

"Mais oui," Gelsey replied.

"You're hiding all sorts of secrets, aren't you?"

Her expression suddenly turned serious. "We all have secrets. I suspect you have a few of your own."

"No," he said.

"None?"

"Well, when I was fourteen, I wanted to be James Bond. I mean, the bloke was a god with the women."

"And you weren't?"

"No. Far from it. I'd never kissed a girl before. And then, that summer it happened and after that it was a brand-new world."

"Tell me about it," Gelsey said.

He glanced over at her. "I suspect you know how it goes."

She drew in a sharp breath. Was he referring to the kiss they'd shared all those years before? Did he remember her? She'd been so young. Eleven years old and all arms and legs. And so flat-chested she was sure she'd never grow breasts.

"Sure," Gelsey said. "It's always very clumsy at first. But you obviously got the hang of it. In fact, you're quite an expert now."

She glanced into a shop window as they passed by and then stopped short. "Look," she said, pointing to the hand-lettered sign: Help Wanted. Enquire Within. Gelsey stepped back to look at the sign hung above the door. "Maeve Dunphrey's Potions and Lotions," she read.

"You don't want to go in there," Kellan said.

"It looks nice. And she's looking for help."

"Trust me, there are lots of other places that would be better suited."

"But this looks like fun. She sells soap and hand lotion and perfumes. I know about those things."

"All right. But before you go in, you should know that she's crazy. A complete nutter. Gone in the head. She thinks she's a Druid priestess. She makes all sorts of potions. She almost poisoned Billy Murphy with a love potion once."

"Really?" Gelsey reached for the door. "She sounds very interesting."

"And I doubt that she has any money to pay you. She

barely scrapes by and no one really visits her shop any-more. Those who do, buy her things just to be chari-table."

"Then she really needs my help," Gelsey said. She pulled the door open and stepped inside. It was apparent from the outset why her shop wasn't doing well. It was a top-to-bottom mess. Beautiful old display cases were overflowing with jars and tins and boxes of homemade beauty products. Some looked as though they'd been there for years and others were wrapped in brightly col-ored paper and tied with little bits of string.

"Hello." An elderly woman dressed in a long tap-estry robe appeared from the back of the shop. "Wel-come." She tipped her head and smiled, blinking at Gelsey through horn-rimmed glasses. "You must be the one they've been talking about. The one who came to us from the sea."

"And you must be the priestess," Gelsey replied.

"That I am." Maeve motioned her forward. "Let's have a look at you. I must say, I have been a bit curi-ous since I first heard your story from Doc Finnerty. He comes in for my sea-salt scrub. His wife loves it for her feet. Keeps them soft."

Maeve made a careful study of Gelsey, then nodded. "You're quite a beauty. I expected nothing less. It's a fortunate thing Kellan found you when he did."

"I'd like to inquire about the job," Gelsey said. "The sign in your window says you need help. And I think I could help you."

"Oh, dear. That sign has been there forever. And you're the first person who's come in."

"What are the job requirements?"

Maeve looked around. "I suppose organization would be crucial. As you can see, I'm not much with that. I need someone who is creative. I've always thought I could do a better job with my displays, but I haven't the patience or the time."

"I could do that for you," Gelsey said.

"I can't pay much and I'm not sure how long I'm going to keep the shop. I've wanted to sell it for a while now, and move to Galway to live with my sister. But with help, I might be able to shine the place up a bit."

"I'm your girl," Gelsey stated.

Maeve reached out and took her hand. "I do believe you are."

"When would you like me to start?"

"How about next week? We're closed on Mondays, so Tuesday morning. How is ten?"

"I'll be here at nine," Gelsey said. She shook Maeve's hand, but then couldn't control herself and threw her arms around the elderly woman. "You won't regret this. I promise." Embarrassed, Gelsey stepped back. "Sorry. I'm just very excited. I didn't expect it would be this simple."

"Yes. Well, having a mermaid in the shop might liven things up a bit." She paused. "Oh, and one more thing." Maeve hurried over to one of the display cases and picked up a small jar, then handed it to Gelsey. "I can see you haven't been getting much sleep lately. Try this. It does wonders for bags under the eyes."

"Thank you," Gelsey said. "I will try it tonight. And I'll see you on Tuesday."

When she walked out of the shop, Gelsey jumped into Kellan's arms and yelled, "I got a job!" She gave him a long, lingering kiss. When she finally drew back, she looked around to find several people staring at them. "Well, that will give the townsfolk something new to talk about," she said.

"Yes, I suspect it will. And congratulations—I think. Can we go home now and have some lunch?"

"All right. But I want to do something more. I'll cook for you tonight. A wonderful gourmet meal."

"That's not necessary," he said.

"But I want to." She pushed up on her toes and gave him another kiss. "This has been an amazing day. I think we need to celebrate, don't you?" Gelsey paused. "She mentioned the mermaid thing. You don't think she'll fire me once she realizes I'm not a—"

"I think everyone knows already," Kellan said. He dropped another kiss on her lips. "But that's not going to stop them from talking about it. Twenty years from now, you'll still be known as the mermaid girl."

_____4_____

THE ONLY LIGHT in the cottage came from the peat fire flickering on the hearth and an oil lamp Gelsey had set on the floor. Outside, a roaring wind from the sea scoured the windows. Though they had a perfectly adequate table at which to dine, Gelsey had chosen to spread their gourmet dinner out on the floor in front of the fire, creating a much more romantic atmosphere.

As Kellan poured her another glass of wine, he studied her features, still rendered breathless by her beauty. What bit of luck had brought her into his life? He could have walked in the other direction that morning. She could have climbed up the cliff on her own and disappeared again, without the two of them getting a second chance. But something had brought them together and he couldn't help but wonder if there were magical forces behind it all.

Kellan groaned inwardly. This was exactly how it began for his brothers. He'd listened to Riley and Danny tell their tales and he'd heard them both blather on and on about the incredible power of love. And now he was doing the same thing. Turning himself inside out over a woman he barely knew.

Clenching his fist, Kellan fought the urge to reach out and touch her. Was it even possible to resist anymore or was he completely lost? Yes, the sex was incredible. And he did enjoy spending time with Gelsey, talking to her and kissing her. But that didn't mean he was falling in love.

Still, he couldn't help but admit that everything that passed between them was different, as if it had been touched with something extraordinary, some little bit of magic.

She drew a deep breath and sighed, stretching her bare legs out in front of her. Gelsey was dressed in nothing but one of his oxford shirts. "I feel like a stuffed hen. I knew I could cook, but I didn't expect it would turn out so well."

"It was pretty amazing. That sauce on the salmon was incredible."

"Capers and lemon," she said, scooping up a bit on her finger and holding it out to him. "It's one of the first sauces I learned. I told you I was good with fish."

He took her finger into his mouth and enjoyed another taste of the sauce. "And potatoes. And turnips. Even the salad was perfect."

She grinned seductively, then crawled over the remnants of the meal on her hands and knees to drop a kiss on his mouth. "Are you ready for dessert?"

He glanced down, taking in the view. His shirt gaped

at the neck and he could see her bare breasts. The long tails covered her backside. "Would that involve taking your clothes off?"

"I don't know. It would most definitely involve taking all your clothes off." She reached out for the hem of his T-shirt, then pulled it over his head. Her attention focused on his chest as she smoothed her hands over his shoulders. "I've had a good day. The best day in a very long time."

Kellan nuzzled her neck. "I'm glad." He pressed his lips to a spot just below her ear. "And what made it so good?"

"Everything. And nothing at all," she said.

Kellan stared at her. "Where did you really come from, Gelsey? And why are you still here with me?"

"I think I might belong here," she said. "I don't want to go back."

"There's no one waiting for you? Wondering where you are?"

"No." She sat back on her heels and looked into his eyes. "I promise. There's no one. The only person I want to be with right now is you." She ran her hands through his hair, smoothing it away from his face. "I don't care about your past, Kellan. Nothing that happened to you before you met me makes any difference at all. We started the moment you rescued me from that beach."

"And how will we end?" he asked.

"I don't know. We don't need to worry about that right now. I'm happy and you're happy and we should leave it at that." She drew in a long breath. "You are happy, aren't you?"

Of course he was happy. What man wouldn't be? He had a beautiful, sexy woman in his bed every night, a woman who fascinated him, a woman who drove him wild with desire. And yet, he knew nothing about her. But then, maybe she was right. What difference did it make? There was very little he could learn that would change his feelings for her.

Gelsey leaned in closer. "Can I ask you a question?"

"Only if I can ask one in return," Kellan said.

"When you found me on the beach, why didn't you just take me to the hospital?"

Kellan thought about his response for a long moment. "I don't know. I guess I was curious. I wanted to know what happened, how you got on that beach and why. And I knew if I took you to the hospital, I might never see you again." He kissed her, his lips brushing against hers. "I lost you once, I didn't want to lose you again."

"You lost me?"

"My turn," Kellan said, quickly shifting the subject.

"Make it good," she warned. "You only get one."

"What really sent you out to that beach?" he asked. "It must have been something pretty upsetting."

She shook her head. "Funny, it was then, but now, I barely think about it."

"It or he? Answer the question," Kellan demanded. "Honestly. Was it a man who did that to you?"

"I did it to myself. Up until that moment, I really

didn't like the person I was. I think there's a bit of magic in you finding me on the beach. I'd like to believe there still is."

Kellan slid his fingers through her hair and drew her lips to his. She went soft in his arms and on a sigh, she parted her lips to offer him a taste. Everything about her was perfect, Kellan mused. When he touched her, sex suddenly made sense. It meant something, something deep and reassuring.

Kellan knew the risk he was taking. She'd dropped into his life so unexpectedly and he suspected she'd leave in the same way. For all he knew, he'd wake up one morning and she'd be gone. And without knowing anything about her, he'd have no way to find her again.

Grabbing her waist, he pulled her close, then threw his thigh over hers, trapping her in his embrace. He reached for the buttons of the shirt she wore and slowly undid them, kissing a path from the first bit of exposed flesh to the last.

"Who are you?" he murmured, his lips pressed against the soft flesh of her belly.

Gelsey groaned, her fingers smoothing through his hair as he moved lower. "I don't know," she whispered.

She was the woman he wanted more than any other. She was the woman whose touch could send his need over the edge. And she was the woman who was becoming a part of his life he didn't want to lose.

Kellan found the spot between her legs and gently caressed her with his tongue. Gelsey arched toward him, her fingers clenching his hair. He knew exactly how to control her release and Kellan took every advantage, knowing that it might be the only thing in their relationship that he did control. But was mind-blowing sex enough to keep her with him forever?

Her breath began to come in desperate gasps and Kellan knew she was close. He drew back and traced his way up to her neck. Her body was made for his touch, her skin so pale and smooth and her limbs long and lithe. He drew a deep breath and pulled her closer.

"Maybe we should go into the bedroom," he murmured. Kellan got to his feet and reached down to help her up. But instead of taking a step toward the bedroom, she wrapped her arms around him and kissed him, her tongue teasing at his.

"Take your clothes off," she whispered.

Kellan reached for the button of his jeans, but she was there quicker. She unzipped them, then pushed them down over his hips along with his boxers. Kellan stepped out of them, then pulled her body up against his, her shirt falling down around her elbows.

"Now that you have me naked, what are you going to do with me?"

She gazed up into his eyes, a smile twitching at the corners of her mouth. Then she grabbed his hand and dragged him toward the front door. The moment she opened the door, a huge gust blew icy-cold rain into the cottage. "It's freezing out there," he said. "And raining."

"I'm used to cold and wet," she said. Gelsey slipped out of her shirt. "Come on. Let's go commune with nature."

"Humans are not made for this kind of weather," he said, motioning down to the erection that had grown so quickly the moment he'd kissed her.

Gelsey reached down and smoothed her hand along the length of his shaft, her touch warm on his already chilly flesh. "It will heighten the experience," she murmured. Kellan reluctantly surrendered. There was obviously something in Gelsey that was fed by pushing the boundaries and taking risks. But how far would it go?

"All right."

"You first," she said.

With a shout, Kellan ran outside, his bare feet skidding on the brick walk. When he was nearly to the gate, he turned around to find Gelsey watching him from the doorway. The feeble light from the cabin outlined her nakedness so perfectly that he felt the breath slowly leave his body.

"Aren't you coming?" he shouted, the rain stinging his skin.

"No! It's freezing out there."

Kellan ran back to the door and stepped inside, pulling her along with him. "I didn't want to go out there in the first place!"

"I know," she said. "But I wanted to see how far you'd go for desire. Now I know."

"This was a test?" he asked.

She slowly slid down along his body until her hands rested on his waist. He watched as she drew her tongue along the length of his shaft, the warmth causing a rush of desire to race through him. The feel of her mouth on his cold body was like nothing he'd ever experienced before. Every nerve in his body was alive, his skin prickled with goose bumps and shivers skittering down his spine.

Kellan closed his eyes and leaned back against the door, losing himself in the feel of her mouth surrounding him, drawing him in deep and then drifting away. And when it was too much to take anymore, he pulled her to her feet and spanned her waist with his hands.

In one smooth motion, Kellan picked her up and wrapped her legs around his hips, pressing her against the door until he was positioned at the damp spot between her thighs. Slowly, he entered her, inch by inch until he was buried deep within her warmth.

"You were right," he murmured, his mouth pressed against the curve of her shoulder. "It does heighten the senses."

He drove deep and then withdrew and Gelsey gasped. "Now you can take me to bed," she whispered.

"I think I'm fine right here."

KELLAN LEFT EARLY in the morning, after he and Gelsey shared a quick breakfast together. He'd promised to help Riley with some painting at the cottage that he and Nan had just purchased in Ballykirk. Riley had hoped to have the place ready by the end of December, just in time to move in after their New Year's Eve wedding. Before leaving, he extracted a sleepy promise from Gelsey that she'd meet him for lunch at the pub.

Though Gelsey curled back up under the covers, she wasn't able to sleep. Her mind was spinning with all the possibilities that life now offered. She'd start a new job next week. She was excited at the prospect, but she was also a bit scared. She'd never held a job before. Would she actually know what to do, how to behave? What if people didn't like her? Worse yet, what if someone recognized her?

With a curse, Gelsey sat up in bed and pushed her tangled hair out of her eyes. How hard could it be to sell face creams and body lotions? But obviously Maeve didn't sell much from her shop. What if she too turned out to be a sales failure?

The first thing she needed to do was find something appropriate to wear. She couldn't go to her first day of work wearing Jordan's and Nan's hand-me-downs. She'd just have to make a quick trip back to Winterhill. Looking around the bedroom, Gelsey searched for something to write on.

She found Kellan's sketch pad on the floor next to the bed and flipped through it for a clean sheet of paper. The pencil that he'd been using last night wasn't on the floor or on the top of the nightstand. Gelsey rolled onto her stomach and pulled open the bottom drawer.

She pushed aside a rusty old tin box and searched the drawer. Then she opened the box, hoping there might be a pencil inside. Gelsey's breath caught in her throat as she recognized the objects in it. "Oh, my," she murmured, pulling out a length of braided yarn.

In a single moment, she was taken back to that day,

running through the meadow with Kellan chasing her, the old biscuit tin clutched in his hand. Time seemed to stand still as she pulled each item out of the box and examined it. These were all her magic talismans, bits and pieces of life that she'd kept for the powerful memories they held.

The day he'd chased her hadn't been the first day she'd seen him. She'd watched him from behind the rocks before, fascinated by his quiet confidence and beautiful face. He'd been her first crush, the very first boy she'd ever wanted to kiss and she'd done just that.

Gelsey smiled at the memory. She'd buried the tin just for him, hoping that he'd find it and touch something that she held dear. It was such a silly idea from a silly young girl, but now Gelsey had to wonder if the magic she believed in back then had actually worked.

She pulled out a shell and held it up to her ear, listening for the sound of the sea. If she could only go back to that time in her life, back before everything had turned upside down. Where had she gone wrong? Had there been a single event that had put her on the path she'd taken?

Her parents' divorce hadn't helped, but plenty of children survived that. Was it the endless supply of money? Had she faced her fears and insecurities rather than trying to hide them beneath a party-girl veneer, perhaps she'd have more to show for herself at age twenty-seven.

Gelsey groaned, tipping her head back and closing her eyes. All that time lost. All that money spent. And she still felt like a seabird buffeted by the wind and unable to find a place to land. What if things didn't work out in Ballykirk? What if this was just another disaster in a long line of disasters?

And how would Kellan feel about her once he found out who she really was? There'd been so many men, so many silly choices—and all of them captured in the tabloids. And the money. How could she ever justify it? It made her look so vacuous and incredibly careless.

And then there was the "incident." How would she explain that to him? She'd tried to put it out of her mind, but if things didn't go her way, she might have to spend some time in jail. Gelsey closed her eyes. How could she have been so incredibly stupid? So wrapped up in her silly little world that she'd done something with real and awful consequences.

Perhaps she'd just have to wait to tell him until it didn't matter, until he loved her so much that nothing she said would drive him away. And if it never got to that point, he'd walk away, none the wiser, and she'd be able to keep her awful secret.

As Gelsey looked through her childhood treasures, she heard a car pull up outside the cottage. She jumped off the bed and peered through the slit in the curtains to see Kellan striding up the garden walk. With a soft curse, she quickly restored the tin to its spot in the bedside table.

"Gels? Are you up?"

With another curse, she quickly pulled a T-shirt over her head and then stood beside the bed, carefully arranging the covers. Kellan walked in. "Hi," she said. "Just making the bed."

He grinned, then circled around and grabbed her waist before he pulled her down onto the bed. "Don't. We'll just mess it up again."

Gelsey smoothed her hand over his temple, brushing aside a lock of hair. "Why are you back here so soon?"

"I missed you," he said. He pulled her body against his. "I missed this. You've made it impossible to think about anything else."

"I find that hard to believe," she said, unable to hide a smile of satisfaction.

"It's true. No matter where I go, I'm thinking about your mouth…" He dropped a kiss on her lips. "And your shoulders…" He pulled aside the T-shirt and gently nibbled on the curve of her neck. "And your impossibly beautiful breasts." Kellan wriggled down until he could nuzzle the swell of flesh beneath her T-shirt.

"You're pathetic," Gelsey said, laughing.

"Yes. Yes, I am." He glanced up at her. "Actually, I came back here to get you. Jordan and Nan are helping with the painting and they insisted I bring you down. They're making a party of it."

Gelsey reached out for a pillow and brought it down on his head. "So you weren't thinking about my naked body? About the naughty things I did to you last night? About the words that you whispered in my ear while you were coming inside me?"

He frowned, then groaned softly. "I wasn't. But I am now."

She got up on her knees and pulled her T-shirt over her head. "So, what are you going to do about it?"

His gaze slowly skimmed over her body, as exciting as a caress. Gelsey felt a familiar knot of desire tighten inside her at the look in his eyes. It was so easy to make him want her. It didn't take much to have him hard and ready.

"Take off your clothes," she murmured.

As she watched him slowly undress, Gelsey thought of the young boy she'd first met on the cliffs. He was still there, in the twinkling blue eyes and finely sculpted mouth, in the boyish curl at his nape and the grin that made her weak in the knees.

This was fate. They belonged together. And nothing she could say or do would shake a bond that had survived so many years. She wanted to believe it was so. She needed to believe it.

"They're going to wonder where we are," Kellan whispered as he pulled her down onto the bed and settled himself above her.

Gelsey drew her legs up along his hips, her toes skimming along his calves. "I'm sure we can keep it under five minutes."

Kellan gasped, then braced himself on his elbows. "Five? Really? Why even bother, then?"

"Because five minutes in heaven is better than a day in the ordinary world." She drew him closer and then arched against him, his shaft pressing against her sex. Slowly, he pushed inside her, filling her with his heat.

"Don't move," she said.

"If I don't move, we'll be here all day."

"Five minutes." Gelsey pulled him close and kissed him, lingering for a long time over his mouth until she was sure he was properly distracted. And then, in a soft voice, she began to tell a story of man and mermaid, an erotic story of two people swept away by desire. She didn't leave out any detail, teasing him with a story of the seduction that had gone on between them from the moment they met.

His eyes were closed and Gelsey knew he was caught up in the images racing through his head. Her lips on his shaft, his teeth grazing her nipple. They didn't need to do it in order to experience it.

She shifted beneath him, just slightly, and his breath caught in his throat. But still, she wasn't ready for him to move. Every word she spoke was designed to bring him closer, to make his release come not from physical sensation, but from his imagination.

She sensed when he was close and then whispered in his ear. "Now you can move."

He drew back and then drove into her in an almost desperate search for pleasure. Again and again, she felt him deep inside her and then, in a single, silent instant, he was there, tumbling over the edge in a powerful orgasm.

When he was finally sated, he collapsed on the bed beside her, his leg thrown over her hips. "I stand corrected. I'm powerless against your rather considerable charms, my dear."

Gelsey smiled and dropped a kiss on his lips. "Five minutes."

"Good to know," he said. "Good for those times when we're waiting for the water to boil for tea or for football to come on the telly. Hell, it sometimes takes five minutes to get a pint at the pub. And there's a perfectly good closet just near the kitchen where we can—"

"Stop," Gelsey said. "We're only allowed to use the five-minute rule in emergencies." She sat up. "Come on, quick shower. And then we're going to go help with the painting."

"What about you? Should we take another five minutes for you?"

"You can take care of me in the shower," Gelsey said, jumping up from the bed. She grabbed his hands and pulled him to his feet, then wrapped his arms around her waist. But Kellan quickly turned her around in his arms, pressing his softening erection into the small of her back.

His hands smoothed down her belly to rest at the juncture of her thighs. He slipped a finger inside her, gently caressing her and before long, Gelsey felt her knees growing weak and her body surrendering to his touch.

His power over her body was just as startling as hers over his. She dissolved into deep soul-shattering spasms, grasping the bedpost to keep herself from collapsing. Breathless, she leaned back against him, wrapping her arm around his neck.

This had all begun with a simple kiss years ago. And yet, try as she might, she couldn't imagine a future without him, without this passion they shared. He had the power to give her incredible pleasure. But Kellan also had the power to break her heart into a million pieces.

KELLAN GLANCED OVER at the three men sitting at the end of the bar. Known as the Unholy Trinity, the trio of pensioners were regulars at the pub. Markus Finn, Dealy Carmichael and Johnnie O'Malley stopped by every day for a pint and a chat with whomever was available to listen to their brand of malarkey.

"What are you three gawkin' at?" Kellan asked from his spot at the opposite end of the bar. He'd been enjoying a quick beer while he waited for the takeaway lunch Riley had ordered for them all.

Markus leaned forward. "We hear you caught yourself a mermaid."

Kellan groaned. He couldn't go anywhere in town lately without having to answer questions about Gelsey. "She's not a mermaid," he said.

"How do ya know?" Dealy asked. "Have ya ever come 'cross a mermaid before?"

"No," Kellan said, trying to tamp down his irritation. "I just know. I've gotten a good look at her and there are no gills or scales or any such thing on her body."

"Of course not," Johnnie said. "There wouldn't be then. They disappear once she's on land."

"She's not a mermaid," Kellan insisted.

"I once saw a mermaid. Of course, I was three sheets to the wind, but it looked like a mermaid to me."

"Supposin' she was a mermaid," Markus said. "Just theoretically. Supposin' our little village of Ballykirk had its very own...what would we call it, lads?"

"Tourist attraction," Dealy said. "That's what you'd call it."

Markus stood and quickly moved to the stool beside Kellan. "Just hear us out, boyo, for it's an opportunity we'd be offerin'. You might already know that our little town got some money to help promote tourism and they made me head of the committee. And we've been looking for something that sets us apart from every other fishing village in Cork. And now we have it."

"You want to use Gelsey to bring tourists to Ballykirk?"

"In a word, yes!" Dealy said.

"You're crazy. She's not a mermaid," Kellan repeated.

"Well, I know that and you know that. Everyone in town knows that. But the tourists don't. That silly Blarney stone makes millions every year and we need a share of the money bein' thrown about. People come to Ireland because of the leprechauns and fairies and all those other silly legends."

"I realize that," Kellan said. "But I don't think Gelsey is interested in that kind of attention. She seems to be a woman who values her privacy."

"It's not like we'd be askin' her to swim around in a

giant tank all day," Markus said. "We just want to explore the marketing possibilities."

"Yeah," Dealy said. "The marketing possibilities."

"Do you have any idea what that means?" Kellan said.

Markus shrugged. "It was in the pamphlet the tourism board sent. But I know what I know. There's bleedin' leprechauns all over this island. But nobody has a mermaid." He shrugged. "You could mention it to her? See what she thought?"

"She has enough going on already. She took a job at Maeve's shop and—"

"She's workin' for Maeve?" Johnnie frowned. "Oh, Jaysus, that's not good. A few days with her and she'll be running as fast as she can from Ballykirk. The woman is mad as a hatter, that one."

"Not necessarily," Dealy said. "Maeve has been talking about selling her shop. We need to convince the mermaid to stay. What if we talk Maeve into selling the shop to Gelsey? A new retail establishment run by a clever little mermaid. The tourists will flock to Ballykirk."

"That's it," Markus said. "Now we have a plan." He clapped Kellan on the shoulder. "And just to make certain, we'd like you to hide the clothes you found her in. This whole scheme will go to hell if we lose her. I don't want to be takin' any risks."

"If you three start bothering her, she might decide to leave."

"Well, then, it's your job to keep her happy," Markus said. "She's...*community property.*"

"Maybe it is best that he talk to her about our scheme, boys," Johnnie said. "He's the one who rescued her. So she is beholden to him."

Dealy nodded, his expression serious. "Feel her out. Find out what she's lookin' for. She could make a real nice home for herself here in Ballykirk. And we could help her out. It would be mutually beneficial."

"Yeah," Markus said. "Tell her that. Mutually beneficial."

Katie appeared from the kitchen with their lunch order. She set the food in front of him, paper-wrapped sandwiches and bags of crisps tucked neatly into a box. Kellan drained the rest of the Guinness from his glass and pushed to his feet. He winked at Katie. "Thanks, love."

Katie grinned at him. "Bring your girl down to the pub for dinner so we can all get a look at her. We've got herring on the menu tonight. And Danny says she's a right vixen, she is."

"You, too?"

"Ah, I'm just playin' with you," Katie said. "Everyone is talking. We're all a bit curious about the girl."

Kellan headed to the door. Their offer was made. But Kellan was willing to consider anything that might keep Gelsey in Ballykirk. He didn't hold out much hope for her work at Maeve's—the woman had been a bit daft for as long as he could remember. But with Gelsey's beauty and charisma, it might just work.

Kellan recalled the phone conversation he'd heard the first night Gelsey had stayed with him. She had at least one person who cared enough to worry over her and maybe a place that she called home. But for some reason, she'd decided to stay in Ballykirk, at least for the near future.

Tucking the box under his arm, Kellan strode toward the waterfront. Riley and Nan had purchased a small cottage overlooking the harbor at Ballykirk. It was about the same size as the Quinn cottage on the hill, but it was in much worse condition. Riley had already replaced the roof and refinished the floors, but both the exterior and interior still needed painting and the windows were a mess.

Kellan had already contacted a few of the contractors who'd worked on Castle Cnoc and they'd agreed to do new plumbing and electricity at a bargain price. He'd decided it would be his wedding present to the happy couple.

When he arrived at the cottage, his brothers and the girls had decided to start work on the facade. The sun had warmed that side of the house and the breeze had died down, taking the last bit of chill out of the air.

"There he is," Riley called. "Poor Nan is about to faint from hunger."

Nan took a swipe at Riley with a paintbrush. "Hush."

Kellan glanced back and forth between the two of them, watching a pretty blush stain Nan's cheeks. "She's been working hard," he said. "She deserves a break for lunch."

"Oh, it's not that," Riley said.

"You said you were going to wait to tell them!" Nan cried.

"Tell us what?" Jordan asked. Danny and Gelsey joined the group with curious looks on their faces.

Riley slipped his arm around Nan's shoulders and grinned. "Nan is eating for two."

"Oh, don't worry about that," Jordan said. "I ordered two sandwiches, too. All of this outdoor work makes me so hungry."

"Don't mind her," Danny said. "All this fresh air has made her a bit cabbaged."

"What's cabbaged?" Gelsey whispered. "Why is she cabbaged? I ordered two sandwiches, too. Is that bad?"

"I expect this isn't about sandwiches. Riley is trying to tell us that Nan is going to have a baby," Kellan explained.

"Oh, my God," Jordan shouted. "Is that true?"

At Nan's nod, the entire group surrounded her for hugs and kisses. Even Gelsey offered her congratulations before stepping back to slip her arm through Kellan's. She looked over at him and smiled. "It's wonderful news."

"Yes." Kellan added, "Riley will make a fine father." He drew in a deep breath. The news had hit him in an odd way. He was happy for the couple, yet he felt a bit strange that Riley would experience fatherhood before he did. Kellan had always been the oldest boy, always been first at everything. But now, he seemed to be trailing behind in his brothers in all the important things.

"I'm going to fetch us a few more beers," he said, setting the box of sandwiches down on the front step.

"None for me," Nan said. "You can bring me a soda. I'm sorry, a mineral," she corrected, using the Irish word.

"You want to give me a hand?" Kellan asked Gelsey.

She followed him inside. The house was nearly empty, except for a few pieces of tatty furniture and the tools Riley was using to renovate the place. But there was a functioning refrigerator in the kitchen and it was stocked with cold drinks.

"Beer for me," Gelsey said.

He opened two bottles and handed one to her. "Are you having fun? Or is this too much too soon?"

"I like your brothers," Gelsey said, stepping across the kitchen to give him a kiss. She ran her hand along his cheek. "And I like Nan and Jordan, too."

"The two of them together can be a bit intimidating. They're both American and when they have an opinion they tend to just throw it out there for everyone to hear."

Gelsey shrugged. "I don't have many girlfriends," she murmured. "I think I'd like having a girlfriend if they were like Nan or Jordan."

Kellan leaned back against the refrigerator and watched a wistful expression dance across her pretty features. "You don't have any girlfriends?"

Gelsey shook her head. "No. Women usually don't like me."

"Why not?"

"Did you get me a corned-beef sandwich?" she asked, deftly changing the subject. "I love corned beef." Gelsey took the other beer from his hand, then headed for the door. By the time he joined her with the rest of the drinks, she was seated on the step, unwrapping her lunch. He gave his brothers each a beer and handed the mineral to Nan, before he sat down beside her.

Gelsey grabbed half the sandwich and bit into it, then groaned softly. "Oh, this is lovely. Are there any fries?"

Fries. Though he could detect a hint of an English accent in her speech, she sounded more like Nan and Jordan than any Brit he knew. But there was something else there. Occasionally, he caught her talking to herself in French or Spanish. "No chips, just crisps."

She looked at the bag. "Those are chips," she said.

"Ah, another little clue," Kellan said. "You reveal yourself a bit more every day. If you call crisps *chips* and chips *fries,* then you've spent time in the States."

"Very astute, Sherlock Holmes," she said. "My mother is American."

He leaned back and watched her eat, pondering the information she'd just revealed. It was the first real clue he had to who she was. "What about your father?"

"British," she said. "Interrogation over." She took a huge bite of her sandwich, then grinned at him.

Kellan chuckled at the funny face she made. For someone so slender, she certainly enjoyed a good meal now and then. She gobbled down her first corned-beef sandwich in just a few bites and then started on the second.

"Where do you come from?" Kellan asked.

She blinked as she looked at him, continuing to chew. "Come from?"

"You heard me. I don't get the accent. It's not Irish, I know that. It's not entirely American, either, or English. So what is it?"

She shrugged. "Lots of different things. A mash-up, really."

"Of what?" Kellan could see that she didn't want to reveal any more. But the woman was living in his house, eating food that he'd provided for her, socializing with his family. The least she could do was fill him in on a few details.

"Does it really make a difference?" she asked, watching him suspiciously.

"I'm just curious."

Her chin tilted up in defiance as she swallowed. "I spoke French as a child."

"You don't want me to know anything about you, do you? Why? What are you trying to hide? There's no reason. After a week together, we know each other about as intimately as we can."

She reached for a crisp and nibbled at it, considering her answer silently. "Can't we just leave it at that? We're both getting what we want out of this, so—"

"What *I* want? You're the one who crawled into bed with me that first night. I didn't invite you." Kellan cursed beneath his breath. "You know they're talking about you all around town. Markus Finn wants to capitalize on all this silly mermaid stuff. He thinks you could be like Ballykirk's very own Blarney Stone."

A gasp burst from her lips and then a giggle. Before long, she was laughing so hard, she had to set her sandwich down. "Really? But I'm not a mermaid." When she regained her composure, she drew a ragged breath and nodded. "Sorry. I didn't mean to laugh."

"The tourists wouldn't care," Kellan said. "They come to Ireland because of all the magic."

"So, what would I do?"

"He and the tourism committee are hoping you'll stay and maybe buy Maeve's shop from her. She's had it for sale for a few years now."

Gelsey crumpled the empty wrapper from her sandwich, then pulled her knees up to her chest, wrapping her arms around her legs. "I—I really don't know what my plans are," she said. "I'm not sure I could make a commitment like that right now."

"A commitment to Ballykirk or a commitment to me? You can tell me the truth."

"If I tell you the truth, you'll *want* me to leave," she countered. Gelsey raked her hands through her wavy hair, sighing softly as she tipped her head back. "I just need to have a moment to myself, a chance to take a breath without someone expecting something from me."

"Are you married?" Kellan asked.

"No!" Gelsey looked surprised. "No, there's no one. Not anymore."

"But there was?"

"It's over. Completely over. I swear to you."

A long silence grew between them. Gelsey reached out and took his hand, carefully lacing her fingers through his. "What difference does it make who we were?" she asked. "We began when you found me on the beach."

Kellan's gaze fell to her mouth, and without a second thought, he slipped his hand around her waist and pulled her into a long and languid kiss. She was right. He didn't care about anything beyond what they'd shared together. And though he knew she wasn't an amnesiac or a mermaid, that didn't matter, either. She was here with him now and that's all he cared about.

5

THE HILLS WERE SHROUDED in a dense mist as Gelsey navigated the battered Fiat toward Winterhill. She'd spent her last four or five Christmases skiing, surrounded by snow and plenty of twinkly lights. It was a bit odd to be staring out at fog.

Kellan had invited her to accompany him to Cork to pick up a set of plans he'd been waiting for and do a bit of Christmas shopping, but Gelsey had decided to take the morning for herself.

Everything was moving so fast in Ballykirk. Her feelings for Kellan were growing deeper with each day and night they spent together. And though he still questioned her about her past, he seemed to take her evasive answers with less frustration. So, had the time come to just be honest with him?

Their nights in bed were proof of his desire and their easygoing way with each other outside the bedroom marked a growing trust and friendship. But passion and friendship didn't necessarily add up to a future together. Gelsey had been through enough "relationships" to know how easily they fractured. And how quickly she grew bored.

She slowed the car as it neared a curve, sighing softly. How nice it would be to believe in love. To know that there was a man out there who could ensure complete happiness for the rest of her life. She'd been chasing that dream her entire life, but had never really believed it would come true.

At least she could make a real life for herself, a life with a job and a place to live, important things to occupy her day.

She'd stopped at the shop that morning, just to chat with Maeve about her job responsibilities. Though Gelsey couldn't offer any retail experience, she could offer enthusiasm and she saw incredible potential in the business that Maeve had started. When Maeve mentioned she was interested in selling the shop, the foundation of a new life had begun to take shape in her mind.

Why not make a life in Ballykirk? She could live at Winterhill and turn the shop into a thriving business. There was a huge market for unusual boutique skin-care products, especially those made of natural ingredients. She knew women who paid thousands of dollars for a small jar of sheep placenta.

But until her problems in Italy were solved, until she faced the consequences of what she'd done, there could be no future for her in Ballykirk and no future with Kellan. The thought of jail, for something as silly as a punch in the face, was almost more than she could bear. She wasn't a criminal, but she'd done something that had broken the law.

Six months had passed and it still loomed over her like a big black cloud, obscuring any sunshine or hope she had. Antonio had been there and up until their fight, had promised to testify to what had happened. But now, she wasn't sure he'd hold up his end of the bargain.

The stone pillars flanking the driveway at Winterhill appeared out of the fog. A feeling of relief washed over her at the sight of the old stone house. This was the only home she'd ever really known. Every summer, she'd arrived still dressed in her school uniform, ready to throw aside the rules and regulations for a summer full of fantasies.

Her grandmother had died six years ago, and since then, she hadn't been back. But three months ago, it had been the only place left to her, the only place in the world she could hide. Gelsey still expected her to be waiting at the door when she drove up to the house, her arms thrown wide and her eyes filled with tears of joy.

This would be a good place to start again, Gelsey mused. She could be happy here. She honked the horn, then smiled as the front door opened. Her grandmother's housekeeper came rushing out, her hands clutching her apron. Gelsey stepped out of the car only to be enveloped in Caroline's embrace.

"Oh, I should be livid, I should," Caroline said in her

thick Irish brogue. "Why haven't you phoned more than once? I've been worrying myself sick."

"I told you I was safe," she said.

"Safe? Look at this car you're drivin'! It's an accident waitin' to happen."

Gelsey looped her arm through Caroline's. "Come on, then. Let's have a cup of tea and I'll tell you all about my adventures in the real world."

"I'm not certain I want to hear," Caroline teased. "Are you driving without a permit?"

"No, I have a Spanish driver's license. I think it's good here."

"And where does that car come from?"

The housekeeper knew all of Gelsey's problems. Confession had been good for the soul and Gelsey had needed at least one person who understood what she'd done to her life. But no she couldn't wait to tell Caroline about her job and all the possibilities for her future in Ballykirk.

"Your mother and father have been calling," Caroline said. "They've been keeping up with the news on your case and they're worried."

"It's my problem," Gelsey said. "I'll deal with it."

Caroline gave her hand a squeeze as they walked to the front door. "Now, I want you to know that I haven't finished yet."

"Finished what?" Gelsey asked.

The housekeeper threw the door open and Gelsey stepped into the spacious foyer. "Christmas."

Gelsey gasped as she saw the beautiful pine garlands and twinkling lights. "Oh, look at this." Slowly, she took it all in, then stopped in front of a Christmas tree that sat just inside the parlor. It was decorated in an old-fashioned style, with faded blown-glass ornaments and tinsel and real candles on the tips of the boughs.

"Your grandmother used to insist that we do it up well," Caroline explained. "Christmas was her favorite day of the year, except for the day that you arrived at Winterhill for your summer holiday."

"I remember these," Gelsey said, reaching out to touch one of the candles. "I spent Christmas here one year when I was—"

"You were seven. I wasn't sure that you remembered."

"Oh, I do," Gelsey said. "It was magical."

"I thought, since you might be spending the holiday here again this year, I'd do it up, like your grandmother did." She gave Gelsey a quick hug. "Come, let's have tea. I want to hear all about this man you've met."

"Man? I didn't mention a man," Gelsey said.

"What else would have kept you away?"

Gelsey groaned as she walked back to the kitchen. "All right, there is a man. But it isn't want you think. At least, not entirely what you think."

She followed Caroline back to the kitchen, then sat down on one of the stools that surrounded the huge worktable in the center of the room. Cupping her chin in her hand, Gelsey watched as the housekeeper placed a plate of shortbread biscuits in front of her, then fussed with the preparations for tea. When the pot was filled and the tea steeping, she set it down on the table and joined Gelsey.

"Where have you been?"

"Ballykirk," Gelsey replied. "I've been staying with…with—a friend. His name is Kellan Quinn."

"Quinn? My cousin Aina married a Quinn from Ballykirk. Jamie Quinn."

"I haven't met him, though I'm sure there are a lot of Quinns in Ballykirk."

"Oh, they don't live in Ballykirk anymore. They moved to Galway years ago. I wouldn't think you'd have found Ballykirk very exciting."

"There's something in Ballykirk that I'm very interested in." Gelsey explained her hopes for Maeve's Potions and Lotions, describing the shop and Maeve's merchandise and the potential to turn the business into something special. When she finished, she looked at Caroline, waiting for her opinion.

"What is it?" Gelsey asked at the odd expression on the housekeeper's face. "I know it's silly to make plans with everything hanging over my head as it is. But I want to think positively. I need to believe that everything will work out."

"Oh, it's not that. You look…different." Caroline reached out and smoothed her hand over Gelsey's cheek.

"I do?"

Caroline nodded, her silver curls bobbing. "You look happy. Relaxed."

"I am," Gelsey said. "So do you think I should do it?"

"Let me ask you one question. How much of your interest in staying in Ireland has to do with this Quinn bloke?"

"I suppose some," Gelsey admitted. "But I'm not really counting on that for the future. I think it's time I begin to plan my life for myself and not whatever man I happen to fancy at the moment."

"Antonio has been ringing here, trying to get in touch. It sounds like he's very sorry for what he did and he wants to make amends."

"Of course he's sorry. All men who cheat are sorry. And I suppose I shouldn't blame him. I ran away to Ireland and he needed someone. In his case, anyone would do."

"He wasn't ever right for you, Gelsey."

She drew a deep breath and nodded. "I know. But after the fight we had, I'm not sure he's going to want to testify for me in court. He was there when it happened. He saw the whole thing."

"Perhaps you should try to smooth things out," Caroline suggested. "For the sake of your future."

Gelsey shook her head. "I'm done with Antonio," she said. "And that life. I want to start a new life, here at Winterhill."

Caroline took her hands and gave them a squeeze. She stared down at Gelsey's ring finger. "Where is your engagement ring?"

"I threw it in the ocean," Gelsey said.

"That was a foolish thing to do."

"I suppose I should have kept it. I could have traded it for all the things I left at his villa in Portugal."

"That would have been the sensible thing."

"Agreeing to marry a Spanish race-car driver with an ex-wife, an ex-mistress and a girlfriend on the side was not sensible. From now on, I'm going to make myself happy first." She paused, then grinned. "Not that I'm giving up men entirely."

"Well, I think that's a grand plan," Caroline said. "Just grand. I have always thought that you deserved more happiness than you allowed yourself." Caroline's eyebrows arched. "Now tell me more about this man."

Gelsey laughed. "He's very sweet and far too serious for me. And, even though I'm afraid I'll find some way to muck it all up, he makes me feel…safe." She shook her head. "I've spent my life living dangerously and now I'm happy with a cozy cottage and handsome architect in my bed. How strange is that?"

"You haven't had an easy time of it, Gelsey. I've been witness to that. But it would fulfill your grandmother's fondest wish if you could find some happiness here."

Gelsey drew a ragged breath, then smiled. "I love this house. Maybe that's why I came running here when things with Antonio fell apart."

"Well, I'll make sure everything is just so for you," Caroline said.

"And I'm going to help this year."

"You're going to come back, then?"

Gelsey thought about it for a long moment, then nodded. "Yes. And I'm going to bring Kellan with me. Just as soon as I tell him who I really am."

"Just who does he think you are?" Caroline asked.

Gelsey winced, then shrugged her shoulders. "At first, a mermaid. But now, probably an escapee from a mental hospital."

"Oh, dear," Caroline said. "It's going to take more than a pot of tea to explain that."

"WHAT THE HELL are we doing here?" Danny grumbled.

"Waiting," Kellan said.

"I can see that. What are we waiting for?"

"I'm not sure."

"When you asked to borrow my car, you told me you had an errand to run. We're not running. We're sitting here at the side of the road staring at a huge house. Who lives there?"

"I don't know," Kellan muttered. "Do you?"

Danny shook his head. "Not really. I'm not sure anyone lives there, at least not year-round. But it looks like a nice place. Well tended. The ironwork on the gates looks original. I'd like to get a closer look at those hinges." He reached for the door handle, but Kellan grabbed his jacket sleeve.

"Wait," he said. "Look. There's someone coming outside. Pull ahead and then turn around."

"Who's coming?" Danny asked.

"I don't know. Someone that Gelsey knows. She came here this morning. Drove the Fiat over. I couldn't stick around because she would have recognized my car, so I decided to come back and check it out once she returned to Ballykirk."

"You followed her here?"

"Not exactly," Kellan said. Then he cleared his throat. "Well, yeah, I did. I was driving back to the cottage to try to convince her to go to Cork with me after Jordan canceled. And I saw her turn down the coast road, so I followed her—at a discreet distance. I was curious. And this is where she came. To this house."

"What kind of sick obsession is this?" Danny said.

"I was beginning to think she *was* a feckin' mermaid. I'm losing my mind, here. She won't tell me anything about herself. I decided to find out on my own. Now I just have to figure out why she came here."

"Maybe it's where she lives?"

"If she lives here, why is she staying in the cottage with me? This place looks a lot more posh than anything I can offer. Look at the bleedin' chimneys. There must be five or six fireplaces in that house."

"Look, a woman's come out," Danny said. "She's putting a wreath up on the door. I'm going to go talk to her."

"No!"

"I'll just tell her I'd like to take a photo of her gates. I do it all the time."

Danny hopped out of the Land Rover and started off toward the woman, leaving Kellan no choice but to follow him.

"Hello, there!" Danny called, striding confidently

up the driveway. "We were just looking at your gate. I'm a blacksmith. Would you mind if I took a photo?" He glanced back at Kellan and motioned him forward. "Do you have your mobile with you?"

Kellan reached into his pocket, then handed Danny his phone. "Just flip it open and press that button on the side. Then press it again to take the photo."

"Would you mind?" Danny asked again.

"No, not at all," the old woman said.

"How long have you owned the place?" Danny asked.

"Oh, I don't own it. I work here. I'm the housekeeper. For thirty-five years. My mother worked here before me."

"Big house," Danny said. "A lot to keep up with, I'd reckon."

"Oh, it's not all that bad. The owner only comes now and then. She's here now, so I've been a bit busier."

"She?" Kellan asked.

"Yes. Miss Gelsey. I've know her since she was just a wee baby."

"Really."

"Her grandmother owned the house up until the time she died. That was six years ago. She was Lila Dunleavy Woodson. Her husband was a surgeon in London and they kept a summer home here. Her son, Gelsey's father, became a diplomat with the British Foreign Service and married an American." She chuckled. "You wouldn't need to know all that genealogy just to look at a gate, now, would you?"

"I guess not," Danny said. "I'll just get a few snaps and we'll be on our way.

By the time they got back in the car, Kellan's mind was spinning. Woodson. Her name was Gelsey Woodson. She had parents and a home—a very lovely home from the look of it. And she had a housekeeper. She'd obviously come home to pick up the expensive clothes, expensive clothes that had magically appeared in the wardrobe sometime before lunch.

Kellan stared out the window, watching as the scenery passed by. "What the hell am I doing?"

"You are definitely in love with this girl," Danny said. "I've never seen you so out of joint over a woman." He gave Kellan a sideways glance. "She did seem a bit more posh than the average girl. She has good manners. Jordan even mentioned that the other day. Nan thought she might be a ballerina because she has such nice posture, but Jordan guessed fashion model. I figured she was rich from the way she talked."

"I don't even know why I'm interested," Kellan said.

"Because she's drop-dead gorgeous. Hell, Kellan, you'd be an eejit if you walked away from a goddess like her." Danny pointed up the road. "Are you coming into town with me or should I drop you at the cottage?"

"Let's go to the pub," he said. "I think I could use a pint or two. And I left my car there."

When they arrived at the pub, they found a crowd inside, oddly large for a Monday afternoon. But as

Kellan stared at the group clustered around the bar, he suddenly realized why they had all come.

"Looks like your mermaid is holding court," Danny said.

Gelsey was perched on a bar stool with the Unholy Trinity lined up to her left. Doc Finnerty occupied the stool to her right and a small group of townspeople filled out the rest of her circle.

Kellan strolled to the end of the bar to greet his mother. "How long has she been here?"

"About an hour," his mother said. "Where have you boys been?"

"I've been draggin' Kellan around the countryside looking for leprechauns," Danny said with an exaggerated Irish brogue.

Frowning, Kellan watched as Dealy and Markus commandeered the conversation. If they were bothering Gelsey with their plans, he was going to put an end to it right now. He pushed away from the end of the bar and strode through the small crowd to stand in front of Gelsey.

Reaching up, she threw her arms around his neck and gave him a quick kiss. "You're back," she said. "I came in here looking for you, but your mother said you and Danny had left together."

"I thought I'd find you at the cottage."

"I walked into town to talk to Maeve, then decided to stop here after. Then these gentlemen came by. They said you sent them."

Kellan glared at the trio over Gelsey's shoulder.

"They did, did they? Well, that's interesting. As I recall, I haven't spoken to them since the day before yesterday when I told them to keep their silly plans to themselves."

Gelsey glanced back at Johnnie, Markus and Dealy. "But they've been wonderful," she said. "They thought I might be interested in a business opportunity and I told them I was."

"You don't need to listen to these gits," Kellan whispered.

"Really," Gelsey said. "It's an interesting plan. One I've actually been considering." She grabbed Kellan around the arm and pulled him along with her toward the door. "It was a pleasure meeting all of you and I'm sure I'll see you again soon. And thank you for the beer, Mrs. Quinn."

"No trouble," Maggie Quinn called, a satisfied grin on her face. "Come back soon, Gelsey."

When they got outside, Kellan drew her along to his car, parked just a few steps from the front door of the pub. He opened the passenger side. "Get in," he muttered.

Gelsey hopped inside and a few moments later, Kellan got behind the wheel, gripping it with white-knuckled hands. "Gelsey, I don't want you perpetrating this mermaid stuff anymore. It might have been fun at first, but it will only make things difficult for you."

"I wasn't," she said. "And it's just silliness. No one really believes I'm a mermaid. Why are you so angry?"

Kellan's jaw twitched. That was a good question.

He'd become so protective of Gelsey, yet he couldn't figure out his motives. He cared about her, yet he'd been very careful about letting himself feel too much. He enjoyed her company and didn't want anyone or anything interfering with that. And he sensed that she was searching for something, something she'd never be able to find in Ballykirk.

"It is an intriguing opportunity," she said. "And with the proper marketing, it might bring more tourists into Ballykirk. The mermaid thing would just be a...what did Dealy call it...a hook, to get people interested."

Kellan glanced over at her. "I thought you couldn't commit to something like that. Isn't that what you said?"

Gelsey nodded. "Yes. But I have to make a life for myself somewhere. Why not here?" She swallowed, forcing a smile. "Unless, of course, you don't want me to. You can tell me, if that's the case. I'm perfectly fine with that. And don't think that, just because I buy the shop, I expect us to continue a relationship. I know what we have might not be..."

"What do we have?" Kellan asked.

"You know."

"No, I'm not sure I do. At least, I'm not sure what you think we have. What would you call it?"

She thought about her answer for a long moment. "Did you ever see the film *Roman Holiday,* with Audrey Hepburn and Gregory Peck?"

Kellan shook his head. What was this about?

"It's about these two people who know that being

together is probably impossible, but they spend a wonderful two days together in Rome. She was a princess and I'm not. And they never had sex. And we've been together a lot longer than two days, but…" She cursed softly. "It's the idea of it. We can still be great together even if it isn't meant to last forever. Does that make sense?"

Kellan frowned. "It might make better sense if I watched the movie."

"Well, maybe we should find a place to rent it and we can watch it tonight. It will all make sense then."

The only thing that would make sense to Kellan would be a complete explanation of who she was and what she was really doing in Ballykirk. And if it took watching some silly chick flick to get her to talk about herself, then he was prepared to do that.

"Our library has a decent collection of DVDs," Kellan said. "Maybe we can find it there."

"THIS IS NOT ANYTHING like *Roman Holiday*," Gelsey said. She was curled up against Kellan's body, her gaze fixed on the laptop that rested on his belly. She reached for the popcorn bowl and grabbed a handful, then slowly munched. "This has cowboys and covered wagons. *Roman Holiday* has ancient ruins and Vespas."

"The library didn't have *Roman Holiday*. But Gregory Peck is in this one."

"*How the West Was Won*," Gelsey said. "Couldn't we have at least gotten a romance? Or a Christmas film?

It's a Wonderful Life or *How the Grinch Stole Christmas.*"

"I like this one," Kellan said. He glanced over at her, then reached for the computer and closed the top. "All right, we probably could have done better for our first movie night."

"Next time, I get to pick," she said.

It was odd how something as simple as movie night was so satisfying. For so many years, her idea of an exciting evening involved an expensive dress, an even more expensive bottle of champagne and a nightclub filled with handsome men. Tonight was just one man and a movie and it was perfect—except for the movie.

Kellan leaned over and kissed her, his tongue tracing the shape of her mouth. "Next time, you can choose." He set the computer on the floor, then crawled beneath the bedcovers. Gelsey stretched out beside him, slipping into the curve of his arm, her head resting on his shoulder.

"I had a really good day today," she murmured.

"Yes?"

"Yes. And I think tomorrow is going to be even better." She glanced up at him. "I get to start work tomorrow. I have a real job and I'm going to be gainfully employed."

"Not everyone is so excited to go to work," he said. "Are you really serious about buying her shop?"

"Maeve would sell me all her recipes," Gelsey said. "And we would manufacture them at the shop to start. We'd have to update the jars and the labels. I know they'd sell at five times the price, especially in some of the exclusive shops in Europe." She paused. "I have a lot of ideas."

"So, you'll look for investors?"

She shook her head. "No. I won't need investors."

"How will you pay for it?"

"I'll figure that out," she murmured. It was an awfully big hole in her plan, at least from his point of view. "I have a little money of my own."

Kellan cursed softly, then tossed the bedcovers aside and got out of bed. He grabbed his jeans from the floor and pulled them on. "I could really use a walk. I'll be back in a bit."

His sudden change of mood stunned her at first. But then she realized that this was bound to happen sooner or later. "I'll come with you," she said.

"No, I need some time to myself."

"You're angry."

Kellan gritted his teeth, then shook his head. "What kind of game is this?" he asked. "And why the hell have you decided to play it with me?"

"I—I don't know what you mean," Gelsey said, avoiding his gaze. She knew exactly what he meant, but she wasn't sure she wanted to admit that.

"I don't know who the hell you are," he said, pacing back and forth at the end of the bed. "We share the most intimate things and yet, I don't know anything about you."

"What's wrong with that? What difference does it

make? The past is in the past. Why are you so determined to dredge it all up?"

God, he was so beautiful when he was angry. Kellan was always so controlled, so sure of himself. She wanted him to crawl back into bed and make love to her, to turn all that anger he felt into passion.

"And why are you so determined to hide it? You're playing a dangerous game here, Gelsey."

"I'm not afraid," she retorted.

Kellan drew a long, deep breath, then shrugged. "Well, maybe I am. How the hell am I supposed to figure this all out if I don't have any of the facts?"

"What do you need to figure out?" she asked. "Can't you just be happy living in the moment?"

"No," Kellan said. "That's not who I am. I'm a thinker and a planner and an organizer. I don't like... ambiguity."

"Not everything is worth knowing."

"You think this is some game? Well, I don't want to play anymore. It's over. The clock's run out. And I think it's time you told me."

Gelsey felt her anger rise. She didn't owe him any explanations. She shouldn't be forced to admit all the mistakes she'd made in her life, especially not to a man she'd only known for a week. "What do you want me to say? I'm married. I'm engaged. I've slept with hundreds, no, thousands of men. I've danced naked for strangers...and money. I've tried every illicit drug known to mankind. And I'm really a man trapped in a woman's body."

"Is any of that true?" Kellan asked.

"No. Aren't you glad it isn't? The truth is much less interesting. And if you really cared about me, it wouldn't matter."

He circled the bed and sat down beside her. "You're afraid," he said. "You're afraid that I'll find something about you that I don't like."

"No," Gelsey said. "I just don't care about who you were before we met. That part of your life didn't involve me. Our lives began that morning on the beach. We're like…goldfish."

"Goldfish?"

"They live completely in the moment. If you watch a fish in a bowl, by the time he gets across the bowl, he's forgotten where he was. It doesn't matter to him."

"That's bollocks," Kellan muttered. "I don't live like a feckin' fish. I'm willing to take the good with the bad. If we don't start to be honest with each other, then we don't have any chance to make this work."

"You want to make this work? What does that mean? It already works. If you try any harder, you might wreck it."

"Maybe so. But this is it, Gelsey. This is the deal breaker. I need some answers."

She considered his demand for a long moment, then nodded. "Have you ever played the game Twenty Questions? It's a game I used to play with my nanny."

"You had a nanny?" Kellan asked.

"Yes. Her name was Marie and she was French. She's the one who taught me how to speak French. My mother thought it was important. That's one question. And I'm only giving you five. So you have four left."

"What's your name?" Kellan asked.

"I'm Gelsey Evangeline Woodson. I'm named after my mother's favorite ballet dancer and my father's favorite poem."

"Where are your parents?"

"I have no idea," Gelsey said. "My mother is probably in New York. And the last time I heard, my father was in Hong Kong. We don't really communicate. They have their lives and I have mine." She sent him a sideways glance. "See. Some of the answers aren't very pretty. My parents divorced when I was eight and sent me off to boarding school. I used to come to Ireland every summer to stay with my grandmother at Winterhill, her house."

"Boarding school?"

"Yes. And that's four. In Switzerland. It's as awful as it sounds. I was lonely and homesick and I had trouble making friends. Last question."

Kellan considered his options silently. "I think I'll save my last question," he said.

"You can't. It's against the rules. You have to ask me now or lose the question."

"This game has rules?" Kellan chuckled. "Doesn't that go against the whole 'living for the moment' thing? Why not seven questions? Or eleven? Who cares how many questions were asked in the past? I say that we should play with forty-six questions. Just to live in the moment."

"Ask your last question," she said, bristling at the sarcasm in his voice. "Or don't." Gelsey crawled out of bed and picked up her clothes from the floor. She tugged on her shirt without putting on a bra, then pulled on her jeans. "I think I'm going to go."

"Go where?"

"Home," she said. "And that's your last question." She brushed past him. She found her boots at the door and slipped her bare feet inside, then put on her jacket. But by the time she opened the door, Kellan was beside her, pushing it shut again.

"Don't go," he murmured.

"I don't want to do this. I don't want to fight with you." This was all so familiar, she mused. It had happened with every man she'd ever known. Accusations, recriminations. Why did every man have to dwell in the past?

"I'm sorry. It's just difficult for me."

"Why? It's so easy. We know how we feel, right now, in the moment. And in a few minutes, it will all be forgotten."

"Is that the way it works? You'll forget that I've been a bloody caffler?"

"I don't even know what that is," Gelsey said.

"An arse of the highest order. An eejit. A proper prick."

She smiled. "Yes, I believe the description suits you quite well."

He slipped his arms around her waist and kissed her, lingering over her mouth until she parted her lips. The kiss was perfectly executed to make her forget the argument they'd just had and by the end of it, Gelsey was convinced.

"Stay with me," he murmured. "I don't want you to go."

"If I stay, no more questions."

"No more questions."

"All right. I'll stay."

Kellan picked her up and wrapped her legs around his waist, then carried her into the bedroom. "Gelsey Evangeline Woodson," he murmured, kissing her neck. "I like that."

"My friends used to call me Gigi," she said. "But I hate that name now."

"I like Gels," he said. "Will that do?"

6

KELLAN STRODE INTO the Hound, searching the dimly lit interior as he walked to the bar. Overnight, the place had been decorated for the holidays with twinkling garlands draped from every spot possible and a Christmas tree sitting in the corner.

But there was something a bit nicer about it all, he mused as he took it all in, he could see Jordan and Nan's influence on the family business already. Kellan recognized his brother's Christmas CD playing over the sound system.

Riley was washing glasses and nodded at him as he approached. "Big brother, what are you about on this fine day?"

"The place looks grand," Kellan said. "Very festive. But the music is crap."

Riley chuckled. "Thanks. I'll let the management know."

"Have you seen Gelsey? I stopped up at the cottage to pick her up and she wasn't there."

"She's over at the church. The ladies' guild is meeting this afternoon and they asked if she might come and speak to them."

"About what?"

"I guess what it's like to be a mermaid?"

Kellan ground his teeth. "If I hear that mermaid shite once more, I swear, I'm going to pummel someone. It's not funny anymore."

"She's over there demonstrating something…something to do with kelp?" Riley chuckled. "I find it quite amusing that she gets you so riled up. I have precious little entertainment here in Ballykirk, but you've been providing more than enough these past couple of weeks."

"How would you feel if Nan went about telling everyone she'd once been a seal?"

Riley thought about that for a moment, then shrugged. "I see your point. But, hell, if it sold more Guinness at the pub, I'd be all for it. Who cares what a bunch of tourists believe? And I hear that business is booming at Maeve's and she's only been working there a week. Five customers yesterday. That's more than Maeve used to have in a month."

"Well, the ladies' guild isn't a bunch of tourists." Kellan pushed away from the bar and walked back outside, then headed toward the church, all the while thinking about what he was going to say to her. She'd told him the truth a week ago. He knew where she was from and how she grew up. He'd just assumed that the mermaid stories were finally going to stop, at least to the locals.

The ladies were gathered in the meeting room of the church. Kellan threw open the doors only to be greeted by surprised silence and twenty or thirty pairs of inquisitive eyes.

"Perfect!" Gelsey said. "You're right on time." She hurried up to Kellan and grabbed his arm, pulling him into the room. "Now, ladies, as I was saying, all these products work just as well on men as they do on women. Many of your men are exposed to the elements every day in their work world and the skin can become wrinkled and leathery. It's no good walking around town with a man who looks as if he's twice your age, right?"

This brought a chorus of approval from the women. Gelsey shoved Kellan into a chair. "What are you doing here?" he murmured.

"A product demonstration," she whispered. "If they won't come to the shop, then the shop will go to them." She turned back to the audience. "Now, the first thing we'll begin with is this sea-salt exfoliator. We just apply this all over the face, with gentle fingers, avoiding the eyes, nostrils and mouth, of course." She looked down at Kellan. "Tip your head back. You'll like this."

"You're not going to put that on my face," he muttered.

"Of course, Kellan, being the typical male, will probably resist. But it's your job, ladies, to make this a pleasant experience. Put on some soft music, maybe

dress a bit provocatively. And get close. Get very close."
She stepped over his lap, her legs on either side of his.

"You'll like this," she whispered. "I promise."

Reluctantly, Kellan closed his eyes. Slowly, she
began to massage the gritty cream into his face, her
fingers dancing over his skin and smoothing across his
forehead. After only a few seconds, he found himself
relaxing, enjoying the touch of her hands.

"This really can be quite sensual, ladies. So, I'd suggest that you reserve this treatment for a time when the
two of you can truly appreciate all the benefits."

Kellan tried to keep his pulse from racing, but it was
no use. Thankfully, the front of his jacket would cover
any unexpected reaction, although from the way Gelsey
was talking, that's exactly what she was looking for.

"Now, I have some lovely samples for all of you in
these little gift bags and I want you all to try them on
yourself and on your man. I've also included a sprig
of mistletoe. I'm sure you know what to do with that.
Remember, all our products are one hundred percent
natural. No artificial colors or scents."

Kellan tried to look at her, but a tiny bit of salt
dropped off his lashes, burning his eye. "Gels," he
murmured. "I think it's time to get this off." But from
what he could hear, Gelsey had wandered off to talk
to some of her potential customers and forgotten all
about him. Kellan got to his feet and blindly searched
for a towel to wipe his face. He banged into a table,
then nearly tripped over a chair before he felt Gelsey's
hand on his arm.

"Come on, then," she said. "Sit down and I'll finish your treatment."

"Don't you dare," he warned. "You're not going to seduce me in the parish meeting room."

"I meant your facial treatment. It doesn't always have to come with sex, you know." She gently wiped the salt mixture from his face and he opened his eyes. "There you are," she murmured. "Handsome as ever." She bent closer and brushed a kiss across his lips.

Kellan slipped his arms around her waist. "Did you really need to put that stuff on my face?"

"I'm selling product," she said. "If I'm going to take over Maeve's store, I'm going to need to get out and stir up some business, especially from the ladies in the area. Regular customers are important. I've already lined up a presentation with the ladies' group over in Glengarriff. Mrs. Murphy's sister is on the program committee and they're always looking for speakers. It would help if you'd come with me."

"You don't need me," he said. "I saw how you were with the ladies. You're good at this, Gelsey. People like you."

"You really think so? You think I'm good?"

Kellan nodded. The simple compliment brought a beautiful joy to her face. That's all it took for him, he thought. As long as she was happy, so was he. Simple, but now he was beginning to understand her approach to life. Dwelling in the past only made the present miserable. She'd forgotten their argument minutes after it had happened and hadn't brought it up since.

"I'm not sure what my schedule is going to be like after the first of the year," he said. "I've got to go back to work soon."

"Where?"

"We bid on a museum project in France. In Brittany. I'm not sure we're going to get it and—"

"You're going to France? For how long?"

"We don't have the job yet," Kellan said. In truth, he wasn't sure he wanted it anymore. Gelsey was here, in Ballykirk. And her plans to buy Maeve's shop would keep her here. France was a long way from Ireland.

He'd been thinking a lot about business. He had some savings and contacts with good investors. Maybe it was time to take that risk, to put his own cash behind a project and reap the profits. After all, Gelsey was used to a comfortable lifestyle. And he couldn't really offer her as much doing just design and engineering on a project. He needed to make some real money.

"Don't worry," he said. "It will work itself out." But as he reassured her, Kellan knew that it wouldn't be so simple. He'd become accustomed to coming and going as he pleased, without a thought to anyone else's feelings. If he and Gelsey were together, then all of that would change. His whole life would change.

He watched as Gelsey packed her boxes and collected her papers. Already, he could see the changes in her. She was confident, so different from the nervous woman he'd sent off to her first day at work just a week ago. In truth, she seemed completely in her element.

"Can I buy you lunch?" he asked.

"I'm going to buy you lunch," she said, waving a stack of cards at him. "I made over a hundred pounds in sales today."

"You don't have to do that," he said.

"No, I want to. Maeve gave me an advance on my pay and I have just enough to buy you lunch. She's been very pleased with my work. That's important. I'm not sure she'd sell to someone who wasn't passionate about the business."

Kellan helped her carry the boxes out to the battered Fiat. "You're going to have to get yourself a better car," he said.

"I know. I've never had a car of my own. But there is a car at Winterhill. I'm not sure it runs anymore. It belonged to my grandmother."

"You could get it fixed," he said. "I could help you out with that."

Gelsey opened the back hatch of the Fiat and put the box she carried inside. Kellan dropped his box next to the first and shut the hatch. But the catch didn't always work and it took three tries before the hatch stayed closed. "Yeah, you definitely need a better car."

She slipped her arms around his neck and kissed him. "Have I told you what a good man you are?"

"I believe you have," Kellan said. "Usually in bed. I think this might be the first time outside the bedroom."

"I've never said that in the bedroom."

"Not in those exact words," he said.

"What words did I use?"

"Little words," Kellan teased. "Like…*oh* and…*yes.*

And then sometimes you say my name over and over. I may be wrong, but I assumed you were telling me I was a good man."

Gelsey laughed. "You assumed right. But I think I need to say it out loud more often." She tipped her face up to the sun. "Kellan Quinn is a very good man," she shouted.

"He's a feckin' gobshite."

The voice came from the direction of Danny's smithy and Kellan shrugged. "I guess we have other opinions on the subject."

"That's because they've never spent a night in bed with you," Gelsey replied.

"Actually, my brothers and I used to share a bed when we were little."

"You know what I mean," Gelsey said.

"I know exactly what you mean."

THE LATE-AFTERNOON SUN shone through the plate-glass windows of Maeve Dunphrey's shop, illuminating dust motes with every movement that Gelsey made. She pushed up on her tiptoes to grab a box from the top shelf of the old wooden wall displays, then carefully made her way down the wobbly ladder.

"Some of this stuff has to be forty years old," she said, setting the box on the counter in front of her. "I suppose we should try to salvage some of these jars. They're so pretty and, technically, they are vintage."

Jordan walked over and pulled a jar of lavender-scented lotion from the box. She screwed off the top and gave in a sniff before wrinkling her nose. "Yeah, this is pretty far gone. But the jar is lovely."

"I can go see if they have an old bucket at the Hound," Nan offered. "We can dump the stuff in there and then put the jars through the pub's dishwasher."

Gelsey nodded, grateful for the help that Nan and Jordan had offered. She'd spent a fair bit of her first week of work just cleaning, going through boxes and crates, discarding old inventory and taking stock of what was available in the store. When Nan and Jordan had stopped by a few days ago, they'd offered to help and had returned every afternoon since, making the job much more pleasant.

Nan stood in the center of the sales floor, her hands hitched on her waist, and surveyed the nearly tidy shop. "It's actually starting to look good," she said. "All these old wooden cases look beautiful, once you can see them."

"Thank you so much for helping out," Gelsey said. "You girls really didn't need to do this."

"You helped paint my house," Nan said.

"And hopefully, you'll be around when I have some tedious chore to do," Jordan added. "Are you really thinking of buying this place?"

Gelsey nodded. "Yes. I think I could make a success of it. There's a little shop like this on the Rue des Arts in Paris and women flock to it. They send their empty jars from all over the world to get them refilled. I bought night cream from them all the time, even when I was living in Portugal with Antonio."

Nan and Jordan glanced at each other. "You lived in Portugal?"

Gelsey blinked, surprised that she had been so honest with them. Over the past few days, they'd become good friends and she hadn't thought to continue the pretense. And now, in a single unguarded moment, she'd given it all away. "That was a lifetime ago." She laughed softly, shaking her head. "It's beautiful there. Very…sunny. Much like Spain. I lived there for a time, too."

Nan glanced at Jordan again, then looked back at Gelsey. "We know about Portugal. And Antonio. We've sort of known the truth from early on."

"You did?"

Jordan walked over to the counter and retrieved her purse then rummaged through it. A few moments later, she pulled out a magazine clipping and handed it to Gelsey. "I came across that while I was waiting to get my hair cut in Glengarriff. It's from *Hello!* magazine from a year ago."

The picture wasn't one of her best, Gelsey thought as she examined it closely. She was wearing a designer dress that barely covered her ass, an ass that was quite visible in the photo. A champagne bottle dangled from one hand and a cigarette from the other. "I was so drunk, I don't remember anyone taking this photo," she murmured, handing it back to Jordan. "It doesn't even look like me."

"You're Gigi Woodson," Nan said.

"I *was* Gigi Woodson."

Jordan crumpled up the clipping and tossed it into a nearby rubbish bin. "Does Kellan know?"

Gelsey winced. "No. But I'm pretty sure he's about to find out."

"We're not going to say a word," Jordan said. "We promise."

"If you know about Antonio, then I'm sure you know about the incident with the Italian photographer?"

Nan shook her head. "No. And you don't have to tell us. We really don't need to know."

"Thank you," Gelsey said. "I suppose I should be glad I managed to get away with it for this long. I assumed someone would recognize me sooner or later." She raked her hand through her hair, then forced a smile. "I guess I haven't changed all that much."

"You look completely different," Jordan disagreed.

"Completely," Nan added.

"I felt like I recognized you when we met," Jordan continued, "but I couldn't figure out where it had been. And when I saw the photo in *Hello!*, it just clicked."

Suddenly, a rush of emotion overwhelmed Gelsey. She fought back tears as she picked up the crumpled clipping. "You can show him," she murmured, holding it out to Nan. "I—I don't care. It really shouldn't make a difference." Gelsey felt a hand on her back and she found Jordan standing behind her. "I just really wanted to start over."

"We're not going to say anything," Jordan said.

"Not even to Danny and Riley?" Gelsey asked.

Nan laughed. "Are you kidding? Those two are horrible at keeping secrets. But to be honest, I don't think it's such a big deal. Kellan loves you. He won't care."

"He doesn't love me," Gelsey said. "And you've only seen one photo. There are hundreds out there. And none of them make me look very good. At least, not to a guy like Kellan." A tear trickled down her cheek and she brushed it away, embarrassed by her show of emotion. Drawing a ragged breath, she forced a smile. "I think we should call it a day. It's nearly four and you two have your own things to do."

Nan patted Gelsey on the shoulder, then thought better of it and gave her a clumsy hug. "It will all work itself out," she said. "You'll see."

Jordan gave her a hug, as well. "Kellan is a good guy. He wouldn't let something like this change his feelings for you."

The girls grabbed their jackets and purses and headed out the front door. Gelsey waved to them as they passed by the windows, going toward the pub. She had at least a few more hours of work ahead of her, but it was better to pass that time on her own, rather that be faced with more explanations.

Maybe Nan and Jordan were right. Maybe her past wouldn't make any difference to Kellan. At least at first. But once everyone else knew, once the press figured out where she was, Gelsey couldn't guarantee that he'd feel the same way.

She'd fought a five-year battle with the paparazzi and in most of the skirmishes, she'd lost badly. In the end, Gigi Woodson sold papers and that was all that mattered. They'd followed her through two broken engagements, a stint in rehab and a very ill-conceived six-day marriage to an already married Argentinean polo player. The end of her third engagement had sent her running back to Winterhill, out of sight and hopefully out of mind.

She was startled out of her thoughts by the sound of her mobile. Gelsey found it sitting on the counter next to the cash register and glanced at the screen. Her stomach twisted into a knot as she recognized the name of her attorney in Rome. She set the phone down, not ready to deal with whatever he had to tell her. She'd call him back later.

The bell above the door jingled and Gelsey spun around to see Kellan standing at the front of the shop, a surprised expression on his handsome face. "Bloody hell, look at this place. You've done wonders."

Gelsey felt her spirits brighten. "I know. Not alone though. Nan and Jordan have been helping out a lot. We've almost got all the old inventory cleared away. Next week, I can start to do a little decorating. Jordan has already given me some great ideas. And Nan thinks we ought to carry some books and CDs, too. Kind of a whole holistic approach."

"Sounds grand to me." Kellan walked toward her, then slipped his arms around her waist. "Nan and Jordan are back at the pub. I thought you might like to join us there. The family is getting together for dinner. My sister Shanna and her husband and kids came down from Dublin and they're staying the night.

It's my niece's birthday. Lily. She's five. And my sister Claire will be here with her kids. I'd like you to meet them all."

"Really?"

Kellan nodded. "Yeah. You've met the rest of the family, why not them?"

"I—I really should stay here and get some more done. We have a sale starting and tomorrow the shop will open early. We want to lure in a few Christmas shoppers and—"

"You have to eat dinner," Kellan said.

"I know." Sometimes it felt as if they were hurtling toward a cliff, unable to stop themselves from falling completely and utterly in love. It was one thing to spend time with Nan and Jordan and his brothers. But it was a whole other thing to become friendly with his parents and his sisters.

Expectations were difficult enough to meet, never mind the fact that none of the Quinns knew who she really was. They were just a regular family and she didn't want to do anything to change that. But how long would she have to wait until no one in the world was interested in where she was and who she was sleeping with? Would the press give up after a year? Or would it take longer?

"I'm just all grimy from cleaning up the shop and I'm tired and I don't think I'd be very good company and—"

Kellan pressed a finger to her lips. "No worries," he

said. "You don't have to come. I don't want to pressure you to—"

"No!" Gelsey cried. "It's not that, it's just—"

"You're right," he said. "There's no reason for you to spend time with my family."

Gelsey bit her bottom lip, knowing that whatever she said next wouldn't come out right. She'd fallen into this relationship so quickly and so easily and never thought about the repercussions. She'd taken advantage of Kellan, used him for a place to escape, and now she'd become a part of his life. "Maybe it's too soon for all this?"

His fingers tangled in her hair and he gently turned her face up until she looked into his eyes. "I'll go have dinner and I'll meet you back at the cottage later." Kellan brushed his lips against hers. "Maybe we'll bring in the tub and make you a nice bath. Right in front of the hearth."

"That would be nice," Gelsey said.

A frown worried his brow and he studied her shrewdly. "Are you all right?"

"I'm fine," Gelsey said. "Just a bit tired."

"We should get some sleep tonight," Kellan murmured. "We have been keeping rather late hours, considering you're a working woman now. You'll need your rest if you're going to get this place in shape." He bent closer and kissed her again, drawing his tongue along the crease of her lips. And then, as if he couldn't resist, he pulled her against him and deepened his kiss, his tongue invading her mouth, desperate to taste and possess.

When he was through, Gelsey was left breathless, her mind spinning. It was so easy to get caught up in the desire and the way their bodies melded so perfectly. But she and Kellan had been living in a fantasy that was slowly being unraveled by reality.

Kellan pressed his palms to her temples and smoothed her tangled hair away from her face. Then he kissed each eyelid, the tip of her nose and her mouth. "You do look tired. I'll eat quick and bring you something from the pub. We'll have a lazy night at home."

Home, Gelsey mused. Is that what they had together? Had they made a home? Did he think of her as part of that home or was she still just a visitor? "That sounds nice. I'll see you in a little while."

She walked him to the door then gave him a quick kiss before he left. Sighing softly, Gelsey flipped the sign in the front window to Closed and pulled down the shade on the door. This was real life now. She couldn't hide from it. And either she'd make a mess of it, or she'd carve out a place for herself.

And somewhere along the way, she'd figure out exactly how she felt about Kellan Quinn.

KELLAN STOOD in front of the hearth, staring into the glow of burning peat. With a soft curse, he glanced at his watch for only the fourth or fifth time in the last few minutes. He'd returned from the pub to find the cottage dark and empty. Assuming that Gelsey had been delayed at the shop, he'd hauled the tub in from the pantry next to the kitchen and filled it with a hose from the kitchen sink.

But after an hour of waiting, the water was cold and the fire was dying. Kellan strode to the door and pulled it open, staring down the road that led from the village into the hills above town. The Fiat was gone, so she wouldn't be walking back. He paused. Unless she wasn't able to get it started.

The first thing on his list of things to do would be find a more dependable car for her to drive. Kellan grabbed his jacket and headed for his own car. He'd drive to the shop and fetch her, before she completely exhausted herself. Since she'd begun, Maeve had decided to make a quick visit to her sister's place, leaving Gelsey with long hours and no days off.

It took just a few minutes to drive into the village, but when he rapped on the shop door, it went unanswered. The Closed sign was hanging in the window and from what he could tell, all the lights were off.

Kellan tried the pub next, thinking that Gelsey may have changed her mind and they might have just missed each other. But when he walked in, his family was still gathered at the tables they'd pushed together, finishing up their dinner as the pub began to fill with the Friday-night crowd.

"Hey, you're back," Danny called from behind the bar. "Did you bring Gelsey?"

"She's not here?" Kellan asked.

"No. I thought you said she'd decided to go home after work."

Kellan leaned on the edge of the bar. "I was up at the cottage and she wasn't there. Is she with Nan or Jordan?"

Danny cocked his head toward the kitchen. "They're still here. They're in the kitchen getting Lily's birthday cake ready." Danny motioned Kellan to follow him to the end of the bar. "I'm glad you came back. I have something I have to show you."

"I really don't have time," Kellan said. "I need to go find—"

"It won't take but a minute. Jaysus, Kell, your woman can certainly survive on her own. Don't be so possessive. It's not good for a relationship."

"What are you, a feckin' psychiatrist?"

"I'm just statin' a fact," Danny said.

"Why don't you tell me your meaning so that we don't have to waste breath figuring it out."

"You're lookin' like a man desperately in love."

Kellan shook his head, fixing his brother with a dismissive glare. "And you're full of shite, you are."

"I don't know," Danny said. "You're getting yourself all bothered about a girl that you've been sleeping with for a couple weeks, all worried when she isn't where she's supposed to be."

"We have an understanding," Kellan said. "Neither one of us is planning our future together."

"Hey, maybe you should be. I know I'm going to

marry Jordan. If I were you, I wouldn't let a girl like Gelsey get away, if you catch my meaning."

"This is none of your business," Kellan said. "Hell, I'm not going to lie. I like having her around. We get along great. We're very…compatible. But we're a long way from spending our lives together."

"Hey, we're all just trying to help you out here," Danny said. "You could at least be grateful. We're all doin' our part to get her to hang around."

"What the hell are you talking about, brother?" Kellan leaned forward and grabbed his brother's arm. "Explain yourself."

Danny cursed beneath his breath and shook his head. "Nan and Jordan think she's just grand. They're helping her dust out that shop. And Markus and his committee are determined to get her to buy it from Maeve." He drew a ragged breath. "Perhaps you might want to make an effort on your end. I mean, it's clear to me that you're in love with her. I see the way you look at her. It's the same way Riley looks at Nan and I look at Jordan. No use denying it, Kell."

"So you and the rest of the town have my whole life planned out for me?"

"No," Danny said. "Well, maybe a bit. But you've got to take it from here, mate."

Kellan stood up and pressed his hands along the edge of the bar. "Why don't you all just bugger off and leave me to my own life."

"So you are in love with her, then," Danny said.

A long silence grew between them. He wanted to

admit that his brother was right, but Kellan had always expected that love would be a concrete concept, that he'd never have any doubts once he found it. He was in love with the Gelsey he knew, the woman who curled into his naked body at night, the woman who could merely glance his way and make him burn.

"I'll take that as a yes," Danny said.

"So, what am I supposed to do about this? She might as well be a mermaid for all I really know about her."

"And if she has some horrible past? Would that make a difference? Would it make you want to walk away?"

"No. As far as I'm concerned, we began the day I found her on the beach." He paused, wondering if he ought to reveal more. "Or maybe we began years ago."

"How is that?" Danny asked.

Kellan braced his elbows on the bar and leaned in, lowering his voice to a whisper. "Do you remember that day when we were lads and we found that box buried in the sand at Smuggler's Cove?"

"Why are we whispering?" Danny whispered back.

"Remember the girl? The one who buried it?"

"There was a girl?"

"Yeah. She ran off and we chased her. I caught up with her and she kissed me. That was the first time I ever kissed a girl."

"What does this have to do with Gelsey?"

"That was her," Kellan said. "At least I think it was. I can picture that girl in my mind and Gelsey is just an older version."

"Have you asked her about this?"

Kellan shook his head. "No. Because if it was her then this thing between us becomes something very different." He scowled at Danny's puzzled look. "Don't you get it? It's destiny."

"Oh. Like Jordan and me. And Nan and Riley." Danny glanced both ways, then reached into his pocket and pulled out a small box. He pried open the top to reveal a diamond ring. "I'm going to give it to her for Christmas," he whispered.

Kellan stared at the ring. "It's grand. She's going to love it."

"Get things settled with this girl," Danny warned, "or you might lose her."

Kellan pushed away from the bar and turned for the door. He'd like nothing more than to get things settled between them. But Kellan didn't have a clue how Gelsey felt about a future together. She obviously planned to stay near Ballykirk, at least for a while. But did her plans include him? Somehow, Kellan knew it would be impossible to get a straight answer from her on that subject.

He jogged back to his car and got inside, then turned toward the cottage. There was one thing he had to check before continuing his search. As he drove up the hill, Kellan decided there was only one other place she might have gone—back to Winterhill.

She'd acted strangely distant when he'd stopped by the shop, been preoccupied with something other than business. And she was usually so happy to get out and socialize.

He pulled up in front of the cottage, then jumped out of the car, leaving it running. Throwing back the front door, Kellan called her name, but there was no answer. He headed directly for the bedroom, then opened the wardrobe and dug into the clothes inside.

He found the green dress exactly where he'd put it the night they met. It was still flecked with sand and bits of seaweed. Clutching the wrinkled fabric in his fists, Kellan chided himself for even considering the possibility. She wasn't a mermaid and she wouldn't leave him to return to the sea.

"Winterhill," he murmured.

The sun was already sinking beneath the western horizon as he drove along the coast road, through Derreeny. On the far side of the village of Curryglass, he turned onto a narrow country lane and followed it as it wound between two dry stone walls.

The lights from the house were visible from the road. He swung the car into the driveway and breathed a sigh of relief when he saw the Fiat parked in front of the house. As he got out of the car, Kellan realized that he'd need an explanation for how he knew where she was. Though she'd mentioned Winterhill in her answers to his five questions, she hadn't given him directions.

He strode up to the front door and grabbed the cast-iron knocker, but the door swung open before he could signal his presence. The gray-haired woman he and Danny had met earlier smiled warmly up at him as she wiped her hands on her apron. "Hello," she said. "You've come back."

"Yes," Kellan said. "I—I'm here for Gelsey. I'm—her friend."

An eyebrow rose slightly and she regarded him with a suspicious eye. "You're Kellan."

He nodded. "Yes, I am. She's mentioned me?"

"Once or twice, in passing." She held out her hand. "I'm Caroline. I'm the housekeeper. We've met before. You were the young man with the camera, the other day."

"I was. She's here?"

"She is. But I'm afraid she's sleeping. She stopped by to pick up some old Christmas decorations for the shop and when I went upstairs to check on her, she was curled up on her bed, sound asleep."

"May I go up and see her?" Kellan asked.

"I suppose it wouldn't hurt. You two haven't been arguing, have you?"

Kellan shook his head. "No. Everything is fine. She's just been working very hard lately and I'm a wee bit worried."

Caroline stepped aside and allowed him to pass. "Top of the stairs, second door on the left."

He took the stairs two at a time and found her room. The door was ajar and he silently pushed it open. Gelsey was curled up on the bed, still in her shoes and socks and the clothes she'd been wearing at the shop. Kellan carefully sat down on the edge of the bed, but she didn't stir.

Holding his breath, he pulled the down-filled duvet up from the foot of the bed and stretched out beside her.

Kellan watched her sleep for a long time, wondering at the life she'd lived before him. From what he knew of it, it hadn't been particularly happy.

He could give her more than what she'd had. He could make her happy. Unable to help himself, Kellan leaned forward and touched his lips to hers. The contact startled her and she opened her eyes, staring at him incomprehensibly. "Hello," he murmured.

Gelsey frowned, pinching her eyes shut and then opening them again. "Is it you?"

"Yes," Kellan said.

"What are you doing here? How did you find me?"

"I followed you here the other day. I guess I got a little impatient and couldn't help myself. Does it make a difference?"

"No," she said softly.

"Can I stay here with you tonight?"

She nodded then reached out and touched his face. "I don't want to fall in love with you. But sometimes you make it impossible not to."

"I know exactly what you mean," Kellan said. He captured her mouth in a long, deep kiss.

Slowly, they tugged at clothes, undressing each other beneath the duvet. He curled up behind her, his mouth pressed against her nape, and a moment later, he was buried in her warmth. Kellan moved slowly, enjoying the sensations that pulsed through his body with every lazy stroke.

He skimmed his hands over her hips and along her belly, then found the spot between her legs, damp with her desire. He touched her there, gently caressing her until her breath quickened and her body arched against him.

They reached their release together this time, with barely a sound between them and when it was over, he wrapped his arms around her and waited until she fell asleep, the two of them still joined.

He'd fallen in love with her. Danny was right and there was no denying it. But how had it happened? They'd only known each other two weeks. Or maybe they'd known each other since that summer day he'd chased her across the meadow.

There was only one thing that Kellan was sure of. He intended to keep Gelsey in his bed and in his life for as long as she'd have him. If he was lucky, that would be a very, very long time.

7

THE DARK PANELING in the conservatory was draped with fresh greenery, holly and pine mixed with red twigs, putting Gelsey in a cheery mood. Caroline had laid out a sumptuous breakfast on the small table and Gelsey poured herself a cup of hot chocolate, wrapping her hands around the bone-china cup. "Try the scones," she said, reaching for her favorite, a candied-cherry scone. "They're still warm."

Kellan sat across from her, his hair sticking up in spikes, a sleepy look in his eyes. He took a sip of his coffee and smiled. "I like this."

"What? Being waited on hand and foot?"

"No. Sitting here with you, reading the newspaper, watching the rain come down outside, thinking about Christmas."

They'd both fallen asleep sometime around eight the previous night and slept soundly until seven the next morning. Since it was Saturday, Gelsey didn't need to be at the shop until noon, so a leisurely breakfast was exactly what she needed.

"I can't believe how well I slept," she said, breaking off a bit of scone and slathering it with butter.

"I know. Me, too. I guess we really should try to get to bed early at least one night a week."

"You think so?" She pushed the plate of scones in his direction. "Try one. I used to live on these when I was younger. Caroline used to send me boxes of them at boarding school, although they never taste really good unless they're right from the oven."

"So this is where you spent your summers?" He nodded approvingly. "It's a beautiful house, Gels. Classic country architecture. It's the kind of house everyone wants these days but it's impossible to replicate."

"It is nice. Whenever I think of home, this is the place I think of. Even though my parents never lived here."

"I grew up in the cottage."

"Our cottage?" she asked.

Kellan nodded. "Yeah. The seven of us in that tiny little cottage. It seems impossible when I think back on it, but it was fun. After we all left home, my folks moved to one of the flats above the pub."

"How long have you been here? I mean, this visit?"

"I've been here for about three months. I was staying with a friend in Portugal. We were in Rome for a few days, then back to Portugal. And then I came here."

"And you left Portugal for the damp and rainy west coast of Ireland?"

"Yes," she said. "It was time to leave and I wanted to spend the holidays at Winterhill."

"So you have a house and you're going to own a business soon. I guess that means you're planning to hang around county Cork for a bit longer?"

Gelsey nodded. "That's the plan for now."

He bit into a scone. "Good. I like that."

Gelsey reached for the salver in the center of the table, loaded with all the dishes in a traditional Irish breakfast. She filled a plate for Kellan and set it in front of him. "Here. Eat. You're going to need your strength."

"Why is that? Are we going back to bed after we're finished eating?"

"No. You're going to help me out at the shop today. I have some heavy lifting to do."

The wood fire in the small hearth popped and snapped, creating a relaxing counterpoint to their conversation. Gelsey was glad he'd come to Winterhill. He needed to know what her life had been as a child in order to understand how it had gone so badly off track as a young adult. It wasn't an excuse for her behavior, simply a point of reference.

A knock at the front door echoed through the quiet interior of the house and Gelsey frowned. "Who could that be?"

A few seconds later, Caroline came hurrying in. Her face was pale and her hands were twisted tightly in the front of her apron. "Oh, dear," she muttered. "I'm afraid I've made a terrible mistake."

"What is it?"

"At the door. He called yesterday and I told him you weren't home and that I hadn't seen you for days. He said he'd call every day until he had a chance to speak to you."

"Antonio?" Gelsey asked, her stomach twisting into a knot at the mention of his name.

"Who's Antonio?" Kellan asked, his mouth full of buttered scone.

"Tell him I'm not here," she said. "Send him away. I don't want to see him or talk to him. It's finished. And if he wants his ring back, he can find it at the bottom of the Atlantic just off..." She turned to Kellan. "What's that place called again?"

"Smuggler's Cove?"

"Yeah," Gelsey said. "Smuggler's Cove."

"All right," Caroline said. "But how should I explain the extra cars in the driveway?"

Kellan pushed his chair back from the table. "Go back to the kitchen. I'll take care of this."

A voice echoed through the house. "Gigi! I know you are here. This is childish. We have to talk."

Gelsey shot up out of her chair. "You will not. Sit down." She pointed to his chair. "Sit!" She neatly folded her linen napkin and dropped it next to her plate. "I'll take care of this."

In truth, she should have done this months ago. Rather than running away from him, she should have explained why she was leaving and how it was impossible for her to continue with such a destructive relationship.

It was his fault she was in trouble with the Italian police. He'd started the argument with the photographers and she was only trying to defend herself. Unfortunately, she'd been the one to break the photographer's nose, not Antonio.

Though Antonio could be stubborn at times, he was smart enough to see that they weren't right for each other. But she'd played games with him in the past, taunting him with threats of leaving just to get him to behave himself. Now that she'd finally done it, it was no wonder that he didn't believe it was real.

"I'll be right back," Gelsey said. She strode through the dining room and into the foyer. As expected, Antonio stood in the doorway, handsome as ever, impatiently tapping his foot and cursing beneath his breath. He froze when he saw her.

"Dios mio," he muttered. "You *are* here."

"I am," Gelsey said, nodding.

He grabbed her arms and pulled her into a kiss, but Gelsey twisted away, holding up her hand in a warning. "Don't do that again."

"Why not? I have missed you, my love. I have been so lonely without you."

"You're going to have to get used to that. I meant what I said on the phone. We're finished, Antonio. You know it, I know it. By now, the rest of the world probably knows it. There's nothing left to talk about."

Gelsey heard footsteps behind her and a moment later, Kellan's arm slipped around her waist. "Is there a problem here?" he asked.

Gelsey looked back and forth between the two men as they sized each other up. Kellan had no idea who he was dealing with. Antonio was known for his quick temper and it didn't take much provocation for him to throw a punch. He'd been sued by at least three photographers for doing just that. "Kellan, I think you should go back to our breakfast."

"Your breakfast?" Antonio shouted. "I see how this is. I am not a fool. This is the man who replaces me, no?"

"Yes," Kellan said.

"No," Gelsey countered. "You were out of my life before I even met him."

"I think it would be best if you left," Kellan said.

"You think I should leave?" Antonio asked. "You think *I* should leave?" He lunged at Kellan, but Kellan quickly stepped aside, shielding Gelsey behind him as he did. Antonio stumbled forward, nearly losing his balance, before he turned around again.

He wasn't expecting the quick jab from Kellan. Blood erupted from his nose and he stopped, holding his hand up to his face, stunned by the turn of events. Kellan quickly handed him the linen napkin he still held and Antonio stuck it under his nose.

"Sorry, mate," Kellan said, his demeanor deceptively calm. "But if you try that again, it will be much worse the second time. Gelsey and I are together now and if I have to beat the shite out of you to make you see that, I don't have a problem doing that at all. So, do you want to fight, then, or will you just be saying your goodbyes and go on your merry way?"

Antonio's eyes narrowed and he looked at Gelsey. "You will want me back," he said. "You forget, you need me. Without me, your whole life falls apart. Are you willing to risk that, Gigi? It would be a terrible mistake. A year of your life is a terrible thing to lose, no?" He walked through the door and slammed it shut behind him.

Gelsey and Kellan stood next to each other, silently watching the door, Gelsey's heart slamming in her chest. Well, at least she had her answer. Unless she made nice with Antonio, he had no intention of testifying on her behalf. She heard a car start and then it roared off down the driveway. She released a tightly held breath. "I suppose that could have gone worse," she murmured.

"Will there be any more of those types coming around?" Kellan asked.

"No," Gelsey said.

"Good. Not really the way I like to start my day." He frowned. "What did he mean about a mistake? What about a year of your life?"

"It's nothing," she said. "Old arguments." Gelsey drew a ragged breath and closed her eyes. Why not tell him? At least he'd understand her reluctance to commit to staying in Ballykirk. If the trial didn't go her way, she could spend some time sitting in an Italian jail.

The tabloids were all hoping for that. Not a month or a year, but at least a few weeks so they might get some good photos of the "criminal" going in and coming out. Gigi Woodson in jail would sell a lot of papers.

They walked back to their breakfast and she sat down across from him, watching as he finished his scone.

"What would you do if I had to go back to Europe for a while?" Gelsey asked.

He looked up. "For what? To see him?"

Gelsey shook her head. "Just to tie up some loose ends. Would you forget all about me?" She held her breath, waiting for his answer. Kellan wasn't the kind of man who'd wait forever and he'd already grown impatient with her refusal to consider their future together.

She couldn't imagine wanting a man more than she wanted him and there were times when a future with him seemed like the perfect way to spend a lifetime. Would her old life always come back to haunt her? Could she really start over again? Was "normal" was even possible for Gelsey Woodson?

"I don't know. How long would you be gone?"

"Not long," she said.

"I suppose I'd miss you. But then, I could always come with. When are you planning to leave?"

Gelsey pushed out of her chair and circled the table, then crawled onto his lap, wrapping her arms around his neck. "Never," she whispered. "I want to stay here forever." She snuggled against him, pressing her face into the curve of his neck.

"I'd like that," he said.

She sighed and hugged him tighter. For now, she'd

ignore the dark cloud looming on the horizon. If she wished it hard enough, maybe it would just dissolve before it ever reached her. Or perhaps, by the time it moved overhead, she'd know exactly what to do. She kissed his cheek. "You're pretty good with your fists," she said.

Kellan held up his right hand. "Fist. If I would have used them both, the guy would be headed for hospital right now."

IT HAD TAKEN HIM the entire afternoon, but the cottage looked perfect. Kellan smiled to himself as he went around the room and lit the candles he'd bought. A big bouquet of flowers sat in the middle of the table and he'd brought out the old copper tub and placed it in front of the fireplace, ready to be filled for a bath.

This was the night, Kellan mused. He and Gelsey were going to determine once and for all what this relationship meant to them. He needed to know if there was a real future with her, because if there was, there were plans to be made.

He glanced over at the table and sighed. He'd been offered the museum job in Brittany and was waiting to sign the contract. He'd also met with some potential investors about a castle renovation near Killarney. A month ago, he would have jumped at the chance to take a job outside Ireland, searching for any excuse for a change. But his life *had* changed and now, he wanted nothing more than to spend all his time near Ballykirk.

Kellan walked into the kitchen and pulled open the

refrigerator to check on the temperature of the champagne. He'd never really done it up proper with a woman before, pulling out all the romantic stops. But there was no doubt in his mind that Gelsey was the girl for him. He wasn't sure how he knew, but he knew, deep down in every corner of his soul, she was the one.

He ought to be surprised at how quickly it happened. Although Riley and Danny had found love at lightning speed, Kellan had dismissed the possibility as a rare occurrence. But now, he'd experienced the same strange phenomenon.

He heard the sound of the Fiat chugging up the hill to the cottage and walked to the door. He opened it and waited as Gelsey pulled the car to a stop at the garden gate. She stumbled out, dragging a canvas bag behind her. The moment she saw him, she stopped and gave him an exhausted smile.

"Long day?" he asked.

She nodded. "Excruciatingly long. Please tell me there's a large glass of wine waiting for me."

"Better than that," Kellan replied, holding out his hand. He drew her inside and closed the door behind her, then helped her out of her jacket.

"What's this?"

"Just a little holiday from all the hard work you've been doing," Kellan explained. "Tonight, I'm going to wait on you hand and foot. I'll make you a bath. I have champagne and candles, and dinner is warming in the oven."

"It all looks so wonder—" she began, before fighting

back a yawn. "Can we just lie down and have a quick nap before we get started?"

"Sure." He took her hand and led her into the bedroom, then sat her down on the edge of the bed. Kneeling, he pulled off her shoes and gently massaged her feet. "How's that?"

"Heaven," she murmured, flopping back on the bed.

He stretched out beside her, lying on his side as he toyed with a strand of her hair. "Can I get you anything?"

"A kiss would be nice," she said, turning to face him. Gelsey pointed to her bottom lip. "Right here. This is the only place on my body that isn't utterly exhausted."

Kellan leaned forward and gently nibbled at her lower lip. A long sigh escaped her body and he wove his fingers through her hair and kissed her again, this time more purposefully.

"Oh, that's much better," she said, smiling. "A girl could get used to this."

"That's what I want to talk to you about," Kellan said.

Her brow wrinkled into a frown. "You look so serious." Gelsey reached out and smoothed her fingers over his forehead.

"I am. But you don't need to look so worried. We've been living together for almost a month now and it's been grand."

"It has."

"And I was talking to Danny the other day and he

plans to ask Jordan to marry him at Christmas and I'm reckoning we ought to make some plans ourselves."

"Plans?"

"Yeah. Maybe it's time we…formalize things between us."

She pushed up on her elbow, her frown deepening. "Formalize? What does that mean?"

"Make a commitment to each other."

"How would that change anything?" Gelsey asked.

Kellan was confused by her comeback and at first, didn't have an answer. "I—I guess it wouldn't. But I have to make some plans with my work and I—"

"What kind of plans?"

"I've got to make a decision on the job in France. It would take me out of Ireland for a long time. You'd be here. I'd be there."

"Do you want to take the job?"

"I don't know," Kellan said. "I don't want to leave you."

"How would your decision change then?"

"I guess I wouldn't leave you."

"See. That wasn't so difficult. We don't need to decide anything right now. We'll just do what we feel."

Kellan sat up and shook his head. "No. I don't want to turn this job down and then have you run back to Europe. That's not the way it's supposed to go."

"You know exactly how it's supposed to go?" Gelsey asked. She sat up beside him and folded her hands in her lap. "Tell me. I'd like to know, too. I've been trying to figure it out for the past ten years and haven't gotten it right yet."

He could hear the sarcasm in her voice and for a moment, he thought better of continuing the conversation. But this was a matter that they needed to resolve. "There's just a certain progression that most people follow. Like...Riley and Nan and Danny and Jordan. They've decided that they want to spend the rest of their lives together and—and everyone knows it."

"So a public announcement will make it all work out for us?"

Kellan cursed beneath his breath. Was she deliberately trying to start an argument? The last thing he wanted to do was fight with her. She was tired and tended to get a bit irrational when she didn't have enough sleep.

"We should probably discuss this later," he dodged. "After you've had a kip. Why don't you crawl under the covers and I'll let you sleep for a bit."

She shook her head. "I think we should get this settled."

"No," Kellan said. "You're in no mood to talk."

"I'm in the perfect mood." Gelsey stood up and began to pace back and forth. "Let me see. I've been engaged three times in the past seven years. Married once."

Kellan gasped. What the hell? This was definitely not going the way he'd planned. "You've been married?"

"Yes. To someone who was already married, so

it wasn't legal. I was twenty-three and very stupid. I thought I was in love, but I was proven wrong. I thought I loved them all and in the end it didn't mean anything."

"Why haven't you told me this?"

"Because it's in the past," Gelsey said. "And I wanted to start fresh. But I can't do that if I keep making the same mistakes over and over again."

Kellan grabbed her hand to stop her pacing. "All right. We're done. This isn't the right time or the—"

"No. We should get this straight. I don't want you to plan your life around me, Kellan. I want you to do what makes you happy. And if that means going to France to work on a project then that's what you need to do." She shrugged. "I'm not sure I'll even be here. If I am, when you come home, we'll take up where we left off."

"And in between? We just forget about each other?"

"No, of course not. You know I care about you."

"But you don't love me."

"That has nothing to do with this conversation. You're talking about commitment. I can love you without making a commitment to you, can't I?"

"Yes," he said. "Of course, but—"

"No buts." Drawing a deep breath, she turned and straddled his legs, then sat down on his lap. Wrapping her arms around his neck, she kissed him, her mouth trailing from his lips to his ear. "I'm happy now. I don't want anything to change."

She tipped her head as she stared into his eyes. But his anger must have been evident in his gaze, because she suddenly stood up. "But then, maybe it would be good to have some time apart."

Kellan gasped, stunned by the turn in the conversation. He stood also, catching her off balance. Gelsey stumbled back and he caught her arm. "How did we get from that to this? We love each other but we should spend some time apart?"

Gelsey nodded. "I think I'm going to spend the night at Winterhill. You can think about what you want to do and I won't be here to…distract you."

"I don't think that's a good idea," Kellan countered.

"Sure it is. Besides, I have some business I need to take care of tomorrow morning at the house, so I won't have to get up early and drive over there."

"Why do I get the feeling that I just turned everything arseways between us?"

"You didn't," Gelsey said. "Nothing has changed."

Kellan didn't believe her. In truth, he could see the confusion in her eyes, the frantic way she kept avoiding his gaze. Hell, she'd been engaged three times? This was a woman who was pathologically frightened of commitment and here he was, pushing her to declare her feelings and plan a future with him after they'd only known each other less than a month.

Jaysus, could he be much more of a gack? How had his brothers managed to find mates when all he could do was stumble around and blather on about his plans and his needs. "If you want to go, that's fine," he finally said. "I'll stop by the shop tomorrow. Maybe we can have lunch?"

"Yes," Gelsey said. "Lunch would be perfect." She kissed him quickly, then slipped into her shoes. Reaching out, she placed her palm on his cheek. "Don't look so worried. Everything will be fine."

As she walked out of the room, Kellan sat down on the edge of the bed. Raking his fingers through his hair, he cursed. This was not the way it was supposed to go. He'd finally found a woman he could love and he'd made a complete mess of it.

He heard the car start and walked to the window. Watching through the lace curtains, Kellan willed her to come back inside, to forget everything that he'd said to her. But instead, she drove off down the hill toward the village and the coast road to Winterhill.

Kellan wandered out into the great room. He felt as if he'd just gone ten rounds in a feckin' boxing ring. His head hurt and he couldn't put a coherent thought together. "I need a drink," he muttered.

Grabbing his jacket, he opened the front door and stepped out into the evening chill. There was plenty to drink down at the Speckled Hound. And maybe his brothers might be able to explain exactly where he'd gone wrong, because he sure as hell couldn't figure it all out.

"DANNY SAID you've moved out of the cottage."

"Where did he hear that?" Gelsey asked.

Jordan shrugged. "I think Kellan told him. He stopped by the pub a few nights ago and got really pissed. Danny had to drive him home."

Gelsey picked at a piece of lace on Nan's wedding dress, smoothing it down until it lay perfectly on her shoulder. "I didn't exactly move out. Some of my things are still there. I'm just staying at my place for a while until we sort out our...issues."

They'd gathered at Danny and Jordan's cottage behind the blacksmith's shop to look at the dress that had just arrived from a bridal shop in Cork. To Gelsey's eyes, it was the perfect dress for the perfect bride. Nan had chosen a simple fitted sheath, bare at the neck with handmade Irish lace covering her arms and shoulders. It hugged the curves of her body, flaring out at the knees, making the dress both sexy and conventional at the same time.

Jordan groaned. "No, you can't have issues. We don't want you to have issues." She paused. "What are your issues?"

"It's nothing serious, really," Gelsey said. "He just wants everything to be...official. Written in stone. And I'm just not sure I can do that. Every time I've tried that in the past, it's blown up in my face."

"Antonio?" Nan asked.

Gelsey blinked in surprise.

"Kellan told Danny who told Riley. He thinks you're going to go back to him."

"Danny?" Gelsey asked.

"No, Kellan. He thinks you're going to go back to Europe and to Antonio."

Gelsey stepped away from Nan then took in the sight of her new friend, dressed in the gown she'd be married in. "You look beautiful." Tears pressed at the corners of her eyes. How had it been so easy for Nan and Jordan to surrender to love? And why did she find it so impossible? Surely, they'd made mistakes in the past. How could they be so certain it was the right thing to do?

If Kellan truly loved her, then he'd have to accept her the way she was, with all the baggage that came along. And if she had to spend some time in an Italian jail, then he'd be there for her when she got out. And he'd be there for her every day for the rest of her life.

It took so much courage to put her life, her future happiness, in his hands. At this moment, she felt as if she could get out without mortal wounds. But if she went on much longer, leaving him would destroy her.

"I'm sorry," she murmured, brushing a tear from her cheek. "I don't know why I'm so…silly." Her voice wavered. "I'm usually not so emotional."

"It's all right," Nan said. "You don't have to hide it with us. So, he knows about your life in Europe? The tabloids?"

Gelsey shook her head. "We haven't really discussed it."

"And what about the thing with the photographer?" Jordan asked.

Gelsey gasped. "You know about that?"

Jordan nodded. "You mentioned it that time we talked. Nan saw it in *Hello!*"

"Yeah, well, it's the truth. I have to go right back into that mess with the photographers and the reporters and all the people who want to examine my life with a microscope. Nobody knows me here and it's been wonderful."

"We know you," Nan said. "And Kellan knows you. And everyone who knows you cares about you. We don't care about that other stuff."

"I haven't told Kellan about court," Gelsey said. "I just know everything is going to change once I go back. All the magazines will have pictures and I don't want him to get caught up in that. He doesn't deserve that."

Jordan slipped her arm around Gelsey's shoulders. "I think you should tell him. He would want to know."

Gelsey forced a smile. They were right. She didn't want to keep him in the dark any longer. Kellan would understand and he would see why she couldn't make any commitments until after the last part of her past was dealt with.

"Can we just get back to your wedding plans?" Gelsey said, reaching out to grab Nan's veil. "You need to put this on. Are you going to wear your hair up or down?"

Nan stared at her reflection in the mirror. "What do you think?"

"Down," Gelsey said. Jordan seconded her choice. "But maybe with a bit of curl?"

Nan nodded. "I always expected that I'd be a bag of nerves before my wedding day, but I feel strangely calm."

"You do?" Jordan said. "How can that be? I get nervous just looking at you."

"I know I'm doing exactly the right thing," Nan said, a serene expression on her face. "I have no doubts. I was meant to marry Riley, the same way you're meant to marry Danny."

"He hasn't officially asked me yet," Jordan said. "But I suspect there's a proposal coming soon. He's been acting weird lately. Staring at me all the time with this dopey smile on his face." She shook her head and turned to Gelsey. "And then comes you and Kellan."

"We'll see about that," Gelsey said. "It's just not going to be as simple for us."

"Do you love him?" Nan asked.

"I think I do. I tell myself I do, but I've never said it out loud. But then, I've fallen in love so many times, I'm not sure I really know how I'm supposed to feel. I guess I'm just waiting."

"For what?" Jordan asked.

"I'm not sure. Maybe a sign? Or a moment of clarity? I don't know what it is, but there has to be something that will make me sure of my feelings. Something that I never felt before with the others."

Nan and Jordan both turned to look at her, shared concern evident in their gazes. But Gelsey waved them off. "Don't look at me like that!"

"Well, we've been ordered to bring you along to the pub," Jordan said. "We're all going to have dinner there and then go into Cork to catch a late movie. A triple date."

"Does Kellan know about this?"

"Of course he does. He said he's barely seen you this past week."

"We were supposed to have lunch on Monday, but he had to cancel. He said he needed to spend some time in Dublin before the holiday." In truth, Gelsey wanted to see Kellan. Over the past few days she'd been left to wonder whether his feelings for her had cooled.

He called her a few times at the shop, just to check in, but his tone had been distant and his mood unreadable. She needed to look into his eyes, to hold his hand, to kiss him again if only to reassure herself that he still loved her.

Nan turned back to the mirror. "All right. I'm going to have to take this dress off, even though I adore looking at myself."

Jordan adjusted the veil. "You do look beautiful."

"Wait!" Gelsey cried. "I have something for you. I can't believe I almost forgot!" She grabbed her bag and rummaged around in it until she found the flat velvet box. "I know you need something borrowed and if you like these, then I want you to wear them on your wedding day."

Nan took the box from Gelsey's outstretched hand and slowly opened the top. Her breath stalled in her throat as she caught sight of the ruby necklace and matching earrings.

"I know you're using red in your bouquet and I thought this might go. You don't have to wear them if you don't like them."

"No!" Nan cried. "They're beautiful. Where did you get them?"

"My grandmother left me a lot of beautiful jewelry and I've never thought to wear any of it. I sat down and looked at it the other day and thought this would be perfect for you."

Nan pulled Gelsey into a fierce hug. "Thank you. Gosh, I feel like royalty now."

Gelsey helped her put the necklace and earrings on, then nodded. "I thought so. They do look lovely."

"Jordan!"

The sound of Danny's voice echoed through the quiet cottage. "We're in here," Jordan called from the bedroom.

A moment later, Danny appeared in the door, breathless, his hair windblown. "Gelsey, there's a guy in town who's been looking for you. I think he's a photographer. He's been hanging around asking questions. Kellan sent me over here to get you."

"Oh, dear," Nan murmured.

"I guess my past has just caught up with my present." Gelsey was resigned. "I think it would be best if I got out of town as quickly as possible."

"Kellan is waiting for you behind the pub. He told me to bring you to him. He'll get you out of town."

Gelsey picked up her jacket and purse, then gave Nan and Jordan a hug before she hurried to the door. "I'll see you both soon. Thanks for inviting me."

When they got outside, she and Danny walked along the back side of the cottage and the smithy, through an alleyway behind the bakery, and then over a low fence to the small garden behind the pub. Kellan was waiting there, his back braced against the side of the building.

"You're back," Gelsey said as he took her hand.

"Just," he murmured. "Lucky thing."

"Where is he?"

"Out front. Riley has been keeping him occupied. Although, he did manage to get a fair bit of information from Maeve, before she realized what he was doing in town."

"How did he know I was here?"

"I suspect Antonio sent him. The guy probably started asking questions in Curryglass and worked his way down the coast. He's got pictures he's showing everyone."

"I'm sorry," Gelsey said.

"For what?"

"They're not going to leave me alone. Now that Antonio's talking, it makes the story even better. I'm sure he's giving them all sorts of juicy details."

"What kind of details does he have to give?"

"The kind that sell papers," Gelsey replied. "There are some things I haven't told you, but I really want to. First, though, we need to figure out how we are going to get out of here."

"We aren't," he said. Kellan pointed to a stairway that led up to the second floor above the pub. "Riley has a flat next to my parents' place. He'll come and tell us when the guy leaves and then we can leave."

"Where are we going to go? He'll find me whether I'm at Winterhill or here."

"He can't be everywhere at once. And everyone in town knows to send him in the wrong direction. After a few days, he'll be so mixed up, he won't know which way to turn."

"Or he'll call in a bunch of his friends," Gelsey said. "They rarely travel alone. It's always in packs."

He started up the stairs in front of her, holding her hand as they climbed. "Why do they even bother? You're not living that life anymore, not that I really know anything about that life." He turned to face her. "I don't care, you know. We all make mistakes and then we move on."

"My mistakes will follow me around forever," she said.

When they reached the landing, Kellan opened the door and stepped aside. Gelsey walked into the kitchen of the small flat. It wasn't at all what she expected for Riley's bachelor flat, then she realized that Nan was living there with him. She heard the door click shut behind her.

In an instant, his hands were on her waist, spinning her to face him and picking her up at the same time. Kellan wrapped her legs around his hips and set her on the edge of the kitchen table.

"Wait," she murmured. "We need to talk."

"I don't care what you have to tell me," Kellan said. "I don't need to know. It doesn't change this."

Gelsey held tight as his mouth came down on hers in

a desperate kiss. All the doubts and insecurities she'd felt over the past few days dissolved and she surrendered to the pleasure that raced through her body at his touch.

She reached for the buttons of his shirt, needing to touch warm skin and hard muscle. Her lips trailed her fingers as she tugged the shirt from the waist of his jeans. Frustrated by her pace, Kellan shrugged out of his jacket, then tore the shirt off his body and tossed it aside.

A long breath slipped out of her body as she ran her hands over his naked chest. It had been only a few days, but it was as if she were parched with thirst for the sight of him, the scent of him, the taste of his tongue in her mouth.

He slipped his hands beneath the hem of her skirt, sliding it up along her thighs as he stepped between her legs. Her fingers trembled as she worked on the button fly on his jeans.

"God, I missed you," he murmured as Gelsey skimmed his jeans down over his hips.

Grabbing her legs, he pulled her against his body and a heartbeat later, he was inside her. Gelsey moaned softly as he began to move, her body falling into a familiar rhythm. How had she ever done without this? Every nerve in her body cried out for his touch, and the ache deep inside her was suddenly soothed with each stroke.

This man was all she ever needed and everything she'd ever wanted. Yet she couldn't bring herself to believe that the feelings between them could last. This desire could…but desire was a very different thing than love.

8

A SMALL CROWD WAS GATHERED on the main street of Ballykirk as Kellan drove into town. "What the hell is going on here?"

Danny peered through the windscreen. "I don't know. Isn't that Maeve's shop?"

Kellan had left Gelsey asleep in the cottage that morning while he and Danny drove to Bantry to pick up supplies for the pub. They'd had a late night, having waited until nearly midnight before leaving the flat above the pub and sneaking back up the hill to the cottage.

Rosie Perry, the owner of the only bed-and-breakfast in Ballykirk, had passed along a message that the photographer had taken a room and was planning to stay for at least another day or two. She'd promised to call Kellan with any news of his movements.

Kellan reached into his pocket for his mobile, then cursed beneath his breath as he noticed the battery levels were dead. "Can you see what's going on?"

"There's the photographer," Danny said. "And it looks like Gelsey is there along with Dealy, Markus and Johnnie. Maeve's there, too."

Kellan pulled the car up to the curb and hopped out, closing the distance between him and the crowd in a few long steps. Strangely, Gelsey didn't seem to be in any distress. She was smiling for the crowd as she spoke.

"Maybe you can get a photo of Maeve and I under the sign." She pointed above her head and the photographer reluctantly focused on the pair of them and clicked his shutter.

"What about you and Antonio?" he said.

"Oh, that's old news. Now, let me tell you about our new product line. It's all natural, made from a special kind of kelp harvested off the coast of the Aran Islands. Here, get a photo of this jar. Isn't it beautiful? Mrs. Logan has tried the facial scrub." She drew Ardelle Logan out of the crowd. "Tell this nice gentleman what you thought."

Ardelle Logan held the jar up for the photographer, smiling as she spoke. "It made my skin so wonderfully soft. It doesn't smell very pretty, but it works."

"Perhaps we can get a photo with our tourism committee too," Gelsey suggested.

"Do you have any plans to return to Europe, Gigi? Maybe to see Antonio? Is it true that he came here looking to take you back?"

"Oh, no. I'm happy right here. Helping Maeve turn this shop into everything that it can be. Would you like to come inside? I'd love to show you around. Wait, maybe we should get a few more photos outside."

"And what about the charges that are still pending against you? There's been talk that after the criminal trial, the guy is going to sue you."

The crowd around her went silent and Kellan glanced over at Danny. "Charges?"

"I—I'm sure that I'll be cleared of any wrongdoing," Gelsey said.

"And what if you're not?" the photographer asked.

Kellan pushed through the crowd to Gelsey's side. "Listen, I think you got what you came here for. It's time to leave, mate."

"Who are you? Are you and Gigi together? Does Antonio know about this, Gigi?"

Kellan grabbed his arm and pulled him along through the crowd. "She doesn't want you here. Leave her alone."

The photographer wrenched out of his grasp and began to snap pictures of Kellan. But within seconds, most of the men in the crowd surrounded them both, moving in on the photographer.

He held up his camera. "All right, all right. I get the message." He hoisted it over his shoulder, then nervously walked through the crowd. "She's turned into a crashing bore anyway. She was much more fun when she was drunk." He turned back and looked at Kellan. "You're not Quinn, are you?"

Kellan shook his head. "Rooney is the name. I run the petrol station near the docks. You're welcome to come down and take a few snaps of my place." He slipped his arm around Danny. "This is my brother. He helps out."

"Do you know Kellan Quinn?"

"Oh, he doesn't live here. He lives in Dublin," Dealy said.

"That's what I've been told," the photographer replied.

"I'm sure he's in the book," Markus added. "K-E-double L-A-N. Ring him and he'll probably let you take his picture, too."

"Either you're all crazy or you're acting like you are," the photographer said. Kellan watched as he strode down the street to his car, got inside and headed out of town.

The crowd slowly dispersed, chatting amongst themselves about the possibility of being on the cover of *Hello!* or the *Tattler*. They didn't seem to care about the bomb the photographer had just dropped. What kind of trouble was she in? And why would it require a trial?

Before long, Gelsey was the only one standing in front of the shop. "I'm going to take the car down to the pub," Danny said.

"Great. I'll meet you there in a few minutes." Kellan stepped up to Gelsey, then looked over his shoulder to make sure there weren't any other photographers lurking about. "Are you all right?"

She nodded. "He'll be back. Don't think he believed that story you told him. They're much smarter than that. He'll pay someone for more information and he'll catch a photo of us together and he'll have his picture and story to sell."

"What story? We're not doing anything wrong."

"Gigi Woodson hiding out in Irish village with new boy toy. Do you really want to be known around the world as my boy toy?"

Kellan chuckled softly, then leaned close to drop a kiss on her lips. "I don't know. Do I?"

"Definitely not," she replied.

"So, now that you're the biggest celebrity in town, I suppose you're not going to want to go out to lunch with me, are you?"

Gelsey shook her head. "Maybe we should—"

"Why not?"

"I just think we ought to—"

"But I'm really hungry."

Gelsey reached into the pocket of her skirt and pulled out an envelope, waving it in front of her face. "All right. My paycheck. Maeve gave it to me this morning. I'm pretty sure it should buy us lunch."

"Where are you going to take me?" he asked.

"There's only one place in town that serves lunch. It's called the Speckled Hound. You ever been there?"

"I don't believe I have," Kellan said, playing along. "Lead on."

She slipped her hand into his and they walked down the street. "How was your trip to Dublin?" she asked.

"Good," he said. "Everything went well. It's another job, this time just outside Waterford."

"What about the job in France?"

"We're still considering that," Kellan said. "It's a big commitment and I'm not sure Jordan wants to spend that much time away from Danny."

"Right," she murmured. "I guess she wouldn't."

"And what about you?" Kellan asked, turning to face Gelsey and pulling her to a stop. "I understand you have a little problem with the law in Italy?"

Gelsey stopped short. "Now you want to talk about that?"

"Do you?"

"Do you want the long story or the short?"

"Short," he said.

"I accidentally hit a photographer and broke his nose. He's filed assault charges. Antonio is my only witness. The hearing for the case is scheduled for January. If I don't win, I might have to go to jail—for a little while." She drew a deep breath and let it out. "There. That wasn't so bad."

"Is this why you've been so reluctant to talk about the future?"

Gelsey shrugged. "In part. There are some other things that we probably should talk about. Stupid things that I've done. I just didn't want you to think less of me. And sooner or later, someone is going to tell you these things or you're going to read about them and maybe you won't like me as much anymore."

"Well, I don't think that will happen. But it might help if we didn't have to sleep in separate beds. Hell, in separate houses. Why are we doing that?"

"I guess I'm wondering that, too," Gelsey said. "But

it's different now. Before, I was staying with you because I was running away from my old life. Now I have a new life and I have to figure out how I want that life to be."

"What do you need to figure out, Gels? It's not that difficult."

"All right. Where do we live? You have a place in Dublin, we can't live there. The cottage belongs to your parents, we can't stay there forever. I have a house, we could live there, but I'm not quite sure I'm ready for that."

"I see your point," Kellan said. "But we can spend a few nights a week at your house and a few at the cottage until we decide what to do."

He pulled open the door to the pub and they walked inside. Gelsey saw Danny behind the bar and smiled at him, but Kellan led her to a booth on the far wall, a spot that offered them the maximum amount of privacy.

Sitting down across from her, he grabbed her hand and brought it to his lips. Their gazes met and for a moment, Kellan saw the fears vanish from her gaze. He was making progress in the right direction. Very slow—but positive—progress.

"Maybe we ought to start dating," Kellan suggested. "Forget about the sex and the sleeping together. We never really started at the beginning. Maybe that's the problem."

"What are we going to do around Ballykirk that we haven't already done?" Gelsey asked.

"There are plenty of things to do. We can sit down

at the harbor and watch the fishing boats come it. We can walk to the library and look at the new books. The greengrocer teaches a cooking class every other Wednesday night. And there's always Tuesday-night bingo at St. Margaret's."

"Bingo sounds lovely," Gelsey said. "And I'll drive. Now that I have my own car, I can pick you up."

"You're driving a forty-year-old Bentley. That thing should be in a museum, not on the road. Do you know how much that car is worth?"

"No. It was my grandmother's. She loved that car. It was just sitting in the carriage house, so I thought I'd drive it."

"And then there's Nan and Riley's wedding. I don't have a date for that and I was hoping you'd agree to come with me."

Gelsey smiled, then twisted her fingers through his. "I suppose I could be convinced. I don't have any other plans for New Year's Eve."

"That would be a rare one for me," Kellan said. "I never have a date for New Years."

Danny appeared at their table, a pad and pen in his hands. "I'd assume the two of you are here for lunch? We have a lovely shepherd's pie, bangers and boxty, and salmon patties with chips. And the regular sandwiches and salads."

"Shepherd's pie," Kellan said. "And a half pint of Guinness."

"Same for me but water," Gelsey said.

After Danny had gone to put in their orders, Kellan asked, "How has work been?"

Gelsey pulled his hand toward her. "Good. Well, maybe not good, but it's improving. We've had a lot of new customers come in. After this morning, I'm sure we'll have more."

"That's good."

"There's going to be all sorts of talk, Kellan. It doesn't bother me, but I don't want you to get caught up in it."

"It'll be good for business. Have you thought anymore about buying the place from Maeve?"

"I have. But it's a little difficult to make plans with everything hanging over me."

"Then don't let it bother you. Go ahead and make plans. Buy the shop. And if things don't go well in Italy, then figure that out when you have to."

"I suppose I could do that," she murmured.

They chatted about the shop until Danny brought their food. As Kellan watched Gelsey dig into her shepherd's pie, he nodded. "I think we should call this our first date."

"Why is that?"

"Because a girl like you probably doesn't kiss on the first date. I'm thinking I might get lucky on our second."

"You had all the luck you could handle the night we met," Gelsey teased. "I'm going to take things much more slowly this time around." He felt her bare foot slowly creep up the inside of his calf until she rubbed his thigh.

Kellan grabbed her ankle and placed her foot squarely in his crotch. "I can see you're the kind of girl my mother warned me about." He rubbed her foot over the front of his jeans. "It's a rare pleasure to meet you, Gelsey Woodson."

CHRISTMAS WAS ONLY two days away and Maeve Dunphrey's Potions and Lotions was experiencing what could only be considered a holiday rush. They'd had customers waiting that morning when Gelsey opened and there had been a steady flow of people in and out of the shop, picking up late gifts for friends and relatives.

Gelsey had picked up some colorful wrapping paper and ribbon in Bantry and for the last week had been wrapping every purchase that left the store. To her surprise, customers were stopping in to buy just because of the free gift wrapping.

She had hoped to find a moment to talk to Maeve. After a lot of thought and a few phone calls to her banker, she'd decided to make an offer on the shop. Kellan had been right. She needed to think beyond what would happen in January and this was an opportunity she couldn't pass up.

She had a life here in Ballykirk. She had friends, a man who loved her, people who were happy to see her each day. And even after the entire town found out who she really was, it didn't matter. They still treated her like the girl Kellan saved from the sea.

She hadn't told Kellan about her decision yet. She'd become superstitious since the arrival of the photographer, just waiting for the other shoe to drop. But now she felt confident that no matter what happened, this was exactly where she belonged.

"I haven't see the shop like this in, well, it's been years," Maeve exclaimed. "I bless the day I hired you, Gelsey. Look what you've done. It's a miracle."

"The shop just needed a bit of modernizing," Gelsey said as she arranged a display of natural sponges in a wicker basket. "I'd like to sit down and talk with you after the holidays. I'd like to make an offer to buy the shop. I'll give you a fair price. Enough for you and your sister to take ten cruises around the world."

Maeve picked up a pot of beeswax lip balm and slowly turned it over in her hand. "About that," she said. "I—I'm not so sure I want to sell anymore."

Her words hit Gelsey like a slap in the face. "What? I don't understand."

"Well, everything is going so well. We've had so many new customers stop in and the shop has never looked better. And I've never really gotten on with my sister. She's bossy and stubborn and she spends far too much time in front of the telly. We'd never be able to live together."

"But, I thought—"

"I know. And I am sorry, dear. This is just so much fun now and I don't want to give it up. You understand, don't you?"

Gelsey felt the frustration bubbling inside her. *She*

was the reason the shop was doing well, *she* brought the customers in, *she* gave them what they wanted. Without her, Maeve would have still been digging herself out from beneath dusty boxes of ten-year-old product.

"I'd still love you to work here," Maeve continued. "The customers adore you. And of course, we'd renegotiate your pay. But, if you want my advice, dear, you're much too clever to stay in this small town. You should be running your own place in London or Paris."

Gelsey opened her mouth, ready to argue her point, but then she snapped it shut. "I'm going to take my break now," she said, trying to keep her voice calm and her manner indifferent. It wouldn't do to burn any bridges right now. Perhaps Maeve could be persuaded to change her mind.

Maeve glanced at her watch. "Go right ahead. I think I can handle things. And when you come back we'll discuss that raise."

Gelsey grabbed her coat and pulled it on over the cashmere sweater and skirt she'd chosen that morning, then retrieved her purse from behind the counter. She couldn't get out of the shop fast enough, but when she reached the safety of the street, she didn't curse or scream. Instead, tears erupted from the corners of her eyes and there was nothing she could do to stop them.

She headed toward the pub. Her immediate reaction was to find Kellan and tell him what had happened. But as she walked, Gelsey realized that this wasn't his problem, it was hers. She'd been the one to naively put all her efforts into improving the shop. She'd been the one to spend her own money on gift bags and wrapping paper and real grosgrain ribbon for the boxes.

She'd dusted and mopped and toted and carried until every muscle in her body ached and she'd been rewarded with happy customers and increased sales. Maeve was right—she was clever. And she did know what she was doing.

Gelsey wiped away her tears. Why was she crying? She didn't need the job. She had plenty of money left in her trust find.

She walked past the pub and down to the waterfront. The smell of the sea was thick in the damp air. She sat down on a bench that overlooked the harbor, fixing her gaze on a fishing boat that was chugging out of port.

People went to work every day and some of them worked at jobs they barely liked. But she'd wanted to find something to make her life meaningful, something that made her proud of what she did with her day. She'd wasted so much time, and now that she'd finally decided on a future for herself, it had been snatched away from her before she'd even begun.

The tears started again and Gelsey didn't try to stop them. She was alone. And the emotional release was the only reaction she could muster. But when she saw Dealy Carmichael and the rest of the Unholy Trinity approaching, Gelsey quickly composed herself and pasted a smile on her face.

"Good morning, lass," Markus called. "What are you doing out here on a chilly day like today?"

"Just admiring the view," Gelsey said, forcing a cheerful tone into her words.

"We're working on a shopping brochure for the town," Dealy said. "We'll be sure to add your shop to the map."

"Good. I'm sure Maeve will appreciate that."

They continued past her, fishing poles in hand. Once they were out of sight, Gelsey drew a ragged breath. Closing her eyes, she tipped her head back and tried to relax.

How had she managed to fool herself yet again? She'd convinced herself that she could live happily ever after in Ballykirk. But she should have known that nothing ever worked out in her favor.

Another sob rocked her body and she covered her face with her hands, her cheeks already growing wet with tears.

"Gelsey?"

The sound of Kellan's voice startled her and she sat up and wiped her face with her palms. "Hi. Sorry, I was just resting my eyes."

"The boys told me you were down here," he said, sitting down next to her. "What are you doing? Aren't you supposed to be at work?"

"No."

"But it's the Friday before Christmas."

"Just go away," Gelsey said. "Leave me alone."

He reached out to pull her closer, but she fought his embrace, moving to the other end of the bench.

"Would you like to tell me what this is about?"

"Maeve doesn't want to sell the shop anymore. Now that it's doing so well, she's decided to stick around. Of course, she wants me to continue working there. With a lovely raise."

"That's good," Kellan said.

"I don't want to be taking orders from Maeve for the rest of my life. She knows that I'm responsible for all the new business, but it's still her shop. I guess I've done my job too well."

"I'm sure that's true," Kellan said. "Maeve may be a big crazy, but she's not blind. She'd be lucky to have you."

"I'm not going back there. I don't want to work for Maeve. She's a lovely woman, but I need to do something for myself."

"Gelsey, I know you haven't had a job in the past, so you might be a bit naive about how things work in the real world. This happens all the time. Employees are taken advantage of, are underappreciated and overworked. That's just the way the world operates." He finally got hold of her hand and this time Gelsey didn't pull away. "My first job, I was amazing. I did brilliant work. But my boss took it all and passed it off as his own. In the end, his boss found out, he was sacked and I moved up into his spot. I had a choice and I decided to stay. But you can do anything you want."

Gelsey laughed. "You say that as if it's the easiest thing in the world to do. I liked Maeve's shop. I knew I could make a success of that."

"So, open up your own shop."

"Selling what? I don't think Ballykirk can support two shops selling kelp facial masks and sea-salt scrubs."

"Gelsey, if you're going to let this stop you, then you aren't cut out to run a business."

Gelsey snatched her hand away. "Whose side are you on?"

"This isn't about sides. It's about business. You can do anything you want. You just have to decide to do it."

"I did decide and it blew up in my face."

"I think you're being a bit dramatic," Kellan said.

Gelsey stood, her tears now replaced with anger. She'd at least thought that Kellan would understand, but he seemed to be taking Maeve's part, which only added to her anger. "I have to go. I don't want to talk about this anymore and I don't want to talk to you."

"Come on, Gels. Don't get mad. This isn't a big deal. You pick yourself up and you move on."

"No? It's a big deal to me. A really big deal. And if you don't understand that, then you don't understand me."

"You're mad at me?" Kellan asked. "Just because I disagree with the way you're handling this?"

Gelsey walked by him and started back toward the shop. "Don't even think about following me," she shouted.

To her relief, Kellan didn't. She managed to make it to the Bentley without having to talk to anyone. Gelsey tossed her purse inside, then got behind the wheel and started the car. The mechanic she'd hired to look at it had encouraged her to get it tuned up before driving it, but she hadn't had time.

The engine sputtered at first, refusing to start, but after the sixth try, it roared to life. She put the car in gear, made a wide U-turn on the street in front of the shop and headed out of town.

He was right. She'd just have to find another opportunity, a better chance to make a future for herself. But would that be in Ballykirk? And would it be with Kellan?

Gelsey scolded herself. She shouldn't have reacted the way she had. He was only trying to help. But Kellan knew what he wanted from life. It had always been easy for him. Since she'd come back to Ireland, she'd been living in a strange kind of limbo, waiting for everything to make sense.

"I don't need him," she murmured to herself as she steered the car along the coast road. "I can take care of myself."

"Here it is," Kellan said. "What do you think?"

Jordan stared at the facade of the shop, nestled between the Ballykirk post office and Roddy Murphy's Sporting Emporium, a confused expression on her face. "About what?"

"The possibilities," he said. He pulled a key out of his pocket and pushed it into the lock on the front door, then stepped aside so Jordan could enter.

"Are you going to bid on the renovations? Who is this for?"

"A friend," Kellan said.

Jordan sucked in a sharp breath as she caught sight of the cluttered interior. Everywhere they looked, old appliances were stacked and scattered, some in pieces. "Is this for Gelsey?"

Kellan nodded. "Yeah. You probably heard about what happened with Maeve. Gelsey quit her job there after Maeve decided she didn't want to sell the shop."

"I know. Nan told me. It happened yesterday and it's all around town. People are plenty angry with Maeve, but she seems as happy as a clam with all her new business. Is Gelsey even interested in staying in Ballykirk now?"

"She was before," Kellan said. "And I hope she hasn't changed her mind. I'm going to do everything I can to give her a reason to stay."

"You're going to buy her this shop?"

"No. She's going to buy the shop. I'm going to renovate it for her." Kellan stood in the center of the huge ground floor. Up until a few months ago, it had housed Eddie Farrell's appliance-repair shop. Eddie had heard about Maeve's change of heart and had come rushing over to the pub last night with an offer of his own. "What do you think?"

Jordan walked along one wall lined with shelves that were filled with old toasters. "I don't know what to think. It's hard to see past the junk."

"Eddie Farrell is ready to sell. And he won't be changing his mind. He's offered to include his inventory, but I'm not sure it's worth keeping."

"It would take a lot of work," Jordan said. "Much more than Maeve's place. But look at these shelves. They're original. And these cases are beautiful."

"I know. That's why I need your help. We're going to need to find more display cases and shelving units and tables. I know you've been all over Ireland looking for furniture for Castle Cnoc. I'm hoping you can find what we need to make this place work."

"I already know of a few places to check." Jordan grinned. "This is going to be a fun project. So what is she going to sell?"

"I don't know," Kellan said. "She'll have to figure that out. But at least whatever she sells will be here in Ballykirk." He turned to face Jordan. "Do you think you could make some sketches? Maybe choose some paint colors and put together some boards. I want to set something up so that when I bring Gelsey here, she'll be able to see the potential."

"Today?"

"No. I was hoping to show it to her on New Year's Eve. After the wedding. I want to get some of this junk cleared out first."

"That would be perfect," Jordan cried. "Wow, you are a romantic, aren't you."

He couldn't help but laugh. The notion was so absurd, but he'd spent a lot of time considering what approach would best appeal to Gelsey. "I'm learning."

"Every woman appreciates romance," Jordan said, patting him on the arm. "Even a good attempt is appreciated. When Danny and I were living at Castle Cnoc, he used to bring my coffee up to the bedroom in the morning so I could wake up slowly. All those little gestures add up and one day, it just hits you square in the face. Oh, my God, I'm in love with this man."

"That's the way it went?"

"I really knew it when we were dancing naked in the rain," she said.

"Danny?"

She nodded. "Don't you ever tell him I told you that." Jordan went silent for a moment and then giggled. "He looked so sexy."

Kellan thought about the night Gelsey had sent him out in the rain. She'd stood in the door and watched him, her eyes alight with amusement. Would she remember that moment in the same way?

"Will Gelsey be coming for Christmas Eve tonight?" Jordan asked.

"I haven't talked to her since yesterday. I decided I ought to give her a chance to cool off. But I'm going to drop her Christmas present at Winterhill later this afternoon. Hopefully, she won't slam the door in my face."

"Why would she do that?"

"Because, in addition to being a romantic, I can sometimes be a Bombay shitehawk."

"And what exactly is that?"

"An arse of the first order," Kellan replied. "I didn't really handle the situation very well yesterday. She didn't take kindly to my suggestions. And I guess I don't blame her. She has plenty of money, so she doesn't have to keep a job for the wages."

"You better take more than a gift over there," Jordan warned. "You better have a full-blown apology ready." She glanced around once more, then nodded. "Have you taken measurements?"

"I have," Kellan said. "I'll text them to your mobile."

"And I'll get to work on the boards. I can probably have them done in three or four days, unless it gets too crazy before the wedding." She pushed up on her toes and kissed Kellan's cheek. "Dinner is at seven, gifts at nine and Midnight Mass after that. Don't be late. Your mother has been working all week on this."

"I won't. I'm going to head over to Winterhill right now. I'll be back in plenty of time."

Kellan wandered through the shop once more, making mental calculations of the cost for renovation. Though Maeve had an existing business, it might appeal to Gelsey to build something from the ground up. He walked to the rear of the shop and looked through the window in the door. An old stone building that used to serve as a carriage house stood close enough to connect the two. If Gelsey wanted to make a product, he'd design a beautiful workroom for her, too.

But as Kellan walked back through the shop to the front door, he realized that before he could sell Gelsey on staying in Ballykirk, he'd have to convince her of his feelings for her. There was one gift that could do the trick, one thing that he had in his possession that would prove they were meant to be together.

Winter had arrived in southwest Ireland. Rain was coming down in sheets and it was almost cold enough for snow. A white Christmas was a rarity in county Cork, but Kellan never stopped hoping.

He jumped in the car and headed for the pub. His mother would have wrapping paper and ribbon, something he couldn't find at the cottage. She also made the best fruitcake. It probably wouldn't hurt to take a loaf along for Gelsey's housekeeper, Caroline.

The wind blew in behind him and Kellan shook the water out of his hair as he stood at the door. Christmas Eve was always celebrated in the large room at the pub. The door was closed to the regular patrons at three in the afternoon and Maggie Quinn took over, arranging gifts under the tree, setting the long string of tables for dinner and finishing the last of the meal preparations in the kitchen behind the bar.

"Hey, Ma."

"Oh, you're here. Come help me with these tables. Every one of them wobbles. I swear, I'm tempted to toss them all out on the curb and have your father order new."

"You could just buy a few long tables to use for the holidays," Kellan suggested. "I've got a few in my office in Dublin that we use for blueprints."

"I'll put that on my list for next year."

Kellan helped her shove folded cardboard beneath the wobbly legs and when they'd made a table long enough for eighteen, he watched as she laid the table linens over them all, turning the scarred pub furniture into an elegant dining table.

"Look what Jordan found," Maggie said, holding up a length of red fabric. "Chair covers. They'll make the table even more beautiful. And a table runner. She has such good taste, that girl. Not that Nan doesn't. She's picked out music for us tonight." Maggie glanced over at Kellan. "And what about Gelsey? Will she be joining us?"

Kellan shook his head. "No. I don't think so."

"There's plenty of room at the table."

"I know. But we're taking a bit of a holiday from each other. I'm going to drive over to Winterhill and drop off her gift. I'll invite her, but I wouldn't plan on her coming."

Maggie paused. "Is everything well with you, then?" she asked.

Kellan nodded. "Yeah. I love her, Ma. She's really something. And you'll love her, too."

Maggie reached out and placed her palm on his cheek. "If you love her, Kellan, I know I will. Just follow your heart and you'll never go wrong."

"Thanks, Ma," he murmured. "Now I have to steal some paper and ribbon. I have to wrap her gift."

"Upstairs on the kitchen table. Take the silver foil and the gold ribbon. And one of those little gold glitter bells to make it pretty. What are you going to give her?"

"Something that I've been holding on to for a very long time."

9

GELSEY SAT IN THE DARKENED ROOM, staring into the flickering fire. Nearby, an elaborately decorated Christmas tree twinkled with tiny white lights. Everything was exactly as she remembered it, the house smelling of freshly baked gingerbread and pine boughs.

She'd driven to Cork to shop that morning, picking up presents for Caroline, Nan and Jordan. They lay wrapped beneath the tree. She'd struggled with a present for Kellan, unable to decide on anything suitable. She'd looked at expensive watches and interesting books, designer clothes and antique fountain pens, but nothing seemed right.

It might have helped if she knew where she stood with him. But since their argument the day before, Gelsey had been too embarrassed to call him. And he'd obviously been too angry to call her. Things had been so perfect between them and now everything had fallen apart.

She pressed her palm to her heart, aware of the ache

that had settled there. Over and over, she'd questioned her feelings for him, but now, faced with a life all alone, she'd come to realize that she was in love with Kellan.

Her days and nights meant something when she was with him. She wasn't just racing through life, she was actually living it, breathing it all in and savoring each moment. She'd tried to think about her time with Antonio and not one second could be marked as memorable. But every moment with Kellan had been etched into her mind, a vivid picture of perfect happiness.

Last Christmas had been spent on a beach in Thailand, drunk on champagne after Antonio had presented her with a diamond engagement ring, the same ring she'd thrown into the sea. Everything in her life had changed and yet, she didn't regret a single decision she'd made.

She took a sip of her wine, then stretched her stocking feet out to the warmth of the fire. She picked up her magazine and flipped through the article on Irish linens. Since yesterday, she'd been racking her mind trying to come up with an alternate plan for a shop, but everything she thought of just didn't seem to excite her. Irish linens, rare books, designer fashions, Gaelic art, hand-crafted jewelry... She had lots of ideas, but no passion for any of them.

Her mind wandered to thoughts of Kellan. That's where her passion focused. She could imagine the Quinn-family Christmas, laughing and teasing, everyone in a boisterous mood. Gifts spilling out from under a tree, endless plates of food. She'd never had a Christmas like that, with boundless happiness. The holidays had always brought tension between her parents, before and after the divorce.

But this Christmas would be a fresh start. From here, she'd begin to build a life for herself. And if it couldn't be in Ballykirk, then she'd find another spot, maybe Bantry or Glengarriff. This next year was going to be even more exciting than the past month had been.

"I'll get that," Caroline called, poking her head in the room.

Gelsey looked away from the fire. "What?"

"The door," Caroline said. "There's someone at the door."

"Oh," Gelsey said. "Fine." A pair of photographers had camped out on the road in front of the gate, waiting for her to come out, but she didn't plan to give them the satisfaction. Maybe one of them had decided to venture up to the door. "If it's a photographer, call the garda."

Caroline disappeared and Gelsey went back to her contemplation of the fire—and of Christmases past. A smile touched her lips. "Deck the halls with boughs of holly, fa la la la la, la la la la." She took another sip of her wine. After dinner, she and Caroline would share dessert and a glass of sherry and then they'd both go to bed. And one more Christmas in her life would be over.

"Gelsey? You have a visitor."

Gelsey twisted around. "A visitor?"

"It's Kellan. He's brought a gift. He'd like to see you. Can I show him in?"

She hesitated. "Sure. Tell him to come in."

She got to her feet, the wineglass still clutched in her hand, and sat on the arm of the sofa. When he appeared in the doorway, her breath caught in her throat and she had to remind herself to take another. "Hi."

"Hi," he murmured. "I hope I'm not disturbing—"

"No, I was just sitting here having—"

"It's Christmas Eve and—"

"Would you like a glass of wine?" Gelsey jumped up to fetch him a drink from the small table against the wall. When she'd filled the glass, she held it out to him. "Sit. The fire is warm. It's so damp outside. Your hair is wet."

"Are we actually talking about the weather?" Kellan asked.

"I hope not." She sat down on the sofa and he took a spot next to her.

"I'm sorry about yesterday. I should have been more supportive."

"No," Gelsey said. "I was acting like a spoiled brat. You were right. I don't know anything about having a job. These things happen all the time. I need to learn to adjust my plans."

"It's caused a bit of a stir around town," he said. "I spoke to Dealy this morning and he and the rest of the tourism committee are very concerned. The only one in town who seems happy about your leaving is Maeve."

"Well, I'm glad that I could help her out. Maybe she'll keep some of the changes I made."

"Have you decided what you're going to do?"

Gelsey shrugged. "I'm going to take my time and explore all my options."

"Would one of those options be spending the rest of your life with me?"

Reaching out, she took his hand in hers. "I do love you, Kellan. I'm certain of that. But—"

He put his finger over her lips. "No buts," he said. "Let me just let that first part sink in for a few moments." He closed his eyes, a smile of pleasure curling the corners of her mouth. "Yeah, that was nice. You love me."

"I do," she said from behind his finger. Gently she pulled his hand away. "But I've got to take some time to get to know myself."

"We could do that together," Kellan said. "I hardly know you. We could kill two birds with one stone."

Gelsey laughed. "I suppose you're right. But I'm not sure you're ready for the person I might be. I've done a lot of really idiotic things in my life and living a true and real life is probably going to be difficult. I'm going to get frustrated and impatient and I know I'm going to say stupid things."

"Gelsey, I love you exactly the way you are. I wouldn't have you change a thing. And if you can put up with me, then I can certainly put up with you."

"I'm just not sure I'm ready for a relationship yet," she said. "I don't think I've ever *not* been in a relationship. I've just moved from one man to another. I broke my engagement to Antonio one night and met you the next morning."

"So, if we aren't together, maybe we could just be friends. You don't have a lot of friends around here, except for Nan and Jordan. We could spend time together, maybe have dinner a few times a week and—"

"I thought you might take a project in France," she said.

"I decided against that," he replied. "I'm going to be sticking close to home for a while."

"Is that because of me?" she asked.

"No, it's because of me. I'm doing it for purely selfish reasons. And I've got a job in Ballykirk that will keep me busy for a while." He glanced down at the gift he held. "I brought you something. A Christmas gift. Even if we are just friends, I wanted you to have this." He nodded. "Go ahead, open it."

Gelsey neatly pulled away the silver paper to reveal the old biscuit tin she'd buried on the beach. She smoothed her hand over the dented top, the illustration faded by time. "I gave this to you the first time we met," she said. "I buried it in the sand hoping you would find it."

"Me?"

"I used to watch you and your brothers from the top of the cliff and I thought you were the most beautiful boy in the entire world. I was madly and hopelessly in love with you."

"Have you known it was me this whole time?"

"I think I did. But I found the box in the bedside table, and then I knew for sure." Gelsey glanced up, tears clouding her vision. "You were the first boy I ever kissed."

"You were the first girl I ever kissed. And I was in love with you, too. I went back to the cove every time I could, hoping you'd be there again. But you never came back."

Gelsey slipped her fingers through his, her gaze fixing on their hands locked together. "Thank you for bringing it back."

"There's something inside," he said. "Besides your treasures. Open it up."

She pulled off the lid and recognized all the contents except for one thing. Gelsey pulled out the key and held it up. "What is this for? The cottage?"

Kellan shook his head. "No. It's for your future. If you decide to stay here, to make a life here, then that key will open up an interesting opportunity."

"What is it?" she asked.

"You'll just have to come to Ballykirk and find out for yourself."

"I'm coming for Nan and Riley's wedding," she said. "Before that, I'm going to New York to see my mother. My father will be there, too. He has some meetings in Washington after the first of the year."

"You are coming back," Kellan said.

She nodded. "Yeah. I'm just going to be gone a few days."

Kellan slowly stood. Gelsey wanted to pull him back down, to stay with her for the rest of the evening. But she knew he had places to be. Christmas with the family and church after that. "Thank you for coming," she said. "I'm sorry I didn't have a gift for you."

"But you did." He pointed to her face. "That smile. I'm going to enjoy that for weeks. And you said you love me. That's better than a lump of coal in a guy's stocking. I guess I'll see you at the wedding then," he said.

"I'll walk you to the door." Gelsey slipped her arm through his and they slowly strolled out into the foyer. She wanted to lead him right up the stairs and into her bedroom. She didn't want him to leave. Yet, she had to force herself to let him go. Making love to him now would only confuse matters.

When they reached the door, he turned to face her. "Happy Christmas, Gels."

"Happy Christmas, Kellan."

They stood there for a long time, just looking into each other's eyes. "Where is the mistletoe when you really need it?" he murmured.

She laughed softly. "I think a Christmas kiss wouldn't do either of us any harm."

With a low sigh, Kellan cupped her face in his hands. Her gaze fixed on his and he bent close and kissed her, lingering over her mouth for a long time before drawing away.

"There. Now the world is right again," he said.

"Please give your family my best wishes," she said.

"I will." He reached for the door, then paused before he opened it. "I love you, Gelsey. I hope you won't forget that."

"And I love you," she said.

He nodded, then opened the door and walked out. Gelsey watched him as he got in the car. Kellan gave her a wave before he drove away. She smiled to herself. It was a beginning, like the kiss they'd shared in the meadow all those years ago.

She glanced down to find that she was still holding the tin in her hand. "My box of dreams," she said. Funny how her dreams had grown so large that a tiny box could never contain them now.

KELLAN STOOD in the front of the church dressed in his best suit and tie. Danny stood beside him in Kellan's second-best suit and tie. Guests had begun to arrive a half hour before the wedding ceremony and he scanned the crowd, searching for Gelsey. She sneaked into church just before the bride started down the aisle, and Kellan realized she'd probably been helping Nan and Jordan get ready.

"You can take a breath now," Danny whispered. "She's here."

"Yeah," Kellan said. "All right. So things are definitely looking up."

As the organ began to play the processional, the three brothers walked to the railing and waited there for Jordan and the bride. Riley and Nan had planned a simple ceremony, but they'd spent time decorating the church with vivid red poinsettias, fragrant pine garlands and hundreds of candles.

Nan looked beautiful, but Kellan's full attention was

focused at the rear of the church, on Gelsey. She wore a fashionable hat and pretty green coat, almost the color of the dress she'd been wearing the morning he found her on the beach.

When Nan took Riley's hand, Kellan was forced to turn around, but not before talking one last look. She smiled at him and gave him a little wave and Kellan sent a silent thanks to the heavens. She'd shown up and she was smiling at him. Things were going quite well.

Throughout the ceremony, Kellan was tempted to glance back at her, anxious for another look. Although the focus of the guests should have been on Riley and Nan, Kellan got the impression that there were just as many people wondering about the state of the relationship between him and Gelsey. The town of Ballykirk missed their very own celebrity, almost as much as Kellan missed Gelsey's presence in his bed and in his life.

To his relief, the ceremony was short and sweet. Vows were repeated, rings exchanged and before Kellan knew it, Nan and Riley were husband and wife. They walked down the aisle hand in hand, as happy as any two people ever deserved to be. Kellan and Danny followed the couple down the aisle with Jordan walking between them.

"Gelsey is here," Jordan murmured as they walked out of the church.

"I know," Kellan said. "I saw her."

"Everything is ready at the shop. Are you going to take her there now or later?"

"Aren't we supposed to hang about for photos?" he asked.

"We're going to take those back at the pub. Nan and Riley will stay here for a formal portrait."

"What are you two whispering about?" Danny asked.

Kellan frowned at his brother. "Didn't you tell him?"

Jordan shook her head. "He can't keep a secret. He was supposed to wait until Christmas morning to ask me to marry him. He had the whole thing planned and then he asked me the day before, right before we walked over to the pub. Needless to say, I was surprised when he got down on one knee as I was curling my hair."

"It was like the ring was burning a hole in my pocket," Danny commented. "I couldn't wait anymore. I couldn't stop thinking about it."

The moment they got outside, Kellan wandered through the crush of guests, looking for Gelsey. He found her standing near the bottom of the steps, her green wool coat draped over her shoulders. To his surprise, she wore the green mermaid dress beneath it.

"Gels!" he called.

She waved and waited for him to make his way over to her. When he stood beside her, Kellan gave her a quick kiss on the cheek. "Hi. You're here."

"I am. I wouldn't have missed it for the world. Nan looks so beautiful. And Riley. He looks so happy."

"How have you been?"

"Good. My trip to New York was nice. My parents were…well, they were civil to each other. My mother has a boyfriend and she's thinking of getting remarried, which would mean my father would be free of alimony payments, which seemed to put him in a cheerful mood. They didn't get into a screaming match, so I'd say the trip was a success."

"You're staying for the party, aren't you?"

"For a little bit," she said.

He took her hand, then drew it to his lips and kissed the tips of her fingers. "You look beautiful."

"So do you," she said with a smile. "Can I give you a lift back to the pub? I'm parked just down there."

"It's not raining. Why don't we walk. I have something I'd like to show you. Something I need your opinion on."

"What is it?"

"It's right down there," he said.

"Come on, then, let's go."

They strolled silently in the chilly night air, each breath they took clouding in front of their faces. Gelsey looked up at the sky. "I wish it would snow."

"We don't get snow very often."

"I know. But it would be nice just this once. There was snow in New York."

Kellan slipped his arm around her shoulders and pulled her close. "I've never been to New York. Maybe we ought to take a trip there, after your case in Italy has been dismissed."

"How did you know it's going to be dismissed?" she asked.

Kellan stopped short. "It is?"

"We're working out a deal. The photographer is considering dropping the charges in exchange for some exclusive photographs."

"What does that mean, exclusive? Does that mean naked?"

"No! It means…exclusive. He's the only one who gets a chance to shoot."

"Shoot what?"

"Our wedding." This time, Gelsey stopped short, grabbing his arm and turning him to face her. "I know that we haven't really talked about marriage, and I guess that's why I thought it might be an empty promise. And I don't want you to be angry, but I had to offer him something worthwhile. A picture like that could fetch a lot of money." She watched him warily, as if she was waiting for him to explode in anger.

"I think…I think I'm fine with that plan. More than fine. Hell, I don't care if you invite every photographer in the world. I'm just happy that you might marry me someday."

"Someday. Maybe," she said, starting off down the street again. "But don't get your hopes up too high. I might not be the marrying type."

"What does that mean? I might not be the marrying type, either."

When they reached the post office, Gelsey continued to walk, then noticed that Kellan had stopped just one door down. "Right here," he said. "This is it."

Gelsey frowned. "What?"

He reached out and grabbed her hand, then led her

to the front door. The shop was dark inside and Kellan was glad for the element of surprise. When he turned the lights on, he'd know immediately how she felt. "Did you bring the key?"

She nodded. "What is this place?"

"Unlock the door and see for yourself."

Gelsey slipped the key into the lock and turned it, then pushed open the front door. Kellan reached for a light switch and the old fixtures hanging from the ceiling flickered to life.

He heard Gelsey draw in a quick breath and he gave her hand a squeeze. "It's going to take more work than Maeve's shop, but this way, you can do it exactly like you want to." He led her over to Jordan's boards, leaning up against the wall. "You can see a few ideas of what you can do. Jordan drew those."

"You didn't buy this, did you?"

"No, you'll have to take care of that yourself. It's your business and you should own it, although I have negotiated a rather reasonable price for you. I'll take care of the renovations. Jordan can help you decorate. And Dealy says they have some tourism money for advertising. The point is, you have friends here in Ballykirk—good friends. And we all want to help you get your business started."

"I—I don't know what to say," Gelsey murmured. "It's all too much."

"No, it's not. It's exactly what you need. I want you to stay in Ballykirk, I want us to work together on this place and I want you to believe that we have a future together. And when—"

"I do," Gelsey interrupted.

"You—"

"Do," Gelsey said. "I've been thinking a lot over the past week and I do want a future with you. And I don't want to wait. I want that future to start right now. I've wasted too much time already. I know I love you, Kellan. And it isn't some silly fantasy love that I think is going to solve all my problems. It's real and I can feel it deep in my soul. I'm not going to run away from this."

He smiled, relief racing through him until he wanted to shout for joy. He slipped his arms around her waist and picked her up off her feet, kissing her until they were both breathless. "So, I guess my plan worked."

"Your plan? It was my plan," Gelsey teased.

"This? The shop was my plan."

"All right, the shop was your plan. I'll give you that."

"And what do you think you want to sell?" he asked.

"Well, I've been doing a lot of research and I couldn't come up with anything. But then I was walking around Winterhill and I started noticing all the special little things that my grandmother had collected over the years. And I realized that's what I wanted to sell. Beautiful things that make a home warm and cozy. I'll have some antiques. And some Irish linens. Maybe some furniture and crystal. But it will all be Irish. I've been surrounded by all my grandmother's things at Winterhill and I didn't realize how important they were until now."

"I think that's a wonderful idea," he said.

"I had a plan, too," Gelsey said, wrapping her arms around his neck.

"You did?"

She nodded. "The plan started long before you found this place, which is perfect, by the way. The plan started the first time I saw you at the cove, when we were kids. I decided that we were going to spend the rest of our lives together and here we are."

"I guess it's fate then that I found you on that beach. And that I kept that tin box all these years."

"Fate or magic," she said. "Or a bit of both."

"So, if we're going to live together, where will it be?"

"I have a house that's big enough for two," Gelsey said.

"And I have a flat in Dublin, for those times when you need to go in to the city."

"Are we going to live happily ever after?" she asked.

Kellan took her face between his palms and gently kissed her again. "Absolutely. What other possibility would there be?"

"There's always blissfully happily ever after," Gelsey whispered, pulling him into a long and languid kiss.

"Mmm." Kellan drew back. "I think I can make that happen, too."

* * * * *

"I'm ready."

Demi went in the therapy room, almost used to the sight of Colin's incredible physique all laid out for her to touch. *Almost.*

Candles lit, music on, hands oiled, she started with the sweeping motions that would improve circulation to his muscles. He was so much looser than when they started three weeks before. Unfortunately it was even more of a pleasure to touch him, and stupidly she gave in, allowing herself sensual enjoyment.

For some reason, as she worked, instead of loosening, his body stayed tight; his breathing picked up.

"You're not relaxing."

"I'm…a little uncomfortable." His voice was low.

"How can I help?"

"I could tell you exactly how." His tone was humorous. "But I'm pretty sure you wouldn't like the idea."

Demi's hands stilled. *Oh.* He was aroused.

Because *she* was touching him? No, no, he could be enjoying her massage and fantasizing about anyone. Except, this was the first time she'd been so flustered.

And so tempted…

Dear Reader,

It's always bittersweet when a miniseries ends. I get so fond of the characters, and even though I take care to send each couple off into the world's most romantic sunset, I do miss them. The Friends with Benefits quintet were particular favorites.

Feels So Right is physical therapist Demi Anderson's story. She was a bit of a mystery in the first two books (*Just One Kiss* and *Light Me Up*) and it was great fun for me to explore her more deeply. Having been a painfully shy kid myself, I know how hard it is to navigate certain social situations, even as an outwardly confident adult.

In injured Ironman triathlete Colin Russo, Demi finds a personal and professional challenge—like how to keep her hands off him when it's her job to touch him everywhere!—but he also helps her feel comfortable in her own skin. True love should always bring out one's better self.

I hope you have enjoyed this miniseries!

Cheers,

Isabel Sharpe

www.IsabelSharpe.com

FEELS SO RIGHT

BY
ISABEL SHARPE

First published in Great Britain 2012
by Mills & Boon, an imprint of Harlequin (UK) Limited,
Eton House, 18-24 Paradise Road, Richmond, Surrey TW9 1SR

© Muna Shehadi Sill 2012

ISBN: 978 0 263 89395 3
ebook ISBN: 978 1 408 96951 9

14-1212

Harlequin (UK) policy is to use papers that are natural, renewable and recyclable products and made from wood grown in sustainable forests. The logging and manufacturing processes conform to the legal environmental regulations of the country of origin.

Printed and bound in Spain
by Blackprint CPI, Barcelona

Isabel Sharpe was not born pen in hand like so many of her fellow writers. After she quit work to stay home with her firstborn son and nearly went out of her mind, she started writing. After more than twenty novels for Mills & Boon—along with another son—Isabel is more than happy with her choice these days. She loves hearing from readers. Write to her at www.isabelsharpe.com.

To Dad, who would have read this one, too

1

ARGH, THE PHONE. Wasn't that always the way? After a long day at her physical-therapy practice, followed by a good hard run and a quick dinner, Demi was just settling in for a short relax-break with her knitting and an audiobook of a suspense novel. Her business line had been quiet for hours, but of course the second her butt hit her overstuffed, supercomfortable chair...

Local caller. She didn't recognize the number. "Demi Anderson."

"Yeah, hi." A deep male voice, familiar, but she couldn't place it. "This is Colin Russo. You treated me back in August."

Demi sat up straight, heart accelerating. Well, well. The cranky triathlete was back. After a few sessions for ruptured disc pain, and her confirmation of his doctor's bad news that he wouldn't be competing in any more Ironman triathlons, Colin had exploded with anger and frustration, and stalked out of her studio in search of a practitioner who'd tell him what he wanted to hear.

Yeah, good luck with that.

"Hi, Colin. What can I do for you?"

"I'd like to see you."

"Sure. Let me look at my schedule." She pulled up her calendar, wondering what had made him come back. Elite athletes took the longest to accept new limitations. If Colin had changed his attitude she could do him some good. Otherwise...

"On Thursday I have—"

"Anything sooner?" He was speaking in a clipped manner that suggested he was either angry or hurting. Probably both.

"You're in pain." She made sure she spoke matter-of-factly. Sympathy didn't go over well with these types.

"Yup." The syllable was abrupt.

"How about..." She ran over the next day's schedule. Busy, but she could give up her lunch hour. "Noon tomorrow?"

"Good."

"Okay, see you then." She hung up the phone and sat for a few quiet seconds, annoyed at the way her pulse was still racing, then jumped up and crossed to her window. She looked out at the street below, Olive Way where it intersected with Broadway in Seattle's Capitol Hill neighborhood. A few cars, headlights on. Not much traffic for a Monday evening. Maple leaves turning color, a light rain typical for October.

Colin Russo.

He'd been a challenge on multiple levels. Demi worked with and treated many athletes, had seen plenty of people hurting, plenty upset at having to confront lifestyle changes after an injury. Like other professionals in the medical field, she had to balance appropriate levels of caring and involvement with enough distance to keep clients' problems from taking her over. Colin had so bravely tried not to show his physical or emotional pain that his rage had touched her, though she'd been taken aback by the suddenness and intensity of the blowout. Humans who felt helpless often turned fear into anger.

Then there was that other problem, one Demi didn't like admitting. She'd found herself reacting physically to touching Colin's body, was too aware of his smooth skin, his remarkable athletic build, his masculine aftershave-and-soap smell. Found herself reacting emotionally to the way he betrayed discomfort only by tightness around his mouth or the occasional quicker-than-most breath. To the sleep-deprivation circles under his eyes, the low, sad set of his brows.

Demi prided herself on treating not only the injured part, but the whole person. Part of her job with Colin, as it had been with so many others, was to make him understand that injury didn't mean the end of his life. Eventually he would be able to compete in triathlons again—though substantially shorter ones. He'd be able to work, marry, have kids—all things vital to being human. This was a message she'd had to deliver many times to many people. She'd just never before pictured herself doing it with her body curled around the client to comfort him.

Part of her had been relieved when Colin disappeared. With any luck when she saw him this time, the unwelcome feelings would have disappeared, too. Luckily painful childhood shyness had made hiding herself second nature. Colin would never know she considered him hot enough to boil water.

A glance at her watch told her a meeting of the five Come to Your Senses building residents started soon. She just had time to call her friend and former client, Wesley, for his inevitable told-you-so. After Colin's dramatic exit in early September, Wesley had predicted with absolute certainty that he'd be back. Demi had been equally sure pride wouldn't let him return. The stakes had been the usual: coffee or a beer at their favorite café, Joe Bar on Roy Street.

She dialed, grinning. "Hey, Wesley. Good news for you. Colin Russo just called. Wants to come in tomorrow. You win."

"Ha!" Wesley's voice was jubilant. Demi had won the last two bets: whether a mom at Angela's bakery downstairs, where they were having coffee, would give in to her screaming toddler and buy him a cupcake—she didn't—and whether Wesley's ex-girlfriend would wear black to a mutual friend's wedding—she had. "I knew I'd win this one. He wasn't going to find hands like yours anywhere else."

"I don't know about that." She felt herself blushing and was very glad Wesley wasn't in the room. Something about Colin...

"Did he say why he was coming back?"

"Just that he was in pain and needed to see me. Must have been bad. He sounded as if he were talking through his teeth."

"Furious he had to crawl back to you."

"Could be." She immediately had to banish an image of Colin, shirtless, on his knees... "I can't talk long, got a Come to Your Senses meeting in a few. Just wanted to let you gloat."

"I'm gloating, I'm gloating. When do I get my drink at Joe Bar?"

"Whenever you want it." Like all introverts, she was protective of her alone time, but she always made the effort to see Wesley, a former marathoner. His running career had ended with a car accident—much worse than Colin's fall from his bike—and head injury that ensured he'd never run again, though he credited Demi with helping him relearn how to walk. For a brief time, maybe two weeks after his therapy ended, they'd tried dating, but it had never felt right and they'd happily gone back to being friends.

"What's tomorrow, Tuesday?" he asked. "I have a date. How about Wednesday?"

"Wednesday's fine. You seeing Cathy again?"

"Yup. See if she can fall in love with a guy who shuffles instead of walks."

Demi grimaced in sympathy. Wesley had been remarkably free of self-pity during his recovery, but it must be agony as a former athlete to walk as if he'd just learned how. Which he had in a way. "If she can't handle a good shuffle, she doesn't deserve you."

"You're a good person, Demi. Remind me why we're not dating?"

"I think it was the lack of desperate need to jump each other."

"Oh, right. That. We're not quite old enough to settle for peaceful companionship, huh."

Demi snorted. "I'm *never* going to be that old."

Wesley burst out laughing. "That's my sex fiend. Okay, go meet with your business partners. And don't let that Bonnie woman get to you."

"I promise." Demi grinned. Wesley was always watching out for her. Whoever he landed would be one lucky woman. She hoped Cathy had brains enough to see that. "Bonnie isn't terrible, she just doesn't know what to make of me. The woman is totally out there, and I'm totally in here."

"No excuse. She gives you any more trouble, let me know."

"See you Wednesday." She disconnected the call, put aside her knitting—a short-sleeved cotton sweater in an easy zigzag pattern for spring—and went in search of her shoes, which she found in her room, one on the floor, one on the bed where she'd kicked them off.

Ready. Sighing, she exited her second-floor apartment and headed down the hall. Bonnie had painted the walls with twining rose vines and, for Jack and Seth, who'd been disgusted by the girlie touch, a line of tanks along the baseboard. At the end of the hall was the apartment the five of them shared as a common area, though Demi didn't spend much time there.

Jack, Seth, Angela and Bonnie had been four of the original five University of Washington alumni who bought and renovated the building, naming it Come to Your Senses when they realized their five businesses represented the five senses. On the first floor was Angela's bakery, A Taste for All Pleasures. Across from that, Bonnie's flower shop, Bonnie Blooms, smelling wonderful. Farther down the hall, Jack Shea represented sight with his photography studio, and Demi's physical-therapy practice was all about touch. She'd bought the space from Caroline, one of the original five investors, who'd moved out of town to get married. Upstairs, Seth Blackstone—representing sound—lived and composed music in the largest of the apartments.

The other four residents were already seated in the spacious living room, drinking soda and/or beer from the refrigerator they all chipped in to keep stocked. Likewise they'd each donated old or unwanted chairs and tables to furnish the place. Feeling out of place and nervous as she always did around her building-mates, Demi grabbed a Sprite from the refrigerator and plunked down on the room's newest and ugliest piece, a black-and-white, futuristic leather love seat she'd gotten from one of her sister Carrie's I'm-bored-with-my-furniture remodeling fits.

Seth, Jack, Angela and Bonnie had been close friends for six years; they shared a boatload of history, in-jokes, stories—it was hard not to feel like an intruder. Given that Demi's shyness made her feel like an intruder in pretty much every social situation anyway, this one was particularly difficult. Angela had been sweet to her, as had Jack and occasionally Seth. Bonnie would be the toughest to melt, but Demi hadn't given up yet.

"Hey, Demi, how's it going?"

"Fine." She nodded stiffly at Angela; the chestnut-haired beauty was sitting on the beaten-up rocker in the corner of the room. The question always made Demi feel she should come up with thrilling new daily developments. The truth was, her life was pretty simple and pretty fulfilling—except in the romance department. It just didn't make good press.

Jack grinned at her from his signature overstuffed wreck of a chair. He'd always been friendly, but was much more relaxed and outgoing since he met and fell in love with a woman named Melissa. He'd been photographing her without her knowledge at Cal Anderson Park for weeks before she walked into his shop, saw pictures of herself and freaked out. Happily, he'd quickly gained her trust and eventually her heart. "How's things in the physical-therapy world?"

"Okay. Thanks." She felt herself blushing, hating the stilted way she spoke, hating the awkwardness that had risen inside her since she was a child, which made the easy banter others took for granted so impossible for her. Once she was comfortable with people, once she trusted them, she was fine. But with Bonnie all but rolling her eyes at Demi's presence in the room, she couldn't unbend enough to sound like a normal person. Which of course made Bonnie's scorn worse. "People keep getting hurt. Keep needing me."

"Have you seen that gorgeous guy again?" Angela was all ears. "If he's been around lately I've missed him."

"Colin?" Demi felt a funny jolt of adrenaline. How weird

that Angela would bring him up today. "I'm seeing him at noon tomorrow."

"Ooh!" Angela waggled her eyebrows. "Bonnie, we're going to have to line up in the hallway and watch this one go by."

"I have to take a rain check." Bonnie shook her head regretfully, glancing at Seth, who sat next to her on the old green couch. "I have a lunch date tomorrow."

"Yeah? What's this one? Garbage man? Prison guard?" Seth tried to look casually interested, but was clearly wary, or at least it seemed that way to Demi. Seth and Bonnie—some romantic history there, Demi was sure of it. Sparks and intimacy flew between them, and whenever they were together they were either fighting or laughing, never indifferent. But with Bonnie signed up on Seattledates.com, they must be on the outs.

"His name is Don." Bonnie lifted her chin, smoothing folds of her bright, outrageously patterned top. "He's a lawyer."

"A *lawyer*." Jack rolled his eyes. "*That'll* be fascinating conversation."

"Maybe he'll show you his briefs," Seth added.

"Oh, that is just the *most* clever line I've ever heard a *million* times." Bonnie sighed.

"Yeah, it was lame." Seth hoisted himself off the couch, stretching his over-six-foot lean frame. "I must need another beer. You want anything, Bon?"

"No. Thanks, Seth." Bonnie glanced tenderly at his back; she was clearly capable of deep loyalty and affection—just not for Demi.

"Good luck, Bonnie," Jack said. "You certainly deserve a normal experience."

"No kidding." She rolled her green eyes. "It's been one disaster after another."

A snort from Seth, who was at the refrigerator. "Anyone else need anything?"

"No, thanks." Angela opened a folder on her lap. "But I have an idea I want to share with you guys. Actually Melissa got me thinking about it."

"Uh-oh." Jack's dark eyes turned warm. He was totally hot anyway, and looked even hotter when he thought about Melissa. Demi wouldn't mind some guy turning liquid on her behalf. She'd had one long-term boyfriend in college, one a few years after, then some casual dating but nothing for a while. At twenty-eight, she was starting to wonder about settling down, having babies, the whole deal. Too bad she couldn't just snap her fingers and find the perfect mate. That's what her older brother and sister had done, once again demonstrating their ability to sail effortlessly through life. She had no idea how they did it. Everything she accomplished seemed to require superhuman effort.

"Last summer Melissa had that idea about making Come to Your Senses a one-stop bridal-pampering place, remember?"

"I loved the idea." Bonnie nodded enthusiastically. "Flowers from me, cake or pastry from Angela, a portrait by Jack and music from Seth, our very own YouTube sensation."

And...? Demi sat silent, not able to tell if the omission was deliberate, unsure whether pointing it out would make things better or worse.

"And a massage from Demi," Angela prompted gently.

"Right." Bonnie thwacked her forehead. "Sorry, Demi. I forgot you."

"'S'okay." Demi kept her eyes down. The closest she and Bonnie had gotten to friendliness was when Angela and Bonnie bumped into her on their way to go dancing one evening last summer and had dragged her along. It had been one of the most fun nights Demi'd had in a while. She loved to dance. That night alcohol and circumstances had made Bonnie actually pleasant, a start Demi had hoped they could build on afterward.

Not so much.

"So, anyway." Angela broke the awkward silence. "I was thinking we could take the same package idea, but have it available as a holiday special from Thanksgiving through New Year's Day. We can charge a flat rate and sell certificates people can buy for themselves or as a gift. What do you think?"

"Wow. I love that idea!" Bonnie grinned, eyes alight, and looked at Seth and Jack for their reactions.

"Same here," Jack said. "Get us new business and reward our existing customers. Win-win."

"I was talking with Daniel about it last night as a wedding package and whining that we'd missed the summer bridal rush and then it came to me…the holidays!"

"I love the idea, Angela." Demi smiled at her. She looked so amazingly happy these days. Last spring she'd fallen for a guy who'd come into her bakery for white cupcakes to commemorate his late fiancée's birthday. Angela had sneaked in a chocolate cupcake to cheer Daniel up, and ended up doing a lot more than that. On her right hand she wore his diamond promise ring. "It's brilliant."

"I've got the perfect jingle." Seth got a faraway look in his narrow gray eyes, then cleared his throat and started a jazzy tune. *"Spend holiday money on your sweetest honey. The cash you've paid will ensure you get lai—"*

"Stop!" Angela and Bonnie yelled at the same time, then tried to restrain their giggles.

"What? What did I do?" Seth dropped his innocent look for a grin and squeezed Bonnie's shoulder. "Okay, maybe it needs work."

"We should plan this out." Angela started counting on her fingers. "Make posters, work on a jingle for a radio spot—G-rated, thank you, Seth. I also think it's time to bite the bullet and come up with a communal website. Right now we each have our own. What do you think?"

There was general assent, lots of joking, lots of constructive brainstorming and thorough planning. Demi was, as always, impressed by the quartet she'd signed on with. They worked hard and had all done well, though she wasn't sure about Bonnie, who always went oddly quiet when the others discussed their good fortune. She'd also dropped quite a bit of weight in the last six months or so and never seemed terribly busy in her shop. Demi hoped she was just angsting about her romantic life. Maybe she'd fall in love with a nice rich guy. Demi's sister had done that. Boy had she. And didn't let anyone forget it for more than twenty seconds.

The meeting broke up; Demi left the four of them still chatting. She was tired, anxious to get to bed, a little flustered at the idea of seeing Colin again the next day. Often she'd dream about whatever she concentrated on at night, powerful dreams that affected her the whole next day. Tonight before she went to bed, she'd imagine him toothless with bugs crawling all over him. That way she might be able to turn him into an object of disgust.

Yeah, and if *that* worked, she'd try walking on water next.

Half an hour later, she was snuggled in bed, listening to the October rain tap on the window, concentrating on Colin, not the way he was, but the way she wanted to dream about him.

Big brown eyes—make those piggy, puffy red ones. His fabulous male scent—now eau de skunky hangover. His rare smile—brown and broken. His build—flabtastic.

Plaid pants, platform shoes. Flowered shirt unbuttoned to his waist.

Gold chains...

She gave a huge yawn and nestled deeper under the covers, smiling faintly.

Long, greasy hair.

Another yawn. Take that, Colin...

Morning already? Couldn't be. Somehow Demi was in her office suite without getting out of bed. Her waiting room, normally a cool, refreshing blue-green color, had been repainted violet with rainbows and pictures of clowns. She glanced at her watch, not the gold one she'd bought for herself, but pink glowing plastic with a picture of Barbie on it. Noon! Colin was about to show up.

A knock on the door. She tried to say, "Come in," but couldn't make a sound. The door opened. Colin! Except he was about four foot five, wearing a clown costume—white with huge red dots and yellow ruffles, floppy black shoes, giant red nose.

This must be her dream. Perfect.

Lie down, she told him without sound. *I'll work on you.*

"Sure." His voice emerged without problem, deep, resonant, very sexy. Oops, she'd forgotten to change that to an appropriately girlie squeak.

You can keep your clown suit on.

"No." He moved his hands to the back of his suit.

She tried to say yes, but couldn't make herself understood, and frowned at him instead, frantically gesturing that he should stop.

Wait, was he growing taller? He was, no! Taller than she was, up to his real height, just over six feet.

Bad clown, bad.

The silly suit melted off. Instead of proper clown underwear, he was wearing boxer briefs that molded to a decidedly not flabby body. The violet walls changed to trees, and suddenly Demi and Colin were lying in a meadow on a blanket, picnic basket nearby, holding glasses of champagne.

Uh-oh.

Then the champagne was gone and he was kissing her tenderly, his body warm and solid against the length of hers...which no longer had any clothes on it. And his briefs were gone, too.

Oh, no.

His mouth tasted hers languidly—upper lip, bottom lip, this corner, that. Then he pulled back and gazed at her from under his brows, causing her blood to race, her body to arch toward his.

Oh, yes.

He rolled over her, the width of his shoulders making her feel protected, surrounded. She felt him hard between her legs, opened hers wide to welcome him inside.

Then he was pushing into her, filling, stretching, setting her nerve endings on fire. She clasped him around the back, lifted her knees high and wide to bring him in deeper.

He said her name over and over, increasing the pressure and pace until she was gasping, reaching for her climax, reaching, reaching, feeling it start to grow, to burn through—

"Demi, I love you."

Say what?

Demi woke with a jerk, staring with wide eyes up at the ceiling, breath coming fast, body still hot with arousal. Instinctively, her hand went between her legs, and then she stopped herself.

No.

There was no way she could get herself off right now. Because if she did, she'd be imagining Colin making her

completely crazy with lust, and when he showed up for
real in—she blinked at the clock—six hours, there would
be no way she could look him in the eye. And no way she
could put her hands on his back and think of anything but
the way she'd clasped that same back while he was hot and
hard inside her.

Bad, bad clown.

COLIN WOKE WITH a jerk, staring with wide eyes up at his
ceiling, breath coming fast.

A dream. Damn it all to hell. He'd been on the last leg
of the Ironman World Championship triathlon in Hawaii.
He'd already sailed through the two-point-four-mile swim,
powered through the one-hundred-twelve-mile bike ride
and was approaching the finish line after the twenty-six-
mile marathon barely out of breath, legs still strong, in first
place by a hundred feet.

What a high. What a feeling. His body ultrafit, lean and
strong. All those hours, all those years of training, coming down to this one explosive sprint to victory that would
make him world champion. Just him, on top of the field,
the dense crowd at the finish line already cheering for him.
Stephanie was there, too, long blond hair swept back in a
ponytail, blue eyes glowing, beaming with pride. Her man
was number one and she was crazy about him.

Then he'd woken up, not on a triumphant path to victory,
but in bed, back muscles contorting in agony, pain shoot-
ing down his right leg.

From king of fitness to short-term disability after falling
off his bike like a six-year-old just learning to ride.

They said he was done. They said his back was too
messed up ever to be able to ride long hours bent over his
handlebars. They said disc injuries like his could be controlled but not healed.

Bull. Maybe some people could hear "no" and accept it, but Colin wasn't one of them. "No" just meant he'd have to work harder, train harder. Fine by him. He was no stranger to hard work.

But he shouldn't have tried to get back to training so soon. Demi had been right, damn it. He'd left her in exasperation last summer, disgusted that an athlete of his caliber should be doing exercises a couch potato could do without effort. Infuriated by her insistence he'd have to cut his recovery expectations to a more "realistic" level. Frustrated that she didn't understand why his level of fitness couldn't be compromised, not now, not this year, not when he had so much to accomplish. So he'd left. Tried another therapist, then another, both of whom had babied him even worse than Demi had. Finally he'd decided he could manage his own damn recovery. Who knew his body better than he did?

Pain shot through him, and he tried like hell to breathe through it, not to tense into the spasms, which made them worse.

Yeah, guess what, managing his own recovery had been a bad idea. Everything sounded like a bad idea these days. Including going back to see Demi.

Because there was another reason he'd left her. By the last of—what was it, three, four appointments? maybe five?—he'd spent the entire session desperately trying to keep from having an erection. He had no idea what she did to him, but it was hell. Demi couldn't hold a candle to his ex-girlfriend Stephanie's fresh California-girl beauty. Demi was dark; he preferred blondes. And she was withdrawn, where he liked a woman with spirit. She was decently attractive, but not beautiful, with wide eyes and a faint cleft in her chin. She had style and grace to burn, and she exuded peace that both stirred and soothed him.

And her hands...

Not going to think about that. The only thing on his mind in her studio today would be multiplication tables and baseball statistics. Unless the crazy attraction had run its course and he'd react more normally this time. That would be good.

He waited for the attack of pain to subside, then drew one knee up slowly toward his chest to stretch, barely able to get it halfway. His flexibility was crap. He couldn't work. Couldn't train.

This sucked.

Yeah, he was being a big poor-me baby, so sue him. He had good reason.

His cell rang. The act of twisting his head to locate his phone on the bedside table caused another spasm, this time in his neck and upper back.

Thirty-four years old and he was falling apart.

Gritting his teeth against the pain, he picked up the phone. Nick. His erstwhile training partner, and the other half of the collision that had pitched Colin off his bike. Nick had skinned his knees. Not that Colin would ever wish this injury on anyone else, but sometimes life was damn unfair.

He took a deep breath, willing his voice to sound normal. "Hey, man."

"How's it going?"

"Not bad." He didn't dare use long sentences in case he had to break off and groan in agony.

"John and I are going to run some hills. Wondered if you'd like to meet up for lunch after."

Yeah, he'd love to. Sit there, the sad cripple, while they exulted in how well their training was going.

"Can't today. Got an appointment."

"Yeah? You back at work?"

"Nah. Physical therapy."

"Dude, you're doing that again?"

"Yup." He didn't feel like explaining.

"Okay. So, uh…" He cleared his throat awkwardly. "You heard from Stephanie lately?"

"Nope." This conversation was not making him feel any better. His girlfriend of four years had gotten sick of his bad attitude and his misery and dumped him on his ass, ironically just as he was seriously considering giving her what she wanted: a proposal.

Stephanie was a marathoner and they'd done a lot of training together. Colin should have noticed how hard it was on her that he was suffering, but he'd been a selfish jerk for quite a few months now. He figured it was only a matter of time before Stephanie came back to him. No doubt in his mind that he could make things right when she cooled off. She loved him. He loved her. They liked the same things, shared friends—at least they had before the breakup. What more did they need? Maybe the relationship had gotten a little stale, but the initial excitement never lasted. He needed to settle down if he wanted kids, which he did, and Stephanie would make a good mom and a solid partner.

One thing at a time. "Have a good lunch, Nick. Maybe I'll be up for it next time."

"Sure. Sure." His tone made it clear he wasn't holding his breath. "Nice talking to you."

"Same." No, it hadn't been nice for Nick. It wasn't nice for anyone to talk to Colin lately. His mom had told him he needed to see a shrink. Dad, predictably, told him to suck it up and be a man.

Yeah, well, he'd never been the kind of man Dad wanted him to be, so why start now?

He closed his eyes, smiling grimly. His level of cranky misery was even disgusting him.

After a few more careful stretches he'd loosened his

muscles to the point where he could just manage to get out of bed. A stunning victory, one that lifted his spirits at least a little. The visit to Demi, if she could help him, would do more of the same.

For the past decade Colin's pursuit of physical power and endurance had dominated his life. He'd been something of a missionary about the miracle of fitness, becoming a personal trainer to help others find the same high of good health and solid self-esteem he'd been able to achieve through working his body.

Now what he could reclaim of his old life rested in the talented hands of a woman he'd sworn never to cross paths with again.

2

DEMI GLANCED AT the clock on the wall of her office, embarrassed to be so jittery. Two more minutes until Colin arrived. *Stay cool, girlfriend*. He was just another client, a man in pain, one of the many she'd treated, one she'd be able to help. For today she'd ignore her whole-client philosophy and concentrate on seeing his body as a collection of muscles, tendons and bones. There would be time for worrying about his brain later—if he stuck with the therapy.

Mysterious, this upset to her system. Demi knew what kind of guy attracted her, and the überjock was definitely not it. Besides, Colin had a serious girlfriend. Sharon or Tiffany or something. A marathoner. Not that he'd look at a woman like Demi twice anyway, especially after she'd pissed him off so badly last time by gently trying to get him to face the truth about his recovery—or lack thereof.

Another glance at the clock. One more minute. Would he be out in her waiting area already? Her studio space, originally a two-bedroom apartment, had been renovated into a waiting room, office, one small room for examination and massage and a larger one for exercising, with a gym mat, treadmill, stationary bike, and the free weights, balls and other tools of her trade.

The minute hand of the clock joined the hour hand at twelve. She gave up her rather lame attempt at updating her previous client's file and stood. *Ready, set, go.* Reminding herself of Colin's anger and poorly hidden contempt at their last meeting, she lifted her chin and opened the door to the waiting room.

Her body went on an immediate adrenaline fizz.

Yeah, he was there. And he was still gorgeous.

At least she'd prepared herself. The first time she'd opened this same door to him back in August, she'd been so flustered by the intensity of his brown eyes and the sheer beautiful size and shape of him, she'd blushed, dropped her gaze and mumbled like a complete geekazoid.

"Colin, hi, come on in." She smiled and gestured toward her massage room, this time blushless, in control and professional.

He nodded and stood slowly, hitches in the motion indicating muscles lashing out at him.

"Uh-oh." Demi's smile faded when she saw what the movement cost him. "You don't look so good. Bad pain?"

"It's—" His response was cut short by what must have been a killer spasm. "Not the greatest."

Translation for a normal human: nearly unbearable. When it came to pain, elite athletes spoke a different language.

"I'll work on that today—should be able to give you some relief." She followed him into the small room where she did her massages. Decorwise, she'd worked to achieve a balance between clinical and luxurious. Half examining room, half spa, with softer lighting than one would expect from a medical office, and nice touches like fresh flowers courtesy of Bonnie Blooms, a CD player for music and a light scent she sprayed on the bedding, floral for women, spice for men. "You know the routine. As many clothes off as you're comfortable with, under the sheet on your stomach. If you need help getting on the table, yell and I'll come in."

"Right."

She smiled and left the room, waiting outside the door, knowing he wouldn't call even if he was in agony. Honestly. What an ego. Risking serious injury to avoid asking for help? Crazy. But he wasn't the first and wouldn't be the last. She'd gotten used to people's peculiarities. Women who hated being touched, men who liked it way too much…

"Ready," he called. Sooner than she'd expected.

She waited three beats and went in. Colin lay with the sheet down to his waist, shoulders as broad as the table, looking like a sexual invitation—or he would if his body wasn't stiff with pain. She eased a cushion under his hips to relieve pressure on his back, opened her heated cabinet and took out a blanket, pulled the sheet up to his neck and draped the warm cover over him. She was glad to hide him from view while she collected herself, cranky that this difficult man provoked such a strong reaction and that she couldn't seem to control it.

Heading for the hand sanitizer she abruptly rechanneled her brain when she found herself wondering how much Colin was still wearing under the sheet. "How have you been?"

"Fabulous," he growled.

Ah. Still Mr. Sunshine. Okay, then. She'd stick with his physical problems today, give him some relief and worry about the rest of him another time if he gave her that chance. "Can you describe your pain? Any particular location?"

"Down my right leg. Neck. Shoulders. Back."

"Doesn't leave much, does it." She suppressed a very tempting told-you-so and turned on her CD player, which filled the room with a bland but relaxing tune she'd heard so many times it barely registered. "The leg pain is from nerves pinched by the disc bulging in your spine. The rest is sympathetic reaction from other muscles, which—"

"I know where the pain comes from."

Grrr. Demi sent him a poisoned glance he couldn't see. Lovely, lovely man. Just as well. If he had an appealing personality to go with those looks and that body, he'd be much too dangerous to have around. Not fair for one person to have that much going for him, anyway. "I'll see what I can do today about loosening you up."

"That would be good." His voice was softer.

Well. Not exactly charming, but better. Demi pulled her bottle of peppermint-scented oil from its warming stand and poured some onto her hands, concentrating on the familiar routine. "I'll start with a light massage, then we'll go deeper. You let me know when it's too much."

As if he would. She could probably light matches and stick them under his fingernails and he'd pretend not to notice.

"Okay." His voice was strained now.

Hands oiled, she had no further excuse to avoid touching him.

So.

This was about his back. Just a back. She'd seen many beautiful backs before, athletic and otherwise. This was nothing different.

Demi laid her hands on him gently, started light sweeping motions following the muscles, encouraging blood flow and warmth, forcing her mind to register only the muscular system beneath her fingers. Trapezius. Latissimus dorsi. Deltoid. Teres major and minor.

So far so good, but she was keeping her movements brisk and mechanical, something she generally avoided. Slow stroking did a lot to bring comfort and pleasure to people in pain. Colin was a client like any other, and Demi wanted to bring him that pleasure.

Uh. She should not have phrased it that way.

Lips determinedly tight, she slowed her movements, traced his muscles more sensually. Colin needed as much TLC as anyone, maybe more, since the macho guys seldom knew they needed it and even fewer knew how to ask for it.

Her fingers relaxed into the slow pace of the music. She dipped them again in the peppermint-scented oil and moved up into his neck, appalled at the tension. This guy was suffering.

Back and neck warmed up, she moved downward to his gluteal muscles, blocking out the fact that he wasn't wearing anything but skin under the sheet, blocking out any picture in her brain but those suitable for an anatomy class, because otherwise her thoughts would go down an entirely different path.

They did anyway. Colin let out a groan of pleasure, and Demi had the absurd urge to lean down and press her lips to the small of his back, let her hair sweep over his—

For heaven's sake.

Gluteus maximus. Largest of the butt muscles, supporting the pelvis, vital in maintaining an erect—

Torso, Demi. Torso.

Moving on, probably sooner than she should have, she swept over the long muscles in the backs of his thighs, the biceps femoris. He seemed to be lying easier now, already more relaxed.

"Better?" She moved up toward his back again. "I'm going to go deeper now, put strong pressure on the spasming muscles. It won't feel good while I'm doing it, but you'll heal faster in the long run."

"I can take it."

Demi rolled her eyes. Of course he could. She could drop

an anvil on his head and he'd insist it was a mild bruise. Guys like him reminded her of the scene in *Monty Python and the Holy Grail,* one of Wesley's favorite movies, in which a battling knight with amputated limbs insisted he was suffering only a flesh wound.

The next part would be a lot easier on her nerves. Neuromuscular therapy was substantially less sensual than the stroking involved in Swedish, and she had hard work to do, going for the most problematic muscles with fingers, fist or elbow, holding strong pressure until they relaxed and gave. Slowly, carefully, she worked on him, finding the process deeply satisfying. Time flew, and she managed to keep her thoughts strictly G-rated.

Well…maybe PG. One PG-13 when she was working on his butt the second time.

"Okay." She trailed light fingers over his back, then laid a firm hand between his shoulder blades before she lifted it off. Done. It was over. She'd survived. "You'll be sore tomorrow, maybe the next day, but after that you should start feeling looser."

He lifted his head, turned it experimentally, pushed cautiously up onto his elbows. She covered his body immediately with the sheet and blanket. "Feels better already."

"Good." Ooh, he'd said nearly a whole sentence. "We'll do this again, then get you to where you can start on some exercises."

"Gee, really?" He rolled cautiously onto his side. "Ten whole minutes on a stationary bike? Two or three sets of leg lifts?"

Grrr. "Gotta start somewhere, Colin."

"I know, I know." He lowered his head back down to the table. "Sorry."

The word came out as if it hurt worse than his back, but it did come out, and made him human enough for Demi to experience a quick pang of empathy. "In the shape you're in, you'll come back fast, Colin. Sprint triathlons are a sure thing, I'm betting within the year."

He grunted and managed to sit up, keeping the sheet safely tucked around his lower half.

Unfortunately, this gave her a superb view of his impressive chest. She spun around and busied herself arranging the scent bottles on her counter, which were already neatly arranged. Sprint triathlons were a hell of a comedown for someone hoping to qualify for the Ironman World Championship. A quarter-mile swim, twelve-to-fifteen-mile bike ride and three-mile run. He could do that in his sleep.

"I know. Doesn't seem much of a challenge. But it's better than being out of the circuit entirely."

"Whatever."

Demi should have known better. Colin was still grieving hard over his loss; he wasn't ready to see any of the positives yet.

"You should be able to whip a couple of old ladies your first time out." She held up a hand. "I know, I know. You think I'm just trying to build your hopes up, but I'm not kidding."

Astoundingly, she heard the beginning of a chuckle. "Don't even talk to me."

Demi handed him a bottle of cold water, grinning. "Come into my office when you're dressed."

"Right."

She left the room and strode into her office, congratulating herself. *Excellent job, Demi Anderson.* A whole hour and she hadn't once sexually harassed him. A fine day's work. She should call Wesley or her friend Julie and go out for a celebratory drink. *Guess what? I had Colin Russo in my office and didn't grab his crotch! Yay!*

She giggled, imagining their faces, and wrote some notes

on Colin's chart, not that she was liable to forget their session by the next appointment—if he came back.

In pain. Uncommunicative. Hotter than a blast furnace. Identifies self strongly as triathlete. Must work on emotional acceptance of injury and its fallout as well as standard treatment for L4-L5 disc rupture.

Okay, she didn't really write the part about the blast furnace.

"I'm here."

She looked up, still refusing to blush, and gestured Colin into the chair set in front of her desk, wishing she'd thought to move it back several feet. But at least being behind the desk gave her a feeling of safety and authority. "You're moving easier."

"I feel better." He sat without as much effort as he'd used to stand, and rested his hands easily on his thighs. Demi felt as if the walls of her office had closed in a foot at least.

"You'll want to be on anti-inflammatories the next couple of days."

"Okay." He held her gaze steadily, as if he expected something from her. Demi opened his file, picked up a pen, took off the cap, wrote, *What the heck is he thinking?* in her most professional scrawl, then put the pen down.

"Colin, maybe we should talk about why you left. Why you came back. What you want from me and this treatment and how you feel about both."

"My feelings?" He looked disgusted. "This is *physical* therapy, right?"

Grrr. Demi needed to set boundaries right now or this would never end. Taking her sweet time responding, she leaned back in her chair and pretended to study his file. "You probably didn't know this, but I'm a betting woman."

"And…"

"And I bet I can tell you exactly how much your parents enjoyed your teenage years."

His silence made her wonder if she'd pushed too far, if they were about to embark on Colin Russo Tantrum, Part II. But when she glanced up again, he was looking amused for the first time. The expression changed his whole demeanor, got rid of the grouchy-brows and downturned mouth, relaxed his forehead and eyes. And made him even better looking, less sulky and more vibrantly male. She could only begin to imagine his magnetism when he was operating at one hundred percent. "I was hell on wheels."

"Not surprised."

"I still am, I know that. This is not easy."

"I am not suggesting it is, or that it should be."

"But I don't need to beat you up with it?"

She shrugged. "I think I could do you more good without that, yes."

"Okay."

Demi raised her eyebrows. "It's that easy? I say 'please play nice' and you do?"

"I tried doing this my way, and figured out when I could barely get out of bed this morning for the fifth time this month that my way doesn't work. My body isn't behaving the way it has for the past thirty-four years. The rules have changed. I have to get to know a new person but it's still me."

"It won't always be this bad. But yes, it's tough for athletes. You have such intimate knowledge of bodies—your bodies." Oh, geez. Did she have to phrase it that way? He looked mildly surprised, still amused, his deep brown eyes intently focused on her. Demi was so flustered she had to look back down at his file. "Now that has changed, you'll have to form a different kind of intimate…relationship."

Stop. Just stop right now. Except he wasn't saying anything and she couldn't stand silence.

"I know you can do it." She closed his file, folded her hands on top of it and determinedly met his eyes again— then wished she hadn't when she found them full of mischief. Her brain mushed on her. "Your discipline is already there. It's just a change. You won't be able to stay training… to keep so hard anymore. Hard on *yourself*."

Okay, her face was officially on fire. All pretense at cool was gone.

"I give up." She lifted her hands, let them smack down on her desk. "You're hurting but it will get better. That's all I'm trying to say."

He was chuckling for real now, his face relaxing further. "I think it was funnier when you were telling me I'd have trouble staying hard again."

"No, no." She shook her head, hands up and out. "That is not my expertise. If you'd like me to help with your pain and the management of your injury, I can. But only if you are realistic about what we can accomplish and how far you can come back. That's going to be much more difficult than the rest of it."

His expression turned grim again. "So I'm discovering."

"Now." Demi composed herself, relieved they were back on familiar ground. "You're a personal trainer and health-club manager."

"Was." His jaw set again. "Will be again."

"You enjoy it?"

"When I can do it, yeah."

She nodded thoughtfully. "The first thing we need to focus on is getting you out of this rut of only thinking about things you can't do. To all my clients I preach the gospel trinity. Positive thinking, can-do attitudes and silver linings. These are the only ways your life can become better after a big change like this."

"Right."

She expected the cynical reaction. "Any hobbies?"

"Swimming, biking and running."

"Uh-huh." Somehow she kept from gritting her teeth. "Anything you did before you took up triathlons? Something you'd enjoy rediscovering?"

His eyes lit for a brief moment before he could resolutely shut down into misery again. Aha. There was something. Good thing, because he definitely needed a jump start back into feeling productive.

"I used to play alto sax." He laughed without humor and shrugged. "I was pretty bad."

"Doesn't matter. If you still have the instrument, bring it by in a week or so when you're standing easier. What else?"

His eyes narrowed. "Bring it here?"

She returned his gaze calmly. Was he going to fight her on everything? "How much does an alto sax weigh, about ten pounds?"

"Not quite."

"Heavy enough. I want to watch you play to make sure you're handling the instrument in a way that isn't going to sabotage your progress. What else?"

His expression grew darker; clearly he thought her questions a waste of time. She had to remind herself to focus on that glimmer of mischief and good humor that had transformed him. She wanted to bring that man back, healed, whole and happy. Because if he stayed like this, she was going to have to medicate herself to be anywhere near him.

"I used to have another hobby."

"Yes...?"

"I made knives."

"Knives." She wasn't sure what to think about that. "Tell me more."

"More?" He shrugged. "I made knives."

Grrr. Just talk to me. "What kind?"

"Kitchen, hunting, whatever."

"You make them from scratch? Blade and everything?"

"Everything." A glint of pride. "Handle, blade…yes."

"How cool." She let the silence go a few seconds. "Why did you stop?"

"Ran out of time."

"Would you say making knives brought you some of the same satisfaction as—"

"Here we go again." He sent her a mocking look. "Is this *physical* therapy or—"

"Okay, okay." She waved his question away. "My point is—"

"That my life isn't over. I have plenty to live for, and though it might seem bleak right now it's always darkest before the dawn and the world is my oyster."

"Colin." She looked at him disapprovingly. "You forgot every cloud has a silver lining and when God closes a door He opens a window."

He actually grinned at that, making him even more irresistible. "I guess I did."

"All joking aside, positive thinking, can-do attitudes and looking for silver linings are the tenets my practice is built on, so you can expect to hear about them until you're ready to scream. When do you want to come back?" She pulled her calendar up on her iPhone before he could make fun of her again. "Next week I've got Wednesday open at two o'clock."

"I'll take it."

"Good." She stood. "We'll make progress. Just please don't push between now and then. Once the pain is gone, and I mean gone, not bearable, you can ride your bike ten or fifteen minutes, easy, sitting up straight. If that goes well, we'll increase. Also, once the pain is gone, do a few, just a few, core exercises to keep those muscles from deteriorating too far. We need them strong to keep the pressure off your spine."

"Right."

"No cheating. No superhuman stuff. Baby steps at the beginning until the swelling is down."

"Right." He walked to the door, obviously in a hurry to escape her lecture, which, perversely, made her talk faster.

"Heat if you're stiff. Ice if the pain seems new."

"Right."

"Colin." Instead of kicking him in the gluteals, which she wanted to do, she gave him an encouraging smile, trying for supportive counselor and trusted medical adviser. "You're going to be okay. Better than okay. You're going to—"

"Right." He opened her door and took off down the hall, still walking stiffly but looser than when he came in.

Demi strode back into her office, closed the door and slumped against it. Colin was going to be tough. She wanted to heal him and let him see enough progress that he could shake off his despair. He needed self-motivation and spirit to do the hard work of fighting back to his new normal. She hoped she could be enough coach, inspiration and taskmaster to help him—while keeping herself and her goofy crush under control.

Every part of her hoped that Colin's recovery was smooth and quick. For his sake and hers.

Because if it wasn't, there was a good chance one of them would lose it.

3

"HEY, BONNIE, how's it going?"

Bonnie turned from a bucket of irises she was arranging in her shop, Bonnie Blooms, and grinned at Seth. He looked devastatingly handsome as usual in jeans and a gray shirt that matched his eyes. He could have been a model if he hadn't wanted to be a musician. "Hey, there."

Nothing in the world gave her as much pleasure as being able to greet Seth without feeling wistful and lovesick. Five years ago they'd broken up, after one year of dating in college that ended when Bonnie got serious and Seth got itchy. Since then, especially once they'd both moved into the Come to Your Senses building, they'd been dancing a painful and cautious circles-around-each-other minuet that had ended last August when Bonnie had finally, *finally* signed up for Seattledates.com.

Not only that, but now, a month and a half later, after many disasters, some comical, some cringe-worthy, most just bland, she'd finally, *finally* had a good date. A really good date. Extremely fun, in fact, with Don Stemper. She'd dated a few guys in the five years since she and Seth broke up, but this was the first time she had her head together and could give a new relationship one hundred percent.

"What's happening?"

She glanced pointedly at the flowers in her hands. "I'm arranging irises. What's happening with you?"

"I'm standing here talking to you."

"Ha-ha." She cut off an inch from one stem and replaced the bloom in water. Her shop was full of buckets of various flowers set at different levels, to give the shopper the impression that he or she had just walked into a carefully landscaped garden or an outdoor flower market. Bonnie was incredibly pleased with the effect. Unfortunately shoppers hadn't exactly been showing up in droves. Wedding season, in full tilt over the summer, had tided her over, brought some of her debt under control, and she was almost current on her payments, but business had slowed again, and she was in no shape to ride out bad times.

The one downside of her life right now, which she didn't like thinking about.

"You seen that guy again?" Seth spoke so ultracasually she knew immediately whom he meant.

"Don?"

"Yeah, whoever." He was practically growling, eyes stormy, his short, dark hair even more disheveled than usual, as if he'd been yanking on it all morning while composing his songs—a sure sign he was upset.

Bonnie wished she could feel vindictive and triumphant at the switch—for a change, *she* was moving on and *he* was left behind. Instead, she felt tender and guilty. Guilty? Ha! As if! She had nothing to feel guilty about. Seth had ended their relationship, not her. He was the one with the issues. If he was still in love with her and wanted her, he knew how to get her back. With a big fat until-death-do-us-part commitment. Bonnie would trust nothing less. But he'd shown no signs of wanting anything more than to get all stressed out about her decision to date, though to his credit, he'd done nothing to dissuade her and seemed to understand and support her decision.

They'd had one good nostalgic tumble in August, a strangely freeing experience that had been, in effect, a goodbye.

Mmm. A damn good nostalgic tumble. She'd been bent over the arm of the couch with her legs hooked around his back and he'd been—

Oof. Better not to think about that.

"Remember Matti?"

"Matti?" Of course she did. One of those unbearably gorgeous "friends" Seth kept coming up with. This one he'd bumped into in a bar, which apparently in his world constituted friendship. Matti had been interested in renting space in Bonnie's shop to sell perfume, which would have been incredibly helpful to Bonnie's bottom line. She'd agreed to consider it after Seth assured her he wasn't out for Matti's "bottom line" himself. "Nope, never heard of her."

"The perfume lady."

"Ohhh." Bonnie repositioned a group of alstroemeria in its bucket, pretending to be only half listening. For too long she'd hung on to Seth's every word, eagerly looking for any possible sign that he was weakening, that he realized how special their relationship was, that he wanted to take it to the next level. In the past six months, he'd seemed to be making snail's-pace progress, but she had been hurt too many times to trust any of it. "Yes, I remember now. What's happening with her?"

"She decided not to rent space in your shop. Sorry about that."

Bonnie rolled her eyes. "Given that it's been over a month since you mentioned her, I'm not exactly shocked."

"Not a month." He looked stunned. "Has it been? I thought it was— Wait…"

She laughed, shaking her head. "Someone's had his brain immersed in his music."

"I guess." He pulled a pink rose out of a nearby bucket and handed it to her. "For you."

"Awww, thanks, Seth." She made a big show of rolling her eyes, cursing her traitor heart for beating the tiniest bit faster when he handed her the flower.

"I was thinking…"

She snorted. "Don't strain anything."

"I have the perfect Christmas present for you."

Bonnie stiffened. Oh, no. He was not going to start with this seduction crap again, was he? Not that it mattered. She had Don to think about now, to fantasize about, to talk to and confide in. His profile had said he was looking for marriage, right there in black and white, and wow, men could do that? In every way he was better for her than Seth Blackstone, no matter the size of Seth's…trust fund.

"That idea Angela had, about the Come to Your Senses holiday promotional? I can pay your share of the group advertising." He shrugged. "No wrapping or ribbon, but I thought you might like that."

She put the pink rose back into its bucket, incredibly touched, and yes, feeling guilty for assuming Seth had been about to bribe her with some expensive gift. Instead, he was trying to help out, knowing she struggled to keep up with expenses others could take on without blinking. "Seth. That is so sweet. But I can't let you—"

"Hey, this is a present." He gave her a severe look, which made him so fiercely sexy she wanted to attack him. But, being newly-in-control Bonnie, she didn't. "Very rude to turn it down."

"How about a loan?"

"How about a gift?"

"How about half of the cost?"

"How about all of the cost?" He put a finger to her lips as she was about to speak again. She tried very hard not to shiver, and nearly succeeded. "Look, Bonnie, I have unfair amounts of money, you're struggling right now, this would make me happy, and it would make it possible for you to be part of the Come to Your Senses special, which you should be because it makes brilliant business sense. So stuff the pride down your pants and say, 'Seth, you utterly astounding man, I bow to your mind-blowing brilliance and accept.'"

Bonnie bit her lip, thinking it over. If the group did a lot of advertising, which they should, the costs would probably add up to the total of what she had in her savings account. A loan would help. An outright gift would help even more. Seth had offered financial assistance several times and she'd always turned him down, but she did desperately want to be part of the event. "How about a simple thank-you?"

"Hmm." He pretended to consider. "So a blow job is out of the question?"

"Seth!" She cracked up, knowing he was kidding, pushing away the image of that incredibly sexy look he got on his face when she— "It is most definitely out of the question."

"Okay, okay." He grinned, which turned him instantly from bad boy to farm boy, a transition that never stopped amazing her. "I'm glad you'll let me help."

"I'm really grateful, Seth. You know I am."

"Yeah…" He dropped his head and rubbed the back of his neck, which meant he had something emotionally risky or otherwise difficult to say. "So you seeing that Don guy again?"

"I am." Sadness started building in her chest just when she most wanted to feel happy. She turned away, moved to a bucket of gerbera daisies, unable to face him. "We're going out to dinner tonight."

"That's fast. Didn't you just have a first date with him?"

"Fast?" She glanced at him over her shoulder. "You and I were in bed within a week."

"Geez, Bon." His voice was tight. "You're going to sleep with him?"

Bonnie's throat cramped. Ironic that she so hated causing him pain, since he'd caused her so damn much so many times.

"Seth." She turned to find he'd come up behind her much closer than she expected. With buckets at her back, she couldn't move away, had to tip her head to meet his gray eyes, which showed a flash of entirely uncharacteristic vulnerability. "I am a grown woman who has met a man I really like. If I continue to really like him then yes. Sleeping together is a natural progression."

The second the words were out of her mouth she regretted them. No, not quite regretted. She'd spoken the truth. But this was Seth. A man she cared for...*had* cared for very, very much. And the way his beautiful tough-guy eyes had just gone dead and his strong jaw had turned to stone, she knew she was hurting him. But since, in his typically caveman way, he was having trouble accepting the idea of Bonnie with someone else, she might as well be blunt, even if it seemed cruel.

And frankly, she'd spent the better part of the past nearly two years since moving into this building watching Seth parade around with one stunning woman after another, so she couldn't say she was totally dying of sympathy. Maybe now he'd start cluing into what her life had been like so many times after he left her. Not that she'd ever want to be vindictive about this. Just pay him back a little. Which was different. Sort of.

"I was wondering." He had his hands in his pockets and was looking down at her with that magnetic gaze that used to regularly set her on fire. "If you wanted to have dinner sometime. Maybe Friday? Either out or at my place?"

She gaped at him, heat flooding her face. Never in the five years since they'd broken up had he ever issued an advance invitation like this, as if he was asking her on a formal date. In fact, not even while they were dating. Their plans were always made last-minute. Hey, let's do this, let's do that, here's what I feel like, how about you?

"Wow. Seth, that is really sweet. And you are the world's greatest cook. I just don't think it's a good idea."

"Why?" He put his hands on his hips, which seemed to broaden his chest, make his proximity even more intimate. "Did you and Don agree not to see other people?"

"No, no." She laughed nervously. "A little too soon for that."

"So you're open to dating other men?"

"Well, yes, but, Seth—"

"Am I not a man?" He glanced down at his pants suspiciously. "I'm pretty sure I qualify."

Did he ever. "Seth, come on. It's different with you and me."

"How about if it wasn't?"

She frowned at him. "What do you mean?"

He took a deep breath, clearly struggling. "How about if we erased everything and started over? You and me. A first date."

She narrowed her eyes. What was this about? He'd told her a couple of months ago that he was starting therapy, to learn why he was resisting her. Had his invitation evolved from that process?

"I'm sorry, Seth, I don't think that would be a good idea."

"You afraid?" His eyebrow quirked; he was already

gaining confidence, knowing how much she hated that particular taunt.

"Of *you?*" She threw out a loud and unconvincing "Ha!"

"Prove it. Have dinner with me." He was too close, the pull of his body undeniable. "Upstairs, my place, Friday night."

He was right. She was afraid. Terribly afraid. Afraid of falling for him again. Afraid of being hurt. She'd come such a long way, had worked so hard to be at peace around him. No way was she going back to vulnerability and pain. He and his therapist might like the idea of starting over, but you couldn't chuck as much baggage as they had just by wanting to.

"Sorry, can't."

"You mean won't?"

Bonnie nodded brusquely, lump the size of Cleveland in her throat, wanting to have dinner with him, hating that she did and that he was making her choose yet again. "Won't."

"I was planning to make shepherd's pie. With chocolate hazelnut cheesecake for dessert."

She glared at him. "You like to fight dirty."

"Seven o'clock?"

"I'm not coming."

"Think about it."

She rolled her eyes. When he got like this, he wouldn't let go. Probably because he sensed her hesitation, sensed her slight weakness. Seth knew her way, way too well, and having grown up extremely wealthy, he was used to getting what he wanted. Though his parents had skimped on the things that really mattered, like love and attention. "I won't change my mind."

She saw the triumph in his eyes. He thought he had her.

If he was talking about the chocolate hazelnut cheese-cake, he might be right as far as her appetite went. The rest of her? He couldn't have that. She was keeping that safe. Safe for a new man and for herself.

TEARS RAN DOWN Demi's cheeks, which she bravely ignored. She and Wesley were sitting at her kitchen table shoveling in mouthfuls of the incendiary Noodles from Hell from their favorite Thai restaurant. They both adored and suffered through the dish, though they considered it a badge of honor not to wince or admit to the chili-induced agony. Demi had bought Wesley his drink at Joe Bar, and they'd come back here for dinner and dessert, in the mood for some edible torture.

"So tell me something." Demi cheated just a little by pushing aside a particularly large chunk of red bird's-eye chili pepper. Big difference between brave and suicidal. "Why is it that men are considered strong if they don't show emotion? Who decided that was masculine?"

"Hmm." Wesley stifled a gasp and poured half a beer down his throat. "If I had to answer that…"

"Which you do because I asked."

"I'd say because children have no control over emotions and women have less control than men. Women and children are weak and need protecting—" He held up his hand to stop Demi's outrage. "Calm down, I'm speaking biologically."

"Okay…" She grudgingly let him continue.

"So in order to be least like women and children—in other words, the most masculine—men have to be strong and emotionless."

"Doesn't that seem stupid to you?"

"Extremely." He ate another mouthful, chewing cautiously. "If it was up to me, we'd change it. But for some reason it isn't."

Demi frowned at him, thinking he looked better and

stronger every time she saw him. "We need to put you in charge, Wesley. Of the globe. Would you mind?"

His blue eyes went wide. "Could I still have ice cream?"

"Absolutely." She took a sip of beer and pushed her plate away, tired of her dinner giving her first-degree burns. "How did you escape the Culture of Macho?"

"I wouldn't say I escaped." He rubbed a hand thoughtfully through his thick, dark hair. "Though I did cry during one of our appointments."

"I remember." She reached to squeeze his hand. "Nearly broke my heart."

"Softie."

"Me? I'm hard as nails. But we were talking about you."

"As we should be." He smiled his easy, dynamite smile. "I had three sisters, for one. And my dad was emotional. He was also crazy about my mom and we got to see that. He cried when he was really sad, and acted as if that was completely normal."

"Which it is."

"He helped around the house in nontraditional ways, too."

"My dad didn't do squat. My sister-in-law is finding out what that's like, too, since my brother takes after him." She gestured to Wesley with her beer. "Your wife will be one lucky woman."

"So will your husband." He laughed at the sight of her startled face. "Scared you, huh."

"Husband? *Husband?*" She clutched at her chest. "I'm too young. Husbands are for grown-ups."

"In some cultures twenty-eight would make you a hopeless spinster."

"I'd make a good one."

"No, you wouldn't, Demi." His dark-lashed eyes took on

a warmth that made her blush. "Too much passion in you to waste on sexual aids."

"Oh, geez." She made a hideous face, hiding giggles.

"So…" He spoke so casually she went on instant alert. "Demi…"

"Wesley…?"

"What brought up all this talk about the Culture of Macho and marriage?" He put a long finger to his cheek and tipped his head. "Could it have anything to do with yesterday's visit by Colin 'Ironman' Russo?"

"Of course it does. Well, no, not the marriage part." She gave an exaggerated shudder. "But the guy can barely move. I worked really deeply on him and he does this whole stoic statue thing. It just seems stupid he couldn't yell, 'Ow, that effing hurts!'"

Wesley looked at her skeptically. "Would *you* do that in a professional office?"

"Nope," she said cheerfully. "That's partly my point, too. It's ridiculous for anyone to hide normal feelings of pain."

"Your studio would get kind of noisy."

"At times." She twisted her mouth, pushing her unused knife back and forth on the tablecloth. "Truth is, I'm not sure what to do about him."

"Jump him?"

She wasn't going to dignify that with a response. "He's not only hurting in his body."

"I'm not surprised." Wesley drained his beer, his handsome face shadowed. "Tough journey out of that pain."

"He wasn't hurt nearly as badly as you were, but like you his athletic career meant everything to him."

"He just thinks it does."

"Yes, he just thinks it does. That's my point. You found coaching. I'm not sure what he'll do." She swirled more pasta onto her fork, mouth craving another shot of pain. "I wonder if he should meet you and hear about—"

"Ha!" Wesley was already shaking his head. "Hear about my sad story? So you can say hey, guess what? Instead of being a world champion triathlete, you could be a suburban high-school track coach. He's not ready for that."

"He might be."

Wesley gave her a look.

"At some point he might be," Demi said.

"Then at some point I'd be happy to."

"He'll get there. I just need to make sure I don't push him too hard." She laughed. "I mean emotionally. I don't think I *can* push him too hard physically. He'd work until both legs dropped off and barely notice."

"Exercise addicts are like that."

"Exactly." Demi stood and carried their plates to her sink, surprised at how rattled she felt by this discussion. "Want some ice cream?"

"Is there any answer possible besides yes?"

"Nope." She opened the freezer. "Häagen-Dazs Vanilla Swiss Almond?"

Wesley groaned. "Do you know what it's like having to cut back from a three-thousand-calorie diet?"

"Nope." She pried the top off the carton. "One scoop or two?"

"Two." He sighed resignedly and patted his flat stomach. "Already gained ten pounds, what's a couple more?"

"Yeah, but you were down way low from running, Wesley. You look great." She tried not to compare his lean, slender frame to the broad torso and hard muscles of her triathlete obsession. She should picture Colin hugely obese.

That didn't work, either.

"What does this god among men do besides work out?"

Demi served him a glare along with his ice cream and

a spoon. "He used to play sax and he made knives from scratch before he became a triathlon junkie. Maybe he can go back to that."

Wesley's silence made her look up from scooping her own ice cream. He was staring at her, shaking his head. "Strange."

"What is?"

"I don't ever remember you talking about a client so much."

Blush. Inevitable. Unwelcome. *Grrr.* "He's an interesting case."

"Uh...ruptured disc? Dime a dozen."

"No, but I mean..." What did she mean? She sat down and lost herself in her first bite of Häagen-Dazs heaven instead of trying to figure it out.

"What else could be unusual?" He pretended to count on his fingers. "Had to give up an athletic career, I think you've seen that before. Trouble adjusting to new reality of his body, ditto..."

"Yes. I know, but—"

"Me?" He put his counting fingers away and dived into his dessert again. "I think you're hot for this guy."

"No. No way. No. That is ridiculous. Completely—" She broke off, wrinkling her nose. "I'm objecting too much, aren't I."

"You said it, not me."

"Okay, okay." She licked her spoon and heaped up another bite, making sure it had plenty of chocolate-covered almonds in it. "He's hot. So what?"

"So what are you going to do?"

"Do? I'm going to help his pain, teach him how to manage the injury, try to show him that his life isn't over and wish him well. What did you think?"

"I don't know, ask him out?"

"A client? Don't think so."

"We went out."

"You asked me. *After* we finished working together."

"Make his treatment short, then ask him out. Or I know." He brightened. "Send him to a friend. What about whatsername, Julie, who you used to—"

"He came to me, I'm his physical therapist and I will treat him."

"Ooh." Wesley narrowed his eyes. "Mighty possessive, aren't we."

"Professional. Why are you so anxious to foist me off on this poor man?"

He reached across the table and ruffled her hair, chuckling. "Because I know you well enough to know that the more you like a guy—if the way you acted with me was any indication—the colder and more professional you become. So he probably has no idea that you're leaving drool spots on his blanket."

"Am not." She gave him a sidelong glance. "Okay, that one was a mistake."

Wesley cracked up. "Okay, okay. But I'm right. So think about it."

"Yes, master." He was right about the way she acted around guys she was attracted to. In high school, for four long years she'd been passionately in puppy love with Brad Johnston. Time after time she'd been in situations where she could have gotten to know him. School paper. School plays. Social-activity committee meetings. But the more she adored him, the less she spoke to him. So guess what, they never went out. Someday she was going to run across him, grab him and plant on him that kiss she'd fantasized about every night. The guy would have no idea what had happened. He probably didn't even remember her.

However, in this case, her shyness was a good thing. If

Colin caught wind of her attraction he could cause unpleasantness that would damage her professional reputation.

"In any case, I'm mostly interested in helping him."

"I know. That's what I love about you." Wesley let his spoon fall back into his bowl and heaved himself out of the chair, something he couldn't have done that well even six months earlier. "I should go. This was fabulous, thanks. Need help with the dishes?"

"Nah. They all go in the dishwasher."

She gave him a hug, congratulated him again on his successful second date with Cathy the previous evening and sent him shuffling off. His balance was much improved from when she'd started working with him two years earlier, but his gait was still not the graceful stride he must have had before the accident. She hoped Cathy fell madly in love with him. Hell, she wished *she* could have fallen madly in love with him. But Demi too often seemed to go for men who wouldn't look twice at her. Sometimes she thought she was sabotaging herself. Other times she figured it was because she essentially made herself invisible around the guys she wanted.

Love and relationships were so confusing, sometimes she wished she didn't want either one.

She carried the ice-cream bowls to the sink, rinsed and stuck all the dishes in the dishwasher, then curled up in her favorite recliner with her knitting and the audiobook she'd been making piss-poor progress on in the past few days ready to play on her iPod. Great story about a guy who thought he—

Phone.

She sighed and put down her knitting. She looked at the display and sighed again, louder. Carrie, her sister. Demi wasn't in the mood. But if she didn't answer now, Carrie would call back and leave increasingly hysterical messages about how she was starting to picture Demi lying dead in her apartment. Carrie never used to be *that* neurotic, but in the past few months she'd gotten more clingy and more intensely…herself.

"Hi, Carrie."

"Hey, little sister. How's everything?"

"Good." She braced herself. Of course she'd have to ask the question back, only her sister wouldn't be able to answer in one syllable. She'd need at least a hundred. And all her "problems" would be these amazingly impressive ones that made Demi feel like cow poo. "How about you?"

"Crazy, crazy busy. Dan got another promotion, which means he's traveling nearly the entire week every week, and keeps missing the kids' school stuff. Rachel got the lead in their second-grade play, and Boris started the Suzuki violin program at his preschool. I'm actually busy selling houses, which I can't believe, considering how strange the market has been."

So strange she had to give up one of her twice-weekly massage appointments. "I'm glad to hear that."

"Oh, and guess what? My black-forest cake took first place twice at our Oktoberfest celebration! Once for taste and once for appearance. I tweaked Mom's recipe, and then I made the cake in the shape of a Bollenhut!"

"A what?"

"The traditional Black Forest hat." As if Demi should know that, as if everyone else on the planet did and what was wrong with her?

More to the point, what was wrong with Carrie? It was as if she'd gotten stuck in her highest gear. In a normal family, Demi would simply ask what was bugging her. But her family wasn't normal; they didn't discuss emotions. "That is fabulous, Carrie. Congratulations."

"Aw, thanks. So tell me more of what's going on with you?"

Demi closed her eyes wearily. This happened every time. What was Demi doing? Not being promoted, not raising overachieving kids, not baking prizewinning from-scratch cakes. "Same ol' same ol'. Working, hanging out."

"You dating anyone?"

"Not right now, no."

"Are you *trying* to date anyone?"

"Not really."

"Why?" Carrie was clearly aghast. Their parents had married in their teens, as had Carrie and their brother, Mike. Once again Demi was struck by the amazing irony that Carrie and Mike, the children her mom and dad adopted when they thought they couldn't have children themselves, were much more like them than Demi, the "surprise!" daughter they had conceived naturally a few years later.

"I don't know, Carrie. If I meet someone I'm not against starting something, but—"

"What about online dating?"

She made a face. After what Bonnie had gone through, the idea appealed not at all. The concept of structuring her life around achieving or failing to have a relationship bothered her, too. "I'm sure I'll meet someone when the time is right."

"You have to go after what you want, Demi."

"Yes." She spoke tightly. Going after what you wanted was a lot easier when you were endowed with beauty, strong extroversion and an unshakable self-confidence. Demi had done just fine considering she had none of those. "I always have. But what you want isn't necessarily what—"

"You don't want to be happy?"

Demi indulged in her most exasperated face for a good three seconds, wishing she had a mirror since she was pretty sure this was one of her best ever. She had plenty of experience making them while talking to her sister. "Of course I want to be happy. It's just that what makes you happy isn't what—"

"Hang on, doorbell. Rachel's being dropped off. Can I call you back?"

No. "Um, I'm about to go to bed."

"Bed *now*?"

"Yeah, long day." She faked a yawn that was pretty good if she said so herself.

"Oh. Okay. *Coming*. Listen, I gotta go."

"Sure, Carrie. Talk to you later. Thanks for calling."

She hung up the phone, found herself clenching her abdominal wall, and pretty much every muscle in her neck and shoulders, and forced herself to relax.

You don't want to be happy?

Honestly. No, she wanted to spend the rest of her life as miserable as possible. Which she would be if she tried to do anything her sister recommended.

Except maybe dating. Maybe. But every time Demi thought of signing up for a dating site, putting herself out there to be judged, found lacking, found appropriate, found whatever…ugh. Bonnie had the motivation and the stamina for that experience. Demi was pretty sure it would either make her crazy or crush her.

But her reaction to her sister's suggestion—the anger, the impatience— She hadn't majored in psychology for nothing. Carrie had hit a nerve.

Okay. Demi would look honestly inside herself and ask the magic question.

Why wasn't she dating?

She was twenty-eight and did want to marry and have children. But there weren't any men she was even attracted to…

Oh, great. One possibility popped into her head with such speed it startled her, though given Wesley's recent teasing it shouldn't have, and just as quickly made her laugh. Right. Good idea. Complete pipe dream even if he was single, and if that wasn't enough, add unethical and—gorgeous male body notwithstanding—not an appealing personality.

Colin Russo, cranky ex-jock with abs of steel and a crappy attitude.

Only in her dreams.

4

DEMI ANDERSON HAD the greatest hands in Seattle. Colin would argue with anyone on that point. He was lying on her massage table, that horrible music playing, candles lit. The usual spicy too-rich smell of whatever she was spraying in the room mixed unpleasantly with the peppermint oil she rubbed all over him.

It was just that the rubbed-all-over-him part was really, really good.

She'd been right that he'd be sore after their first session. He'd woken up the next morning feeling as if he'd been beaten up by a gang. But she was also right that his muscles would loosen, and after she'd worked on him deeply again last week, things were getting better. He still felt like an old man, but at least he had hopes of becoming young again.

Her hands moved down to his lower back. Colin suppressed a groan of pleasure. They'd mostly done exercises today, but Demi always finished sessions with a brief massage.

Fine by him.

Her hands were strong, supple. She hit the perfect balance between keeping her touch clinical and making him feel as if she was touching him because she enjoyed it.

Now that he wasn't in so much pain, he *definitely* enjoyed it.

Her hands continued down, following the path of his gluteals.

This time he couldn't keep the groan silent.

"You okay?"

"Fine." He spoke abruptly so as not to betray what was happening to his body. Five times six was thirty. Five times seven, thirty-five. Five times…um…

Her hands slowed, dug in deeper, kneading the muscle.

Eight times nine, uh…was seventy…something.

Oh, man.

The pain in his back might have eased but he was going to be experiencing quite a bit in a different place if he didn't stop thinking about where she was touching—

"Turn over for me?"

"Uh…" Colin tensed, which was the last thing he wanted to do. Demi had never asked him to turn before. "I can't right now."

She made a sound of concern. "Where is the pain?"

How the hell was he supposed to answer that? *Between my legs* would be the most honest. *As if I'm lying on a tree root.* But he wasn't going there. "Give me a minute."

"If you tell me where—"

"It's fine now." His annoyance and embarrassment were already minimizing the problem, but he still moved slowly, glancing at Demi, who was frowning worriedly. "You just had me in an, uh, altered state."

Her face relaxed; she nodded, then pushed a strand of hair behind her ear and held it there for a second, as if hoping it would stick with enough pressure. She wore black today, as always. The color brought out her hair and brows and made her pale skin paler except for her mouth, which was a soft rose color. A full, sensual mouth. "It's good that you can disappear into the massage. I think the more you can leave yourself the better."

"Yeah." Leave himself? What did she mean by that? It made no sense that he was still attracted to her. The first day or two, okay, but by now...they had less than nothing in common.

"So how about..." She gestured for him to lie down.

"Uh. I'm actually done for today." No way in hell was he lying on his back with a sheet over him. *Demi, if you've ever wanted to see a pyramid, today's your lucky day.*

"Done?" She looked surprised, then shifted her features into neutral. "Sure. See you in my office. Take your time getting up."

"Right." Getting up wasn't the problem.

He dressed, pleased to be able to step into his jeans and pull them up in less than a minute, which was still a hell of a long time when it came to pants, but better than it used to be. Baby steps for old man Colin.

No, he hadn't lost his impatience, but he had to say that being in the calm, capable hands of Demi, forcing himself to accept her treatment plan, being able finally to hear and understand the stages of recovery he still had ahead of him—yeah, he was doing better.

If only he could stop thinking about her. While he was at home exercising, he was imagining her encouragement, her corrections, her concern. While he was walking in his neighborhood or in a nearby park, he heard her voice correcting his posture, urging him to be patient, not to extend himself too far. He felt as if she were personally invested in his journey back to health. Even knowing that acting that way was part of her job, Colin couldn't help responding. She had a rare gift.

Yeah, so did he: for feeling sorry for himself. If nothing else, Demi was helping to get him out of that rut bit by bit. He should know better, being a competitor. Negativity helped nothing, could sap all chance of accomplishing goals. Slowly, he was absorbing her trinity: positive thinking, can-do attitudes and silver linings.

He left the small room, which had seemed oddly diminished by Demi's absence, and sauntered over to her office, where he'd left his sax earlier, looking forward to their postsession consultation. He had a growing and unwelcome need to get behind her calm, professional exterior and discover what she was hiding.

Crazy talk. He needed to get out more. He should throw his stupid pride and pain under a bus and meet with Nick and their training group sometime for a drink. Or two. He should call Stephanie and pretend he was just wondering how she was, testing the waters for their eventual reconciliation. Anything but fixating on some schoolboy thing he had for his PT.

In Demi's office, he sat in his usual chair, careful not to slouch or she'd get on him about "stacking his vertebrae." He felt sorry for whomever she married. The guy would have the posture of a ballet dancer or get nagged to death.

"You seem better, that accurate? Both in body and attitude?" She turned a page, seemingly absorbed in some report. The woman sure loved her paperwork.

"If that's what the sacred file says, it must be true."

She rolled her eyes. "What do *you* say, Colin?"

"I say yeah." He couldn't help a smile. "I am doing better, thank you for asking, Ms. Anderson."

"Honestly." Demi bent down and retrieved his sax, passed it across the top of her desk as if she was handing him a revolver for their next round of Russian roulette. "Show me."

He opened the case and hauled out the instrument, put it together, stupidly nervous. He wasn't auditioning for Duke

Ellington here, just making sure he could play the thing without hurting himself. Last night he'd perversely resisted practicing to prove he wasn't out to impress Demi, so he hadn't touched the sax in years. She'd have to deal with that.

Taking the reed, he stuck it in his mouth, wetting it to vibrate properly. The taste and feel of the slender wood piece brought back countless memories, from serenading Stephanie to avoiding his father's disapproval by practicing in the basement of his childhood home, pretending to be John Coltrane or Charlie Parker.

He fitted the wet reed into the mouthpiece, tightened it in place, put the strap over his head and stood, adjusting the instrument's neck until its angle suited him. The sax felt good against him again, familiar in his hands, like a reunion with an old, true companion. Though it remained to be seen how the quality of their friendship had withstood the separation...

"Here goes." He closed his eyes, running his fingers over the keys, hearing the tune in his head before he played.

When Sunny gets blue...

The instrument squawked, then again, but after the first phrase Colin got the feel back in his mouth and hands, got into the music. No, he wasn't Charlie Parker, would never come close, but playing felt damn good. Demi didn't stop him, and once he started playing, really playing, he didn't want to stop himself, either. He blew the melody slowly and simply, then repeated it with flourishes and embellishments, jazzy, soulful, whatever came to him.

But of course he had to stop eventually. The last note faded; he opened his eyes, letting the sound fade from his mind as well, then turned to Demi.

She was watching him, color high in that pale Snow White face with the rosy lips and dented chin. For a crazy few seconds their eyes held, and something deeper than their gazes connected. Emotions flooded Colin's brain and heart, like the deluge ending to a long dry season. Then Demi blinked and looked down at her beloved files, her refuge, and he slowly took the instrument off his neck, still in some kind of weird music—and Demi—induced trance.

When she looked back up it was all business again; the flood receded abruptly.

"That was really good, Colin. You have real musical talent."

"Yeah, thanks." Her goal was to rebuild his self-esteem, make him think about something other than being a failed triathlete. She'd compliment him no matter how he played. What annoyed him was that he found himself wishing he knew if she meant the words sincerely. Why would he care what his PT thought of his playing? He played first and foremost for himself. Always had.

"You're holding the instrument fine. I'm guessing that you have to keep good posture in order to breathe well. Just make sure you don't sway around too much yet. Otherwise great."

"Okay." He packed up his saxophone and glanced at the clock, shocked to realize how long he'd been playing. "I went over our time."

"No problem. I'm taking lunch now."

"Then I cut your lunch short." He closed the lid of the case, even more annoyed now. Holding the instrument in his hands again had fed something he hadn't realized was hungry. He didn't have any right to involve Demi's personal time in his epiphanies. "Where do you eat?"

"I bring a lunch or buy takeout and eat at Cal Anderson Park." She spoke matter-of-factly, but blushed. She was fine putting her hands all over his body, but admitting she ate alone in the park embarrassed her? It didn't embarrass him.

It made him feel protective of her. He scoffed at himself. What, like she was a baby rabbit or something? *Come on.*

"I'll get going, then." He thanked her for the session and strode out into the hallway, pausing outside Bonnie Blooms, idly imagining Demi with a blossom pinned into her hair.

With a what? *Blossom?* What the hell was wrong with him?

Lunchtime. He needed food. But at his condo right now there was only peanut butter, cheese, pickles, emptiness and boredom. He pushed out of the building and stood on the front steps for a minute or two, breathing in the soft, fresh air. A beautiful, warm fall day—in the mid-sixties, he'd guess. Eating outdoors wasn't a bad idea.

The door opened behind him. Demi came through, saw him and stopped in her tracks. He reached to hold the door over her head before it hit her.

"Oh. Hi." She was clearly as caught off guard as he was.

Colin responded with a nod, let go of the door after she moved through. Out here, away from her territory, they weren't client and physical therapist anymore. What were they? Not strangers. Not friends.

"So…are you meeting someone?" she asked.

"Nope." He saw the question in her eyes. *Then why are you standing alone on the steps?* "Just indecisive. What's good to eat around here?"

"You like hot dogs?"

She surprised him. He'd expected her to name some vegan place where he could get tofu twenty-four ways. Fine by him, he loved tofu. But he also loved hot dogs, though he hardly ever ate them because they were loaded with God knew what, and like most athletes, he put into his body what he wanted to get out of it. Feed your body crap, it performs like crap. Right now, however, a big, juicy dog sounded like heaven. "Bring 'em on."

"How do you like them?" She quirked an eyebrow at him. Clearly this was a test. "Loaded or un-?"

"Loaded, baby."

"Ah." She pointed down Broadway, obviously approving of his choice. "There's a cart near the park that sells big natural-casing dogs, the kind that explode juice in your mouth when you bite. Awesome white bakery buns, not too fluffy but not heavy. And the toppings..."

Her eyes were bright, and a small smile curved her mouth as she spoke, gesturing with her hands. By the time she got to "toppings," she was practically sighing in ecstasy. Colin was fascinated and mildly aroused. Demi Anderson turned sexual over hot dogs. Intriguing. "They're that good?"

"Chili; sauerkraut; jalapeños; onions, grilled or fresh; mustard, yellow, brown or Dijon; ketchup; barbecue sauce; shredded cheddar; cream cheese; pickles; coleslaw—you can have pretty much anything."

"Oh, man, I'm dying." He put a hand to his rumbling stomach. "Is that what you're eating?"

Her features froze, as if she'd been caught in an unexpected trap. She nodded stiffly. "Yup."

"You want some company?"

Demi blinked twice, her color deepening. The blush was cute, softened her further, made him feel big-brother protective. No, not brother. More like her big brother's best friend. Who'd discovered his buddy's little sister had done some growing up.

Crazy. Women with spirit attracted him, women who challenged him. Stephanie had done that constantly, sometimes with shows of temper or hysteria that Colin had learned to roll his eyes at and tolerate. She always calmed down.

"I don't— I can't be with— You're a client."

"And?" He set his jaw. He hadn't asked her to sleep with him, just eat a freaking hot dog.

"I'm not…" She took a deep breath, pushed hair behind her ear. Colin waited, but she was clearly too flustered to explain further.

"Okay. Not a big deal. I'll see you next week." He went down the steps, more annoyed than he should be. She had her code of ethics, this crossed it for whatever reason. He didn't have to pout as if she'd rejected him personally. He'd buy his own damn hot dog and they could eat on opposite sides of the park.

"Colin."

He turned. Demi still stood at the top of the steps wearing a determined expression. "Lunch would be nice. Thank you."

Unexpected pleasure. He found himself smiling somewhat goofily. "Well, good."

"Okay, then." She smiled, too, then laughed. First time he'd seen her let loose even halfway, and it nearly blew him over. From mousy mystery to a vibrant, magnetic woman.

"Hot dogs." He gestured toward Broadway, feeling unaccountably giddy. "Let's go."

They walked down the street, somewhat predictably discussing the nice weather, until they passed a shop window and he realized he'd lost Demi to the pull of whatever was in it.

Edwin's Jewelers. Another surprise. He'd never noticed her wearing jewelry, though now that he looked she did have on small silver earrings in the shape of some flower.

"Look at that." She pointed when he came up beside her and he followed her finger. Draped around one of those weird headless models was a necklace of twisted silver that grew into a delicate floral vine studded with diamonds. "Isn't that gorgeous?"

"You going to buy it?" he teased.

"I've got nearly a dozen."

Colin's eyes shot wide. The piece would sell for thousands. "You've bought a dozen—"

"No, no, I don't buy them. I collect them." She tapped her head and smiled self-consciously. "Mentally. It's a game Mom started when I was a little girl. She or my sister would see something one of them liked and we'd pretend we were going to buy it."

He squinted at the necklace, trying to imagine her and a dark-haired sister holding their mother's hand, ogling jewelry. He'd sort of pictured Demi as a tomboy. "Wait, didn't *you* ever see anything you wanted?"

"Not usually." She spoke matter-of-factly, still staring at the piece on the decapitated model. "I wasn't that into jewelry or most of the girlie things Mom and Carrie enjoyed. Sometimes I felt as if I came from a different planet than the rest of my family."

"That's tough to handle." He felt sudden strong empathy. Boy did he know what that was like.

"Anyway. It's a silly game. Not sure why I still play it."

"Because it's fun?"

"It is and it isn't." She grinned wryly. "Not so great to spend time focusing on what you can't have. Know what I mean?"

He sent her a look. "Is this going to be lunch or more can-do therapy?"

"Lunch. I promise." She gave the necklace one more look before moving away. His picture of her with the flower in her hair zoomed back for a wider shot; now diamonds sparkled against her skin. Because she was wearing a dress with a plunging V that was…very nice.

"Did your parents play games like that with you?" She ambled along and he found himself liking the feel of her next to him, liking the way she moved and the way their shoulders bumped occasionally.

He was really losing it.

"My parents weren't much for games. Dad was a pretty serious guy. Mom did whatever he wanted."

"No good strong female role models for you, then?"

He hadn't thought about it that way. "I don't know. I had a kick-ass female sax teacher. She'd been everywhere, done everything. Used to let me drink beer after lessons."

"Underage?"

"Yeah. Betty Sandison. I thought she was the coolest thing ever."

"Betty Sandison is not a beer-drinking name. I'm thinking aprons with ducks on them and meat-loaf dinners."

"Definitely not this Betty."

"Is your girlfriend more like your mom or like her?"

Colin gritted his teeth. He did not want to talk about Stephanie with anyone and especially not with Demi and double-especially not now. "What's with all the questions?"

"What's with the fear of answering?"

He stopped on the sidewalk, faced her with hands on his hips. She had him off balance and he didn't like that, wasn't used to it. "I am not afraid of answering."

"Good to know." She broke into that surprise smile and pointed left on Howell Street. "Hot-dog cart is at the end of this block."

He followed her, wondering if she'd agreed to have lunch with him in a purely professional capacity for the purpose of digging deeper into his psyche, and then wondering why that bothered him.

Too much bleeping wondering. When his body was static like this it left his mind too much to do.

Happily, within a few minutes, his mind was busy choosing toppings for his dogs. Sauerkraut, mustard and jalape-

ños on one. Chili and cheese on the other. Demi ordered
hers with coleslaw and pickle, a combination Colin reminded himself to try next time. Chips and drinks next,
then he pulled out his wallet to pay the weathered guy
manning the cart.

So did Demi.

"Let me buy you a hot dog."

"No, no." She shook her head and fumbled for bills. "I'll
pay mine, you pay yours."

"Forget it." He shoved a ten at the vendor, having expected her reaction. "It's a few bucks. You can deduct it
from your bill if it's that important."

"Well…" She frowned, bunching her rosy mouth.
"Thank you."

"You're welcome." He picked up the bag, pleased she'd
let him win that one.

The Howell Street entrance brought them into Cal Anderson Park by the cone-shaped fountain, its waters flowing
into a long stone channel that emptied into a rectangular
pool. Two women were just leaving one of the benches by
the pool. Colin and Demi quickened their steps and grabbed
it, beating out a couple of suited businessmen by seconds.

"Big score," Demi said. "These benches are never available, even in winter."

"You sit out here all year?"

"Unless it's really cold or really hot." She took the hot
dog, drink and chips he handed her. "I like being outdoors."

"You like being alone?"

"Don't mind it." She unwrapped her dog. "It's my nature. My parents, brother and sister need people around all
the time. That would exhaust me."

"I'm in between." He took a bite of his chili dog. Spicy,
juicy, hot—she was right. This was a superior fat-and-salt
vehicle. "Oh, man, these are good."

"Told you."

"You did." He grinned at her. "Thanks."

She ducked her head, took a bite of her own dog, retrieving cabbage strands that tried to stay in the bun. A blob of coleslaw fell onto her lap. She picked it off and absently brushed at the spot with her napkin.

Colin grinned. Stephanie would have had a fit about her clumsiness and potential dry-cleaning bills. He liked that Demi didn't even seem to notice. "So what do you do besides heal people and collect virtual jewelry?"

"Oh." The question seemed to take her aback. "Well. I read. I knit. And I run."

He waited. Was that it? No parties, movie outings, dinners, clubs, classes... He felt that same weird jolt of protective concern. A woman like Demi shouldn't waste herself being alone. "Not a partyer, huh."

"Nope."

"Friends?"

She gave him a look. "No. None at all. I hate people."

"Right." Touché. But again he liked that she wasn't apologetic. Most of his friends indulged in competitive bragging over how much excitement they could cram into their lives. Her attitude was refreshing. Books, yarn and running, there it was. Unfortunately, his reading was sketchy, though he'd been doing more since his injury, and he had zero questions to ask about knitting. "How far do you run?"

"Five miles some days, three others." She crunched on a chip and licked a crumb off her finger. "Depends on my energy level and time."

"Do you lift?" He was suddenly having to work hard at focusing on what she was saying instead of imagining her naked. She was slender, tall, probably five foot eight or nine, and her fitness routine meant she must be well muscled under all that black clothing. Plus her tongue looked very hot licking her finger.

He was such a guy.

"Free weights. Just to stay strong. Nothing obsessive. I use muscle at work."

"I've felt that." He finished his chili dog, started in on the kraut and jalapeño combo, glad he wasn't planning to kiss anyone that night.

Which immediately had him wondering what it would be like to kiss Demi. Her mouth was nicely shaped, with wide, curling corners and a full, lush center. Appealing. Sexy even.

Very sexy.

Okay. He wanted her. For whatever reason. He did. Rather badly. First woman in a long time besides Stephanie—whom he'd wanted beyond reason from the second he'd laid eyes on her.

Demi wouldn't want him back. If she had this much trouble having lunch with him, she wouldn't jump on an invitation to…jump on him.

But he was single. And if reading and knitting filled the bulk of her free time, he'd bet she was, too.

Hmm…

"You seeing anyone, Demi?"

"Nope." She said the word a little too loudly and a little too cheerfully. "Why?"

"I wanted to know." He turned and gazed at her directly. "For the record, Stephanie is more like Betty Sandison than my mother."

"Ah." She nodded, sending him a sidelong look from her wide dark eyes that gave him a distinctly animal reaction. Good God. There must be something in his hot dog. And why didn't he mention he wasn't seeing Stephanie anymore? They'd been together so long it felt jarring to admit. As though if he never said it, maybe it wouldn't be true.

"What do you mean, ah?"

"Ahhhh!" She opened her eyes wide, raised her brows high. "Ahhhh!"

He started chuckling, positively smitten now with this alternative version of Demi. How had this happened to him? "You've figured me out, huh."

"Oh, totally."

"Give me a break." He finished his second hot dog, opened the bag of chips. "How come you're not seeing anyone?"

She put down her drink. "That is the world's most annoying question."

"Seriously, why aren't you?"

"Because I haven't found anyone, and no one has found me, what do you think?"

He shrugged. "I don't know, maybe you're asexual."

"Ha. No, I am definitely—" She checked herself visibly. "This is not appropriate conversation."

"No?" Colin thought it was getting quite interesting. *Definitely* not asexual? Gay, maybe? He seriously doubted it.

Well. He put his arm along the back of the bench to see what she'd do. Predictably, she stiffened right up. Avoiding his touch because she didn't want it? Or because she did?

Adrenaline was flowing now. He hadn't felt this alive in quite a while.

"What would be appropriate conversation with me?"

Her cheeks were red. He liked making her blush, liked the way he could get her off balance, too. "The state of the economy. Your mental state approaching your recovery. The migration of tropical butterflies. The—"

"How about when can we have lunch again?"

She whipped her head around and looked at him as if he'd suggested they strip right there and swim naked in the fountain. "This was a one-time thing."

"Why?"

"Because I don't see clients socially."

"You're seeing me now."

"This is a one-time thing."

"Why?"

"Because you seemed to need it."

"*Need* it?" He narrowed his eyes incredulously. "A pity lunch?"

"No, not pity." She made a scornful noise, dark eyes watching him steadily. A breeze blew her hair back from her pale, pretty face. "I don't do pity."

"Then what? *Concern?*"

"Sure." Cool, professional Demi. He was starting to hate her like that. "Why is concern bad?"

He was pissed. He'd been imagining them doing very nice, very adult things together, and she'd been thinking of him as a child who needed mommying. Ego down for the count.

He crumpled his hot-dog wrapper and chip bag and stuffed them in the paper sack, held it out to Demi for her garbage. "Ready to go?"

She gave him a wary look and added her trash. "Sure."

They walked in awkward silence back to Olive Way, where Colin had parked. He shook her hand, ditching his fantasy of ending lunch with a lingering kiss on her cheek. Not likely. "'Bye. Thanks for lunch."

"Thank *you*. I'll see you next Monday."

"Right."

He got into his car. Instead of going back into the building, Demi stood on the sidewalk and watched him. What was she waiting for? What did she want? Didn't she have some other client to go feel sorry for?

Who cared? He pulled out too fast, tires screeching briefly, and was rewarded for the childish gesture and his sulky attitude with a renewed stab of pain through his back.

5

DEMI OPENED HER door, cool smile firmly in place to welcome Colin.

He wasn't there.

She stared at her watch, as if it would tell her anything different from what the clock just had. *Honestly, Demi.* The guy wasn't even late yet.

Dangerous. All morning, Demi could think of nothing but Colin showing up today. She was jittery and fizzing and distracted and for heaven's *sake*. She'd been like this all week, no matter how far she ran, no matter how earnestly she meditated, no matter how many books she read. Knitting was out of the question because it left her mind free to wander. And wander it did, over the way he'd changed into a totally different person playing the sax: sensitive, soulful and sensual. The way he'd asked her to have lunch with him, the way he'd looked so stunned after they ate when she'd hinted she'd accepted his invitation so she could get him talking, find out more about what went on in his head.

Professional curiosity had been part of the reason she'd accepted, certainly. But not all. When did a woman like Demi *ever* get a lunch invitation from a guy like Colin? A guy who could be on the cover of *Men's Health*. Or

GQ. Or *Playgirl*. Which explained why he looked shocked when she didn't jump all over him—though man, did she want to. How could someone like her be indifferent to Mr. Amazing?

She wasn't. She had to keep her guard up so high a pole vaulter couldn't get over it. No flirting. No lingering looks. No hair-flipping, eyelash-batting, luxurious stretches or drawn-out leg-uncrossing.

But Colin was so funny. And so good-looking. And so oddly charming, even when he was cranky and shut down. He'd pulled some pretty hard-to-get-at heartstrings, especially when he'd hinted that he'd grown up, as she had, trying to please unpleasable parents. Boy did Demi understand that pain and frustration.

Bottom line: she needed to stay focused and in control and...

Maybe it was just the mood he'd been in. Pretty day, lonely guy, and Demi happened to be there. Not like he'd pursue her or ask her out again.

Or maybe he would.

She closed her eyes, forcing herself to breathe in slowly, breathe out slowly. She could not, would not, give even the merest hint that she was expecting or craving anything from him. Her only goal was to serve him as best she could in a purely professional capacity.

One eye open, she peeked at the clock. He'd be waiting by now.

He wasn't.

She went back into her office, sat down and stared at his file, trying to concentrate on his treatment plan, on the nature and severity of his injury and the best way she could get him focusing on positive messages...

God he was hot. She wanted him with a fierceness that frightened her. She'd been sexually attracted to plenty of men, had indulged herself happily with a few who'd pursued her. But with Colin she wasn't following her usual pattern, wasn't putting up walls, wasn't violently tongue-tied and awkward. Well, sometimes. She was still Demi after all.

Maybe she felt more confident because he was her client, and she therefore had some authority in their interactions? Maybe. Though the more she'd found herself attracted to Wesley, the more she'd turned stony and unresponsive, and he'd been a client.

So much for that theory.

When Colin asked her to have lunch with him, her familiar self-protective instinct had quite sensibly refused, but it had been completely overpowered by such a strong longing...

Demi got up to compose herself, mildly aroused at the prospect of seeing him, of being able to touch him, smell him— Oh my goodness, she was going to have to suppress every natural impulse she had around him.

Door open.

Not there.

Sick disappointment started to settle in her stomach.

Get a grip!

She turned firmly back into her office. Okay. He wasn't coming. She could use this hour to—

The door to the waiting room burst open behind her. "Sorry I'm late."

Relief, mixed with dread, mixed with excitement, mixed with— Was there medication for this stupidity?

"No problem." She put on her best impersonal smile, which nearly fell off when she turned. Flushed as if he'd been hurrying, he was walking toward her without evident pain, wearing—God help her—tight black biking shorts and a tight blue athletic shirt, hair tousled, eyes full of life and spirit. And if he'd been sexy before...

"I rode over." The triumph on his face made her want to hug him.

"And survived." She shamelessly took the opportunity to check him out. "No pain?"

"Nope."

Uhhh. "None?"

He shrugged. "Some stiffness."

"You rode slowly?"

"Yes." He was already looking annoyed.

"Sat straight?"

"Yes."

"Walked the hills?"

"Sort of."

Demi rolled her eyes. Athletes, ptooey. "You only want to 'sort of' recover from this injury?"

His jaw set. "I walked the ones I needed to walk."

"Hmm." She gestured him into the exercise room, proud of how she was handling herself. "Let's see how much damage you've done."

After she saw him through a solid exercise session and some stretching, it turned out he'd done very little. His flexibility had improved, range of motion, too. She was really pleased for him. "Okay, time for massage. You're doing fine. But don't let this go to your head."

"Ha!" Colin stood carefully. "As if I would?"

"You would." Demi shook her head. "I can smell the testosterone from here. You're getting cocky. Be careful."

"I will." He grabbed his jacket, started rummaging in the pockets. "I'm not interested in any more setbacks."

"Good." She wiped down the mat he'd been using with alcohol and stacked it in the corner with the others, then picked up the exercise ball to find Colin holding something out for her to see. "What's that?"

"Tickets to the Earshot Jazz Festival. Saturday's concert. Full Nelson is playing."

"Oh, you're lucky. I love that band."

"They're for you. I'm giving them to you."

Oh. She put the exercise ball carefully on the rack, unsure how to respond except to say, *Are you crazy?* Why was he doing this? "Colin. That is really sweet, but I'm sorry, I can't accept—"

"Yeah, yeah, right. Take them. I don't know if my back can take sitting for that long yet."

"What about your friends?"

"They don't like jazz."

"Stephanie."

"Stephanie and I aren't seeing each other anymore."

She was startled into facing him. "I'm sorry."

"Don't bother."

Her mind went to high speed. Had he meant to go with Stephanie and couldn't face going with anyone else? What was the right thing to do in this situation? She'd accepted gifts from clients a few times, but only tokens of appreciation at their last sessions.

"No agenda, no strings. I just don't want them to go to waste." He held the tickets out insistently. "Besides, you need to get out and have fun. You can bring your knitting."

She started to get insulted, then saw the twinkle in his eyes and laughed. "One ticket for me, one for a half-finished sweater?"

"Come on. You can land a better date than that. Easy."

Like you? The image came immediately, straight out of the clown-gone-wrong dream, of them lying on a blanket sharing a preconcert picnic and a bottle of champagne…

"At least let me pay you for them."

"Oh, for—" He stared at her, clearly exasperated. "You are a hard woman to do something nice for, you know that?"

Wesley had said the same thing. But Wesley was a friend, and Colin was her client. A new one. One she was wildly attracted to and confused by. And guess what, she wasn't going to admit any of that to him. "I'm your PT."

He made a sound of impatience. "I'm aware of that."

"I'm sorry. I'm not…"

Colin strode forward, took her hand and slapped the tickets into her palm. "They're yours. Just forget it and enjoy the concert."

She stood, indecisive, then caught the stubborn set of his features and relented. Refusing again would be rude. "Thank you, Colin."

"You're welcome, geez." He rubbed his lower back. "All that work made my back hurt."

Demi snorted. "Into the massage room. Undressed and on the table. I'll be right in." She closed the door on him, putting the tickets in her pocket. She shouldn't have taken them. But Wesley loved jazz and his birthday was coming up. Maybe he'd like to go with her. Or maybe he'd like to take Cathy. Things seemed to be going well between them.

"Ready."

She went in, almost used to the sight of Colin's incredible physique all laid out for her to touch. Almost. In a few weeks maybe the novelty would wear off to ho-hum. More likely the best she could hope for was to cool her attraction to a manageable level.

Candles lit, music on, hands oiled, she started with the sweeping motions that would improve circulation to his muscles. He was so much looser than when they'd started three weeks before. Unfortunately it was therefore even more of a pleasure to touch him, and stupidly she gave in, keeping her thoughts in platonic territory, but enjoying the smooth masculine feel of his skin, waiting for the muscles to relax further under her fingers. Up to his shoulders, down to his lower back, onto his finely developed gluteals, which the non-PT part of her would call a fabulous ass.

For some reason, instead of loosening, his body stayed tight; his breathing never settled into its usual slow rhythm, the signal she could start going deeper.

A couple of minutes later she broke off, frowning.

"What's up, Colin? You're not relaxing."

"I'm...a little uncomfortable." His voice was low. Not his usual cadence, but not the way he spoke when he was in pain, either.

"How can I help?"

"I could tell you exactly how." This time his tone bordered on suggestive. "But I'm pretty sure you wouldn't like the idea."

Demi's hands stilled. Oh. He was hard. Because *she* was touching him? No, no, he could be enjoying her massage and fantasizing about anyone. Erections happened now and then with her male clients. She knew the protocol. But this was the first time she'd been so flustered.

And so tempted.

She wanted to dig down under his hips and get to know his cock, take it into her mouth until he was begging for mercy, then straddle him on her table, watching his face, listening to his moans, finally having mercy and making him come.

Instead, she took her hands off his back. "Why don't I step out for a few minutes?"

He lifted his head, watching her intently, a question in his eyes. "Is that what you really want to do, Demi?"

Her mouth dropped open in a tiny gasp she couldn't quite suppress. Was he *hitting* on her? No, no, he couldn't be. Wait, maybe he was. "I'll just give you time to get... comfortable again."

"Yeah, okay." His head dropped back to the table, as if

nothing had passed between them. Had she imagined what he was offering?

For three of the longest seconds of her life she stood there, on fire for this man, craving him, wanting to chuck every professional ethic she'd ever had for one fabulous roll on the massage table.

Then she turned quietly, left the room and fled to her office, behind her solid, respectable desk, breath coming fast, cheeks hot—*everything* hot.

Colin Russo had hit on her, and she couldn't do anything about it. In three minutes she was going to have to go back in there and pretend nothing had happened. In three minutes and at all their future appointments.

How could she stand this?

She had to. It was that simple. She hadn't had the world's most tragic life, but it hadn't been a piece of cake, either. She'd been virtually ignored by her parents. The miracle baby they'd prayed for for so long had chosen a damned awkward time to show up, right after they'd adopted two other beautiful children who'd taken to the family culture like ducks to water. While Demi had twisted and chafed and rebelled and sulked and finally put physical and emotional distance between herself and her past in order to let it rest.

If she could do that, she could go into the room with Colin for the last ten minutes of their appointment and not act like a cat in heat. Right?

Right.

Shoulders straight, chest lifted, she marched back into the room, hoping her still-red cheeks were the only thing that would give away her advanced state of fluster. He was sitting up, his naked back broad and muscled.

"Okay now?" She spoke like a nurse asking after her patient's bowel health.

"Fine." He didn't turn around. His voice was flat, withdrawn. Perfect. That was the way she could handle him best.

"Would you like to continue the massage or—"

"I'm good."

"Okay." She stayed by the door. "Don't be surprised if you're sore again tomorrow after today's bike ride. Take it easy for a few days, just gentle walking, and then you can try riding again."

Silence.

"You can get dressed now, and—"

"Demi." His voice had turned gentle.

She kept hers brisk. "Yes?"

"Sorry."

"No problem." She breezed around him to put the cap back on her peppermint oil. "It happens. Nothing to be ashamed of."

"I'm not ashamed of that."

"Oh." She nodded too many times. "Okay. Well, good. I wouldn't want you to—"

"I was apologizing for coming on to you."

"No. You didn't. Not really."

"Yes, I did."

"Oh. Well." She scrubbed at a tiny drop of spilled oil on her counter as if it were a lake of toxic waste. "I didn't notice, so you don't need to—"

"Yes, you did." He reached and clamped a hand down on her wrist, stopping her frenetic scrubbing before she could process that he'd moved. "I saw it in your face."

She had no choice, couldn't hide herself in useless activity anymore. She gave in and met those deep brown eyes, then wished she hadn't when she could barely get her voice to work. "Saw what in my face?"

A slow, sexy grin spread over his features, making it hard for her to breathe, impossible to move.

"How much you wanted it to happen, too."

DEMI PAUSED OUTSIDE her apartment. She was just back from buying fresh ravioli and sauce for dinner. From the end of the hall in the Come to Your Senses communal apartment came voices and laughter.

She fit her key into the lock and turned it. Paused again. Maybe she should go join them for a while? She never did, always felt like an intruder. But in a frustrating catch-22, she would never be one of them unless she spent time feeling like an intruder first.

Not tonight. Socializing took effort; she was tired. Her cozy chair with knitting and audiobook was calling her name. That, with a nice cup of tea or glass of wine after dinner would hit the spot.

A rumble of male voices, then Angela, shrieking with laughter. Demi pushed into her front entranceway, then put the food away in the kitchen and got herself a beer. Took off the top and stood next to her sink. Had the first cold, bubbly sip.

Another rumble of laughter down the hall. She must not have closed her door. She always closed the front door, immediately. She took a few steps toward it, shoving her hand into her back pocket and encountering stiff paper.

The tickets.

She pulled them out, smoothed them on her counter. Saturday. Five days away. Had Colin been trying to soften her up so he could hit on her? She frowned. It hadn't felt like that. More like he thought she had a boring, pathetic life that desperately needed spicing up.

That better not be the reason he hit on her. Geez, at least she only gave him a pity *lunch*.

A clamor of voices sounded from the end of the hall, as if her building-mates were all trying to speak at once.

She looked around her place: sparsely furnished, semi-neat. The big bouquet of flowers from Bonnie Blooms she insisted on treating herself to graced her coffee table. Book-case, a couple of her sister's more tasteful cast-off chairs around a dining table she'd bought herself.

A nice apartment. For a single woman. Who, yes, prob-ably spent too much time at home. One who'd left her door open to the social noise down the hall. She didn't need her psych degree to figure that out.

Clutching her beer, she marched out into the hallway and headed toward the group's common room before she had time to think and change her mind.

At the doorway, she paused, dreading the moment when they noticed her and conversation stopped, then turned po-lite. Maybe she should—

"Hey, Demi's here. She'll know." Jack beckoned her into the room and pointed to the green couch next to Seth. Bon-nie was conspicuously absent—a guilty relief. "Come on, we need the benefit of your wisdom. We're fighting."

"Okay." She plunked onto the couch next to Seth and clinked her bottle with him when he offered. "What do you need to know?"

"We're *not* fighting, we're *discussing*." Angela glared at Jack. "Why do you think women are more into wed-dings than men?"

"Because men aren't women?" Seth said.

"Because men were out hunting the mammoths and women were stuck in caves." Jack shrugged mischievously. "They had to do something to pass the time, so they de-cided to make the caves pretty."

"What does that have to do with weddings?" Seth asked.

"I think what he means is that the need to make occasions or spaces special and homey evolved as a female trait," Angela said. "Out of utter boredom and total neglect."

"If I may…" Demi pretended to be thinking it over carefully.

"Sure, go ahead, Demi." Jack smiled kindly. "We asked for your opinion and then didn't let you say anything."

"Well, I believe it's more that a woman is really celebrating the joyous day when she finally has cemented in her grip a man whose life she can now proceed to ruin." She waited three beats, then grinned devilishly.

Jack and Seth burst out laughing. Angela, too, though it took her a second.

"While men on the other hand…"

Seth subsided. "Uh-oh."

"…are not taking any of it seriously because they plan to go out and screw the first hot babe they can find no matter what vows they took."

Angela looked stricken. "Demi, do you really believe either of those things?"

"Nah." She grinned, fingering the label on her beer. "I think like any stereotype there is a grain of truth, but it's not true for everyone. According to my mom, Dad was really into all the planning stages of their wedding. Of course he was a control freak. Why were you talking about weddings? Anything I should know?"

Angela blushed. "Saturday night Daniel asked me to marry him."

"Oh, gosh." Without thinking, Demi jumped up and threw herself on Angela in a hug, probably squashing her. "How wonderful. I'm so happy for you."

"Thank you." Angela squeezed her back, laughing with pleasure. "I guess you're not cynical about marriage after all."

"Definitely not. I think it's great. Daniel seems like a

great guy." She wished suddenly that she'd hung around here more, gotten to know him better. So she could say he *was* a great guy, not just that he seemed like one.

"Hey, Demi. How come you never hug *me* like that?" Seth winked at her, which, considering he was one of the best-looking men she'd ever seen, made her want to pull her turtle head back into her shell to avoid answering. Except then he grinned his boy-next-door grin and put her back at ease.

"Hmm. Maybe I will one day."

"All right!" He challenged her with a stare. "When?"

"How about when *you're* getting married?"

"Oh, geez, who am I going to marry? Or more to the point, who'd marry me?"

She sent him the same challenge back. "I'm thinking Bonnie."

For a second she thought she'd gone too far, then a roar erupted from Jack and Angela. Seth, Mr. Cool, Mr. Style, Mr. Mega-Bucks, blushed as if he was fourteen, and thank goodness someone besides her was doing it.

"I gotta hand it to you, Demi." Jack was still chuckling. "None of us have ever had the balls to say it. Hey, Seth, why don't you quit messing around and ask Bonnie to marry you?"

"Seth, I just had a *great* idea." Angela clapped her hands together. "Why don't you quit messing around and ask Bonnie to marry you?"

"Ooh, ooh!" Demi raised her hand as if she were in a classroom. "I had an idea, too. Seth, why don't you quit mess—"

"Stop." Seth looked as if he'd been out in the midday sun for six hours—but he was laughing. "Enough. I'll give it some thought."

The laughter stopped. Angela put a hand to her chest. "You will?"

"There. I just did." He got up and headed for the refrigerator. "I need another beer."

"Get me one, too?" Angela asked.

"Sure. Jack? Demi?"

Demi drained the one she'd brought and nodded, smiling her thanks to Seth, sending silent ones to Colin, who had no idea what he'd started when he handed her those tickets. She was having a good time. And she should also send thanks to Bonnie for not being here so Demi could gain confidence with her other three building-mates before she took on the dragon lady.

"Thanks, Seth." Angela took the beer he handed her. "Here's to your wedding."

"Hear, hear!" Jack raised his.

"Oh, I'm thinking a triple wedding now." Angela set her sights on Jack. "When are you going to ask Melissa?"

"There's the real question," Seth said.

"Ha!" Jack scowled. "When are you going to mind your own business?"

"And, Demi." Angela gestured with her bottle. "How about whatsisname, Colin?"

"You're seeing someone?" Seth seemed surprised.

"No." She shook her head adamantly. "He's a client. Angela has fallen deeply in love with him because he's hot."

"Wow." Seth settled back onto the couch next to her. "That is so deep."

"*I* just look," Angela protested. "*She* gets to touch him. *Everywhere.*"

"Not *everywhere*." Demi was having a hard time keeping a straight face. For some reason, instead of the situation with Colin being an anguished source of conflict, in this company it was simply funny.

"What do you do when you're attracted to a client?" Jack asked. "Can you ask him out?"

"No, no, no." She waggled her finger. "Big bad idea. Prosecutable in fact."

"Now, wait a minute," Angela said. "Bonnie saw you two strolling down the sidewalk together last week. At lunchtime."

"Oh, call the paper," Jack said. "Post on Facebook. Tweet the world. They were on the sidewalk."

"Oh, that. No, that was nothing. We'd finished a session—"

"With *massage?*" Angela asked.

"Yes." Demi stopped the oncoming rush of comments with a raised hand. "I end most sessions with massage."

"I can see it now." Seth framed his hands around a headline. "'Client in critical pleasure condition after massage veers out of control.'"

Demi pretended to ignore him. "We were both hungry and—"

"After a solid hour." Seth had switched to a booming newscaster's voice. "We were still starved for each other."

"—so we ate a couple of hot dogs in the park."

"Authorities believe dogs were involved."

"Eww, *Seth.*" Angela made a face. "That is disgusting."

"I know, I know." He switched to his normal voice. "But it was either that or an eat-my-wiener joke."

"Disgusting too-o!" Angela sang.

"As I was saying." Demi continued to ignore him. "At the park we *ingested frankfurters,* and then he went home."

"Client retreats." Jack took up the newscast. "'She was too much for me,' he admits."

Demi collapsed into giggles with the others, loving the glow of being part of the gang, at least this one time.

"So besides all the perverted male commentary, the

point is, Colin wanted to have lunch with you." Angela was beaming encouragingly. "That's great. Now, if he calls just to talk, you know he wants more."

"He isn't going to call me just to talk. I'm totally not his—"

Her phone rang. A roar erupted in the room. Demi's adrenaline went nuts. She grabbed the phone and stared. Her sister. "It's *not* him."

"Doesn't matter. You should have seen your face." Angela was grinning at her. "Like you wanted to run and hide, and jump up and down with joy at the same time."

"Oh, come on."

"I'm right. And when was the last time all of us felt that way when a certain someone might be calling?"

Jack raised his hand impatiently.

"Let's see…why don't we hear from…Jack." Angela gave him royal permission.

"When I was falling in love with Melissa."

"Correct." Angela pointed to herself. "When I was falling in love with Daniel."

Seth put a hand to his heart. "Last night when I heard my take-out pizza was ready."

"Guys…" Demi gestured helplessly in the face of a triple set of knowing grins.

"It's unanimous. I'm right." Angela pointed a warning finger at Demi. "Trust me here, girlfriend. You are about to enter a brave new world o' man-trouble."

6

BONNIE STOOD FACING Don on the front steps of Come to Your Senses, thinking a good-night kiss was a really good idea. Dinner had been delicious, sushi at Umi Sake House, where they'd had sake until she lost track of how much. Right now she was feeling no pain, the air was bracingly chilly and Don was looking particularly handsome in the building's outdoor light. He was a good-looking guy, a few inches taller than Bonnie, with a solid broad-shouldered build, dirty-blond hair he kept neatly combed and big brown eyes with long lashes. Kind of a Ricky Gervais face, very cute. For their date he'd worn a navy sport coat over dress khakis. She liked that he'd gone traditional. She'd worn a new dress—new to her anyway—one of those miracle secondhand-store finds that fit perfectly and cost nearly nothing. It wasn't her usual wildly patterned Bohemian type outfit, but a light blue knit that clung in very flattering ways.

She was gratified to notice Don had discreetly checked out her bod whenever she stood or leaned over. Dating a gentleman was great, and a wonderful change from Seth the Sexual Barbarian, but Bonnie wanted a guy with a nice, healthy libido, too, and apparently Don had one.

"Don, I had a great time tonight."

"I did, too." He grinned at her. "I always have a great time with you, Bonnie."

"Same here." She smiled back expectantly, willing him to make the big move. She was perfectly able to initiate the kiss, but she was particular about two things in the dating world: that the first kiss and the marriage proposal were the man's jobs.

"Would you like to go out in a couple of days? Maybe Wednesday?"

"I'd love that." She moved a step closer, put her hand on his lapel, looked up invitingly. *Kiss me, you fool.*

"Maybe we could go sailing if it's not too cold?"

"Oh, I'd love that." She blinked. Sailing? On what?

"I have a sailboat. Nothing fancy, but I'd love you to meet her."

She was so thrilled he owned a boat—a boat!—that she ignored him referring to "meeting her" as if it were human.

"I'm not fancy, either, so that works perfectly." She smoothed her hand over his shirtfront. Nice firm chest underneath. Very nice. *Now, Don, about that kiss…*

"You're great, Bonnie. Really great."

"So are you…" She rose on tiptoe toward his face. Apparently she'd have to get this one going by herself.

However.

Once she turned the green-light signal into a roaring bonfire of come-on-already, Don took over.

Oh, boy, did he.

His arms came around her in the kind of hug that let a woman know she was really being held. His mouth found hers perfectly on the first try, and their kiss was soft and lingering, no slobber whatsoever, with promise of good heat to come.

Mmm, yes. Maybe she'd fall for him one day. She really, really hoped so.

The kiss ended slowly, and then there was another one, and another after that, and Bonnie was starting to heat up quite nicely and about to press herself shamelessly against his khakis to let him know, when the door to the building opened behind them.

"What the—"

An angry male voice. Very angry. *Seth*.

Bonnie's instinct was to jump guiltily away, but she managed to squash it in time. Not hard, since Don's arms were still solidly around her and she would have had to shove him to get anywhere.

"What's going on, Bonnie?"

Don turned, keeping Bonnie partly behind him. "Is there a problem?"

Seth stepped forward, gray eyes blazing, nearly a head taller than Don. He was wearing a black leather jacket and gray shirt. Behind him the door swung shut with a melodramatic clank.

"Seth, chill out." Bonnie spoke quickly, putting a reassuring hand on Don's shoulder. "Don, this is Seth, a friend of mine who is being a little overprotective at the moment. Seth, this is Don. My *date*."

She sent Seth a back-off look that had better work, because if he tried to mess this up, she was never speaking to him again.

"Nice to meet you." Don managed to make the pleasantry sound like an insult.

Seth nodded once, lips tight. "Nice to meet you, too."

An even worse insult. Bonnie sighed. Men and their egos.

"Bonnie, you okay?"

"More than, Seth."

"Good." He pushed past them, ran down the steps and stalked off down Olive. Bonnie and Don both turned to watch him go.

"That was weird," Don said.

"Tell me about it."

"You got any more of those *protective* guys hanging around?"

"Nope. Oh." She grimaced. "Well, there's Jack…"

Don looked pained. "Jack, huh."

"He's a sweetheart. And semiengaged."

Don sighed. "I guess it doesn't surprise me. I'd go nuts if I walked in on some guy kissing you, too."

Bonnie bussed his cheek gratefully. He'd dealt with Seth's little tantrum really well. Point in his favor. Maybe he trusted her instinctively. Maybe he just hadn't been bitten by the dark side of love yet, making him suspicious and bitter. Though she couldn't imagine any person single and on the downward slope toward thirty who didn't have scars of some kind.

"I don't think you need to worry." She turned toward him again, heart still thumping from the encounter with Seth, trying to block the image of his tall body all in black, striding away from her.

"No?" Don gathered her close. "No special guy in your life?"

"None." The phrase hurt just a little, but it was true.

Don kissed her again, this time harder, more possessively, and she tried to throw herself into it, tried to banish memories of other lips, and succeeded nicely. Pretty nicely. Sort of nicely. *Oh, Seth.* "I'd like to keep it that way, Bonnie. If you're willing."

She'd already forgotten what they were talking about. "I'm sorry, keep who what way?"

He chuckled. "I know. After that kiss I can't think straight, either."

"No, I know." Oh, dear. That wasn't what had distracted her.

She suddenly wanted the evening over, wanted to go back to her apartment and regroup, process more of this damn endless grief at finally giving up on Seth so she could concentrate on falling for Don. He was really a great guy, generous and funny and sweet.

"I was asking if we could date exclusively, Bonnie. I think I'm fall— I'm crazy about you."

"Oh." She breathed the syllable out, wishing he could have made the declaration about ten minutes earlier, when the evening was still all about him. "Same here. And yes. I'd like that. Definitely. Yes."

"Good." He squeezed her tightly, kissed her with real passion this time, and enough desire that her brain came back completely into the date so she could respond more genuinely. "I'm really happy, Bonnie."

"Me, too." She wanted, suddenly and absurdly, to cry. "Really happy."

"So I'll see you Wednesday, then?"

"Yes. Wednesday."

His eyes were warm, kind, and he gave her a sweet, long kiss before he whispered good-night.

He hadn't hit on her. He hadn't asked himself in for coffee. He'd kissed her, asked permission to date her exclusively and had gone home.

Wow. A nice guy. A really, really nice one. Finally.

She watched him walk away, thinking how great it was to see a guy's back and not feel agony, to trust she'd see him again, and that things between them would go forward until they reached an impasse or they grew old and died.

Normal. Date a guy like him, see if things worked out.

None of the glitches and fears and games and exhausting heart-and-mind gymnastics. For once she felt safe and relaxed going into a relationship.

Imagine that.

Upstairs, Bonnie opened the door to her apartment and was greeted by the basket of laundry she'd intended to get up early and do that morning, then intended to do on her lunch hour, then intended to do before her date...

Oops.

Sighing, she took off her jacket and flung it onto a nearby chair, then frowned down at the basket. Since she was washing anyway, she might as well add the dress.

She wriggled out of it and added it to the pile, then kicked off her shoes and tossed in her stockings and underwear. She'd shower, put on pj's, then do laundry.

Her phone rang from her jacket and she grabbed for it. Seth? No. Geez, Bonnie.

"Hi, Don." She smiled, wondering what he'd do if he could see what she wasn't wearing. "You home yet?"

"Almost. I missed hearing your voice."

"Aww." She grinned and ran her hand over her breasts, imagining him touching them. What would that touch be like? Would he be able to bring her nearly to orgasm with his fingers and mouth on them? "I'm glad you called. I was thinking about you."

"Good thoughts?"

"All good."

"I'm glad. So...listen, that guy who interrupted us."

"Seth?" She tensed, palm still curved around her right breast.

"You used to date him, didn't you."

Bonnie closed her eyes. His tone was calm, but she didn't know him well enough to sense what he was feeling. "About five years ago."

"It's not over for him."

She didn't know what to say. "I don't think—"

"It wasn't a question. I'm telling you, it's not over for him."

"Oh. Well. I suppose—"

"Before I get in any deeper, Bonnie, I need to know if it's over for you." He coughed, cleared his throat, coughed again.

"It's over." She spoke clearly, feeling only slightly sick. It wasn't a lie. She was well on her way to being over Seth, and the more she was with Don, the more distant their connection would seem.

"That makes me really happy."

She smiled; her hand moved over her breasts again. "I'm glad."

"I'm really looking forward to seeing what we can be together."

"Same here." She imagined herself taking off his sport coat, tossing it across the room. Unbuttoning his shirt— would he have hair on his chest or not? "I have to wait for Wednesday to see you again?"

"How about now?" He laughed softly. "Okay, maybe that would be pushing it."

She giggled like a silly schoolgirl, hand drifting down over her stomach. "I'm free tomorrow…"

"I can't." He made a growling sound of frustration. "I have a work dinner. I guess we have to keep it Wednesday."

"I guess." She sighed heavily.

"Bonnie."

"Mmm?"

"I can't wait to get my arms around you again."

"Me neither." Her hand found its way lower. "Maybe we should have dinner at my place?"

Argh! What had she said? She couldn't afford to make

any kind of decent dinner for him with her finances in a crisis state. Cottage cheese with a side of potato chips. Maybe without the potato chips.

"Actually, I was going to suggest I make dinner for you here."

Whew. "I'd love that, thank you." She smiled dreamily. Dinner at his no-doubt fancy apartment, nice wine, then a trip into his no-doubt very masculine bedroom. What kind of lover would he be? Sensitive and sweet, maybe a hidden beast in there somewhere...

Her hand brushed idly across her breasts, back down. "Can I bring wine?"

"I'll have plenty. Come early. We should make a night of it." His voice was low, suggestive.

"Mmm, I'd really like that." She echoed his tone, fingers lingering between her legs.

"Good night then, Bonnie. Sweet dreams. I'll call you tomorrow."

"Good night, Don." She hung up, smiling, and let herself slump against the wall. Dinner, wine, romance. Who could ask for anything more?

She imagined herself under him, his body thrusting hard. Her fingers went to work; she let her head drop back, braced herself, arching her back. What did Don sound like when he came? What did he look like? She wanted to see. She wanted to see him coming, feel him inside her. She wanted him to—

Her door swung open. "Bonnie?"

She gasped. Seth.

Oh, dear God.

For a long moment their eyes held, his gray ones glittering in a face stony with shock. The only sound was Bonnie's loud, irregular breathing.

Seeing him when she was prepared was bad enough.

Seeing him when she was naked and horny and touching herself...

Please, God, give her strength to resist the inevitable. Seth wouldn't let an opportunity like this go by to press his advantage, fight his case, try to get her back with sex, the crazy, irresistibly explosive way they went about it.

Oh, Seth.

His gaze traveled down her body. His eyes closed. His jaw and fist clenched.

"Sorry. I should have knocked."

Then he turned and walked away.

"So THEN MIKE hits a patch of gravel and wipes out." Nick smacked his fist into his palm. He and Colin were walking the three-mile Elliott Bay Trail from Smith Cove Park north then back south, along the railroad and the Sound into downtown Seattle. They had nearly completed the trail and were about to turn and head back. "I'm telling you, everyone there was thinking about you when he fell, but he turned out fine."

"That's good." Colin swung along, his body itching to run. He'd been feeling better every day, looser, in less pain, and had decided to try a walk. At the last minute, he'd called Nick to join him, well aware that asking Nick to take a walk was like asking a master engineer to change a lightbulb. Colin thought he'd be glad for the company but Nick had done nothing but talk training: running, biking and swimming. He might as well have applied thumbscrews, though Colin had the uncomfortable impression that those topics might have been all they ever talked about. Now the story of Mike, who'd fallen a hell of a lot harder than Colin, and was completely fine. Of course.

They turned at the Sculpture Garden and started on the three miles back to Colin's car and Nick's bike.

"I did a personal best in the pool the other day. I was smoking, man. It was like—"

"Want to run?" Colin broke into a slow, careful jog, not waiting for Nick to respond. He couldn't stand it anymore.

"Are you kidding?" Nick's freckled face broke into a grin. "Hell, yeah. That baby pace was killing me."

Baby. Thanks, Nick. Colin accelerated, monitoring his back for signs of rebellion. So far so good. And God did it feel good to move, even running like a beginner. The air blew fresher, the colors around them seemed brighter, the Sound glistened restlessly in the sunlight. Another unusually warm day for late October. The gods were smiling today.

"How's that feeling?" Nick turned to scope out Colin's stride, his sandy curls blowing haphazardly in the breeze.

"Good. Really good."

"Think you can go faster?"

"Sure." He wasn't sure. But why not try? If he felt any pain, he'd slow or stop immediately. Otherwise Demi would have his head on a platter. He grinned at the thought, then forced himself to concentrate on his body and his stride. Demi occupied way too many of his thoughts recently. "You talked to Stephanie lately?"

"Oh. Yeah. I, uh, saw her last night."

"Yeah?" He felt a twinge of jealousy, even knowing it was entirely innocent and bound to happen. Nick and Stephanie ran in the same social circles. Of course they'd bump into each other. "How did she look?"

"Fantastic."

Colin gave him a sharp glance. Nick's response had been a little too enthusiastic for his taste. "Yeah? She seem happy?"

"She does actually." Nick measured his pace to match Colin's. "Really happy."

Colin sped up. He wanted Stephanie to be happy. At the same time, news of her looking miserable without him wouldn't have hurt. "Maybe I'll call her. See how she's doing."

"Yeah. Yeah, sure." Nick's enthusiasm had fallen off.

"Maybe she'd like to have lunch with me."

"Maybe."

Colin inhaled deeply. His muscles were warm, his back was quiet, accepting that this was what it was meant to do. He ran faster and the extra speed fed his energy. Check this out! The King of the Track was on his way back. Not going to compete again? Said who? Look at him! That finish line in Hawaii would be facing him yet. "Damn, this feels great."

"You look good, man. Keep it up."

They kept the pace going, joining the railroad tracks at Garfield and following them until they'd head back south again to Smith's Cove. Demi would be proud of him. Well, no, she'd probably yell at him for taking the chance, but look how it was working—

He stumbled and pitched forward. A stab of pain shot through his back, but he caught himself before he fell. He stopped running immediately to assess the damage.

Nick jogged back to him. "Geez, buddy, you okay?"

"Yeah." He tried to hide the fact that he was breathing a hell of a lot harder than Nick, and twisted experimentally, tried out a few stretches, then grinned. No pain whatsoever. "I'm fine."

"Thank God." Nick slapped him on the back, grinning. "Nothing keeps you down, huh?"

"Nothing." Colin held up his hand for a high five and they kept running, egging each other on to faster speeds until Colin's navy Toyota came into sight next to Nick's bike. Nick sprinted on ahead, as Colin knew he would.

Once a competitor, always a competitor. Though at least Colin had the sense not to join that race.

Nick started laughing when Colin reached his car. "Listen to you, panting like a girl."

"You wait. I'll live to kick your ass at the world championship." He forced his breathing to slow, unlocked the car and grabbed his water bottle. "Want to go for a beer?"

"You kidding? I have many more miles to go before I drink. This was my warm-up, old man."

"Right. Seeya." He waved Nick off, envious that he got to keep going, but determined not to be stupid about this. He'd promised Demi that much, and he owed it to himself, as well. So far everything felt good. Everything. He wanted to run the same trail again right now, then plow into the water and swim to Alaska. He wanted to sit down and indulge his visualization of winning Hawaii.

Instead, he walked until his muscles had cooled, did his core exercises and a series of long, careful stretches before he climbed back into his car and drove home, windows open, radio blasting a Red Hot Chili Peppers CD. He even got looks from a few women crossing the street, something that hadn't happened in a while.

Colin was on his way back!

At home, he took ibuprofen and showered, made himself a late-afternoon turkey sandwich on whole-grain bread bought from Angela's bakery and drank a good quart of water to make sure he stayed hydrated. Then he treated himself to a beer and the newspaper. And another beer. What a great evening. He felt as if he could breathe more deeply; his body felt alive and glowing. God, he'd missed working out. Look what it did for him. He even felt enough like his old self to consider calling Stephanie tonight, see how she was, find out if she was really that happy or if she missed him, if she wanted to get together and talk things over.

After his second beer, he opened a third and picked up the phone, feeling more nervous than he should be. He'd known this woman forever. A lot had changed with his accident, but not that.

"Hey, Stephanie."

"...Colin." She sounded surprised, but not necessarily in a good way. She hadn't expected his call, and undoubtedly hearing his voice brought back a lot of emotion. "I'm out shopping. With Briana. What's up? Why are you calling me?"

"To see how you are." She'd sounded slightly irritated, which irritated him. After all they'd meant to each other, she was cranky he'd interrupted her shopping?

"Oh. Well, I'm fine. Doing really well. Happy."

He hadn't expected that. "Don't miss me, huh."

"We broke up for a reason, Colin." She sounded as if she was lecturing a small whiny boy, even though he'd deliberately kept his voice playful and flirtatious. He'd forgotten how much that tone pissed him off.

"I know." He took a deep breath. "I was an ass, Stephanie. I'm sorry. But things are finally turning around."

"That's great, Colin. I'm glad for you." She didn't sound glad. She sounded like all she cared about was getting back to spending money.

"Yeah, thanks." He was totally disoriented. He'd called to ask her out, start the process of getting back together with her, and now that he had her on the phone, this woman he'd adored and wanted to marry, he felt oddly detached. Wasn't even sure he cared about seeing her again. Wasn't even sure she was the same woman. And yet, of course she was.

Maybe he wasn't the same man.

"Was that all?"

"I was wondering if you wanted to go out sometime. To

catch up." The second the words were out, he wanted them back. This didn't feel right.

"Colin..."

She wasn't going to give him a chance, and faced with that fact, he was stunned to find he didn't really care, not deep down where it mattered. "What, Stephanie?"

"I'm seeing someone else."

"Okay." The word came out automatically. Along with it, a loosening of the tension that had been holding him. "Who? Do I know him?"

"Look, this isn't really the time to have this discussion."

Wariness rose. "Giving me a name is a discussion?"

"You always turn everything into a fight."

"I'm not fight—"

"That looks great on you, Briana. Colin, I have to go. I'll call you later."

No, she wouldn't. He was about to tell her that when the pieces clicked into place. How stupid could he be? "Nick."

Silence.

Oh, for—

"You're seeing *Nick*."

"It just happened, Colin. I'm sorry. Neither of us planned this."

"And neither of you thought it was worth telling me."

"Of course. But— I mean, of course we— It just never seemed—"

"Yeah. Okay, never mind. Keep shopping. Buy out the store." He hung up the phone, already regretting the bitter comment. He should have taken the high road, wished her well, wished her happiness screwing one of his best friends when they'd only broken up a few weeks ago. Or no, months. But after four years of dating—

Nice.

Back when he'd been whole and stepped in bad crap like

this, he'd jump on his bike, take a punishing ride around Seattle's steepest streets, come back utterly spent, then sleep and wake up refreshed and revived. Worked like magic.

But he wasn't whole now. One puny walk/run had used up his allotment of exercise for the day. He couldn't do anything to help himself.

A completely inappropriate urge to call Demi came over him. Geez, he needed a mommy to cry to now?

He'd deal with this like a real man. Get a six-pack, turn on the TV and get blitzed.

Two hours later, the six-pack was gone and he felt like absolute hell. Men were really stupid when it came to handling emotion.

He got up, his body slightly stiff, swallowed more ibuprofen, took off his clothes and crawled into bed though it was barely eight o'clock.

In his dream, Stephanie was stripping for him, tossing the clothes onto his face, then laughing at him because he couldn't have her. He tried to lunge for her, tried to show her who was in charge here, but his body wouldn't move. He couldn't get out of bed.

Then disembodied hands helped lift him. Hands that knew exactly what they were doing, soothing his aches, giving back his power. Stephanie's image grew fuzzy; her hair started turning dark. A dimple dented her chin. The hands on him belonged to Demi now, stroking his chest, flicking over his nipples. Then she was on top of him, her hair dragging across his skin, her mouth reaching his cock, which strained toward her, desperate for the feel of her tongue.

Then he was inside her mouth, so hot and hard that he came almost instantly, in a glorious, pulsing release.

And woke to horrible pain ripping through his back.

7

"Ahhh." Demi relaxed in her chair and pulled her knitting onto her lap. Today had been good. She'd released one client into the world, his frozen shoulder healed to the point where he could manage his recovery on his own now. She loved that, when she'd really been able to make a difference in someone's life. Her client had been so grateful, he'd brought in a bouquet of flowers, which were sitting right now on Demi's dining table. White roses and mini-carnations, blue delphinium and hydrangea. Just gorgeous.

After work, Demi had taken advantage of the dry, warm Tuesday and gone for a long run, then back to Come to Your Senses for a shower and to change into loose, comfortable clothes, followed by a dinner of pasta with mushrooms and greens and a glass of wine. Then another glass. A third sat on the table next to her beside a ripe pear and shortbread cookies. She inserted the earbuds of her headphones and pressed Play to listen to her book. Perfect. A night of quiet relaxing. Just what she—

Her phone rang. Of course.

Demi put her knitting aside—was she *ever* going to have time to finish the sweater?—struggled out of the seductive depths of her chair and ran for her phone, which she'd care-

lessly left on the kitchen counter. When she planned to indulge in an evening of total relaxation, having the phone
within easy reach was vital.

It was Colin. She calmed herself, made sure she was still
breathing normally, and answered. "Hey, Colin."

"Demi." His voice was tight.

Uh-oh. "What's wrong?"

"Can't move."

"You can't move?" Demi frowned, glancing longingly
at her chair. "Want to tell me what you were doing that
brought this on?"

"Sleeping."

"Sleeping. That's it?" Silence. Demi sighed. "That's not
it. Out with it."

"I went running. Slowly. I was fine after that. Then I
took a nap and…uh, when I woke up I couldn't move."

Demi thought that one over. Either he hadn't been running slowly, or something had happened between the nap
and waking up that had trashed his back. She didn't want
to know what. Especially if it involved a hot woman riding him like a pony.

Grrr. She'd told him he had to be careful. "How long
have you been awake?"

"A couple of hours. I thought it would loosen up."

"No." She sighed. "You need to relieve the spasms. Can
you call your doctor or get to a pharmacy? Muscle relax-
ers should help some."

"I can't get out of bed." Spoken as if she should have
figured that out herself.

Demi narrowed her eyes. "So what are you calling me
for?"

"I'll pay you double, triple, whatever you want, if you
come help me."

"Oh, for God's sake. You go out and do something stupid and you expect me to come fix it at ten o'clock at night?"

"I don't *expect* anything. I'm asking. If you can't come, forget it. I'll just lie here until the stench of my corpse brings in the neighbors."

An unwilling chuckle escaped her. He hadn't lost his sense of humor this time. "I don't make house calls."

"Think of it as a mobile-treatment unit."

Demi sighed, wistfully contemplating her wine, her cookies, her chair, her book…

But then there was Colin.

Oh, man. She had to be completely insane even thinking of going over there at this hour. To his house. To his *bedroom*. When last time they'd been together he'd all but asked her to sleep with him.

Completely insane.

Outright bonkers.

Nutty in the extreme.

"Give me your address." She headed for the pad by her kitchen counter and wrote down the address of his building, along with the name of the neighbor who would buzz her in. "Okay. I'll be there in fifteen."

She ended the call and kicked off her ugly fuzzy slippers, the most comfortable footwear on earth, thought about changing out of her sweats to look more attractive, then very sensibly decided against it. After picking up a few supplies, she slipped out her apartment door.

All the way to Colin's house, Demi grumbled to herself. Why was she helping him? He'd fall back asleep eventually. His spasms would work themselves out. She didn't need to be doing this.

So why was she?

Ahem. She should avoid answering that question honestly. Because it had to do with concepts like titillation, temptation and tantalization.

Masochist. She should know better. Except in Colin's case, apparently she didn't. Or just didn't care.

She pulled up to his building, an attractive one on Eighth Avenue in the University District. Having parked in a visitor spot, she went inside and rang his neighbor's buzzer. Seconds later, the front door clicked open and she went inside, took the elevator to the third floor and emerged onto a well-lit hallway with gray carpet and cream-colored doors. She read the gold numbers as she padded by, stopping opposite Thirty-two to retrieve his spare key, which his neighbor had shoved so it just showed under the door.

Okay. Moment of truth. His place: Thirty-four. She let herself in, in full professional mode, keeping nerves at bay by holding on to her irritation that Colin hadn't taken care of himself. Whether it was the run or sex with someone or whatever he'd been doing in bed—she did not want to know—he'd been careless to backslide like this when he was doing so well.

"Hello?" The condo was modern, spare, with a fireplace in the living room and a fabulous view of the city from floor-to-ceiling windows. She put the key on the kitchen counter and crossed the space toward the door that must be his bedroom. Dark.

Oh, boy. She couldn't believe she was doing this. Into the lion's den…

"Colin?"

"Yeah, here. Light's right there next to you."

She flipped it on and walked over the condo-predictable soft beige carpet to the queen bed in the middle of the room, thinking how much more she liked the hardwood floors, worn fixtures and unexpected spaces in her apartment.

"So." She stood by his bed, hands on her hips, feeling suddenly shaky-nervous. "You've done it, huh."

"I guess." His face was pale and drawn, eyes shadowed with pain.

Her heart ached. Yes, he'd been a dummy, but what a tough setback. "Do you have naproxen sodium?"

"No."

"I brought some." She brought the bottle out of her purse. "Two every twelve hours. Starting now."

"Yes, Nurse Anderson."

"I'll get you water." She marched into the kitchen, noticing more this time: his sax on the couch, a neat pile of running magazines on the glass coffee table, modern art prints on the walls—not exactly her taste, but colorful, and a nice antidote to the bland interior. On a table outside the kitchen, a rack of exquisite knives, blades gracefully shaped in assorted sizes, handles of various materials: wood, metal and…bone? Really lovely. How long since he'd made the last one? An unusual talent.

In the kitchen she opened a cabinet. Four glasses, four plates, four mugs and a lot of empty space. Apparently he wasn't much for entertaining large groups.

She filled a glass with water and brought it back into the bedroom. "Here."

"Thanks." He reached for the glass, grunting with the strain, and took the pills.

"Those will help. Can you turn over?"

"No."

"I'll take care of that first, then we'll work on some pressure massage." Demi turned his light back off so the only illumination was outside light coming through the open curtains and the apartment light coming through his bedroom door.

"Don't have any candles, sorry."

She snorted. "Not a problem."

"You can spray aftershave on the bed if you want. And how about some real music?"

"Yeah, thanks, Colin. I think we'll make do with this setup as is." She kicked off her shoes, pulled off her sweater, attempting her very hardest to look nonchalant, and climbed onto the bed next to him. As she helped to roll him over, she tried not to notice the sleepy-clean smell of his skin, the warmth of his body and the cool softness of the sheets. Or that he was stark naked. She was here in a medical capacity, not to take off her own clothes and slide in next to him.

Oh, what a bad idea. And speaking of bad ideas, she shouldn't have had that extra glass of wine with dinner because it was making her wanton thoughts and impulses a lot harder to ignore. The dim light wasn't helping, either, though she felt it important to make him relax.

Not that she'd get wild sex out of a guy who couldn't move.

"Here." She maneuvered one of the four bed pillows under his hips, then knelt beside him and put her hands on his back, finding it very difficult to feel professional when she was in bed with him.

In fact, she didn't feel professional at all.

And when she started to massage, experiencing his tightness gradually release under her fingers, she found herself becoming more and more sensual in her motions, enjoying the texture of his skin, of his muscles, his back, his extraordinary buttocks, his absolute maleness.

What was she doing? What was she considering? She wanted to slide her hands under his hips to feel if he was hard from her touch.

This was crazy. "Better?"

"Mmmm." His voice was a low growl that made her shivery. "Much."

"Good. Can you turn over now?"

"I can, but you probably wouldn't want me to."

"Oh." She closed her eyes. He was hard again. Oh, my.

"Sorry. But you are very sexy, and…we are in bed together."

"We are." She nearly purred the words. *Shh, careful, Demi.*

He turned his head, features just visible in the half light, and for a moment she imagined herself so vividly leaning over to kiss him that she started swaying forward and had to stop herself.

"Help me turn on my side toward you."

"Yes, sir." She covered him to his waist with the sheet and lifted his left side, arranged a pillow at his back and one between his knees. "Okay?"

"Yes. Now lie down next to me."

"Uh, Colin?" Her breath started coming faster in spite of her attempts to stay calm. "I don't think that's a good idea."

"I can't move. What am I going to do to you?"

"I don't want to find out."

"Yes, you do."

Yes, she did. Desperately. She was crazy with hunger for this man, even if he was immobilized.

"Lie down. I want you next to me. Please."

Oh, crap. When would she stop being victim to her hormones?

Telling herself she'd gone completely over the edge, she closed her eyes, slid down onto the mattress a foot away from him, even more stiff than he'd been when he was rigid with pain.

"Closer."

"Don't push it."

"Closer. Or I'll hurt myself and it will be your fault."

"Hurt yourself doing what?"

"Demi." His voice had dropped to a seductive murmur. "Come closer."

She swallowed audibly. Then slowly, with an exhausting combination of reluctance and eagerness, she wiggled closer to his warm body.

"Good." His hand landed on her solar plexus and lay still, exciting and oddly reassuring. "Thank you."

She swallowed again. "Colin…"

"Shh, relax." His hand began to move over her, slowly and carefully, from the right side of her rib cage to the left. "Just let me touch you like this."

Demi closed her eyes, heart beating much too quickly, breath coming much too fast. Caught in the world's oldest dilemma: what she should do versus what she wanted to do.

She wanted him. She wanted his hands all over her body the way hers had been all over his so many times. Only closer, more intimate. Sexual.

His hand veered from its back-and-forth path, making warm circles up under her breasts, down between her hip bones. She felt herself grow hungry, wet between her legs, the area crying out for his hand to explore, his fingers to bury themselves deeply in her.

She swallowed again. This shouldn't be happening. But in his territory, in his bed, want had triumphed. She felt less like his PT and more like…a woman. A desirable, sexy woman, wanted by a much more desirable, sexy man. Who could get enough of that feeling?

Not really excuses for breaking professional ethics to this degree. But she was nearly past caring, on fire for him to touch her, touch her *there*.

He took his time, finally sliding his hand under her soft, worn T-shirt, up between her breasts. Then he stopped; he drew his breath in sharply.

"Colin." She was instantly concerned. "You shouldn't be moving if—"

"No, no. It's not pain." He resumed stroking her, keeping his fingers together, investigating her sternum.

"What is it, then?" she whispered.

"You're not wearing a bra."

"Oh." She moved restlessly, becoming crazy aroused. "I left the house quickly."

"I like that about you. A lot." He spread his fingers, hand still centered between her breasts, but on this stroke his thumb and pinkie slid over her nipples and she was the one inhaling sharply. "You're beautiful, Demi."

She didn't know what to say to that. She was decidedly not. Attractive on a good day. Not beautiful.

His hand slid full onto her right breast. She let out a moan. "Colin."

"Mmm?"

"This...can't go anywhere."

"I think you'd be surprised."

"I mean, I can't and you can't... Your back."

"I know." His hand slid down her stomach; his fingers slipped under the loose waistband of her sweats, just touched the top of her pelvic bone and slid back up.

She exhaled explosively. This was torture. She should stop him. She should get up and walk out. She should...

"Pull down your sweats."

She swallowed again. Pulled them down. His hand followed the motion, roamed over her panties, the heat of his skin penetrating the thin cotton covering.

Demi groaned. All reason had gone, replaced by the searing need to have his hands directly on her.

"Take your panties off," he whispered.

She obeyed, practically weeping with desire.

"Spread your legs for me."

They opened wide off to his right, avoiding hitting his body.

Then nothing. No movement, no sound but their breathing, the room's air cool on her wet sex, sensitivity heightened by arousal and anticipation.

Then his palm gripped her hip bone, fingertips nearly reaching where she wanted them to be.

Nearly.

"Do you want me to touch you, Demi?"

"Yes."

"Where?"

She took his hand, guided it, let out a moan when his fingers found their target.

"Ohhh." His voice was a deep groan of appreciation. "Feel that."

"Yes."

"You're wet for me."

"Yes." She lifted her hips, panting, squeezing her buttocks together.

He gently explored, stroking her labia, lightly flicking over her clitoris, then leaving to explore again, coming back to her clit more and more frequently until he settled in a firm, circular rhythm.

Demi practically lifted off the bed. She barely had time to register the change before her orgasm started to build, then swept over her.

She gave in to the waves of pleasure, cried out his name, losing herself completely to the ecstasy, on and on, while she panted and writhed, and then slowly, slowly came down.

Oh, my. She hadn't come that hard in a long, long time.

"God, you are hot, Demi." His whisper was harsh, choked. "That was… Oh, my God."

She came back slowly to herself, aware of his lingering hand, aware of his body so close.

"What…what can I do for you?"

He chuckled. "You just did it."

"But don't you—"

"Hey, Ms. PT." He spoke softly beside her. "What would be the worst thing for my back right now?"

"Oh." She laughed, put her hands to her face, then let them fall beside her head. "Right. Tension and spasms."

"Uh-huh. I'll take a rain check."

She turned her head, on level with his. "This was not… I mean, I really can't—"

"Can't do this again. Right. And before you did this you couldn't do this, either."

"I know."

"And before we went to lunch you couldn't go to lunch, and before—"

"I *know,* I know."

"Does this feel like a mistake?" He moved his hand to lie possessively across her stomach.

"It will tomorrow."

"Do me a favor."

"Uh-oh."

"Hey." He gave her an affectionate pinch. "Since I just did the hardest work of my entire life staying still with my back relaxed while every instinct was screaming at me to plunge inside you, I think I'm due a small favor."

She giggled. "What?"

"Spend the night."

Demi arched away from him. "Colin, I cannot spend—"

"You know what, Demi?"

She sighed. "What?"

"If you want to be happier, we need to get you out of that rut of negativity, change it to a positive can-do attitude."

Demi burst out laughing. "Oh, really."

"Repeat after me. 'I can-do some sleeping here tonight.'"

"I can see you're completely insane."

"Very good." He squeezed her abdomen. "Next. 'I can-do lunch sometimes with Colin.'"

"I can see where this is going."

"Excellent. And the most important can-do is this one. 'I can-do Colin whenever he wants me to.'"

She was giggling so hard she snorted, which made her giggle even harder. "You always get what you want?"

"Doesn't everyone?"

"No!"

He was still grinning, and he looked so pleasant and relaxed it was impossible to imagine he'd been unable to move so recently. And hard to believe he was the same man who'd stalked out of her office last September and stalked back into it three weeks earlier.

"Stay, Demi." His voice was gentle, nearly tender. He was idly stroking her stomach, brushing lightly over her breasts. "I will need your help again in the morning."

She pretended to look suspicious. "With what?"

"You know, ironing my shirts, cooking me breakfast."

"Ha!"

"Okay, how about another massage? I'm liable to be stiff." He raised an eyebrow. "Of course most men wake up stiff..."

Demi groaned. "Saw that one a mile away."

"Stay. It's cold out. Might snow tomorrow."

"Really?"

"No. Stay."

She laughed, loving this crazy, intimate, funny time. "I shouldn't."

"I know."

Demi sighed, thinking about her career, her absolute adherence to the principles of her practice. How could she toss them aside so carelessly now? Just because Colin was hot?

No. Not just that. Because he was hot and she also suspected that he needed her, and she was starting to wonder if she needed some of what he could give her, too. At least right now. She wasn't the forever woman for him, and he wasn't the forever man for her, but…

"Stay?"

They'd have to talk about this, about him starting up with another therapist if he wanted to keep pushing her over the lines. The idea lightened her mood. She turned toward him, leaned over and kissed his forehead.

"I'll stay. But just this one time."

"Right, Demi." He chuckled in the darkness and put his arm all the way around her. "Just this one time."

8

MIRACLES COULD HAPPEN. Demi knew, because she managed to extract herself from Colin's bed that morning, give him another massage, more medication, help him get up and standing and leave the apartment without jumping him. What's more, he behaved remarkably well, not making more than a token protest at her insistence on impersonal contact.

Not to say this miracle had been easy to achieve. Demi had woken slowly, aware of him beside her as she had been at intervals all night long. The desire to wrap herself around him and fall back to sleep, or slowly stroke him awake to make love to her was so strong she had to force herself to lie still. Even then, she'd spent several minutes listening to Colin's slow breathing, reveling in that lovely feeling of waking up next to someone special. How special? She wasn't sure, couldn't shake the certainty that Colin was attracted to her because of what she was doing for him, and what she was bringing him at a low point in his life, not because of who she was.

Eventually, reason crowded in and forced her out of bed and into efficiency. But those had been really lovely minutes. And she'd guiltily enjoyed the taste of faux-domesticity between them, even if she'd gone firmly into caretaker role the second he woke.

Demi liked him. She really, really liked him. The way her body had responded to his touch...dangerous stuff. But more than that, she'd come to admire and respect his struggle. He was more than the babe-ogling high-fiving dude she originally thought. Much more than the bitter man he'd become when the accident so abruptly took his golden-boy status away.

She brought herself back to reality in her office and glanced at her watch. One more client before the day was over. Maybe she should call Colin and ask how he was doing? She wasn't sure what protocol to follow for clients she'd had sexual contact with because there wasn't any protocol like that. But she couldn't manage to regret what had happened. One slip, one night. If Colin wanted to keep some kind of sexual relationship going, he could find another PT. Otherwise, they'd keep on platonically as before. Either way, she wasn't going to start panting after him. She'd done plenty of panting last night in his bed, with his fingers on her and over her and into her. Oh, my God, she'd already had to duck into the bathroom once today and bring herself off thinking about it. All day today, seasonably cold in the upper forties, she'd been practically running a fever.

Her client was late, as he usually was. Fred Cranger had a rotator-cuff injury that she suspected had healed enough for him to be recovering on his own. But he was a top-notch hypochondriac and kept coming up with new pains in new places that needed her attention.

Shrug. Okay. Her time, his dime...

Fred finally showed up full of his usual apologies and phantom pain. After he left, she headed out for a run, then showered and got ready for a dinner date with Wesley, only checking her voice mail three or four dozen times.

Okay, not that many. But she did check too many times, even telling herself severely that he'd either call or not, and there was no point—

Phone.

She pounced on it, peering at the display screen.

Colin. *Yes.* Demi took a second to breathe so she wouldn't answer too eagerly.

Ready, set, go. "Hi, Colin, how are you feeling?"

"Not terrible."

Just his voice was making her hot. Two words, he'd said. Two! She was really in fantasy-lustland here. "Discouraged by the setback?"

"It's my own fault." Yes, he was discouraged.

"We'll get you back on track quickly. Setbacks are really common. Just keep thinking positive thoughts. And, uh, no more running today…"

He chuckled briefly. "Yeah, I promise."

"Good."

Awkward silence while they were probably both trying to calculate whether it was appropriate to keep the conversation professional or turn it personal. And right there was the reason Demi should have stayed out of his bed.

Except…she'd had so much fun in it.

"I was going to call you earlier but I was afraid you'd have wall-to-wall appointments today."

"I did, actually." She gave a stupid laugh over nothing funny.

More awkward silence.

This was crazy. They'd crossed a line they weren't supposed to, way before they knew each other well enough to, and now they were being exposed by the fact that they had nothing to say to each other.

"I want to see you, Demi."

Demi closed her eyes blissfully, pleasure zipping through

her body and settling in places it shouldn't. *Ohhh, my*. The way he'd said that, as if he couldn't possibly last more than a few hours without her…

Her eyes sprang open. Wait! Brilliant idea! "I'm having dinner tonight with my friend Wesley. Want to come along?"

"Friend?" He sounded skeptical.

"Uh-huh. You'd like him. We're meeting at Joe Bar at seven. I can drive if it's tough on your back." He agreed somewhat hesitantly, and made arrangements for Demi to pick him up at his place.

She ended the call feeling positively smug. Perfect. She could see Colin, but with a chaperone, making it clear this was not a date. *And* she could show him how one of her favorite people had come to terms with life after an injury that ended his competitive career.

First she needed to clear her brilliant idea with Wesley, though she was sure he wouldn't object. She dialed his number, feeling giddy at the prospect of seeing Colin again, even knowing she shouldn't be playing with this fire.

But…since when had she ever been sensible when it came to men? She had girlfriends who could pick and choose, this one, that one, this characteristic, that one. But Demi just felt. And when she felt that wild lust starting for someone, she knew it was trouble. Even throwing herself in that fire time after time and being repeatedly burned to a crisp hadn't diminished her optimism.

Silly girl.

At least she knew right from the outset that there was no happy ever after in the offing for her and Colin. Even if he did decide to find another PT and dated Demi for a while, eventually when he accepted what had happened to him, when he was ready to rejoin life pretty much as he'd known it, he'd naturally gravitate toward other types of women. Hadn't he said Stephanie was more like his beer-drinking sax teacher than his sedate mother? And that she ran marathons? Demi could just picture her. Tall, slender, athletic, big boobs, perfect white teeth, long wavy hair, a penchant for miniskirts and stilettos, which she could walk in like she was barefoot...

Everything quiet stay-at-home Demi wasn't.

Wesley picked up. "Hey, Demi."

"I thought I was going to go to voice mail there."

"I was in the shower. We still on tonight?"

"Absolutely, but..."

"Ye-e-es?"

"I've invited someone to join us."

"To join us? Well that sounds formal. Who is he?"

Demi frowned. "How did you know it's a he?"

"Because if it was a girlfriend you wouldn't be so nervous that you'd say something like, 'I've invited someone to join us.'"

She giggled. "Okay, okay. It's—"

"Colin Russo."

"What?" She pulled the phone from her ear and stared at it as if she was afraid it would bite. "Now you're freaking me out."

"Who else would it be?"

"Come on, there's no way you'd know that."

"Okay, okay, lucky guess. So who did the inviting?"

"He did." She grimaced. "Well, no, I did, sort of."

"Hmmm. Looking into my crystal ball I discover that he wanted to see you, but you said you were already seeing me, and then you invited him because it's—"

"*Where* did you put the surveillance equipment around here?" Demi noisily banged open a kitchen cabinet, pretending to look. "You must have installed it that night you were here eating Thai noodles."

"Nah. That one was easy. You would never initiate social time with a client, so the call must have come from him. And because you are a very ethical woman, and also scared to death of what you feel for him—"

"Now, wait a second."

He chuckled. "Congratulations, Demi! The unattainable hot guy wants you after all!"

She scoffed, feeling an unwelcome thrill. "Like that means anything."

"Okay, Ms. Low Self-esteem, why doesn't it?"

"Think about it. He's miserable, lonely, on the rebound from being dumped, and guess who's here to make him feel better?"

"Demi." Wesley made a sound of frustration. "Either you're hopeless or fishing for reassurance."

"As I recall, you were in the same situation he is. What did you do? You asked me out, too."

"Oh. Uh. Well." He cleared his throat. "So, um, still the same time and place tonight?"

She laughed. "Yes. And it would help if you'd find a nice, subtle way to talk about your new life postaccident and how rewarding it is. No sugarcoating, but some of the positives he can't see yet."

"Ah, Demi. My sweet devious saint. If that eases your conscience over the burning lust you feel for him, then yes, I'm happy to."

"Thanks, I think. See you soon." She hung up the phone, positively giddy. See? This wasn't a date. It was nothing like a date. This was a way Demi the PT could help her client navigate the rest of his life.

And what a damn fine job she was doing.

COLIN STEPPED OFF his building's elevator and went through the double doors into the chilly evening where he'd wait for Demi to pick him up. He was still moving carefully, but he'd come back from this latest injury a lot faster than he'd feared, thanks to big doses of anti-inflammatory meds and Demi's quick intervention. With her magic hands.

From what he remembered, his own hands had done some magic for her, too. *Man.* That was some unbelievably sexy stuff. He hadn't stopped thinking about it since he woke up this morning, to find Demi transformed back into brisk PT Anderson, a persona that had started amusing rather than annoying him.

Because he'd discovered PT Anderson's secret. Under that cool professional exterior, she was one of the hottest, most sensual women he'd ever met. The juxtaposition drove him wild. How he'd managed to lie still watching her come, he had no idea. Fear of pain must be a more powerful driving force than he thought. That, and the certainty that if he'd pushed their sexual contact any further, she'd have bolted.

Her initial reluctance, her gradual arousal, her climax—he might as well have a video of the event, it was so clear in his mind. Not to mention he'd played that mental video over and over and over, hearing her gasps, her moans, feeling her soft skin and her wetness under his fingers. She'd opened completely, lost all inhibition, become a totally sexual creature responding to him.

He wanted more. He wanted it all. He wanted to make love to her in every possible position in every possible location that didn't get them arrested. Starting tonight.

On cue, a car pulled into the circle in front of his building, driven by a dark-haired woman. A bright yellow car. A bright yellow Volkswagen Beetle.

Good God. First he'd break his back getting into that toy, and then it would turn him bisexual.

She pulled up in front of him, grinning, and he forgot all about the ridiculous car, and everything else that his consciousness might be trying to register, because his passionate mystery woman was here. Tonight she wore a turquoise scoop-neck top that made her pale skin even more enticing, and set off her dark hair in a stark and striking contrast. Her lips were a maroon shade that emphasized their beautiful shape and made him realize with a sudden shock that he'd never kissed her.

He would tonight.

"How do you expect me to get in that tiny excuse for a vehicle and ever be able to walk again?"

"There's tons of room. You'll be amazed."

He wasn't sure *amazed* was the right word, but he did fit comfortably, and he liked the intimacy of being in a car with her, even though his masculinity was as threatened by the yellow bug as it was not being behind the wheel on a date with a woman.

Another surprise awaited him: Demi drove like a NASCAR professional. Totally unexpected, but it only added to her allure. A shy woman who in certain areas liked to live on the edge. The road. And the bedroom.

They reached the bar a short time later—certainly shorter than if he'd been driving. Parking was kind to them; she found a space around the corner on Broadway and they walked to tree-lined Roy Street. Joe Bar turned out not to be the hip bar he'd expected, but a neighborhood coffee shop that served beer, wine and food along with various versions of java. It made more sense that Demi would be drawn to a place like this, friendly and low-key, with green walls, dark wood and enough paintings to make Colin suspect it doubled as gallery space.

Her friend Wesley was a tall, good-looking guy with dark hair, blue eyes and an athletic build, who greeted Demi with obvious affection. Colin kept his expression pleasant, hiding the jab of jealousy that sneaked up on him. Good move, because when Demi introduced them and they shook hands, Wesley's eyes were assessing, but friendly, not at all threatened or threatening.

They ordered sandwiches, crepes—Joe Bar's specialty— and beers, chatting easily about a movie Wesley had seen recently with his girlfriend, then about the Seahawks' season. Upstairs, they found a table and arranged themselves around it.

"So I guess I don't need to ask how you and Demi met." Wesley gestured between them with his beer.

"Same way you and I did." Demi smiled at Colin, and turned back to Wes.

"That right?" Colin didn't like thinking of her hands all over Wesley's impressive body, so he decided Demi had treated him for something wrong with his foot, and that he had hideous feet.

"Wes had a traumatic brain injury."

"Damn." Colin sucked air in through his teeth, immediately regretting the childish foot joke. "I can't imagine there's any other kind."

Wesley chuckled. "No, you don't hear about many 'pleasurable brain injuries.'"

"How did it happen?" He lowered his beer. "If you don't want to talk about it…"

"Car accident." Wesley toasted Demi, eyes softening. "She got me walking again."

"You couldn't *walk?*" Colin tried to imagine his body betraying him to such an extent, or the rage and impotence that kind of disability could engender. He'd had a baby booboo in comparison.

"I couldn't move much at all right after it happened. Amazing how you come back from that shit."

"Incredible." If Wesley hadn't told him, Colin never

would have known, though he had noticed a slight shuffle in Wesley's stride. "I bet that took a lot of hard work."

"Yeah." He said it offhandedly, but the expression on Demi's face told him how much Wesley had suffered. "You get used to it. The hardest part was not being able to run anymore."

"You ran?" Colin dragged his attention away from the gorgeous sight of Demi's neck curving down to the low scoop of her top, from which peeked two beautiful breasts his hands had had the intense pleasure of exploring the night before.

"Wes was a marathoner." Demi's voice was quietly matter-of-fact, which was somehow more horrifying than if she'd been pouring on the sympathy. "New York, Boston, all the big ones. He took fourth in Minneapolis three years ago."

"No kidding." Colin took two seconds to be impressed before the obvious hit him. *Was* a marathoner. The accident took that away. His beer suddenly tasted sour. He dug into his sandwich and could barely taste it.

"And you did Ironmen?" Wesley asked.

Did Ironmen. He and Wesley had lots in common. "Yeah."

"I'm sorry." Like Demi, Wes spoke quietly, but it was clear he knew what Colin had suffered, and for once Colin didn't mind the sympathy. "It sucks. No way around it."

Demi was looking at him expectantly, and it hit him why she'd arranged this little evening. Not for herself. She'd done this for him. So he could talk to someone who knew exactly what he was going through.

Part of him was immediately pissed off. She'd manipulated him into this.

Part of him was immediately hurt. She hadn't included him so she could get near him again as soon as possible. She was still treating him. PT Anderson.

Part of him was humbled and pleased. This wasn't part

of her job. She wasn't getting paid for this. She'd gone out of her way to help him in a very personal way. Maybe she did this for all her clients, but he doubted it.

Okay. He took a deep breath. Showing weakness wasn't his strong suit, but he couldn't repay Demi for this kindness by being rude. "How did you come back?"

"Part of me never will. Facing that was the hardest. And because I did come back so far so fast, it's still a battle, because I keep thinking, well, why not keep improving? But brain damage is brain damage and I've got it. I won't run again. But there were some really dark days when I thought I wouldn't even walk again. So I try to be grateful and I do succeed a lot of the time. It's hard to keep that perspective. It's doubly hard to rewire your whole life's focus."

"No kidding."

"And there's that other shit that happens, which people don't tell you about. Even Demi."

"What?" She pretended outrage. "Are you implying I'm somehow imperfect?"

"Of course not." Wesley grinned and briefly stroked her back. Colin managed not to grit his teeth, but he didn't love the easy, intimate way Wesley touched her. That was starting to feel like his job.

"What other stuff?" He had a feeling he knew.

"The way people disappear. Friends you used to train with. You realize that's all you had in common with some of them. And for others, you've come to represent their worst nightmare and they can't handle the change. My girlfriend dumped me. And it was years before my mother could look at me without bawling."

Colin nodded, unable to speak. He was angry on Wesley's behalf and every other poor sucker whose life kicked him in the teeth. And he was suddenly and savagely angry at Stephanie, who ran from his broken body to Nick's still-whole one, as if triathlons were all she valued about him.

"Relax, Colin." A hand landed on his arm, and he realized he was holding his beer in a death grip. "Breathe. I don't want you stuck back in bed."

It took a second for him to focus on Demi and realize what she'd just said, but when it registered, his anger fled, and he gave her a slow, intimate grin. "You don't?"

There. A blush the color of roses. He loved doing that to her. Especially when it was a flush of intense pleasure instead of embarrassment, the way it had been last night.

Wesley was grinning between them, but stopped abruptly when he met Colin's eyes. Not manly to be caught gooping over another guy's budding relationship. Colin respected that. "Sorry to have gone on about the head injury, Colin. I don't mean to be a downer."

"You can't be," Colin said. "I'm living similar stuff every day."

"There are silver linings, as Demi no doubt has told you."

"Oh, only about four million times."

Demi glared at him. "Hey, it helps *and* it's true."

"She's right." Wesley shrugged. "You might not be there yet, but life does get better. You find out who your friends are. You find out who you are. Marathons are what I did, not who I was."

Colin quirked an eyebrow, not sure he was buying all the happy-ending crap. He still couldn't totally let go of his dream of Hawaii. Maybe he never would be able to. "Who are you now?"

"A teacher. A coach. A good friend. A better man."

In spite of his cynicism, Colin couldn't help a flash of hopefulness. "So you're telling me you prefer your life now?"

"In some ways, absolutely. I'm less selfish. I'm more about helping other people, less about what I can do for myself. I discovered I love kids. I discovered I want to be married and have some. Before, it was just about pushing harder, going faster. I like myself better now."

"I like you better, too." Demi grinned at him, then squeezed Colin's forearm. "You think *you* were a pain in the ass…"

He pretended deep offense. "No, I absolutely do not. What are you talking about?"

She snorted. God, she was beautiful. The longer he was around her the more he wanted her all to himself. "Let's just say Wesley made you look like an amateur."

Wesley nodded. "I was pretty angry."

"You were pretty badly injured." Colin lifted his beer in a respectful salute. "I just fell off my bike. Any kid can do that."

"Hey, your injury is a tough one, Colin." Demi plonked her beer down on the table. His heart turned over. Not only because he really wanted to kiss her, but because she always supported him, in her quiet way, didn't let him put himself down or get discouraged. Maybe there was something to that positive-thinking crap.

Demi was a good person. And he really wanted her to-night.

They switched to lighter topics, talking about the up-coming winter, skiing plans that couldn't happen for either guy, alternate suggestions that went from the sublime—a cruise in the Bahamas—to the ridiculous—building igloos up in the mountains.

Not long after 9:00 p.m. the staff started clearing up. Colin wanted to cheer. The place closed early, hallelujah. He'd re-ally enjoyed meeting Wesley, but he was dying to get Demi alone.

They said good-night outside the café, and Colin and Demi walked to the sunshine-yellow abomination that was her car.

"How's your back holding up?"

"Not bad. A little sore. I'm due for more meds." He slid her a sideways grin. "And a long, slow massage would really help."

"Uh-huh." She unlocked the car. "Make an appointment."

"Okay." He climbed in gingerly. "How about my place in ten minutes? Five the way you drive?"

"I'll have to check my schedule."

Her reply was so unexpected he was stunned into silence. Horny silence. She wasn't going to fight him?

The idea made him fold his hands in his lap to hide the evidence of his...anticipation. "Thanks for introducing me to Wesley."

"You're welcome." She glanced at him before she tore out of their parking place and roared down the street. "He's a good guy."

"You were trying to help me."

"Well, yes. Did it work?"

"It did. Not that I had any doubts I'd make it to the other side of this, but..." He shrugged. "Okay, maybe once in a while."

"It's impossible not to doubt."

He nodded, bemused that he could show weakness around her. When had he met someone who simply accepted him as he was? To his parents, he was always the weird kid who didn't march to his father's military drum, a creative dreamer of a boy, more into moving his body than moving his mind, but sensitive and not a joiner. He fit no type his dad could relate to, so it followed Colin was the wrong type. His brothers and his father joined everything that would take them—clubs, military branches, associations, everything—while Colin was in the basement playing his sax, making his knives or alone out on the road, running to exhaustion.

"As I said, I appreciate that you arranged for me to meet Wesley tonight." He sighed loudly and clasped his hands behind his head. "But I kind of hoped you'd invited me because you couldn't wait to see me again."

"I didn't *mind* seeing you again." The look she shot him this time was just shy of flirtatious. "Because I was worried about your physical condition."

"That's it?"

"Oh, yes." Her next glance inched closer to sexual invitation. "What other reason would there be?"

"Can't think of a thing." He wouldn't share his "physical condition" at the moment. A hard-on from contemplating what they might do tonight. "It's nice seeing you in something other than black, Demi. You look beautiful."

"Hmm."

"Hmm?" He reached over and put his hand to the back of her neck, loving the feel of her skin and the softness of her hair cascading over his fingers. "You *are* beautiful."

"You *are* delusional." She put her foot down and they shot ahead, nearly at the exit for his building already.

"In a hurry?"

"No. Why?"

He laughed, massaging the muscles at the base of her neck. "You drive like you're desperate."

She kept her gaze straight ahead. "Not desperate, no."

"I think I am."

This time he earned a frowning glance. "I am pretty sure I don't want to ask this, but for what?"

"To figure out what this is between us." He laid his hand alongside her cheek. "And what we're planning to do about it."

9

WHAT WERE THEY planning to do about it?

Demi took Roosevelt Way to Forty-seventh Street. At Forty-seventh, she'd go left, left again and be at Colin's place.

And then what?

Maybe she already knew the answer to his question, though she'd responded only with a joke about pleading the fifth. Certainly being with him was what she wanted. But not if Colin was going to keep seeing her as a therapist. That one night they spent together had pushed her ethical boundaries to the max. Demi could lose her license if it came out that she'd had sexual relations with a client.

She was just having a hard time seeing how making Colin come so hard he yelled for mercy was wrong in any way.

It was important they talked this out and that both of them were clear on what was at stake, legally, emotionally and, with his back only barely recovering, physically.

How did she get herself into this situation? Anyone in her right mind would drop Colin off, say good-night and drive home.

But around Colin, Demi wasn't entirely sure she was ever in her right mind.

"You can park in the visitor lot there." He pointed to the one opposite the building's entrance.

Demi came to a stop, neither in the lot nor by the entrance. "*Am* I parking?"

"Yes."

"You've decided this, huh."

"Yes."

She turned to him in the dim light of the car's interior. "And what, then I'm coming upstairs with you?"

"Yes."

"For…"

"A private tour of my knife collection." He grinned mischievously. "I want to make one for you. You can tell me what type you'd like."

"More gifts?" She shook her head, clucking her tongue.

"Well, gee." Colin was all innocence. "Making knives again is part of my therapy, right?"

"Hmm."

A car pulled up behind her. Demi turned into the visitor lot, chose a space and killed the engine. "I think we need to talk about—"

"Upstairs." He opened the door and got out into air that had a distinctly wintery bite. "If I stay in your car any longer I'll start wanting to wear pink."

Demi sat for two beats, then sighed and got out. Colin was striding well, tall, straight and almost graceful. He was nearly at the entrance when she caught up to him. He gallantly held open the door to the building's lobby, dominated by a table on which sat an immense dried flower arrangement that looked as if it had done plenty of time there.

In the elevator they were saved from awkward silence by a woman on her cell phone loudly discussing every detail of a so-so date the entire way up. She was still talking when they got off on Colin's floor.

"Remind me not to ask her out." He shuddered, then unlocked his apartment door and pushed it open to let Demi go first. "Home sweet home."

"Thank you." She waited until he'd closed the door, before confronting him, hands on her hips. "Colin, we need to talk about what's going—"

"Let me pour us a drink first." He grinned when she shot him a look. "You like cognac?"

She was taken aback. Her dad had loved the stuff, let Demi taste it now and then, but she didn't know anyone her age who enjoyed it. "I do, actually."

"Good." He moved into his kitchen, reached up to take a bottle out of the cabinet above his refrigerator.

"You're moving well."

"You think so, huh." He winked at her. "I have a damn good physical therapist."

"Thank you." She watched him pour out two good measures of brandy into modest-sized snifters, surprised at how comfortable she was, even though she generally felt a combination of annoyance and unease in fancy condos. And she wasn't sure she should be in Colin's in the first place.

"Let's go in the living room?"

"Sure." She followed him and sat on the couch, half dismayed, half pleased when he sat next to her. Close.

This was going to make it hard to keep her logical mind on full alert for their discussion.

"Cheers." He clinked his glass with hers, looking steadily into her eyes, flustering her further. She watched him sip, watched his very fine mouth savoring the liqueur before he swallowed.

Mmm, yes. Flustered. She raised her glass in self-defense.

The sweet, fiery taste was warming, elegant and comforting. "Very good."

"Glad you like it." He took her hand, held it idly, rubbing his fingers over hers. "So talk to me, Demi. Tell me what reasons you're cooking up for why you can't be with me tonight. Why you can't come into my bedroom and let me undress you, then touch every part of your body. Why it's such a bad idea to invite you to touch every part of mine until neither of us can stand waiting anymore and we give each other enough pleasure to make us scream."

Demi half laughed, half gasped, cheeks hot, chest hot, and everything female about her very, very hot. "You're not playing fair."

"Oh, and by the way?" He toasted her with his snifter. "You're fired."

That got through. Barely. "What?"

"Yup." He was irritatingly cheerful. "You're no longer my physical therapist."

"Wait, are you serious? You're firing me?"

He nodded.

She was totally confused now. Wasn't this what she wanted, for him to make this exact decision?

And yet, as she sat here with him now, it hit her that treating Colin's injuries, helping unlock the man from the bitter cage he was in…that had come to mean a lot to her. And obviously nothing to him if he was happily ditching that relationship in order to get laid. Any woman could help him with that.

"Is there any other way we can sleep together?"

Demi drank more brandy, then drained the glass, swallowing convulsively, feeling demeaned. "No."

"Then that's it. We're clear." His smile died at the look on her face. "Uh…okay, no, we're not clear."

"You're leaving therapy so we can have sex tonight."

"Yes, exactly." He looked hopeful, then gradually more and more pained. "Okay, this is one of those times when I'm being a clueless guy, isn't it. Because I thought you wanted this, too."

"I do."

"So…"

Right. Male logic. Made sense to him. And outwardly to her. But inwardly… She couldn't talk to him about her reaction because it would mean admitting more vulnerability than she cared to.

"It feels as if my body is worth more to you than my… expertise." To her horror, her voice emerged shaky instead of assured.

"Whoa, Demi. No, that's not what this is about." He took her shoulders, tipped her face up to his, warm and concerned. Where had Cranky Colin gone? She'd helped bring this part of him back to life. What would happen to him without her? "I gave this a lot of thought. You're the best PT I've ever had, and I'm not giving you up lightly. But our sessions in that massage room were pure torture. Your hands on me were torture. Then after the other night, when I finally got my hands on you…"

He blew out a silent whistle.

She nodded. "It was hard on me, too."

"Oh, you think so?" He was smugly skeptical.

Demi bristled. *"Yes."*

"Sorry. When it comes to being hard, trust me, I win."

He could make her laugh even when she was anxious and confused. Maybe the more appropriate question was the reverse of one she'd asked already—what would happen to *her* without *him?* "One more thing."

"Go ahead."

"What happens after we do this tonight? We're finished and you rehire me? Or we're done?"

"No. No. Not like that." He dragged his hand down his face. "Obviously I did this all wrong. Here it is, then. I want us to hang out, Demi. I want to ask you to dinner sometimes, or to go biking or eventually running together. We can go to jazz concerts, ball games, movies. Maybe we can go virtual-necklace shopping. Or hey, I know, sit at your place and *knit* together."

Her laughter had a slightly raw edge. "That sounds way hot."

"Bottom line, I don't just want you tonight. I'll want you tomorrow, too. More than once, likely. And the day after that and the day after that…"

She smiled at his eagerness, more confused than happy, and not sure why that was the case. His view was clear. His little speech—of remarkable length for Colin—put to rest her fears that he was rebounding, vulnerable, and Demi just happened to be there. He didn't sound like a man on his way to falling for her. He just wanted company as he went through his recovery. Maybe that would be all right, and they could—

"Stop." He put gentle fingers to her forehead, gazed earnestly into her face. "You're overthinking this."

God, his eyes were beautiful. "You're right."

"It's not that complicated."

His mouth was beautiful, too. "It's not really uncomplicated, either, Colin, because—"

"Shh. Only positive thoughts." His hand moved down her face, his fingers brushed across her mouth, making it tingle.

Then his lips took their place.

Ohhh, my. The second his mouth touched hers she realized they'd never kissed. And oh, how fabulous it was. Lingering, gentle kisses, tasting, tempting her to want more.

"You fired me." She tilted her head to let him explore,

under her ear, down her jaw, then down the length of her neck. "That's never happened to me before."

"I guess no one has wanted you as much as I do."

His words gave her a brief thrill. Yes, he wanted her. Not only in his bed tonight, but again and into the future, as companion, friend, lover... For a time, anyway.

She was still trying to wrap her brain around her reaction to that one, but it had started shutting down functions except pleasure receptors, so she might have to let the concept lie for now.

"Demi." He spoke against her lips.

"Mmm."

"Would you like to move into my bedroom?"

"Well. As a physical therapist, though no longer yours, I would advise you not to try anything athletic on your couch. So yes."

"I'll keep that in mind." He got up, only slightly stiff, and held out his hand.

"So you're not going to show me your knives?"

He chuckled. "How about in the morning."

"I'm spending the night?"

"Yes."

"You're bossy, you know that?"

"Yes."

Then he was kissing her again, long, heady kisses that made something inside her melt and harden at the same time. Which didn't sound possible, but that was exactly how it felt. Maybe it would always be that way between them. The more she felt, the more she'd want to protect herself.

But tonight...she was going to give herself over to this physical experience with him, because they both wanted it, and there was no longer any reason not to, though a court of law might not entirely agree, since she was going to be in bed with him roughly fifteen minutes after their professional relationship ended.

Demi had a feeling Colin wouldn't tell the authorities. She wouldn't, either.

"I'm bossy, too," she announced.

"No kidding."

"And as your former PT, I'm going to insist that we proceed tonight in a way that will put you at minimal risk of further injury."

"Oh?" He backed them up until the bed stopped him. "And what does this plan entail?"

She planted a finger in the center of his chest and pushed gently. "You. Naked."

"So far I like it."

"On your back on the bed, with a pillow under your knees, not moving at all. No matter what I do to you."

"Uh…" He pretended to look alarmed. "I *think* I like it. Do I? You're just bossy, right? Not a sado-dominatrix?"

"Not." She pushed harder on his chest, until he sat on the edge of the bed. "But I strongly suggest you do what I say."

"Or else?" He ran his hands up the outsides of her thighs, clasped her around the waist and nuzzled between her breasts.

She smiled, caressed his head. "Or else you might hurt yourself. And then we wouldn't get to try this again for weeks."

He let go of her abruptly, looked up in mock-panic. "Don't say that."

Demi burst into more giggles. This man was such a far cry from the sour cynic who'd first needed her help. She liked him more and more. "Let's get you out of these clothes."

"Let's." He raised his shirt over his head, and even though she'd seen that torso naked before, touched most every inch of it, she still took in a breath of pleasure at the sight.

"You are a stunningly built man, Colin Russo."

"You." He spread his knees and hugged her between them. "Are so right."

Again she laughed, pushing him gently back on the bed. "Down, ego boy."

He hauled himself up until his whole body was on the mattress, and slid the pillow under his knees as instructed, to help align his back optimally. "I'm down."

"Pants, too."

He pulled them off. "They're down."

"And…" She quirked an eyebrow and pointed to his boxer briefs, snapping her fingers, trying to look stern. My God, the man was a sight. She'd seen parts of him under the sheet while massaging him, but the sight of that torso connecting so gracefully to his gorgeously muscled legs…mmm.

"I'm shy." He was already pulling them off.

"Yeah, I can see that."

"Can you?" He was laughing at her now, half-erect, his penis a thing of awe-inspiring power and beauty.

"Oh, my."

"All yours, Demi." His grin took on a tenderness that made her lower her eyes to collect herself. This wasn't about love, this was about hanging out. And my goodness, was he ever.

"Remember, don't move." She backed up a few steps, holding herself straight, the way she'd learned in the ballet class her mother made her and her sister take. Predictably, Carrie had been a gazelle, Demi a duck. But not tonight. Tonight she was Colin's most fabulous sexual fantasy.

She forced herself to meet his dark gaze again; this time she was ready and the contact no longer overwhelmed her.

This was her show. She might not be one of the red-hot babes he usually dated, but he wanted her, and he was going to get the best she had to offer.

Grateful for the bracing brandy, she grasped the hem of her top and eased it up and off, letting the material muss her hair, not bothering to smooth it back off her face.

"Oh, Demi." He was holding still as instructed, watching intently.

She smiled at him sensually, unhooked her bra and brought her forearms close, letting it slide off while her breasts pushed together in an offering meant to impress.

If the way his eyes bugged out of his head was any indication, it did. And he was no longer riding at half-mast, but full.

Gaining confidence, she drew her elbows back, wet her index finger and painted circles around and over each nipple until a whimper sounded from the bed.

"Don't move," she said sharply.

"You're killing me."

"Am I?" She pretended surprise, put her hands to the stretch waistband of her skirt and eased it off, rocking her hips side to side. "Make sure you're relaxing totally. You don't want to strain—"

"My *back*'s not in danger of straining." He gestured to his rigid cock, thick and golden, his balls drawn tight underneath. "But if you keep doing that, I might have to get a sling for my—"

"Shh. Arm down. No moving."

He groaned. "Yes, ma'am."

She stood before him, naked except for her underpants, and caressed her stomach, undulating her hips, then dipped a hand under the soft cotton of her panties.

Sharp intake of breath from the bed.

"You like this? Me, too, Colin." She spoke in a low, languid voice. "It feels amazing. Very warm. Very soft. And getting kind of slippery."

He responded with something that sounded like "ungh." Demi felt like purring. Modern man reduced to caveman essentials.

"Do you want to see me?"

Another grunt, head nodding, face pained.

She moved the underpants down, then stood quietly, letting him look.

He struggled to sit; she held up her hand. "Stop."

His body fell obediently back onto the mattress. "Help... me..."

She giggled, ruining her seductive-siren routine, but who cared? Colin had responded beyond her wildest dreams, and she no longer felt the need to compete with whatever female she thought he wanted most.

A few steps and she was at the edge of the bed. She climbed up, prowling like a cat about to pounce, pressing kisses to his knees, thighs, hip bones, and then finally, to the beautiful, hard-soft length of his cock, inhaling his male scent.

"Mmm." She ran her tongue from base to tip, took the first inch into her mouth and played there with lips, tongue and teeth. Grasping him gently, she fingered his balls, until his hands curled into fists, and his breath was nearly painful to listen to.

"Demi..."

"Condom?"

"In the nightstand drawer."

"Excellent." Demi retrieved one and rolled it over his erection, lifted her leg to straddle him and positioned herself directly over his penis, where she paused to heighten the anticipation. Then, closing her eyes, she sank one slow inch, thighs starting to tremble as his cock touched her, nudged, pushed just inside her.

"Oh, my."

"Demi..."

Then she made the mistake. She opened her eyes and caught his. In seconds, the most extraordinary wave of emotion tumbled over her. She froze, unable to handle the rush that nearly stopped her breath. What was happening? Was she having an anxiety attack?

His hands landed on her hips; he pushed up, and the icy block broke. She sank down onto him as a grateful moan echoed from his mouth, and they moved together, slowly, gracefully, until his arms came up around her and he pulled her down on top of him. In that position, she could only tip her pelvis back and forth, which ground her clitoris against him. Hearing his quickening breath, she knew he was as turned on as she was. Good. This was safely carnal and hot as hell.

She spoke too soon. He turned her face to his, and keeping up the slow, incendiary rhythm of their lovemaking, he touched his mouth to hers. The kiss went on and on, tongues tasting, retreating, lips fitting, refitting, and all the while the glorious friction of his slow slide inside her.

Their faces separated, their eyes locked again, and she was drawn into the depths of his gaze to a degree that terrified and elated her all at once.

This was too much. Way too much. Too intense and too sweet and not at all what was called for here. This was their first time. They hardly knew each other. They were here for hot sex and good laughs.

She lifted off him and began a strong, pumping rhythm he responded to by closing his eyes and urging her on with his hands.

"Yes. That's... Demi... Oh, yes." His breathing became

harsh; his fingers dug into her ass. Her vagina was on fire around him, and she could feel every inch of him inside her; every thrust pulled on her clitoris, building her higher and higher. Sweat broke out on her body. She felt herself gathering for her climax.

"Colin," she whispered. "I'm going to come. Now. It's starting."

He groaned and pushed up with one furious thrust, then blew air harshly through his teeth. She felt him pulsing inside her at the same time that she surrendered to her own ecstasy.

Afterward, she lay on him, fighting a rush of tenderness. *Do not make more of this than it is, Demi.* This wasn't like her. She was perfectly able to date men casually even when sex was part of the equation.

The problem here was that she'd invested too much emotion in Colin's recovery. So it was a damn good thing he'd fired her. Everything she was feeling right now, no matter how intense, no matter how lovely and how wonderful, she had to back away from, slowly—no sudden moves. Because with Colin in this odd place in his life right now, and her emotional overinvestment in his treatment, nothing either of them felt could be trusted.

10

UH-OH. BONNIE KEPT the polite smile pasted on her face, aware that Don had just asked her something. She desperately hit a mental Rewind to see if she could retrieve any of what he'd been talking about.

Nothing. Her panic grew. It wasn't the first time this had happened, and it was inexcusably rude.

They were sitting in her kitchen on a Friday night, sharing a bottle of wine. She'd lit candles for the table, had brought up a small bouquet of mixed sweetheart roses for the centerpiece, set the stage for a romantic evening between two people who still hadn't become lovers, though not for lack of Bonnie trying, and…

Once again, she couldn't keep her mind on what he was saying.

This was not a good sign.

"Ask me again, Don?"

He looked startled, then confused. "Was there something wrong with the way I asked?"

"No. No. Oh no, of course not." She blushed, shaking her head too many times. Don didn't deserve this. He was incredibly sweet, attractive, intelligent, funny and sophis-

ticated. On paper, perfect. So what was wrong with her?
"I just—"

"Wasn't listening."

She didn't know what to say, how to fix it. She couldn't
lie. Her misery grew. "I'm sorry."

"Nah, it's okay." He took a sip of wine, put the glass
down exactly in the center of his napkin as he always did,
making Bonnie want to knock it askew just to see what
would happen. Would he have a panic attack? Become en-
raged? Or simply cease to exist in a small puff of smoke?
"I kind of go on sometimes."

"I'm distracted tonight. Sorry. Some complicated stuff
at the store."

"Yeah? Can I help?"

*Sure, get me out of debt so I don't have to give up the
shop.* She'd gotten a letter from the bank, and it was not
friendly how's-it-going? correspondence. Bonnie had spent
too long in denial, too long telling herself not to worry
about her financial situation, that something would work
out. It hadn't. "Don, you are so sweet, thanks, but no, it's
my burden."

"Okay."

She drank more of her wine, more than she should, especially since Don had been sipping his and she'd been
slugging back healthy gulps. About three inches left in
the bottle; Bonnie was afraid she'd had most of it. But she
was on edge tonight. It was time she really faced that she
was going to lose her store, that she'd have to leave Come
to Your Senses and find somewhere to start over. Where
would she go? What would she do? The possibilities frightened and exhilarated her—in a manic, unnatural way—and
made her extrasensitized, as if everything around her had
become more meaningful and more intense.

Which also meant little things about Don that didn't deserve to be annoying were annoying her. He'd given up so easily when she said she didn't need help, hadn't asked what was wrong or if she wanted to talk about it. Which was ridiculous because he was probably being respectful of her privacy, assuming that if Bonnie wanted to talk, she would.

Seth would have understood that she needed to vent and he would have listened, then offered a solution, which she'd either accept or reject. But at least she'd end up feeling heard and cared for and therefore stronger.

She sucked down more wine, aware the comparison was unfair. Seth had been a friend first, then a lover and intimate friend, and then a friend again for the five years since they'd broken up.

Except…from the beginning he'd been remarkably tuned in to what she needed, even if he was clueless about understanding what *he* needed.

"We should go to the jazz festival one night."

"Oh." Bonnie nodded, thinking it would have been nice before he suggested the date if he'd asked whether she enjoyed jazz.

She didn't.

Mood plummeting further, she drained her glass. Sometimes alcohol gave her a lift, made her chatty and energized, and sometimes it plunged her into a miserable stupor that was very difficult to dig herself out of.

Today was apparently going to be one of the bad times. She should stop now, while she was only mildly behind.

Instead, she poured herself more.

"Whoa." Don chuckled uncomfortably. "Slow down there, girl."

Bonnie gritted her teeth. If he'd said, "This isn't like you. Why are you drinking so much?" that would have been nice. A simple "Hey, what's wrong?" would have worked, too. Pretty much anything but "Whoa, slow down there, girl" as if he was talking to his horse.

Poor Don. She was not being fair to him.

Or maybe she finally was being fair to herself. She didn't love this man. She never would. Her initial attraction and optimism had paled. When was the last time she went out with a guy several times, had been in his apartment and he in hers, and still hadn't slept with him? They'd made out some, but Don never took the bait, and by now she really couldn't care either way.

That wasn't a good sign, either.

"Sorry, Don, I'm having a rough night, I guess."

"I guess." He chuckled again, a humorless cackle that made it clear he was not amused.

Bonnie's teeth could conceivably crack. No sympathy. No empathy.

Don was a dud.

No, no, he'd be fine for the right woman. One who didn't need a deep physical and emotional connection. Bonnie wasn't that woman. It would be kinder to end it now.

Instead of panic, the idea of being free gave her a jolt of excitement.

Then panic.

So? She'd been single plenty in her life. And there was always Seattledates.com to search for someone who suited her better. Crazy to think she'd be lucky enough to hit the jackpot on the first try. Unless she left Seattle. Unless starting over included a complete change. The possibility instantly appealed, though she knew better than to make any major decisions when she was a tipsy disaster of a person.

In any case, first things first. She blew out a breath, then turned to face the music, who was looking thoughtful. "Don, I've been thinking…"

"Yeah, me, too."

She blinked in surprise. "About what?"

"Us."

"Oh. Me, too."

"Good." He looked vastly relieved. It would be so wonderful if he dumped her right now. Sad, bittersweet—it was always bittersweet when the hopes that rode along with a brand-new relationship were crushed. But if he did the dumping then she didn't have to.

"Go ahead, Don." She figuratively crossed her fingers. Now that she'd made the decision to break up, she wanted the whole thing over and done.

He put his hand over hers, his face wreathed in worry. *No, Don, no worries. Pull that plug!* "I was thinking…I should spend the night tonight."

Oh. Crap.

"I am *really* attracted to you, Bonnie." He trailed his fingers up her arm to her shoulder, then curled his hand in the curve of her neck. "I think you're totally hot. And we've waited long enough."

She sat stiffly. It was as if someone had just lifted her blindfold. "*I* should spend the night." "*I'm* really attracted." "*We've* waited enough." No asking how she felt about it or what she wanted, and not seeming to care that she'd already told him she was upset and distracted by bad news tonight.

"Where do I fit into this?"

He looked startled. "What do you mean? I'm saying I want us to have sex tonight."

She laughed, although nothing about this was funny. "I meant what about what I want to do tonight?"

He dragged his chair closer, put his hand on her thigh and smiled earnestly. "You just have to tell me, Bonnie, and we'll do it."

She groaned and dropped her head back in despair, eyes closed. He thought she was already mentally in bed with

him, working out sexual positions. A spectacular miscom-
munication.

"God, Bonnie." He practically lunged at her, burying
his face in her neck and sucking as if she had a snakebite
he needed to treat.

"Don!" She shoved him away. "What are you *doing?*"

He pulled back immediately, looking stunned. "I'm trying to make love to you."

"But I haven't said I wanted you to."

"You dropped your head back and moaned like you were
getting turned on." He was clearly annoyed now. "What, I
have to wait for written permission?"

"No, that's not what I meant. I just…" She sighed. "Look,
we're not on the same page here at all."

"What's not to understand? I want to make love to you."

"And I want to break up with you."

Silence.

Half an hour later, Bonnie closed the door behind Don,
who clumped down the hall, raging loudly.

Instead of feeling relief and doing a happy dance around
her kitchen, she burst into tears, threw herself on the living-
room couch and began what she was afraid would be one
of those endless cries that stopped for a few minutes, only
to start again.

A knock on her door.

"Go away."

"Bonnie, let me in."

Seth. She lifted her head, eyes streaming. "Go away."

"Let me in."

"Leave me alone. Go write another YouTube hit or something."

"Let me in or I'll break the damn door down."

"You're not going to break the damn door down."

"I'm going to try. Let me in."

"For God's sake." She stomped over to the door, sniffling and wiping her eyes, whipped open the lock and whirled around immediately so she could stomp back to the couch, mumbling about what complete and utter poo-balls men were, and why did she have to want one at all, and maybe she would do better turning gay or giving her life to Jesus.

Seth burst into the apartment behind her. "What happened here?"

"What do you mean what happened here?" She stopped stomping, but she didn't feel like talking to him or anyone.

Wait, yes, she did.

No, she didn't. She just wanted her couch.

No, she didn't.

She started crying again.

Arms came around her shoulders; Seth's wide chest pressed against her back, rocking her. "Hey there, what's going on?"

She shook her head.

"I heard Don crashing out of here sounding angry, so I came down the hall and heard you crying." His arms tightened around her. "He better not have—"

"He didn't." She sniffed, wiping her eyes again. "I dumped him."

Seth went very still behind her. "Why?"

Bonnie shrugged, sniffed again. "He wasn't right for me, what do you think?"

"I think you need a tissue."

She did. Seth knew she'd be better discussing what happened after she'd blown her nose and calmed down. But he'd want to listen, he'd want to know and he'd care. Why couldn't he be right for her when he was so…right for her?

"Here." He pushed the tissue at her, stood watching her dry her face and blow her nose, tall, reassuring, hands on his hips, gray eyes narrow with concern.

"Thanks." She started into the kitchen. "Want some wine?"

"Sure. What are you pouring?"

"Wine." She hid a near-hysterical giggle. Mr. Vintage-Snob would be rolling his eyes. "Red."

"What *kind* of red? Cabernet? Merlot? Shiraz?"

"I dunno." She pointed to the bottle, pretending confusion. "But it was sort of harsh, so I dumped a bunch of sugar in it."

Seth snorted and leaned over for a look, gave a whistle. "Nice."

"Don brought it."

"He knows his wine."

"He knows his wine merchant." She got down a glass for Seth, sat by her half-finished one and released a shuddering sigh, giving in to the heavy peace that came after a good cry.

"So you dumped The Don, huh."

"I did." She stared miserably into her glass.

"Regrets?"

"No." She lifted her gaze to his. "None."

"Good." He reached over the table and took her hand. She let him. "Then it was the right move."

Bonnie nodded, looking down at their joined hands. His were so familiar. The freckle on the back of the right one; the scar where his younger brother had whacked him with a toy truck. He had other scars, too, on his body and on his heart. She knew all of them.

And suddenly she was finished fighting, finished struggling against what she felt for Seth. There would never be anyone else for her. The search on Seattledates had been about regaining personal power and self-esteem, not finding another man. She'd never wanted any other man. Not really.

Her gaze lifted to his again. She knew some of her vulnerability showed in her face, and she didn't try to hide it. No more games, no more hiding. If they were meant to be together, they would be. If not, she'd move out altogether, out of state. Maybe go to the other side of the country, like North Carolina or Maine, and start over. Buy a lighthouse and live there alone year-round, listening to the crash of the—

Good God, she'd go completely nuts. What was she thinking?

Pressure on her hand, then her arm. He was pulling her toward him, onto his lap.

Bonnie went, feeling as if she were going back home. She put her arm around his neck, rested her head against his. They sat that way a long time, Bonnie absorbing his strength, comfort and affection.

"Thank you, Seth." She lifted her head.

"For what?"

"Coming to my rescue, making me feel better."

"You're welcome, Bon." He smiled briefly, the goofy, wonderful smile that lit up his face so endearingly. "Remember, he's not the last man in the world."

"Thank God."

"You'll find someone. You're only just starting to look."

His words hurt, and she realized that subconsciously she'd been expecting him to try to get her back, the way he'd tried so many times in the past few months.

He'd learned. Finally. Good for him. Maybe he could really change. She hoped so. Because some lucky woman out there was going to get the finest man in the world.

"I'm thinking of leaving Seattle, maybe Washington." She couldn't believe she'd blurted out the words. She'd only just had the thought minutes ago. Why was she saying it out loud already?

And yet, as the words left her mouth, they became true

in a way she hadn't expected. Another victory for her subconscious.

"Bonnie." He stiffened in shock. "Why?"

"The shop isn't making it. And I need a change. I want to start over somewhere new."

He opened his mouth, closed it again. Stared at her for a long time, then gently pushed back bangs that had fallen into her eyes. His touch was gentle, tender and so sweet it made her heart ache.

"If that's what you want, then it's a good thing."

Her determination developed feet of panicky clay, and she straightened her spine. No, this wouldn't be the easiest decision, but maybe it was best.

"Thank you, Seth."

"I'd miss you. Like crazy."

"I'd miss you, too." The words came out easily, but they had a surreal quality, as if it weren't really possible for her and Seth to separate, as if somehow, sometime, a director would walk into the room and yell, "Okay, cut. Take five, everyone."

"Where are you thinking of going?"

"I don't know. Maine? My oldest brother went there for college. He loved it."

"Yeah," he said miserably. "But it's on the other side of the world."

"It is." She nodded, wishing for a few seconds that he'd beg her not to leave, insist he'd follow her anywhere, marry her, have kids, get a dog and live happily ever after.

But Seth wouldn't do that. Commitment wasn't his thing. And for her to stay sane, she needed to be as far away from him and what he would never give her as she could.

"One question. Promise you'll answer truthfully?"

"Sure." She lifted her head because she suddenly felt as

if she could never get enough of looking at his face, as if she hadn't already memorized every microinch of it.

"If the store was doing well, would you stay?"

"Seth." She gestured, then let her hand drop helplessly to her thighs. "The store *isn't* doing well. What is the point of—"

"You promised to answer the question."

She studied him for a few seconds, knowing the answer without having to think. Seattle was her home. "Yes."

"Okay. Thank you." He pulled her head down against his and closed his arms back around her once more, making her feel safe, protected and loved.

Bonnie closed her eyes, savoring every sensation as deeply as she could, knowing that in a few more weeks they could be saying goodbye forever.

11

"TA DAAA." Bonnie gestured to her computer. "Our new website. What do you think?"

Demi and the other Come to Your Senses residents peered at Bonnie's laptop in the common room. On the screen was a colorful, funky and appealing drawing of their building. On the sidebar, each business had a link over which was superimposed a cartoon of its owner, with features exaggerated to represent the five senses. Jack's face had large, dreamy eyes. Seth's head was turned in profile so his ears were front and center, Angela had gorgeous, plump lips, Demi was giving a flirty wave with both hands and Bonnie rapturously sniffed at some delicious fragrance. The overall effect was casual fun, colorful and very inviting.

"Bonnie, you did a *great* job." Angela put her hand on Bonnie's shoulder. "Really, that is amazing."

"Thanks." Bonnie's smile was brief. She'd been very subdued lately, had even been pleasant to Demi, which meant either she'd mellowed or had completely lost her mind. Demi couldn't claim to adore the woman, but she was worried about her. And given how the others treated her with kid gloves and traded anxious looks behind her back, they were worried, too.

"I love it," Demi said. "I think it sets just the right tone, perfect for the holiday special but also going forward after that."

"Agreed." Jack tipped his head to study it from another angle. "I like me with Bambi eyes."

"Yeah, real cute, Jack." Seth snorted. "Bonnie, you've outdone yourself."

Angela clapped her hands. "Good. Let's have beer to celebrate. I can go downstairs and get some cookies and a—"

"Not me." Bonnie glanced at her watch and hurriedly snapped her laptop closed. "I have to get going."

"Another date?" Demi asked.

"Sort of. Not really." She shoved back her chair, body tense. "More like a...business date."

Seth picked up her computer somberly. "I'll walk you."

"I'm out, too." Jack got up and stretched. "I'm meeting Melissa downstairs in five."

"Hot date?" Angela asked.

"Not really." His grin was unnaturally wide. "Just going to drive out to Seward Park."

Angela wrinkled her brow. "Didn't you guys do a photo shoot there?"

"Uh-huh." Still grinning. Possibly even wider.

"What about you, Demi?" Angela turned to her. "Want to share a beer? Or a six-pack?"

Demi hesitated, squashing the shy demons that said Angela had asked her just to be polite after the rest of her *real* friends couldn't make it.

Then just as quickly she told herself not to react like that anymore. Positive thinking! About time she followed her own advice. She wasn't meeting Colin for another hour and a half. She had plenty of time for a beer.

"I can't stay long, but I'd love to."

"Got a date?" Jack stood swinging his arms back and

forth. He was definitely on edge tonight. Was something going around?

"I'm going to the Earshot Jazz Festival."

"You're going with Colin." He wasn't asking.

She stared at him curiously. "How did you know?"

"You look like someone is lighting firecrackers inside you."

"Yeah?" Demi pointed accusingly. "Well, so do you."

"I rest my case." He left the room, chuckling.

Demi made a growling noise in her throat and turned to Angela. "How can you stand living with these caring, warm and supportive people?"

Angela burst into giggles on her way to the refrigerator. "I know, I know, it's painful. Jack was antsy as hell tonight, though, wasn't he?"

"Another of his photography shows opening?"

"Don't think so. But he's been doing really well after that big one of Melissa at the Unko Gallery." Angela rummaged in the refrigerator. "Hey, there's some good cheese in here, too. Help me find crackers. We'll have a party."

Demi crossed to the cabinets and began searching. "Here's a crazy idea. Think he's going to ask Melissa to marry him tonight?"

"Oh, my God!" Angela straightened, gasping. "They're going to Seward Park. I bet you're right!"

"Just a guess."

"No, no, I know, we could be totally wrong. But I hope we're not." She laid out the cheese on a plate and added a knife. "I'm not going to be able to stand the suspense!"

"Me neither." Demi brought down a box of crackers and a plate, and started arranging, enjoying hanging out with Angela. She should ask her to lunch sometime, or dinner, or maybe to a chick flick. "How are things with you and Daniel?"

"Blissful. Stupidly, hopelessly, ridiculously blissful. I know it's the worst cliché on the planet, but I'm going to say it anyway. I did not know it could be like this."

"Oh, gosh. That's wonderful, Angela." Demi beamed at her, then resumed her cabinet search and found some pretzels and a jar of mixed nuts to add to the party, thinking of the night she'd spent with Colin, all the overwhelming and exhilarating and terrifying emotions that had buffeted her around endlessly. "Can I ask a dumb relationship question?"

"Well, of course. All dumb questions encouraged. Besides, there's nothing I like better than talking about Daniel, and the other three are sick to death of hearing about how perfect he is."

"How did you know that what you were feeling wasn't just infatuation or lust?" She held her breath, waiting for teasing, but Angela simply passed her a beer, looking thoughtful.

"That's a tough one. Because once you've been around, you know that initial thrill can happen with people who aren't right for you same as those who are. But with Daniel...it was just more. More feeling, more excitement, more fireworks, but also more trust, more contentment, a more conscious awareness that our values and lives and habits meshed really well.

"And I like who I am around him. He doesn't change me, but I've dated other men who did—hell, I *married* one. Around my ex I was a horrible, insecure mess. I'm nothing like that with Daniel. We bring out good things in each other." She opened her own beer. "See? I'll talk about him all day if you let me."

"It's fine. Actually that was perfect. I just feel with Colin..." She followed Angela back into the common room, and set the snacks and beer on the coffee table, then sat on the couch, trying to frame her jumble of feelings into words that might make sense, ridiculously happy that she had someone kind and caring and female who'd listen. "I feel as if it's too soon to be feeling this much, and I can't trust it. As if it's so different that it can't be real, because I can't control it or label it or… I mean, it's like I'm going around and around, beating myself up over— *What* is so funny?"

Angela had her hand over her mouth to keep from spraying beer. "If Bonnie was here she'd die. I was saying exactly the same stuff about Daniel months ago. Seriously, if I had a transcript I think it was word for word. Or close."

"Argh." Demi smacked a hand to her forehead. "But I don't *like* this. It doesn't make sense that someone like him would want someone like me."

Angela's left eyebrow rose. "You mean a beautiful, funny, talented woman?"

"You should have seen his last girlfriend."

"Who he's not seeing anymore."

"Because she dumped him." She started counting on her fingers. "I'm shy, he's not. I'm a homebody, he likes going out. He's rebounding, he's a mess because of his injury, he's—"

"Oh, way to focus on the positives." Angela brought out her counting fingers, too. "How about he likes you, he wants to be with you and you guys are checking each other out to see if there's a fit? It's called dating."

Was it really that simple?

"When we started, it did seem that easy, but…" Her body slumped against the couch cushions. "I don't want to get hurt."

"Aw, sweetie." Angela's face turned gentle. "No, you don't. At the same time, if you want to find out what can happen between you, you can't hold back, either, because then you're cheating each other out of who you really are and you won't get a true picture."

Demi groaned, attacking cheese with the knife. "I liked it better when I thought he was a jerk."

"I know, I know. Dating sucks. And I know you're thinking easy for me to say, I'm happy. But I wasn't for a long time. I know how scary it is. For years after my divorce I didn't date anyone. I thought I was being strong. Nuh-uh. Just chicken. At least you're trying."

Demi passed her cheese on a cracker. "What made you want to date again?"

Angela shrugged, taking on that beaming, melty expression Demi had seen her and Jack wearing multiple times when they were talking about their beloveds. "Daniel walked into my shop. Knocked me for a loop."

Oh, boy. Demi knew what that felt like. Colin had walked into her waiting room. "You think it was love at first sight?"

"Oh, no, just big old lust. Love came later." She grinned. "By the way, I'm so glad you're hanging around with us more, Demi. It's really great. We felt sort of awkward for a while, like you didn't enjoy our company."

Demi's jaw dropped. "You're kidding. I avoided everyone because you were such good friends I thought I'd be intruding."

"No, not at all. I think you're fabulous. Seth and Jack, too. And Bonnie…"

"Yeah, I know. Bonnie hates me."

"Bonnie makes snap judgments. She'll get over it once she spends more time with you." Angela's pretty brows drew down. "I'm worried about her. Something's going on, and I can't get her to talk about it. We've always been close but this is really worrying me. I'm terrified she's sick or something. She's lost so much weight."

Demi shook her head. "She doesn't seem sick to me. Just sad and worried."

"Definitely sad. I wonder if— Oh, geez." Angela jumped, then hauled her phone out of her pocket. Her face lit like the sun.

"Say hi to Daniel." Demi stood up, giggling.

Angela looked startled. "How did you know it was him?"

"Easy." She took one more cheese slice for the road. "Your internal firecrackers."

"Ha! The damn things won't stop when he's around. Have fun on your date!" She gave a brief wave, and answered the phone with a "hi" so blissful Demi couldn't decide whether to giggle or be envious. So she did both.

Back in her apartment, she thought about those firecrackers while getting dressed in black pants paired with a red sweater, and her favorite dangling earrings given to her by her mom for her twenty-first birthday—gold thread twisted around red coral beads. Thought about them as she painted her lips a matching red, squirted on the faintest spray of eau de cologne her sister gave her years ago, which she'd worn maybe three times, and went downstairs to wait, even though it was early.

Everything Angela had said about falling in love with Daniel described how Demi felt about Colin. From the fireworks, to the sense of newness, to the better person she was around him. The way she was conquering her shyness, the way she was free to indulge her sensuality.

Only problem? She didn't want to fall in love with Colin. Because he was only just beginning the process of figuring out who postaccident Colin would be. And because deep down she didn't believe he could truly fall in love with her.

So the best thing she could do, the most sensible, anyway, would be to acknowledge she was developing feelings for him and say, *So what? Que sera, sera.* She'd ride this boat until it got her where she wanted to go or capsized and she drowned.

Her phone rang and she fumbled for it, then rolled her eyes. Carrie. Demi had never returned her last call. She'd better pick up. "Hi, Carrie."

"Hey, little sister. What are you doing?" Her voice cracked; she sounded weirdly manic.

"I'm about to go to a jazz concert." For once she had something exciting to report. "How about you?"

"Oh, that sounds fun. Who's playing?"

"Full Nelson."

"I love them! You lucky. Who are you going with?"

"A guy I'm dating. Colin Russo."

Her sister's scream of excitement made Demi jerk the phone away from her ear. Was there a polite way to tell someone to dial herself down? "Demi, how great! I'm so glad you took my advice."

Her advice? "Thanks."

Carrie sighed dramatically. "I so envy you. Always have."

"Uh." Did Demi hear that correctly? "Did you say you envy me?"

"Your life is still evolving. I mean, you still have so much ahead of you. I settled down so early, and…I don't know. I feel sort of stuck sometimes. Like I'm running in these meaningless circles and not really getting anywhere."

Her sister's speech sounded a little sloppy, and Demi suspected she'd been drinking. This was a totally unexpected side of Perfect Carrie. "You've always made it sound as if you had the ideal life."

"I've been in therapy. I'm working a lot of stuff out. I'm not sure I married the right man, Demi." She started crying. "I'm not sure I'm living the right life for me. I've been trying to be Mom and I'm not Mom. Trying to be someone you're not is a horrible mistake."

"Carrie, honey. Listen, I'm about to get picked up. Why

don't we go out sometime so we can really talk?" She stood on the steps, feeling totally disoriented. Did she really just voluntarily suggest she and her sister spend time together?

"I would love that." Carrie sniffed several times. "I feel like I'm the only loser in the family. Mike is perfect, you're perfect."

"Perfect?" Demi's voice squeaked. "Me? Are you kidding? I'm the alien child. Don't like people. Can't handle parties. Haven't gotten married..."

"None of those are bad things, they're just different."

"Yeah, I'm different all right. You and Mom were in total sync."

"I was copying her," Carrie said glumly. "I have no personality of my own. No talents that matter in the world."

"That's not true." Demi could not take all of this in. How could she not have had any idea how much pain her sister was in? Was everyone in her family this good at hiding their real selves? They should all have been spies. "For one thing, you can make cakes that look like hats, and for another, you can virtual shop for jewelry with the best of them."

Her sister giggled. "That I can do."

Inspiration hit: Edwin's Jewelers. "I know. Come downtown Monday, Carrie, after work. I have this great necklace we can both buy."

"Expensive?"

"Through the roof."

"Diamonds?"

"Dozens."

"I'm there." She giggled again, still sniffling. "Thanks, Demi. You're the best."

Demi hung up the phone, still feeling as if she'd been transported to an alternate universe. Her perfect sister with the perfect life was a mess.

Maybe that was something she needed to keep in mind

when she found herself trying too hard to make her own life about order and logic, and kept beating herself up for simply being human.

Ya think, Demi?

"Want a ride, gorgeous?"

She started, then stood still while, yes, the firecrackers, predictable by now, went nuts inside her. How long had Colin been there?

"Yes, please." She ran down the steps and into his car, grinning at him, feeling freer and happier than she had in a while. Relieved of the burden of judging herself so harshly? Or of feeling harshly judged by others—her sister, the Come to Your Senses bunch. Most likely it was all part of the same thing. "Hello."

"Hi." He leaned over for a brief kiss and pulled out into traffic, then turned left onto Broadway. "You look absolutely gorgeous."

"So do you." She was not remotely exaggerating. He was smoking hot dressed in a black shirt and black pants. "How is your back? I'm asking of course as a concerned friend, not a physical therapist."

"No, of course not. I took a quick run yesterday, a slow half mile, and it was fine. I'm going to build up from nothing if it kills me."

"Oh, don't let it do that."

"I won't." He took her hand, gave it a squeeze. "And neither will your friend Julie, who is not nearly as talented as you, but she's helping."

"Julie is a doll." She sat back, smile permaglued to her lips, feeling positively bubbly. "What else is going on?"

"I'm going back to work next week at the health club. Been practicing my sax. I've started making you a knife."

She touched the back of her hand to his cheek. "Life feeling good these days?"

He pulled up to a red light. "Yeah, Demi. Life is feeling really good."

Joy swamped her. She was practically in tears. "That is fantastic."

"You're responsible, you know." He turned those devastating eyes on her, which made it even harder not to cry.

"Nah." Her voice was shaky. "I might have given you a shove, but you would have found your way back without me."

"It was a good shove."

She beamed at him until the car behind them politely honked that the light had turned green. "Speaking of shoves, was giving me these tickets a little hint that I needed to get out more?"

"Maybe. But I was hoping you'd ask me to go with you."

"Oh, so I fell right in with your diabolical plan?"

He cackled evilly. "You did, yes."

"The same way I fell into having lunch with you, and coming over when you were hurt, and staying the night and—"

"Face it, you have no hope of resisting me." He turned onto Madison. "None."

Demi laughed to cover the fear that he was right. "I better stop trying?"

"I'm telling you, resistance is futile."

"Okay, then." Demi glanced at him again, unable to stop looking. How she was going to bear sitting next to him for three hours, keeping her hands to herself, she had no idea. He'd turned her into a junkie for his body, for his scent, for the way he felt and the way he made her feel.

"Who were you talking to when I pulled up? You looked shell-shocked."

"My sister. She was acting...not like herself. Usually our conversations consist of her making sure I know how much more rewarding and impressive and enjoyable her life is than mine, plus loads of advice on how I could become more like her."

"Not a happy person, huh." He glanced over to get her reaction. "Jealous of you maybe?"

"What— How did you—" She laughed, shaking her head. "Was I the only person who couldn't see that?"

"I'm sure she fooled lots of people." He shrugged. "It's easier to see when it's not your baggage."

"Maybe it's true of your family, too? Your overachiever brothers?"

"Yes, but no. None of them wants to be a half-crippled personal trainer." He flashed her a grin. "Sorry, was I pouting again? I accepted a long time ago that I love my family, but I don't always like them. And I don't need them to like me. It's helped."

Demi nodded. "I think we share that attitude."

"And a lot of others if you've noticed." He turned right on Eighth Avenue and passed Town Hall to park at the garage a few blocks farther north. "Ready?"

"Sure." She climbed out of his car and took his hand, nearly toppling off her heels when he swung her around and dragged her up against him, then kissed her until she could barely think straight.

"Sorry." He released her and gently brushed hair off her forehead. "There was just no way I could make it to intermission without that."

"I'm completely fine with it." Her voice was breathless, giddy. "Anytime, really. Love to help."

He grinned, kissed her again, then drew back. "I like you, Demi."

Oh, my. The phrase went into her ears and triggered in her brain an astonishing array of pleasure sensations. "I like you, too, Colin."

They smiled at each other until it felt horribly awkward, then they laughed at themselves and their goofy infatuation, held hands and flew to the Town Hall.

Flew. Seriously. Demi had never understood the concept of feet not touching the ground, but she wasn't aware of any contact between sole and cement. Ah, the joys of being with this man all in black whose kisses erased her brain.

The Great Hall was packed for the concert. She and Colin had excellent spots on the wooden benches, aisle seats in the front section only a few rows back. This place was one of her favorite concert venues. Not only did it have excellent acoustics, but with its stained-glass windows, vaulting and central dome, it felt like an ancient church more suited to Europe than the States.

Today, however, she barely blinked at her surroundings. Something much more magnetic and compelling was sitting right next to her, not cool stone or dark wood, but hot flesh and pulsing blood.

Oh, my goodness. She had it bad tonight. Lust? Infatuation? More?

Oops. She'd promised herself not to wonder. Just to enjoy.

Full Nelson entered in all its long-haired, tattooed glory, and started to play. Demi knew they were good, but her brain would not pay attention. She could only sit there, experiencing Colin's thigh pressed against the length of hers, the way their hips met, the perfect way her shoulder fit against the side of his chest, the way she wanted to touch and taste every part of him.

This was not a good night for a concert. This was a good night for opening a bottle of wine, building a fire and making love in front of it. For hours.

Oooh, Colin had a fireplace at his condo…

Her thoughts became happily occupied with that scenario. The music drifted past her hearing as she focused on herself and Colin in his condo, wine in their glasses, Colin lighting a blaze, turning out lights, standing tall and proud, slowly stripping off his…everything.

Shirt first, unbuttoning black cotton, widening the V that let his golden skin show, until he slipped it off his shoulders, so muscled and masculine. In her mind the shirt floated to the floor like a leaf in autumn, and his hands moved in an equally leisurely manner to the fly of his black pants, unsnapping, unzipping, showing black material underneath, boxer briefs that clung to his trim hips and powerful thighs.

Down went the pants, unwrapping more golden skin beneath hair that glinted in the light.

Then his briefs went down and down, revealing the perfection of his build, head to toe, the magnificent cock springing free. In her imagination she was drawn over to him, naked herself. She put her hands to his hard shoulders, slid them over his curving solid pecs, let them ski moguls over his abdominals. She knelt and took him into her mouth, feeling the warmth of the firelight at her back, seeing it dance in his eyes when she looked up and—

The audience burst into applause, making her body jerk with panic.

"Whoa." Colin smirked at her. "Did you drift off there?"

"No, no, of course not." She clapped maniacally hard. "That was great, wasn't it?"

"Uh-huh. What was that number at the end of the set?"

"Oh, it was…" She pretended to think. "Hmm, I can't remember the name of it."

His eyebrows rose. "Variations on a little tune called 'Twinkle, Twinkle Little Star.'"

Oops. She wrinkled her nose. "Um, okay, you got me. I was kind of thinking about something else."

"Yeah?" He was clearly more amused than offended as

he put his arm around her and hugged her close. "What were you thinking about?"

"Well…" She leaned up for a lingering kiss and drew her hand down his chest. "You and me. Totally naked. Making love in front of a fire—"

"Excuse me?"

Colin and Demi turned to find a rowful of people waiting to get out for intermission.

"Sorry." Colin jumped up and took Demi's hand, leading her into the aisle. He grabbed his coat and then hers.

"Ready to go?"

"It's just intermission." She gestured to the stage. "The second half…"

"I know." He winked. "Ready to go?"

Her smile grew wicked. "Go where, Colin?"

"My place."

"Fireplace?"

"Yes, ma'am." He practically dragged her down the aisle. "I'm going to drive like you, so we'll be there in about three minutes. Then I want you to show me exactly what you were thinking about."

12

COLIN DIDN'T QUITE get them home from Town Hall in three minutes, but it wasn't a whole lot longer. He loved jazz. He loved Full Nelson. But he'd barely heard a note of the concert. The entire time he'd been aware of Demi sitting beside him, how she breathed, how she moved, how her body felt against him. So when she'd stopped moving, and her eyes had glazed over, he'd realized she wasn't listening to the music any more than he was.

Someday the two of them would be able to get through a concert, but not yet, not when the desire for each other was still so strong.

Someday? When had he started thinking longer-term with Demi? She'd been receptive to his lovemaking, but emotionally neither of them had taken any risks. Maybe tonight he would. Because clearly his feelings for her went beyond the physical. Since meeting her he'd gotten back in touch with someone other than the one-track jock he'd become, unaware of the narrowness of his own life. Stephanie had done nothing to broaden it, and when he'd needed her most, she'd deserted him. With Demi he was discovering how honest intimacy could enrich his life—and him.

For the first time he wondered what he could bring to

her life, and immediately promised himself to make sure there was plenty. He hadn't ever worried about that with Stephanie. Apparently he'd figured the gift of his manliness was enough.

Demi was making him more humble, too.

She was amazing.

He parked the car and took her hand on the way up to his apartment. He was going to take this slowly. He wanted to make love to her in front of his fireplace, just the way she'd been daydreaming about during the concert. He would make the experience between them so erotic, so emotionally charged, that it would be impossible for her not to realize how good they were together and commit to finding out if she could have serious feelings for him. Because he was pretty sure, even in this incredibly short time, that he was damn serious about her.

The thought was so overwhelming, so emotional, that he could only stand there, clutching her hand, watching the floors count higher, feeling like there was a warm honey-covered balloon gradually inflating in his chest. Beside him Demi was also quiet, poised as always, but he could sense her anticipation was as high as his. He could only hope it was for the same reason.

Inside his apartment, he took off his jacket, helped her off with hers, then slid his hand down her cheek. She was so beautiful, so hot tonight, the lady in red. He didn't think Demi had noticed, but she'd caught many men's eyes on the street and in Town Hall tonight, which had made half of him want to strut with she's-with-me pride, and the other half growl with my-woman possessiveness.

Now he had her alone and he was going to make her fantasy come true.

"Tell me what you want, Demi," he whispered. "What were you thinking about during the show?"

Her shy smile made his heart beat almost painfully. Her hands landed on his chest and slid up around his neck. "You *really* want to know?"

"Uh…yeah?"

He loved her easy laugh. "Okay, we were drinking wine here in your apartment."

"Which room?"

"Living. Don't interrupt."

"Sorry, I have to." He kissed her, drawing her close, savoring her soft lips clinging to his. They were good together. She had to realize that. "Okay, interruption over, keep going."

"Well." She was laughing now. "I guess *that* kind of interruption is okay."

"Better than. Go on."

"Okay. The fire was lit, and you were standing by it." Her voice was slow and dreamy. He was getting hard already and they hadn't done anything. "You took your clothes off, piece by piece. I couldn't take my eyes off your body in the firelight."

"Mmm, I like this fantasy a lot."

"Inter-rupting," she sang.

He snorted, nearly drunk with how crazy he was about her. "Sorry, go on."

"I was already naked, by the way."

"You—mmph." Her hand landed on his mouth, so he pulled her hips tight against him instead. Who needed words? The way her eyes widened, then narrowed with pleasure made him even harder.

"So then…" She started circling her pelvis against him, making him groan beneath her fingers. "I went over to you and knelt down in front of you and took your beautiful, hard cock deep in my mouth."

His eyes crossed. She giggled and took her hand away, started to pull back. "You are terrible," she accused.

"You are killing me." He pulled her back against him just this side of roughly. "And you are remarkable. You even give to me in the privacy of your mind, where you can have anything you want happen."

"Yeah." She pushed away again and pulled her sweater up and over her head. "I'm pretty much a saint."

His jaw fell open. No saint. Seriously sexy sinner. Under the sweater Demi had on a lacy red bra that pushed her breasts up into paradise. "Oh, my—"

"C'mon, baby." She posed, her fabulous breasts thrust forward, one leg pointed slightly out. "Light my fire."

"Duh." He pretended stupor. "Soon as my brain reboots."

"Oh, wine, too." She moved her hips in a slow circle. "We need wine."

"Mmmm." He took her shoulders, tasted the soft skin of her neck, bent down to press his face to the beautiful rounds of her breasts. Demi dropped her head back, let him explore.

Oh, what this woman did to him. And what he wanted to do to her…

Somehow he tore his mouth from her skin. "Wine. Fire. Let's do this."

He managed to walk into the kitchen and open the refrigerator. No white in there. He opened the cabinet where he kept his reds.

When he had any.

"Uh. Demi, I'm out of… Does beer work?"

"Beer?" She shoved hands on her hips, pretending disgust. "That's the best you can do?"

"Brandy?"

She looked pained, her brown eyes dancing. "I *guess* that would work."

"Whew." He got down snifters and poured, then led her over to the fireplace. "Epic fail on the wine. But we do have the fire. This will still work. You ready?"

"Oh, yes." She looked like a men's magazine centerfold, red lips matching her bra, her dark hair and pink cheeks contrasting perfectly with the pale cream of her skin. Yes, he'd be very happy to have her kneeling in front of him—what guy wouldn't?—but he really wanted to make love to her. And as soon as her fantasy played out, he'd take her into his bedroom and make sure he showed her exactly how important she was becoming to him.

"Behold. I give you fire." He grinned cockily and flicked the switch. Nothing happened. He flicked the switch off, then on again.

Nothing. Off again. On again. He started to sweat.

Damn it. He hated to disappoint her. Again.

But she was giggling. "Wow, this is *just* like my fantasy."

"Demi, I swear, this has never happened." He flicked the switch again in desperation. If at first you totally screw up… "It's always worked fine."

"I guess you just can't get hot for me, Colin."

"You have no idea."

"Fine." She sighed. "I can see I'm going to have to take over myself if I want to get anything done here."

He flicked the switch one more ridiculously hopeful time, then crouched and peered under the pseudo-logs. Was the pilot light out? Was there some kind of blockage under there? He poked around, trying to see if…

Some instinct told him it would be a very good idea to turn around.

He did.

It was.

While he'd been ineptly staring into his fireplace, Demi had been very ably removing her clothes. She was smiling Mona-Lisa-like, holding her glass, siren-stunning, but also—and this pleased him even more—completely comfortable standing naked in his living room. No shyness, no blushes.

He wanted her here often. She could even have an article or two of clothing on sometimes. Once in a while. Maybe.

"Ungh."

"Sorry?" She sauntered toward him. "Didn't quite catch that?"

"Naked. Woman. Naked."

"Man. Clothed." She pursed her lips in disapproval.

His clothes came off faster than they ever had. Also naked, he stood by the not-fire across from his gorgeous siren, thinking he'd never had so much fun with a girlfriend in his life. Sex with other women had been so earnest and he'd always felt pressure to make it movie-perfect.

"Very nice." She sipped her brandy through those fabulous red lips, eyes enormous in her face. She looked happy. And hot as hell.

"Demi, I know I didn't get the fantasy *quite* perfect, but maybe we can salvage it a little?"

She put her glass down and stood close enough that he could feel the heat from her body and smell her light perfume and her own enticing Demi-fragrance. His cock rose.

"I think we can manage just fine." Her hands landed on his shoulders; she kissed a trail down his stomach, then knelt gracefully and took him into her mouth.

"Oh, Demi." He groaned, closed his eyes, felt her warm tongue on him, her fingers gently fondling his balls. His knees nearly gave out; he shifted and reached out to touch her—

Pain shot through his back; his body jerked uncontrollably and Demi's teeth...

Ow!

"I'm so sorry." She took hold of his rapidly shrinking penis, examining it tenderly. "I *bit* you, my God. I'm so, *so* sorry."

"It's fine. I'm fine." He was. But her fantasy was now officially toast, and he felt worse about that than being bitten.

"Was it your back?" She stood, clearly stricken. "Are you okay?"

"Yes." He gave her a reassuring smile. "Just a quick shot of pain. And teeth marks are the very coolest thing on penises now."

"I feel so bad I—" She must have heard his comment in delay mode, because she suddenly burst out laughing so hard it made him laugh, too. And nothing in the world felt better than sharing a belly laugh with Demi.

Well, maybe one thing. But she might have had enough of that for one evening.

"Oh, my gosh." She giggled a few more times, wiping her eyes. "Can we give up on the fantasy? I think we should just go into the bedroom."

"Maybe it's safer." He pulled her close and kissed her, intending a quick lighthearted peck, but she felt so soft and so right and so…*naked* that he couldn't stop.

"Make love to me, Colin," she whispered.

Who was he to say no to a naked siren he was falling for? In his room they climbed onto the bed and moved toward each other without ceremony, without trappings, man and woman together, natural and right.

When he entered her, her eyes stayed open. It seemed natural to gaze at each other, sharing the wonder of what their bodies were feeling. And sharing something deeper that Colin had suspected was there all along.

He moved slowly, wanting their lovemaking to go on all night, all weekend, all month, maybe forever. She was hot and tight around him, fit him perfectly. She gave herself completely, wide-open to him, letting him know with her hands, her hips, her breaths, moans and whispered words how much he was pleasing her.

Every thrust, every caress, she was right there with him. He'd never felt so connected to another human being. This was what sex was supposed to be like. This was what poets and playwrights went into raptures over, what men killed for.

Not just sex. Making love. He'd never felt such depth of feeling for any other woman before this, and it both scared and thrilled him.

Because there was only one conclusion to be drawn from this experience, from these feelings and from the thoughts he'd started having about a future with Demi in it.

He loved her.

"You're welcome. Enjoy them." Bonnie waved the woman out of her shop and slumped onto the stool behind her counter. Good lord, were pigs flying out there? Should she order up some ice from hell? Bonnie Blooms had been overrun with customers and phone orders that morning—a Sunday. Outside it was dismal, rainy and cold. Usually people stayed home in droves in bad weather, except for special occasions, though some people needed the bright color and scent of flowers to perk them up in grim weather. Maybe that's what was happening today? Bonnie Blooms had been here nearly two years and she'd never had such good business.

The irony of course was that the upturn was happening just as she'd decided to give up on the store, though she couldn't count on the rush continuing. Bonnie didn't need to make bucketloads of money, that was never her goal. She'd just wanted desperately to stay in business. To take her crazy dream and make it work.

But given how badly she was in debt, it would take more than a few days of above-average business to get her out of danger and make her change her mind. She would need the foot traffic to continue, plus several standing orders from companies.

She gazed around her shop, thinking of all the hopes that had gone into it, all the work and the pride.

Might as well admit that for all her excitement over the vague notion of starting over somewhere else, it would rip her heart out to leave this behind.

Another customer walked in. Looked like a college kid, earphone wires hanging from his ears.

"Hey." He grinned at her, bobbing his head up and down like a seal to some beat only he could hear. "How's it going?"

"Fine." She wasn't sure what was wrong with him but obviously something was. He was probably high—Bonnie hoped he wouldn't be violent or otherwise unruly. The last thing she needed after a day like today was someone robbing the register.

"It's really you." He took out his earbuds and pointed at her, advancing slowly. Bonnie gripped the counter, wondering when to start screaming. "From YouTube."

From YouTube? She was from Seattle. "Sorry, you must have me mixed up with—"

"No, no, no." He was still grinning that weird squinty-eyed grin. "It's you. Bonnie from Bonnie Blooms, right?"

"Yeah…" She wanted him to leave. Now. He was creeping her out.

"Your video. About your store. It's really cool. I love that guy. He rocks."

She stared blankly. The kid was out of his mind. How was she going to—

"C'mon. You know who I'm talking about. Seth something."

Bonnie started. "Seth Blackstone?"

"Yeah, yeah, that's the guy. He posts those great songs to YouTube."

"I've heard them."

"There's the one about you."

She blinked at him. "About me."

"Hang on." He pulled an iPhone out of his pocket and tapped the keypad, gazed at the screen earnestly for a minute, then shoved the device into her hands. "There."

Bonnie took it reluctantly and watched the clip stream by, curious at first, then stunned and then very emotional. Suddenly the whole morning made sense. And now that she thought back, a couple of people had mentioned seeing a video. But she'd been frantically busy filling multiple orders—something she wasn't used to doing—and hadn't really paid attention, just nodded politely and moved on to the next customer.

Seth had written a song. A silly, fun, catchy song about a shop on Capitol Hill. How the owner was a lady with special powers to bring joy, comfort and love into the lives of the people who bought her flowers. The video was scattered with clips of her, which he must have gotten over the years and from her parents, interspersed with close-ups of stills. In one clip from her childhood she was dressed as a fairy princess carrying a magic wand. In another she was proudly gesturing to the garden she'd designed in her parents' backyard. Later came pictures of her laughing with employees of Blossoms Dearie and dancing at a Halloween party hosted by Come to Your Senses, dressed as a daisy; and finally, during the closing refrain, a lingering close-up of the picture Jack had taken of Bonnie wearing nothing but flowers. Probably her favorite picture of all time.

Life would be tragic without her sweet magic
My bonnie Bonnie Blooms only for me.

Tears filled her eyes. *Oh, Seth.*

She sniffled and handed the iPhone back to the kid. "Thank you for showing me this."

"Sure." He looked aimlessly around the shop. "Hey, so, can I have some flowers? My girlfriend loves this stuff."

"Absolutely." She could barely concentrate on what he was saying. "How much did you want to spend?"

"Aw, I dunno. Fifteen?"

"Coming right up." She wrapped up an appropriate bouquet on autopilot, though did think to put in a few extra blooms to thank him, and signed a grubby piece of paper he provided for her autograph. Her autograph!

As soon as he left, she rushed to the phone to call Seth...

But more customers came in. And then more phone calls. Apparently his latest upload was also a hit. Apparently people wanted to check her out.

By the end of the day, she'd had fifty-three walk-ins and forty-two phone orders, about triple her busiest day so far. But it didn't stop there. She had a call from a hotel, another from an exclusive downtown women's clothing boutique. Both were looking for a florist for regular deliveries, would she be able to show them what she could do?

It took every ounce of Bonnie's self-control not to shout, "Yes! Please! You have no idea!"

By the time she closed up her store, she was absolutely exhausted and absolutely exhilarated.

And she had someone to thank.

She checked her stock, updated her financial records, wrote out a new order for the wholesale shop and locked up. Instead of rushing upstairs, though, she went out onto Broadway to the specialty grocery store she generally avoided, opting instead to drive to the big bargain super-market some miles away.

Not tonight.

She bought mixed roasted nuts, cheese, champagne recommended by the guy in the wine department, French bread, raspberries, paper-thin slices of prosciutto, a mixed green salad with walnuts and red onion, and one of the gorgeous glazed fruit tarts she'd coveted in the window for months and effing months.

Now it was all going to be hers. And Seth's.

On her way back to the Come to Your Senses building—her home!—she dug out her cell and dialed him. "Hey, Seth, it's me."

"Hi, me."

"You doing anything right now?"

"Just finishing a song."

She grinned. She'd get to hear it when it was finished. This one and all the others he wrote from now on. Maybe they'd end up together, maybe not. Maybe she'd find someone else, maybe not. But Maine could stay right where it was, and she'd go visit when she managed to have a little extra change. She hadn't come this far to give up. Not on Bonnie Blooms. Not on Seth. He hadn't given up on her.

"Feel like having some dinner? My treat."

"Bonnie, I'm happy to buy you—"

"No, no. My treat. Ramen noodles and kidney beans. Can I come up?"

"Always, Bonnie."

She took a moment to close her eyes blissfully, then sprinted up the front steps, charged down the hall and up the staircase, too impatient to wait for the elevator. In front of his door, she put down the grocery bags and no, she didn't knock, she *hammered*.

"Okay, okay." Seth opened the door, looking bleary-eyed and tousled as he always did when he was composing. "What's the—"

She didn't give him the chance to finish, just jumped into his arms and kissed him with everything she had.

The second she finished and pulled away to thank him, he grabbed her back and kissed her with everything *he* had. Which was plenty.

"Okay, now tell me." He loosened his grip, as breathless as she was. "Dinner, kissing...what's the occasion?"

"You did the video! People were coming and calling in all day, and Razia's Dress Boutique and the Greymont Hotel want to see if I can fill regular orders. And it's all because you—"

He kissed her with such relief and passion that she thought she was going to have to scream to let her joy out.

"I had no idea what would happen, so I didn't say anything. I couldn't bear to get your hopes up in case the video tanked."

"It didn't." She laughed from sheer excitement. "All day long I was either making sales or answering the—"

"Does this mean you're not leaving?"

"Hell yes."

He gave a shout and swung her around, kissed her again and again until she considered pleading for mercy. "I didn't see how you could."

"I don't think I really ever was going to. It always seemed a little unreal. I needed an escape hatch, I guess. But the store is everything to me."

He grew still. "Everything, Bonnie?"

"Not quite." She smiled tenderly, messing his messy hair further. "Seth, you are definitely...something to me."

He laughed. "I'll take that for now."

"Oh, I left dinner outside."

"The ramen and beans? Uh, about that. I have some steaks I can thaw in the microwave."

"No, no, this is my treat." She darted to the hall and lugged in their dinner.

"Really, Bon, it wouldn't take me any time and I can whip up a..." His eyes bulged at the sight of the bags. "Holy crap, that is a *lot* of beans and ramen noodles."

"I know." She marched into his kitchen and started unloading, hearing his chuckles behind her. "I splurged just a little."

"I'll say you did."

"You deserve it." She turned and patted his cheek.

He grabbed her hand, held it to his face, then kissed it, slowly, each finger, then her palm, letting his tongue linger on her skin.

Fire started low in her belly, traveled down between her legs. Oh, this man...

He lowered her hand, looking about as serious and sincere as she'd ever seen him. Her heart started beating way too fast. A choice was coming. One that would determine what happened between them for the next few hours, and maybe the next...who knew? With Seth it was always impossible to tell.

"I want to play you this song I wrote."

Bonnie swallowed, disappointed. Maybe *she'd* have to offer the choice, since she was the one who'd walked away this time. "Sure. I'd love to hear it."

She followed him into his studio, thinking fondly of how much time she'd spent up here with him, trying out songs, giving him advice, making him laugh. And that one special time a few months ago, tearing up the room with wildly hot sex.

He took his guitar out of its case, pulled his stool close

to the chair she always sat in and tuned his instrument with unusual concentration, frown between his brows.

He was nervous.

Last time he'd been nervous playing her a song, it had been about falling in love, unusual for him. His songs were all about heartbreak, cheating and doubt.

She'd wondered at the time if that song had been a message to her.

Seth strummed a few chords, readjusted his position. "Okay."

"Okay." She was nervous, too, and she wasn't even sure why. But the powerful sensation was back, telling her the choice would be hers to make—here, and very, very soon.

He started to play a simple arpeggiated line then began to sing. "Roses are red. Violets are blue. I wanted to tell you that I love you."

"Seriously?" She screwed up her face in distaste. He didn't hit every time, but he'd never composed a clunker like this before.

"Shh." He strummed a few more times. "Don't interrupt. There's more."

"Gee, I can hardly wait."

"Violets are blue, roses are red. This song is to ask if you want to be wed."

"Seth. Stop, it's awful. What were you thinking?"

"Bonnie you bloom here in my heart. I cannot bear us to be apart. You're part of me, all warm inside. And I'm asking you to be my bride. You make me laugh, you make me smile, please walk with me down the aisle."

The last chord faded away. He lowered his instrument. "What do you think?"

She was staring, frozen, unable to dare hope.

"Okay, I know it stunk. Let me try again." He took the guitar off his neck, slid from the stool and knelt at her feet, looking up with such vulnerability that she almost couldn't connect him with the man she knew, almost couldn't bear to look.

And yet. It was Seth. On his knees. And if she wasn't mistaken...

"I'm asking you to be with me for the rest of my life, Bonnie. To belong to me the way I belong to you, and have for years, only I was too stupid and scared to be able to handle it. I've been working like a dog in therapy so I could deserve you, so I could feel whole enough to ask for what I've wanted all my life."

Tears first, a steady slide of them down her cheeks. He reached into his pocket and pulled out a velvet jeweler's box, took out a ring with hands that trembled and offered it up to her.

She knelt opposite him and spread the fingers of her left hand, watched him slide the beautiful ring onto her finger, mesmerized by the sparkle of diamonds and by the overwhelming significance of this moment.

Diamonds on her finger. From Seth, Mr. Fear of Commitment.

Diamonds. On her finger.

"Bonnie Fortuna, will you marry me?"

It took three tries for her voice to work. "Seth Blackstone, I would love to."

She kissed him, kissed him again, and even though she'd kissed this man dozens, hundreds, maybe thousands of times, these kisses felt brand-new, stronger and more intimate. Finally, after so much pain, so much growing, so much love, from that moment on, it would be the two of them, for each other, with each other, forever.

Oh, Seth.

13

"SO AFTER THAT Dave was totally wasted. And this ugly chick comes on to him, but he's like, 'Sorry, I'm not into fat girls.' And she goes, 'You are drunk.' And he's like, 'Yeah, but in the morning I'll be sober and you'll still be fat.'" Nick burst into coarse laughter. "The guy is freaking brilliant."

Colin made a sound of disgust. "The guy is freaking plagiarizing Winston Churchill's joke."

He slowed his pace, monitoring his stride and posture. He and Nick were out running the Elliott Bay Trail again, and Colin was determined this time not to let his ego get in the way of his recovery. Knock wood, he'd had two pain-free weeks and was feeling stronger all the time.

Without the pain, sex with Demi was getting hotter and more adventurous and more emotional than anything he'd ever experienced. His whole life was different from anything he'd ever experienced.

"Churchill, huh. Well, it's still funny."

"Yeah, making people feel horrible about themselves is really hilarious."

"Dude, lighten up." Nick scowled at him. "And is that the fastest you can run, grandpa?"

"Yup." Everything about Nick was bugging him today.

He felt as if knowing Demi and meeting some of her friends had deepened and enriched his capacity for healthy relationships. What had he and Nick shared but training and bullshit boasting about women and partying? More to the point, why had that sustained Colin for so long?

It couldn't now.

"So, uh, thought you should know. Stephanie and I aren't together anymore."

Colin felt the very slightest twinge in his chest at that news. More like habit than anything else. "That was quick."

"She's seriously high maintenance. We're together two weeks and she starts acting like we're married."

"Yeah?" He was amused, he had to admit. Stephanie was seriously delusional if she was looking for commitment from Nick. "Like what?"

"Like expecting me to hold my weekends open for her, check with her every time I want to go out, like she holds the master schedule to my life. And man, she is even more competitive than I am. Like, 'You shouldn't be drinking that second beer, you have an event in less than a month.' I'm like, 'Chill out, I know my body.' You know? It's like my triathlon career is suddenly ours. Like it's more important than I am."

"Maybe it is." He tipped his face up to the sun, enjoying the faint warmth in the November chill. What if he'd given in and asked Stephanie to marry him? The accident had spared them both a lifetime of misery or divorce. *Silver linings, Demi.*

"She was talking a lot about you toward the end, though, man. I get the feeling she thinks she made a mistake."

"Yeah?" The news barely registered.

"So if you want her back, you better up your training." Nick threw Colin a contemptuous glance and pulled ahead. "At this pace your next Ironman won't be for three years."

"I'm not doing Ironmen anymore." He felt only a slight jab of regret. "I'll probably be able to do the sprint length, though."

"Sprints?" Nick scoffed. "A quarter-mile swim, twelve-mile bike, three-mile run? What kind of challenge is that?"

"Better than nothing." He found himself speeding up to stay abreast of Nick, and made himself slow. "I'll have more time to do other things."

"You can't be serious." Nick dropped back beside him, shaking his head. "You have lost it, dude."

Colin chuckled. Maybe someday Nick would wake up to a bigger world, but Colin doubted it. "Trust me, I found more than I lost."

"Come on. Are you serious? You live for this. We *all* do."

"I used to. There's other good stuff out there."

"What about Hawaii? What about being the best? You try hard, train hard, you can get back. What do the doctors know?"

For a second, Colin allowed the old visualization back, of himself ahead of the pack, approaching the finish line in Hawaii, fans cheering, women lusting, the championship in his grasp. His adrenaline raced, his gut tightened, his lips tensed in a determined curl, his stride quickened... and his back gave a warning throb.

He deliberately replaced the vision with one of himself wrapping Demi in his arms during a long-weekend getaway in the mountains or on the beach, her head on his shoulder, hair across his chest, her bright eyes gazing at him. His lips smoothed and curved in a smile. His gut relaxed. His back eased.

"Not doing that anymore. I have other goals now."

"Like what? Getting fat and sitting on your ass?"

"No, actually I'm going to ask Demi to marry me, buy a

house and have a boatload of kids and a dog. Get a graduate degree in business and start a new career as an executive."

Nick turned and ran sideways to gape at him. "Say *what?*"

Colin thought he'd have a hard time keeping the smile off his face, but that wasn't the case. At all. He'd deliberately picked the scenario Nick would least expect, but when the words started coming out of him, he was startled to find that they were true. His subconscious knew what he wanted more than he did. Marry Demi. Have kids. Share a house with her. Start a new career that used more brains than brawn. With her in his life, he felt as if anything was possible. "You heard me."

"What the hell would you want to do any of that for?"

Colin grinned, suddenly giddy with this entirely new vision. Coming home to Demi. Kissing their baby. Petting the dog. "What I want has changed."

"No kidding." Nick shook his head in despair. "Well, it's your funeral."

And there it was, the end of what turned out not to have been a beautiful friendship.

"I guess."

"I'll catch you coming back. I can't stand running this slow anymore." Nick took off at a pace Colin couldn't possibly match.

Yeah, Nick could leave him in the dust on any trail in the state, and probably would always be able to. But Colin was beginning to realize that he was the one truly pulling ahead.

"Hi, Colin." Demi sat in her office, phone to her ear, grinning so hard it nearly hurt. Colin lit her up like a floodlight, a lightning bolt, Las Vegas—what else was bright enough? She could see him two hours after their last goodbye and feel as if it was a precious months-later reunion.

So she'd done it. Fallen in love. She thought she'd been in love before, but that had been nothing like this. Around Colin she felt strong, confident, not mousy, not worthless, not alien. Things that frightened her before she tossed off with a laugh. She and Carrie had even had a nice lunch together. They'd never be best friends, but there was a strong possibility of a real sister relationship evolving with her.

Having someone think you were the cat's meow, the bee's knees, a red-hot mama—well, it was hard to keep trying to convince yourself you were anything else. Because who wanted to?

And yet, there was so much to admire in Colin. It wasn't all about how he made her feel. She loved his courage, his determination. He was working regularly with Julie, making great progress, and he seemed to have accepted his new limitations much faster than she'd expected.

However.

There were no concrete signs on his part that he was falling in love with her, too.

Well, maybe there were some signs, but she didn't dare start looking or trying to interpret them, because the only thing worse than knowing your partner wasn't in love with you was spending agonizing time hoping he was.

"Meet me at Cal Anderson Park for lunch today? I want to buy you a hot dog. And I have a present for you."

"Oooh, a present! Yes, I would love to meet you, even without hot dogs *or* the expensive jewels."

"How did you know?"

She laughed. "And furs? And cruise tickets? I require all such things."

"I knew that about you." His voice was soft, tender, and sent shivers through her that were almost as deep and exciting as the sexual ones he induced in her. Quite regularly, in fact.

"What time?"

"I'm on my way. Be there in five, so as soon as you can make it…"

She glanced at her watch. "I'm finishing up some paperwork, so— Oh, guess what, I'm finished. I'll be right out."

His laughter felt like a prize she'd been awarded. They'd known each other six weeks, but she felt in many ways as if it had been much longer.

Stuffing the insurance forms back into their folder, Demi jumped up from her desk, locked her office and skipped down the hall, waving first at Bonnie, who actually waved back—she'd been acting as if she'd won the lottery lately, which she essentially had, thanks to Seth's video. And she had *almost* smiled at Demi the night before during another meeting on the holiday special gift cards, which would go on sale the next day in time for Thanksgiving.

On her right, a wave to Angela and then out the door into the cloudy chill of mid-November, which felt like a sunny day in Florida to her, because guess what? She was seeing Colin when she hadn't thought she would, and that was always a sunny-day kind of experience.

She nearly ran the last several feet toward the hot-dog cart where he was waiting, but made herself stay calm— *yes, yawn, hey, Colin, good to see you*—when she wanted to fling herself in his arms and kiss every inch of him, shrieking that she loved him and would for all time.

Good way to make a guy you're seeing casually feel totally comfortable.

However, when she was a foot away, he lunged at her and swung her around as if she weighed one hundred pounds, which she decidedly didn't. What an extra-nice perk, to have a boyfriend you weighed less around.

"Hi." He kissed her as if he hadn't seen her for a lifetime, when it had actually only been twenty-two hours, five minutes and thirty-two seconds. Or so.

"Hi." She was beaming like a fool, she knew it. Except that he was looking unusually animated, too, so that was fine.

And no, she was not going to read anything into it.

They ordered hot dogs from the same impassive man she'd ordered hot dogs from countless times, who never gave the slightest sign that he recognized her, no matter how friendly and chatty she tried to be.

The benches by the fountain were being used, so they perched on the pool's concrete edge, eating hot dogs and chatting comfortably about their days. Work was going well for Colin. He was back to a full schedule. Demi had gotten a new client with neck issues. They were thinking about going to see a movie that weekend.

She loved having someone to talk to every day. Boyfriends weren't everything in life, but they were really nice. Especially this one, who was close to her like no boyfriend she'd ever had. If only there were some magic place she could dial into and place an order for a guaranteed happy ending. Not that she was dying to get married—okay, the fantasy of marrying Colin had occurred to her and it had been exciting, even though she'd made sure to shut it down right away so she didn't start convincing herself that's what she wanted—but it would be nice not to have an end to this lovely association. Not to mention the lovely screaming-banshee sex. It added so much to life.

"Hey." He stuffed his trash into the paper sack the hot dogs came in and handed it over so she could add hers. "You ready for your present?"

"Well, of course." Her heart beat just a little faster, even as she sternly told herself it could be her favorite flavor of gum.

"Here." He drew a slim package out of his jacket, eyes full of something she couldn't quite identify.

It was probably not gum. "Thank you, Colin."

"You don't know what it is yet."

She started unwrapping, hands a bit shaky, emotions a bit shaky, telling herself over and over to stop imagining. "No, but I can thank you for the thought."

"You're welcome for the thought." His body was tense, which communicated to her that he really wanted her to like his gift, which made her tense, because she really wanted to like it, too, for his sake.

She lifted off the lid and gasped. A knife. No, a work of art. Long, slender shining blade without a single scratch, and a smooth red handle. She picked it up. The weight was perfect in her hand, expertly balanced and gracefully fitted to her grip.

"Colin, this is exquisite." She clutched it to her chest, near tears. "I can't believe how much work you must have put into this."

He was pleased. Really pleased. She could tell by the way his eyes softened, and his mouth tightened, as if he was trying to keep himself from looking anything but man-tough. "Glad you like it."

"No. I love it. Thank you. I'll use it a lot." She held it out admiringly. "Though I sort of feel as if I should put it under glass and display it."

"No. Use it. Enjoy it." He smiled in that way that made it seem the two of them were the only two people in the world, which at that moment, as far as she was concerned, they were.

"Colin! Wow! Hi!"

Demi started, then turned to see one of the most stunning blondes the universe had ever produced. Tall, slender, wearing a skintight running outfit that left no question to anyone with functioning vision that her figure was spectacular.

Demi hated her instantly.

"Stephanie." Colin stood up, smiling the held-back smile he'd just given Demi when he didn't want to show how pleased he was.

"It's *so* great to see you." She hesitated in this perfect oh-gosh sort of way and then stepped forward and kissed him, holding her lips on his cheek a little too long.

No, way too long.

Demi hated her more. And now that Colin was standing there, grinning and not introducing Demi, she sort of hated him, too.

"How are things going?" His voice had become low and gruff. With emotion?

"Fine. Fine." Stephanie brushed a piece of something off his chest that probably wasn't even there. "I broke up with Nick. Maybe you heard."

"He told me." He stuffed his hands into his pockets, which he did when he was uneasy.

Yup. Demi hated them both. And she felt dark and ugly and fat and in the way.

She wasn't supposed to feel that way around Colin.

"Stephanie, this is a friend of mine. Demi. She was my PT for a while."

Oh. Friend. PT. Not lover, not girlfriend. "Hi, Stephanie." Demi stood, feeling like the mutant next to Mr. and Mrs. Universe.

"Hi, Demi." Stephanie linked her arm through Colin's. "Thanks for helping get Colin here back on track."

"You're welcome." She picked up the box to put the knife away. Stephanie pounced.

"Oh, pretty one, Colin. Nick and I were comparing ours the other day. You gave one to Tom once, too, didn't you?"

Demi felt sick. Very nice, Stephanie. Really very nice. Make sure Demi was aware that there was less than no significance to the gift. Colin had probably given one to his garbage collector, too.

"I like making them." His voice was pleasant, but she could read the tension underneath, see it in his body as he extracted his arm from Stephanie's. He wanted one of them gone. Might as well be her. He and Stephanie must have lots of catching up to do. Especially because, guess what, she was available again, and made sure he knew it within the first ten seconds of their joyous meeting.

"I was actually wondering the other day if you'd like to get together sometime, Colin." Stephanie tossed her ponytail, blinked up at him enticingly in that way that only enticing women had. If Demi tried it she'd look as if she had something in her eye. "Talk things over?"

Demi closed her eyes, telling herself murder would only land her in jail and, anyway, she wasn't sure which of them she'd rather take out first.

"We do have plenty to talk about." At least Colin didn't sound warm and sexual the way Stephanie had.

"Why don't you talk now?" Demi put the knife away and rather pointedly handed the bag of trash to Colin. "I need to get back to the office."

"Okay." Colin gave her a perfunctory smile, hands cemented to his hips, barely meeting her eyes. "Thanks for lunch. Nice to see you again."

Nice to see her again? As if they'd just met up to discuss the good old days of his treatment? Ouch. Just ouch.

"Good to meet you, Stephanie. Thanks for the knife, Colin."

She nodded pleasantly to both of them and turned. Before she was out of earshot, she heard Stephanie asking if "that woman" was Colin's girlfriend. Immediately, she pretended her shoe needed adjusting so she'd be able to hear his answer.

It came quickly, in the form she half expected, though a stupid, eternally romantic part of her was hoping for something completely different.

"Demi? No, no, just a friend."

She fled the scene, knowing she had a long day and a long cry ahead of her.

But that was that. She knew where she stood. All dreams she had of getting serious with Colin were over. So either she could hang in there with him, knowing she'd never get what she wanted, growing increasingly unhappy, frustrated and bitter.

Or she could end it. Now. Because unless she'd misread what was going on back there, Colin was about to go back to the woman he belonged with.

COLIN STRODE DOWN Broadway, barely keeping himself from sprinting. He'd been angry before of course. Angry most of his childhood because his father clearly favored his intellectual and successful brothers. Angry when Stephanie dumped him. Angry when he had to give up his dream of running the Ironman in Hawaii. But nothing had felt like this. That Stephanie's body wasn't lying lifeless in the park—figuratively speaking—was only due to him wanting to avoid the mess and trauma. After he told her what he thought of her, which she richly deserved, he spent ten minutes or so listening to her trying to make dewy-eyed apologies and then, when those didn't work, screeching out what she thought of him.

Wow, he sure missed those manipulative hysterics. By golly who wouldn't?

Stephanie had gone out of her way to make Demi feel small, insignificant and less. Less attractive, less grace-

ful, less important than she was. What a joke. Demi was
ten times the woman Stephanie could ever hope to be. Not
stopping her right then and there had been the hardest thing
Colin had ever done. But he knew his ex well. Once she
got a whiff of the fact that he and Demi were a couple, the
claws she'd kept mostly sheathed would have sprung out to
ten-foot lengths and slashed Demi to ribbons.

Seeing Demi's face fall when she didn't understand he
was protecting her, when she must have thought he was pan-
dering to Stephanie at her expense… Colin still wanted to
rip something into unrecognizable pieces. Like Stephanie.

Deep breath. All was not lost. He'd make it up to Demi.
He'd explain. He'd hope like hell that she'd understand,
and if she didn't today, he'd spend however much time it
took convincing her he was crazy about her. After that little display in the park she had every right to think he was
fickle, two-faced and shallow. That he made knives by the
dozens and tossed them around to anyone, when he'd put
more time and love into her knife than anything he'd ever
made. And just like that Stephanie had trivialized his gift.

She was good, he had to hand it to her.

Up to him now to prove to Demi that his feelings were
much more than casual for her.

He passed Edwin's Jewelers, where she'd stood and
talked about buying the necklace. He'd loved that—still
did—about her, the whimsy, the unexpected twists, the
way she gradually revealed the fun and the fire that burned
underneath her cool exterior.

Yeah, he was serious about her. Very serious.

His furious stride slowed. He turned around, retraced
his steps to the jewelry store. The necklace was still there,
sparkling on the headless model.

He opened the door to the shop and strode inside. Demi

would want to know how serious. Right here in this shop, he had the perfect way to show her.

"Hey, Demi, guess what?"

Demi turned wearily. Damn it, she was almost to safety, just outside the door of her apartment, in the act of unlocking it, and look who showed up. About the last person she wanted to see besides Stephanie or Colin. Bonnie, looking as perky as Stephanie, only shorter and wearing a brightly flowered shirtdress. "What?"

"I wasn't sure you knew." She held up her left hand, fingers wiggling. "I thought I told you, but Angela said you didn't know yet. Seth and I are engaged!"

Demi tried to summon every bit of enthusiasm she could even though she was about to burst into tears. "That's great, Bonnie. Congratulations."

She frowned. "You don't seem that happy."

"No, I am. I'm just not in the greatest mood."

"Uh… Yeah, that's what I meant." She looked at Demi as if she only had half a brain. "Which is why I said, 'You don't seem that happy.'"

"Sorry." She put her hands to her temples, sure her head was about to crack into pieces. "I thought you meant I hadn't seemed excited enough."

"Yikes." Bonnie actually looked horrified. "That would have been horrible."

Nothing new from you. "When are you getting married?"

"*Soon.* Like next month." She tried to scowl but there was no way her joy could be covered up completely. "Before the jerk changes his mind."

"He won't."

"And you know about Jack and Melissa's engagement?"

"Jack told me, yes." She struggled to put on a look of delight. "That's great, too."

"You're the only one left!" Bonnie folded her arms over her chest, beaming. "We gotta do something about that."

"*No*. God no." Demi couldn't hold her tears back another second, and when they came, they came in torrents. *Crap.* She turned and blindly tried to locate her doorknob. "I'm sorry."

"Demi, oh, my God." Bonnie followed her inside, the last thing Demi wanted her to do. "There I was completely ignoring the fact that you're miserable, and telling you all this good news, when you'd *told* me you were miserable. But did I take the hint? No. *I'm* the one who's sorry."

"It's okay. But..." Demi gestured back toward the door. "I think I need to be alone now."

"No." Bonnie shook her head. "That is absolutely the last thing you need. I will make you some tea and you will tell me everything. And if you don't want me, I'll get Angela, because she will... Oh, wait. She's working."

Demi sighed, feeling trapped. "Is Bonnie Blooms closed?"

"I hired an assistant," Bonnie announced proudly. "Or more like an apprentice. This wonderful older lady who needs to get out of the house. She works for pretty much nothing."

"That's nice." Her voice broke. More tears.

Bonnie clapped her hand to her mouth, green eyes contrite. "Gah, here I go again blabbering on about me. Now. We're going to fix you. Where is your tea?"

Demi numbly pointed to the cabinet. She didn't have the energy to get into it with Bonnie, and frankly, if Bonnie was finally going to be nice, she didn't want to discourage her. When Colin dumped her she'd need all the friends she could get.

"I assume this has to do with Colin."

"Of course."

"Of course." Bonnie filled the kettle, rolling her eyes.

"How much do we suffer over these damn guys? I wish I knew why we find them irresistible. Life would be so much simpler without them."

"True." Demi stared glumly down at her table, chin propped on her hands, wondering if it was possible to die of a broken heart anywhere outside of an opera.

"Now, what has Colin done that would give the Come to Your Senses crowd license to remove his privates?"

More tears, along with the ghost of a giggle at Bonnie's humor. "His old girlfriend showed up."

"Ooh." Bonnie's face crumpled with sympathy. "Those encounters are the worst. Seth had so many old girlfriends, it happened every time we stepped out of the building."

"I think they're going to get back together."

"Think?" Bonnie jammed her hands onto her hips. "So you're not sure yet?"

Demi told her the story of what had happened in the park, feeling stronger as Bonnie's outrage grew. "That bastard."

"I just can't believe I judged him so wrong." She took the tissue Bonnie handed her and wiped her eyes. "I'm usually good at weeding out the real jerks."

"Yeah?" Bonnie contemplated her thoughtfully. "Well, I can't see how you could have misunderstood the situation, but if your instinct told you this guy was a good one... maybe you should hold off on total despair until you hear his version of the story."

"Maybe."

Bonnie wrinkled her nose. "I admit it doesn't sound good. But even if the worst happens, you still have us."

"Yeah." Demi rolled her eyes. "And you're all engaged."

"Ew, I forgot. That is brutal." She patted Demi's hand, then jumped up. "Mugs?"

"There." She pointed to the cabinet by the sink. My God,

the woman had enough energy to power a windmill. She was exhausting. And also serving as Demi's lifeline to sanity at the moment, for which she was grateful.

"So, by the way, I was pretty awful to you for a long time, Demi. I'm sorry." Bonnie got down two mugs. "I thought you were stuffy and standoffish. You never hung out with us. I thought you had decided we were beneath you."

"I'm just shy."

"That's what Angela said. I have to tell you, she and Jack really whupped me upside the head. Said they'd been spending more time with you and that I was wrong about you and better try to make more of an effort."

"You're doing a bang-up job." The remark came out drily. She couldn't help it.

To her amazement, Bonnie cracked up and turned, still grinning. "Okay, I'm not the most subtle person in the world."

Demi managed a smile, which to her surprise was genuine. "Maybe not. But it's sweet of you to want to help me."

The kettle started screaming. Bonnie grabbed it and filled their mugs, set them on the table.

"I just want you to know if this Colin guy turns out to be the world's biggest jerk, you've got friends here who have your back and always will. I'm going to include myself in that category, too." She picked up her mug and held it up. "Here's to looking forward."

"To looking forward," Demi said. "Which suits me because I don't ever want to think about what happened back in the park again."

Bonnie's gaze jerked suddenly over Demi's head. At the same time, Demi registered the sound of her front door opening. Hadn't she locked it? She always locked it.

"Uh-oh." Bonnie looked like she'd seen a ghost. And

right then Demi knew exactly who was standing behind her, and that her hopes of never having to think about what happened in the park again were about to be crushed under a well-worn size-twelve running shoe.

14

DEMI STOOD INVOLUNTARILY. If Bonnie hadn't grabbed the tea out of her hand, she would have let the mug fall. Colin was here. Her heart rose in her chest until it felt as if it was trying to burst into her throat.

Not a pleasant feeling.

Worse, her brain was registering that he looked about six times as gorgeous as he had any right to, his dark eyes deep and somber, his jaw set, hair windblown. Poor Colin was going to have quite the time dumping her. How he must dread it.

What would he say?

Stephanie and I have so much in common and...

When I saw her today it hit me like a thunderbolt that we're meant to be together...

You and I have always known this was temporary...

It's not you, it's me...

Okay, if he said that last one she was going to kick him where it counted.

"Hi." He stood in her entranceway, hands in his pockets. When his eyes met hers, his face registered shock, then froze into grim stone.

She looked that good, huh.

"I'm Bonnie." Bonnie strode over to him, huge smile in place, and shook his hand.

"I'm Col—"

"I know who you are." She beamed harder, her voice superperky. "And I just want you to know that the four of us living here with Demi take the whole friendship thing very seriously, so if you hurt her, we're going to hunt you down with machetes. Okay?"

Colin glanced past Bonnie at Demi, who found herself out of the kitchen without having been aware she'd moved. Colin was probably wondering what the hell she'd told Bonnie—he didn't know she'd overheard his dismissive comment about her. Demi couldn't feel bad about it. She couldn't feel much of anything. She wanted this over with, wanted him out of here, wanted Bonnie out of here and wanted to collapse into pain for a few months and then get over it. Maybe she'd close her practice for a month and fly to Jamaica to grieve on the beach.

"Machetes. Well. I'm glad Demi has friends who care about her so much." Colin smiled down at Bonnie with distinct affection. Bonnie sent Demi a what-the-heck? look that Demi would have responded to if she'd been able to move.

"Okay, then." Bonnie took a couple of steps back, arms still folded, eyes narrowed in suspicion. "I'll give you two some privacy, but I'm *right* down the hall."

She strode to the door, turning behind Colin to give Demi a look of melting sympathy and a thumbs-up for courage. Then she left. The door closed behind her.

"Would you like to sit in the living room?" Demi gestured him in, feeling like a zombie hostess.

"Demi." He took two steps toward her, reached toward her cheek. She ducked away and headed for the couch.

"We can talk in here."

"You've been crying." His voice was anguished. "That sucked in the park today. The way Stephanie treated you, the way I treated you. I'm sorry it had to be like that."

"I understand." Rock. She was made of rock. Except rock wouldn't know that emotional agony was on its way soon. Rock was very lucky in that it didn't have to feel anything at all. She'd like to stay made of rock for as long as possible. Like maybe until she'd gotten over Colin and was happy again.

"No, you don't understand." He made as if to sit next to her on the couch.

"There." She pointed across the room to a chair, teal with gold, which Carrie had bought in her striped-furniture phase, then decided she didn't like the shape. "You sit over there."

He pressed his lips together, then went to his assigned seat. "Okay."

"Good." No, she wasn't made of rock. Metal. Metal parts. She was a robot.

She wished.

Colin leaned toward her, hands folded, elbows on his thighs. Oh, those thighs. She didn't want them to belong to that woman. "Here's the thing about Stephanie."

Demi's face actually twitched when he said Stephanie. She knew what "the thing" was about Stephanie. She was perfect. "Okay."

"I know her really well."

Yes, and you also know she's perfect for you, so you'll have a perfect wedding and raise perfect brats who will torment you their entire lives.

A girl could always hope. "Okay."

"Stephanie has always been and will always be—"

"Perfect."

"No." Colin looked startled. "Stephanie has always been and will always be about Stephanie."

Demi blinked. That's why he still loved her? That was weird. She wouldn't have thought Colin would fall for someone who—

Her brain screeched as it tried furiously to work again. Wait...

"And I knew if she found out we're a couple..." He shook his head. "Well, let's put it this way. You saw how snarky she was. If I'd let on how I feel about you, she would have turned it up a thousand percent. She can be truly vicious."

We're a couple... How I feel about you...

Demi blinked again and managed to move her head. Deep in her chest, she felt little stirrings of hope. "After I started walking away, you told her I was nothing to you."

"Oh, Demi." He winced as if she'd socked him. "I'm so sorry you heard that. I was protecting me by that time. You have not seen tantrums until you've seen Stephanie's. I wanted to make sure you were far gone before she started."

He was acting so normal. As if nothing had changed between them. "So...you aren't going back to her?"

"God no." Colin shuddered. "Not in a million years."

"Does she know that?"

"Oh, yes. As soon as you were safely away, she found out. I have the hearing damage to prove it." He got to his feet, smile fading. "I hated putting you through that, Demi. I'm sorry she tried to cheapen the knife. The truth is, I only make knives for people and friends I love. And I'm grateful the hilt isn't sticking out of my back right now. I wouldn't blame you."

"I thought about it." Her features allowed the beginnings of a grin. They were just friends. She shouldn't take the *L*-word too literally. "So is this woman going to come after me?"

"No." He sat next to Demi on her couch. Without her permission. Took her hand. Also without her permission.

"She calms down after she's vented. Also, um, I might have said something vaguely threatening."

His hand was warm and dry and comforting; her body and brain started a slow, delicious thaw. "Vaguely threatening?"

"Yeah, you know, implying that it would not be a good idea to bother you."

"I see." She smiled for real; he squeezed her hand. "How did you imply that?"

"Something along the lines of, 'If you go near Demi I'll have Bonnie hunt you down with machetes.'"

She actually laughed that time, and boy did it feel good to have her humanity returning. Except she still wasn't clear on what was going to happen between them, or how they'd go forward. She loved him. His feelings were a big question mark. "So what now, Colin?"

"Now?" He looked very serious. "Now I want to make love to you until you come so loudly all the people in your building call 9-1-1."

"Oh." She got up off the couch, away from temptation. "I'm not sure that's such a—"

"Demi." He stood, too, and pulled her into his arms. "Where is your can-do attitude?"

"I'm not sure." To her horror, tears formed. Again. She still had Colin, which was really good, but maybe only for sex, which was bad. She'd almost lost Colin to Stephanie, which was terrible, and then she didn't, which was good. She loved Colin, which was good, but wasn't sure she could keep him, which was bad.

It had been a long, confusing day. And it wasn't even dinnertime yet.

"Sweetheart." He tucked her head against his shoulder and held her with his strong arms, rocking her back and forth. "I'm so sorry."

For a while she burrowed against him, eyes closed, relishing his strength and familiar smell. Then practical Demi took over. Did she want to get this close again, get used to relying on him, risk falling more deeply in love with him, when the payoff could be getting her heart smashed anyway?

But his mouth found hers, and she surrendered to the sheer bliss of the contact. And then he murmured such sweet and tender things that her stupid hope burned brighter. Maybe he'd grow to love her, too, over the next weeks and months. If she bolted now, she'd never give them that chance.

She deepened their kiss, began exploring the sleek contours of his back and shoulders with her hands, with her mouth, her favorite place between the firm curves of his pecs, pressing her pelvis against him, wanting to lose herself in this man's body and his desire for her.

Their passion mounted, kisses turned fiery, and fingers fumbled with clothing until they were naked, hands all over each other, and Demi finally got so hot she turned in his arms, braced herself against the wall and offered herself to him, needing the rush, the crazy burn of animal ecstasy.

His hands followed the upward line of her arms to rest over her fingers. His body was warm against her back, his penis slid between her legs without entering her. He took her hands from the wall, turned her to look at him. "Not this way. Not today."

She stared back, unsure what he meant.

"Come." He led her into her bedroom. At the edge of the bed he drew her close again, kissed her forehead, her cheeks, her mouth, over and over, slow, gentle, sweet kisses.

Demi felt cherished, adored…but while half of her was saying yes, yes, that this was what she wanted, the other half was retreating, fearful of the vulnerability this exquisite tenderness engendered.

He helped her onto the bed, where there were more kisses, and a long, leisurely exploration of her body with his fingers and his mouth. Gradually she relaxed into this slow, languid pace and allowed herself to open, mindful of the risk, but as always loving the honesty and depth of their connection.

He slid on top of her, kissing her, murmuring endearments she wouldn't ever have imagined could come out of the mouth of her cranky triathlete six weeks ago. She wrapped her arms around his neck, his back, his shoulders, making sure he knew how much she loved the feel of him against her, the warm sweep of his skin, his smell and his taste. For a long, long time they lay like that, just touching, exploring, sharing themselves physically and emotionally to a degree that eclipsed even their previous lovemaking.

Then he put on a condom and lay back over her, one hand pressed to her cheek, eyes steadily on hers, and pushed deep inside her. Demi disappeared into his eyes, into the dreamy intensity of their lovemaking, sure she'd never shared this kind of intimacy with anyone ever before.

Colin.

She had no idea how long they were there, lazily making love, hands never still, arousal constant but in the background as she luxuriated in how tied she felt to this man.

Then finally the background became the foreground, their movements faster. Desperation crept in, up to the final sweep of ecstasy. Colin held back until she went over the edge, then let himself go with her, holding the pleasure between them as long as they possibly could.

With him, Demi understood what sex could be about. Her previous experiences had been shallow imitations of what could happen between two people. She was so grateful to Colin for showing her how much better it could be.

He lifted his head to meet her eyes, and the awe in them was such that she realized Colin hadn't showed her anything. This was something they'd discovered together. This belonged only to them.

Her heart lifted.

"Demi," he whispered.

"Yes."

"That was…" He shook his head, bewildered. "I don't know where we went, but I've never been there before."

"Me neither." She let everything she felt show in her eyes. And there was a hell of a lot.

He moved restlessly. "I have something to give you."

"No." She wasn't ready to let him move yet. "You just gave me the knife a few hours ago. And the best sex of my life a few minutes ago. I don't need anything else."

"Stephanie tainted the knife."

"No." She shook her head. "Absolutely not. I'm always going to treasure it."

He moved off her, sent her a mischievous look. "Well, I'm not taking this present back, so you're stuck."

"Oh, for—" Demi rolled her eyes. "You are so selfish."

"Aren't I?" He drew his hand down her cheek, kissed her lingeringly, then strode out of the room, his body beautiful enough to inspire a sculptor.

He was hers. For only a while, maybe. But hers now.

He came back in, holding a long, thin box, eyebrows up with worry, body tense, exactly as he'd been in the park.

"Another knife?"

"I didn't make this."

"Colin, you're really going to make me feel like I…" Her voice trailed off. She'd seen the box up close. Edwin's Jewelers.

He saw her staring. "Remember when we looked in the window together?"

She gaped at him. He hadn't. Not the necklace. It cost thousands. He couldn't possibly have.

"Remember that necklace you showed me?"

"Colin." She could barely breathe, let alone speak. "You did not buy me that necklace."

"Nope." He grinned and knelt by the bed, placed the box in front of her. "I bought you something else."

"You…" She smacked him playfully. "Don't ever do that again."

"What, buy you jewelry?"

"No, pretend you did." She reached for the lid. "If you'd bought me something that expensive I would have had to—"

She stopped. This time she really couldn't speak. Or breathe. In the box, cleverly attached to keep it from sliding around, was a ring.

No, she was seeing things. It was…

A ring. A diamond ring. The kind a man bought for a woman when he was—

She lifted her eyes to his face, not daring to interpret even this completely obvious…

Ring.

"Demi." His voice came out husky and low. "I've never met anyone who has brought as much to my life as you have. I've never met anyone who inspires me so much, who makes me so happy and so…hot all the time."

A giggle-sob escaped her.

"I admire your talent, your humor, your outlook, your in-cred-ible body, and I can't ever envision a time when I won't want to turn to you, talk to you, make love to you. I love you. Will you marry me?"

She nodded. And then she nodded again. And she really,

really tried to think of something to say that would even come close to the beautiful speech he'd just given, that would encapsulate her feelings so perfectly, show him how important he was to her, how much she admired and adored him.

But all that came out of her was happy tears and one word: "Yes."

His face crumped into relief, he climbed onto the bed and they wrapped themselves around each other as if they'd never, ever let go.

And Demi stopped worrying about telling him all the things she wanted him to know, outlining perfectly all the remarkable and beautiful things he'd done for her and brought to her.

Because she realized she'd have the rest of her natural life to get it absolutely right.

Epilogue

August, the following year

Postmark: Rockport, Maine

Dear Extended Come to Your Senses Family,
Seth and I are loving our honeymoon here in Maine.
The only problem is figuring out how many lobsters
we should eat at every meal. No, really, including
breakfast. This is one of the most gorgeous places
on earth, but we still miss you all and can't wait to
come home. Okay, Seth says that's ridiculous. We
can definitely wait to get home, but it will be easier
to leave this place knowing the rest of you will be
coming back from your adventures, too. Best idea
ever to close Come to Your Senses for quadruple
honeymoons. As long as our customers and clients
don't forget us! Oh, one more thing, Seth was hired
to score that big Hollywood movie even though we
can't tell you who the actor is playing the lead, but if
it works out, I'm going to want to cheat on Seth big-

time. He is making me tell you I'm kidding. Like you couldn't tell.

Love to you all from paradise,
Bonnie

Postmark: Paris

Bonjour, mes amis,
Well, Daniel and I are not going to make it back from Paris, I am sorry to tell you, because we have eaten so much croissant and pastry that the plane will charge us for our overweight butts and we can't afford it. Everything is so ooh-la-la around us, elegant and beautiful, ancient and new, fascinating and delicious. And boy, it's ten times better being here this time with a husband who adores me. Definitely do not recommend marrying ones who don't. Tonight we're going to splurge on dinner at one of the best restaurants in town, which will set us back the price of a small Latin American country, but hey, you only live once. Somehow, even in this fabulous romantic city with this fabulous romantic man, I still manage to miss you guys.

À bientôt, mes bien-aimés,
Angela

Postmark: Athens

Hey all, having a wonderful time. Glad you're not here. I thought I'd seen Melissa at her most beautiful at the wedding, but photographing her against the backdrop of this incredible place, with the clear water and stunning monuments, makes me realize how wrong I was. You think you know someone well

enough to marry her, and then after the ceremony
you realize a whole new depth of intimacy is now
possible, and that fifty or sixty years might not be
enough time to explore it all. And in case that was
too sentimental we had our first fight—over who got
to pose with the juggling monkey. Brutal! I won of
course. Oops. She just told me to stop being a lying
pig. She won. I caved. I've never been happier, and
it's great thinking that the same has to be true for all
of you. We'll have great stories to tell in September
and for the rest of our lives.

Be at peace,
Jack.

Postmark: Kailua-Kona, Hawaii

Dear Angela, Daniel, Bonnie, Seth, Jack and Melissa,
I love this idea of coming home to letters from each
other. But I can't say I love the idea of coming home.
Not right this minute because I'm writing this on the
beach next to the hottest man on the island. No, really.
He's sweating like a pig.

So my control-freak husband wouldn't tell me
where we were going on our honeymoon until we
got to the airport. Such a typical guy. Didn't occur
to him I would need to know climate information to
pack. Prepare for anything, he says. Big help.

Hawaii is stunning. We're here now visiting the
site of the Ironman World Championships. I'm proud
to say Colin only broke down sobbing twelve or
thirteen times. Okay, no, wait. He says make sure
I tell you that manly men like him don't cry. Ever.

Unless I withhold sex.

Being away from you all has made me appreciate

our partnership and friendship all the more, even though I was kind of a late bloomer in that regard. Yeah, okay, wallflower nerd. But I look forward to the years to come, to more holiday events like the last one, which went so well, to more successes, joys and, hey, who's going to have the first baby?

Thanks to all of you, and here's to the bright happy future we're all going to share.

See you soon!

xoxox

Demi

* * * * *

A sneaky peek at next month...

Blaze®

SCORCHING HOT, SEXY READS

My wish list for next month's titles...

In stores from 21st December 2012:

- ☐ The Professional – Rhonda Nelson
- & Feels Like Home – Vicki Lewis Thompson
- ☐ The Mighty Quinns: Dermot – Kate Hoffmann
- & The Mighty Quinns: Kieran – Kate Hoffmann

Available at WHSmith, Tesco, Asda, Eason, Amazon and Apple

Just can't wait?

The World of Mills & Boon®

There's a Mills & Boon® series that's perfect for you. We publish ten series and, with new titles every month, you never have to wait long for your favourite to come along.

Blaze.
Scorching hot, sexy reads
4 new stories every month

By Request
Relive the romance with the best of the best
9 new stories every month

Cherish™
Romance to melt the heart every time
12 new stories every month

Desire
Passionate and dramatic love stories
8 new stories every month

Have Your Say

You've just finished your book.
So what did you think?

We'd love to hear your thoughts on our
'Have your say' online panel
www.millsandboon.co.uk/haveyoursay

- 🌹 Easy to use
- 🌹 Short questionnaire
- 🌹 Chance to win Mills & Boon® goodies

Visit us Online

Tell us what you thought of this book now at
www.millsandboon.co.uk/haveyoursay

YOUR_SAY